Drowning Rose

MARIKA COBBOLD was born in Sweden and is the author of six previous novels: *Guppies for Tea*, selected for the WH Smith First Novels Promotion and shortlisted for the *Sunday Express* Book of the Year Award; *The Purveyor of Enchantment*; *A Rival Creation*; *Frozen Music*; *Shooting Butterflies*; and most recently *Aphrodite's Workshop for Reluctant Lovers*. She lives in London.

Drowning Rose

MARIKA COBBOLD

BLOOMSBURY

LONDON · BERLIN · NEW YORK · SYDNEY

First published in Great Britain 2011
This paperback edition published 2012

Copyright © 2011 by Marika Cobbold

The moral right of the author has been asserted

Bloomsbury Publishing, London, Berlin, New York and Sydney
50 Bedford Square, London WC1B 3DP

A CIP catalogue record for this book is available from the British Library

ISBN 978 1 4088 2194 7

10 9 8 7 6 5 4 3 2 1

Typeset by Hewer Text UK Ltd, Edinburgh
Printed by Clays Ltd, St Ives plc

MIX
Paper from
responsible sources
FSC
www.fsc.org   FSC® C018072

www.bloomsbury.com/marikacobbold

To Michael,

my common frame of reference

One

Eliza

WHAT DO YOU SAY to a man whose life you destroyed? That was the question I asked myself when, out of the blue, my godfather phoned just as I was leaving work at the museum.

'Am I speaking to Eliza?' It was the voice of an old man, a little hoarse, trembling on the last syllable. 'This is Ian Bingham.'

What sun there had been, pallid and diffident, had set a while ago but darkness was banished by the street lamps and cars and, since the weekend, the Christmas lights in the trees and round the ice-rink further up by the Science Museum. I loved that artificial brightness; it softened the blow of night and winter.

My bus drove past, pulling in at the stop just a few yards away but I stayed where I was on the front steps of the building. Sleet was falling from a low sky but in my mind I saw wind-blown ripples of water lapping against a wooden jetty in the monochrome light of a spring evening.

'I expect you're surprised to hear from me.'

Oh yes. The last time we had seen each other had been some moments after he had admitted he couldn't stand the sight of me. He had been inside the house, talking to my mother. I had been sketching in the garden on the bench right outside the open window. Even now, twenty-five years later, I could recall his words precisely; they weren't the kind that you forgot.

'I know it's unfair, Olivia, and I've tried my best, but the truth is that I can barely stand to be in the same room as her. I can't stand looking at her, or hearing her voice.' There had been a pause before he added, his voice lower but not too low for me to hear. 'And the worst of it is I find myself wishing it had been her.'

I didn't blame him for feeling that way; in fact I felt pretty much the same way myself. But it was still hard to hear him say it. For a while, following the accident, the friendship between my mother and Uncle Ian had dragged along, like an injured fox trying to reach the safety of the roadside, snarling and biting at anyone trying to get close. But at that moment, with those words, it died.

'Eliza, are you there?' Uncle Ian asked.

My voice seemed all bunched up in my throat and I had to take some extra breaths before managing a feeble 'Yes.'

'Your mother gave me your number.'

'Oh. She didn't tell me you'd been in touch.' I paused before asking, 'Are you in London?'

'No, I'm at home. In Sweden.'

I hoped he hadn't heard my sigh of relief. A wet snowflake landed on my lashes like an insect and I wiped my eye, smudging the back of my hand with mascara.

'I didn't know you'd moved to Sweden.'

'There's no reason why you should know.' There was a pause. Then he said, 'You'll no doubt be wondering why I'm calling.'

I nodded before remembering the obvious fact that he couldn't see me. 'Well yes, I am. Although it's lovely to hear from you. I mean there doesn't always need to be a reason for calling other than the call itself. If you see what I mean.' I was making the kind of conversation Uncle Ian used to compare to an idling engine.

'I never intended for us to lose touch in this way. Still, better late than never, eh?' He gave a forced laugh.

'No' would have been my honest reply, but as every child knows, there was a time and a place for honest answers and quite often that's a different time and a different place. 'Absolutely,' I said.

'I would very much like to see you.'

'You would?'

'I was hoping you might be able to come over for a visit?'

I switched the phone from my right to my left ear and then back again. My voice sounded like someone else's, high-pitched and anxious as I said, 'A visit? To you?'

'Well, of course to me.'

Annoyance made his voice younger and I thought it was quite comical how, after a quarter of a century, we had managed to pick up where we had left off; as Irritated and Irritant.

'And don't worry about the tickets. I'll arrange all that.'

'I'll get tickets.'

'I am inviting you.'

'Really, I'd prefer to get them myself.'

He sighed. 'You always were stubborn.'

I thought that as reconciliations went this one was definitely not up there with the greats. A second bus passed, its massive wheels squelching.

'My bus is here. May I call you back?' But I didn't board this time either. I needed to stay out in the open. My entire body was itching as if ants were using my veins as motorways. My chest was aching from all the swallowed words and most likely, once this conversation was over, I would have to shout and scream and swear which, were I on a bus, might cause alarm. So instead I sat down on the museum steps, not caring about the cold and wet while all around me the city I thought of as my friend carried on as if nothing had happened.

My phone rang a second time. 'It's, me, Ian. Are you on your bus?'

'Didn't make it.'

'I realised that of course you won't have my number and it won't have come up on your phone as it's a trunk call.'

'Sorry. I didn't think about that.'

'So, you'll come?'

There was a pause and then I asked the obvious question. 'Uncle Ian, what made you decide to get in touch, now, after all this time?'

It was his turn to hesitate before saying in a pre-emptive voice, as if he expected to be challenged, 'It was Rose.'

My heart leapt like a fish in my chest. 'Rose?'

'That's what I said.'

I scrunched up my eyes and the headlights of the passing traffic elongated and merged into a stream of golden light. I pushed a strand of damp hair from my face. 'How do you mean, Rose?'

'I saw her.'

He'd gone mad. Or senile? Please let it be senile. Senile wouldn't be my fault, but grief could make you crazy. 'You've seen Rose?'

'That's what I said.' I could hear he was trying to stop himself from snapping. 'She's angry.'

Rose was angry. Of course she was. I put the mobile down on the step, having decided against throwing it into the road. I pushed my head between my knees, taking deep breaths, one after the other.

'Eliza, Eliza, are you there?'

I realised that I'd been rocking back and forth like some crazy woman. I straightened up and picked up the phone. 'I'm here.'

'As I said, she's angry with me.'

'With *you*?'

'There is no need to repeat every word I say. It's all perfectly straightforward. Rose came to see me. And she is angry with me for neglecting you all these years. She told me to get on and sort it out.'

That last bit dispelled any doubts I might have had as to the state of mind of my godfather. He had gone mad. Rose would never tell him or anyone else to 'get on and sort it out'. Getting on was not what Rose did. Rose rested and she hesitated, she shook her head and hid her face, she wandered and floated but she did *not* get on with it. Nor did she sort things out. Instead she smiled sweetly at a problem. Sometimes she laughed at it. She walked round it and over it and under it. She did not sort it out. That's what the rest of the world had been for.

'Uncle Ian, Rose can't be angry.' I paused. It was hard to go on. 'She can't be anything.'

'I'm telling you that I saw her. You can believe me or not.' This was a man who had worn two watches, each for a different time zone. A man, who when he closed a factory, closed a town; a man who had never to my knowledge sat in a soft chair. I should not let the voice that had become as unreliable as that of an adolescent boy mislead me, nor the fact that he seemed to be seeing ghosts; Uncle Ian remained the kind of man who brooked no arguments.

'She told me to get in touch with you and she was right to do so. My neglect of you, my betrayal of your dear father's trust, has weighed heavy on my conscience and ...'

'But you were entirely right to feel the way you did.' I must have been shouting because the woman hurrying past, laden with Harrods bags, stopped abruptly and stared. Seeing nothing out of the ordinary, just a woman speaking too loudly on her mobile, she hurried on, her expression once more reflecting only the usual despair of the Christmas shopper.

'Rose doesn't think so. She wants me to make amends. And I agree with her.'

I looked around me for reassurance but the world had slipped out of focus and for now, remained that way. The people, the cars, the buildings, all appeared distorted, like reflections in a funfair mirror, the kind that were supposed to make you laugh. Never being able to make amends, I thought, was a particular kind of hell. I said, 'Of course I'll come.'

'Thank you, Eliza,' the old man said. 'I'll tell Rose. She will be very pleased.'

Two

AS WE FINISHED OUR conversation another bus drove up and this time I got on. I rode through the city, gazing at the festive streets. From the hive of electric lights, the energy-wasting, global warming-schwarming two-fingered gesture to the mood of our time that was Harrods, through the grand baubles of Regent Street to the scrappy strings of traffic-light coloured bulbs nearer home, London, like a good old girl, was making an effort.

The day, when it began, had given me no warning that it was going to turn out to be any different from any other Tuesday. I am not a morning person. My natural inclination, when faced with the choice of catching a worm or staying in my warm bed, is to leave the worm for a more deserving, perkier bird. It had been no different this morning when it had taken three alarms sounding in sequence as well as the mantra that never failed to put a spring in my step, 'Get out of bed, you useless lump, and be grateful you're not dead', to get me up.

I had opened the curtains, that were yellow with a pattern of flowers and butterflies in the dragon-reds and blues and greens of Fairyland Lustre Ware, and looked out on to my street. All had been as it usually was: the bags of rubbish drawn to the lamp-post at the corner like party-goers to the most glittering guest, the graffiti taking the place of Christmas wreaths on the row of doors opposite and the large dog of undetermined parentage taking his morning dump in the middle of the pavement while his owner, a fat middle-aged man dressed like a rocker, looked the other way. As usual I had toyed with the idea of sticking my head out of the window and, if not actually yelling abuse, at least asking him, politely, if he would mind clearing up after his pet. As always I decided not to as I didn't want him posting the turd through my letterbox. After my shower I had eaten my usual breakfast of Cheerios with a sliced banana and a large mug of sweet milky tea while I glanced through the paper. It was Tuesday so my day to walk Mrs Milford's dachshund, Jonah. I didn't like Mrs Milford or Jonah, but somehow it had been my idea to set up a rota amongst neighbours willing to walk the damn dog after MRSA following a hip operation had landed Mrs Milford in a wheelchair.

Jonah had, as usual, bitten me as I tried to put his harness on. Jonah was a small dog so his bites, leaving two punctures and a slight swelling, were more like the bites of a mildly venomous snake, but I had been careful to keep up my tetanus shots all the same. I had asked another neighbour on the rota how long a miniature dachshund might be expected to live – Jonah was seven – and she had told me up to seventeen years.

By eight o'clock I had delivered Jonah back home to Mrs Milford and by eight fifteen I was on the bus. At eight fifty-five I had walked through the staff entrance of the museum. I had made my way up the stairs and along the corridors to the ceramic restoration studio, feeling the modest thrill I always felt as I went about my business behind the scenes, as if moving around the intricate works of a beautiful old clock. Diana, one of the other restorers, and I were about to start work on a rare William de Morgan panel. The panel was an exciting find. It had not been thought that any of the panels de Morgan designed for the P&O liners had survived until this was discovered in an architectural salvage yard in Somerset.

I had told my mother all about it a day or so ago. I had sensed I was losing my audience; it might have been the tapping of fingernails against the receiver or possibly the fact that she was simultaneously keeping up a conversation with my stepfather: 'In the drawer. I said in the drawer. No, not that one. The one to the left. Well, right then. Don't be so pedantic.'

I wound up my story of the tiles and my mother had suggested that I go and buy myself something nice to wear. She might not share my enthusiasm for porcelain but she did place great importance on appearance and she seemed to sense the gaps in my wardrobe even from the other side of the world in Australia.

Diana and I had spent most of the day bent over the boxes, unwrapping the jewel-coloured tiles and fragments and placing them on the worktable, where they were left like broken promises. It had seemed no time at all had passed when darkness settled once more and the end of the day had been reached. By six o'clock I was making my way back down the corridors of the museum and on to the street.

So, I thought as I rode home on the bus, it had been a day much like any other, a day giving me no clue that at its end I would be feeling like a glove puppet wrenched inside out, left to gaze uncomfortably at what was hidden inside.

I reached my stop. The sleet had turned to rain and I hurried towards home, clip clop clip clop, in step with all the other drones, heads down, not looking left nor right, expressions blank when eyes accidentally met eyes, wanting only to reach the scents and warmth of home. I expected those others were thinking about what to cook for supper; thinking longingly of kicking off sodden shoes and swapping their uptight work clothes for something soft and loose and smelling of Lenor; looking forward perhaps to something nice on the television. At least, that was how my own thoughts went most winter evenings as I made my way those last few yards to home. But not this evening. Tonight it felt as if my mind were under attack from a swarm of killer bees each carrying its own deadly sting: a laughing girl, a moonlit lake, a cry for help, an angry grieving father, a careless friend who should have known better.

I sang quietly to myself as I marched in step: 'Oh death where is your stingeling-a-ling your stingeling-aling your stingelingaling,' a smile fixed on my lips. Smiles however forced, they had told me at the clinic, brought smiley feelings with them. Just not tonight. I tried another trick: reciting facts, lovely, sure-footed, neutral facts, unchanging unchangeable facts, facts beyond my control. The Loire, France's longest river. Lisbon, located at the mouth of the River Tejos. The Mediterranean, connected to the Atlantic by the Sound of Gibraltar and the Suez Canal. Rhymes were good too, simple, repetitive, constant: *Jack and Jill went up the hill . . . Ding dong dell . . . Humpty Dumpty . . .* no, not that. Humpty Dumpty was nothing but an ode to defeatism. The very antithesis of what a restorer stood for. I would have put him together again. It was what I did.

I reached my front door. My flat was above a bridal shop. It was not a very good shop. Sometimes I would stand at the window looking at the young women arriving with their mothers and sisters and friends, all smiles and excited chatter. Then, some little time later they would come out looking a little bewildered, a little less glossy, as if the lacklustre pick of frocks and veils supplied by the shop had given them a foretaste of the compromises that lay ahead. But the shop was shut for the day and there was no one around now as I let myself in. I had my own front door and a tiny hallway with stairs leading up to the actual flat, that consisted of a bedroom and bathroom, a sitting room and a kitchen.

Once I'd changed into the soft shapeless grey dress that was just respectable enough to open the door in but scruffy enough to count as comfort wear, I poured myself a glass of red wine and switched on the news with its comforting litany of bad tidings and other people's misery: Yes, we were having a cold snap but do not be fooled, the world was getting hotter and in the future wars would be fought over water. There was flooding in the north. The nation's debt was increasing. Greed and folly and abject materialism were to blame. We needed to increase spending on the high street. People were being laid off. And never ever forget to eat your Five a Day.

I found it soothing. I felt detached and blameless. I was not a banker or an MP or a gas-guzzler or a footballer's wife or an oligarch; I wasn't even American and most days I ate not just a banana but also an orange, a carrot and at least two other kinds of fruits or vegetables.

So what did Uncle Ian really want after nearly a quarter of a century's silence?

I turned the sound up on the television: The country had gone from 'A terrorist attack is imminent' alert to 'A terrorist attack is certain but might not happen until next month' alert. I also learnt that the new kind of euro-approved, planet-saving light bulbs do in fact kill on contact when broken and need to be transported by special contamination units to a dump beyond where any government official lives until unearthed by future generations who really won't mind their children being born with six little fingers and six little toes. And don't you ever forget those dinosaurs. They too carried on as if they were going to live for ever, putting their kids through school, planning their holidays and saving for their pensions and then – one little meteor strike and it was all over. That's how fragile it all was.

I switched off. There was only so much good cheer a person could take at any one time.

I wanted to talk to my mother to ask if, when Uncle Ian had spoken to her, he had told her what he really wanted. And why she hadn't warned me that Uncle Ian was going to ring me. She warned me about everything else. Terrorists: on Tubes, buses, airplanes. Flu: Bird, Swine, Spanish. Poisoning: food, spider crossing ocean on bunch of bananas, date rape drugs dropped in one's drink. (The trick to avoiding the latter was to stick closer to your Bacardi Breezer than a starlet to her plastic surgeon.) Radiation: Wi Fi, mobile phone, Radon, Russian assassins. So why had she not tipped me the wink that Uncle Ian was planning to call? But I had to wait as it was only six o'clock in the morning in Sydney and like me, Olivia was not a morning person. In fact, she wasn't much of a night person either, peaking instead in the few hours between a late breakfast and her afternoon nap.

I thought about supper but unusually I wasn't hungry. Instead I brought out my box of broken bits and pieces from its place beneath the kitchen table. With space at a premium, beneath was a very useful place. Next I protected the oak kitchen table top from further damage with a sheet of yesterday's newspaper. Then I laid out the contents of the box. The challenge, as always, was to construct something that was, if not useful, at least decorative, from the shards of coloured glass and porcelain. I liked it best when the resulting piece ended up being *both* useful and decorative. It was this dual quality that attracted me to ceramics in general, the ambition it so often harboured of turning the everyday tools of life, plates and cups, pots and jugs, thimbles and boxes, vases and containers, into things of beauty.

I spent a while arranging the broken bits into different patterns, seeing if an idea would come to me but nothing did. I crouched to the level of the table top and squinted; sometimes interesting shapes appeared that way, but still nothing. No metamorphosis. What was broken tat was still just that. So I put the pieces back in the box. I stared down at the ungrateful shards and for a moment I was tempted to throw the whole thing in the bin but of course I didn't. You don't discard something until it's certain there is nothing left to do. I couldn't free myself from the thought of the maker of a piece. They might have put their heart and soul into the production. They might have looked at the finished article and felt pride at the thought of their work living on and giving pleasure to others. They might have died soon after making that particular pot, mug, plate, making it the very last thing left behind by a once living being. Or, they might have tossed if off with scant thought before taking the bus back home in time for tea. Either way I didn't like to take the risk. So I put the box back beneath the table.

What did Uncle Ian really want?

I decided to call Gabriel.

If Uncle Ian asked about how my life had panned out in the twenty-five years since we last spoke I could at least tell him that although I was undoubtedly alive, things had not gone all my way and Gabriel was a good example of that. Gabriel was tall and fair and handsome, a doctor specialising in that most un-telegenic of fields, geriatrics. Gabriel had been born to be head boy. Born to rescue kittens caught up trees and to befriend the funny-looking kid who everyone else gave a hard time. It was all this goodness, this need to help and manage, that had made him fall in love with me, a woman who had spent years not caring if she lived or died, and if asked would admit to a slight preference for dying, a woman who still somehow always managed to get thrown back into the swim of life like the wrong kind of catch. And it had been these same characteristics that had caused Gabriel to leave once it had become clear that there was not much more he could do and that I was floating, if not happily (exaggeration gets you nowhere) but safely enough, in the shallows of existence. That and a waif-like brunette with a history of self-harm and a great deal of 'cheerful pluck'.

And I could see his point. 'Waif-like brunette' conjured up attractive images of ingénue actresses and who in this world was not drawn to 'cheerful pluck'? The self-harming, well, I would have thought there might have been a certain 'been there, done that, bought the T-shirt' feeling about that for him, but then we weren't talking about what I thought.

'What can I do?' Gabriel had said during that endless month when he had been trying to leave our marriage with his belief in his own goodness intact. 'I'm really worried she won't cope. I mean, really won't cope.'

I had looked up at his handsome anguished face and given a little shrug. 'Let her die?'

Of course he had not thought that especially funny and nor, after two seconds' thought had I, as that is what you could say I had done with Rose. So then I had started crying hysterically and he had wept a little too and we had held each other tight and made love and then the whole damn sorry carousel had started all over again. Until it stopped finally and for the last time.

That was three years ago. I had adored Gabriel. In truth I still did. For the first few weeks after he had left the pain of the loss was such that I hadn't been able to sit or lie for more than a few minutes at a time, day or night. Instead I had walked and tapped and hummed and picked and turned and shrugged and muttered. At work I had ended up over-restoring a piece and had been told to take a week off. At home I made a lot of little clay hearts which I then smashed with a hammer before putting back together in hideous and unnatural shapes. But of course, as usually happens in these matters, it got easier. The sound and the fury abated and settled down to a low hum of distress that was, nevertheless, able to rise back into a crescendo at the most inopportune moments. Eventually, once a year or so had passed, there came a kind of peace. The kind that comes when there's nothing left to fight for.

And we had remained friends. Ours had been the kind of divorce everyone admired for the civilized manner in which it was conducted. In fact, at the time I could have been forgiven for thinking that what everyone wanted most of all for Christmas that year had been a nice new divorce just like Gabriel and Eliza's.

The waif had plumped up and her cuts had healed yet it was she, not he, who had ended the relationship. Gabriel had not come running back to me but he did still phone once a fortnight. I always imagined that these calls occurred at times when he found himself unaccountably out of sick old people, injured birds and kittens up trees, and was at loss as to what to do next. I would tell him that I was tickity boo and tum tiddily tum and never ever better. He would sound satisfied; another unfortunate had been ticked off his list, and then he'd hang up before I changed my mind and told him how I really felt. It was only a week since we had last spoken but after some hesitation I picked up the phone and dialled his mobile. I called him sufficiently rarely for him to sound concerned as he picked up. 'Eliza, is everything all right?'

I told him everything was fine. There was silence as he waited for me to tell him more. So I said that actually I wasn't completely fine and that I would like very much to see him. I never asked to see him. He was just finishing off at the hospital, he said. Then he would be right over.

I remembered that I was wearing my baggy grey dress and went up and changed into a somewhat less baggy grey dress. I added a short string of large fake pearls that, as my friend and colleague Beatrice had agreed when I had showed it to her, might have been taken for Chanel if Chanel made cheap-looking pearl necklaces. I reapplied some lipstick and then I went downstairs to wait.

Three

THE DOORBELL RANG AND I rushed down the stairs, pouncing as if he were prey. He filled up the doorway with his height and the width of his shoulders. He swept his cycling helmet off and raked back his fair hair. His cheeks were pink from exercise. He exuded life and warmth. We kissed, a brush of lips on cheeks.

In the kitchen I pulled out one of the cornflower-blue painted kitchen chairs for him and poured us some red wine. I wondered if he thought about the day we'd got those chairs. We had been wandering around the architectural salvage yards in Hackney looking for fire surrounds and old tiles. The four chairs, spindle-broken and white-chipped, had been huddled together outside at the back. One even missed a leg. But I had felt certain that deep down they were good chairs, they just needed someone to bring them out of themselves. Gabriel had not been convinced but it had been the month anniversary of our wedding and he had been in the mood to agree with pretty well everything I wanted to do. It had taken me the best part of two weeks to restore the chairs, working in the evening and at the weekends, but the result had been well worth it: four French café chairs, two blue and two the yellow of the chair in Van Gogh's painting.

'My godfather called,' I said as I sat down opposite him. 'And you look exhausted.'

'I'm fine,' he said. 'Are you talking about Rose's father?'

I nodded. 'It's been twenty-five years. Well, give or take.'

'Right,' Gabriel said.

'You really do look tired.'

'I told you I'm fine.'

'Well, I think you look tired.'

'Do you want me to be?'

I shrugged. 'Maybe. It would show you're human. I know human is overrated but it would give us a connection at least. As in you're human, I'm human; wow, whoever would have thought it.'

'It upset you to hear from him?'

'Well, yes it did. He was very nice and friendly so it wasn't that.'

'Then what?'

'It's just that it's brought everything back.'

'I thought you'd dealt with all that.'

'I had. Sort of.'

'So the call shouldn't have upset you like this.'

'I know. But try telling that to the call.'

'What?'

'You said the call shouldn't have upset me so I said . . . oh never mind. I shouldn't have bothered you.'

'It's not a bother. I've meant to pop around for ages. So did he say why he was getting back in touch after all this time?'

'He said it was Rose.'

'Rose?'

I pulled a face. 'I know. Is he senile, do you think?'

Gabriel shrugged. 'I would need to examine him in order to establish that.'

'Insane?'

'Same answer, I'm afraid. Did he sound insane or senile to you, apart from the bit about Rose?'

I was not a weeper as a rule but suddenly, and to the surprise of us both, I was crying. It was the shock of the call that did it, that and Gabriel sitting there as if he belonged, the glass of wine in his hand, his legs outstretched, cutting the kitchen floor in half. But at the sound of crying he straightened up like a soldier at reveille and reached across to take my hand. Next he got up to find some tissues. There were none in the kitchen so instead he tore off some kitchen roll and handed it to me. I dabbed at my eyes and blew my nose. I got up and threw the ball of paper in the bin and then I washed my hands.

'Have you eaten yet?' I asked. He shook his head. 'Would you like to stay for supper?' He said he would. I asked him if pasta and tomato sauce was OK. He said it was, which was lucky as that was all I had. That and parmesan cheese.

Saving lives was hungry work and Gabriel ate a whole plateful of the pasta in near silence before saying, 'You shouldn't be worried about meeting your godfather. It's pretty normal, as you approach the end of your life, to want to tie up the loose ends. I see it all the time at work on the wards. It's as if they have a mental list of I's to dot and T's to cross before they feel they can let go.'

I thought how it would be to be thought of simply as a loose end in Ian Bingham's life. Being a loose end sounded relatively benign, and eminently solvable. I reached across and topped up our wine glasses.

He put his fork down and took my hand. His fair hair fell in a wave across his forehead and his blue-grey gaze was fond and my heart beat faster. 'You're not drinking, are you, Eliza?'

I withdrew my hand and straightened up, about to inform him that if what he meant was, was I drinking too much, the answer was no. But just as I was about to speak it occurred to me that maybe I should take on a sad dishevelled look and tell him, eyes downcast, that yes, yes I was, but that the love of a good man would most probably cure me of my filthy addiction now as it had done in the past.

I sighed. 'No, I'm not. Not at all. But thank you for asking.'

'Good.' He smiled at me the way I'd seen him smile at patients, reassuring, caring yet detached. 'Now, what would you like me to do? To help, I mean.'

I smiled back at him. I could do detached myself. 'Nothing at all. I just needed someone to talk to who knew the history.'

Four

THE CAB THAT UNCLE Ian had booked to meet me at the airport was white with a yellow go-faster stripe and a cartoon chauffeur in 1950s uniform emblazoned on the side. They were the official taxis, Uncle Ian had told me, sounding like my mother. Any others might rob me or at least lose their way and end up taking me to Borås. Borås, by the sound of it, had to be a downtown rough-hewn bad-boy kind of place, I thought. I would Google it once I was back home. As we drove out of Gothenburg and into the snow-covered countryside I thought of Grandmother Eva, Uncle Ian's mother, who had been Swedish. She had helped bring Rose up after Rose's mother left. I had been very fond of her and she, although she obviously loved Rose the best, seemed to have had the space to love me too. In that I believe she was typically Swedish: even-handed.

Eva Bjorkman told us stories of dark woods and of meres as deep and as black as night. She told us of the Huldra, the Lady of the Forest who would lure handsome young men deep into the woods using her beauty and the magic of her voice. Sometimes the Huldra made love to the young men and rewarded them with untold riches but sometimes she abandoned them to the deep impenetrable forest from which no human could find their way out unaided. You knew you had been snared by the Huldra when she turned her hollow back on you and showed her tail, which was sometimes that of a cow and sometimes that of a fox. Rose and I had fought over who, in our games, would be the Huldra as opposed to the hapless swain. Rose, with her perfect beauty, looked the part but my singing had been just a little bit better and singing was a good way for a Huldra to lure. Then again my hands and feet were large, which was more the mark of a swain, hapless or not, than a temptress. We had ended up taking turns wearing the old white nightgown donated by Grandmother Eva although we never did manage to work out how to make our backs hollow. However, we had found an old fox's brush in the dressing-up box in Eva's attic and once we'd tied it to the back of a belt the rear view was pretty impressive. As Eva had said, the tail was definitely the most important give-away for a Huldra.

I smiled at the memory of when life had been both simple and full of promise as I sat there in the back of the cab driving me to Uncle Ian's house some thirty miles outside of town. He had moved from the house that he had inherited from his mother, the house I had visited as a child. This new place was not far away, however, and as the car stopped at a crossroads I recognised the small white painted church with its green copper roof and tumbledown graveyard.

The sun sat low above the pine trees, not quite reaching the forest bed but casting pebbles of golden light across the snow that covered the ground like whipped egg white. Every window in every house was lit by a Christmas light. Rose and I had lights just like that for our bedroom windows, wooden with seven electric candles forming a chevron. Rose's had been white and mine had been red. I wondered what had become of them.

The car took another left off the main road and drove down what was little more than a track through the fields. We turned a corner, the car slowed and we had arrived.

Three wooden buildings, dragon-blood red, with white-painted window frames and pine-green doors, were grouped round a slate stone courtyard swept clean of snow. Behind them was the forest. The driver got out of the car, opening the passenger door on the way to the boot. I stepped out, but gingerly, as if the ground were burning. I realised that the driver was speaking and I turned round and apologised. As I brought out my wallet my hands shook.

A door opened and a woman stepped out from the porch, waving. 'Eliza.' She placed the accent on the 'i' just as Eva had done. I squinted against the sun and then I waved back.

The woman was tall and lean but sturdily built. Her steel-grey hair was cropped short and even in mid-winter her skin was tanned. 'The snow's come early,' she said. Then she put out her hand and took mine in a firm grip. 'I'm Katarina. He's inside, waiting for you.'

Our feet cracked the thin layer of frost on the stones as we walked across to the main house. I realised I was holding my breath and I let it go in a puff of steam. If there were such a thing as judgement day, I thought, was this what it would feel like?

'So, Sweden,' I said, 'population 9,208,034. But then you probably knew that?'

Katarina turned with a polite smile. 'No, no, I didn't. Not down to that exact number, anyway.'

We stepped inside into a hall painted golden yellow. A striped rag-rug in red and green lay spread across the floorboards. *The metropolitan area of Stockholm is home to around 22 per cent of the population of the country. In Gothenburg the city proper is home to a population of 508,714 with 510,491 in the urban area and total of 920,283 inhabitants in the metropolitan area.* White lace curtains like bridal veils draped the windows and there were pictures, some watercolours and some pencil drawings, on most of the available wall space. I put my suitcase down but kept hold of my handbag. By now my heart was pounding against my chest like a crazy person against the walls of a padded cell and no one could hear a thing. I continued to focus on the decor. Getting immersed in your surroundings, 'being fully in the now', was another trick, or 'coping mechanism' as they called them at the clinic, for those occasions when what I really wanted to do was to jump screaming from a tall building or drive a car into a tree at a hundred miles per hour. It had worked so far; that and not keeping a car or going near tall buildings. So as I approached the moment of facing Rose's father once more I focused on the decor. The first thing to note was that it was nice. What exactly made it so nice? Perhaps it was the use of colour, joyful combinations a child might use in a drawing before they learnt that pink didn't go with red. Maybe it was simply the very un-beigeness of it all that was so pleasing.

'Would you like to freshen up first?' Katarina asked.

I thought about it. Did I want to delay the inevitable by taking a small detour, the scenic route to the gallows, or was it best just to get it over with? I turned to her with a smile. 'I'm fine, thanks.'

I followed as she led the way through the small library and into a large rectangular room with windows on three sides. I imagined my feet on backwards so that with every step I was actually getting further away.

'And here is the sitting room,' Katarina said. This room was painted in a warm apricot pink and the wooden-framed sofa and two of the chairs were upholstered in pale blue and white striped cotton. The curtains were of the same white lace as in the hall and the floorboards were of the same golden pine. The rugs here were finer, though. Chinese silk in gold and shades of blue from sapphire to dove. There was a tiled stove and a fire warmed the room. The tiles were Delft-blue and white in a delicate flower and bow pattern I recognised as Gustavian. Katarina cleared her throat and the tall figure in the wingchair by the window turned to face me. I heard the soft click of a door shutting and we were alone.

Five

Sandra/Cassandra

I DON'T WANT TO appear big-headed but I always knew I was destined for something special. People around here are nice enough but they're ordinary, humdrum. Their lives are not the kind I see myself living. Most of all I didn't want the life my parents had. They knew that's how I felt and to be fair they understood, which was why they were making the sacrifice.

'We won't see her for dust will we, Derek?' my mother said to my father as I was getting ready to leave. 'She'll be far too busy with all her new friends to have time for her old parents.'

'Oh yes, hobnobbing with all those debs and whatnots,' my father said, and I sighed and rolled my eyes although secretly I agreed with them.

I'd had a brother once but he died, and my father had ambition once, hoping for a promotion and a move to the country but the promotion happened to someone else, and someone else after that, so my mother never got her big garden. So for a long time now I had been the only thing my parents really cared about. It was exhausting, quite frankly. They ruled me with their innocence, controlled me with their goodness and gagged me with their adoration. I couldn't wait to get away.

I waved goodbye to them as they stood on the doorstep of the pebbledash box that was my home. They both had their hankies out. Tears rolled down my father's cheeks. 'Tears of pride,' he kept saying. 'Don't worry, Princess, they're tears of pride.'

I hadn't been able to sleep properly for a week and each morning I had ticked off another day in my diary as if I were a child waiting for Christmas, instead of what I was, a teenager about to go off to boarding school. But seeing them, my parents, standing there so small and, well, humble, I suddenly wasn't so sure I wanted to go after all. I felt like running over to them and putting my arms round them and telling them I loved them. Then I got annoyed. They didn't need to be that pathetic. All that was needed was a flat cap for my father and wrinkled stockings for my mother and they could have walked straight out of *Last of the Summer Wine*. Us not having a car used to really upset me but now I thanked God. If we'd had one they would have insisted on taking me all the way to LAGs. Honestly, I would have died! As it was, Mr Bennings, the minicab driver, was dropping me, for free, at the train station and then the school minibus would pick me up the other end. Apparently there were several girls on that same train from Manchester.

I turned round and looked behind me as we drove off. My parents were still waving. I realised how stooped they both were. Jesus, they were sixty, not a hundred. My father's roses, though, those garish Peace and Queen Elizabeth roses, stood ramrod straight, glad to get rid of me no doubt. They had long memories, flowers, and I suppose they'd never forgotten the weed-killer incident.

I had tried to make my parents see how naff our garden was. 'Like some municipal park with everything in perfect straight lines. Jessica's garden is all wild and overgrown. It's gorgeous.'

'Well, Jessica's parents are very bohemian, aren't they?'

I would have killed to have bohemian parents but instead I had a mother who crocheted antimacassars and a father who used a tape measure when he planted his narcissi.

Three hours after leaving home, I stepped out on to the hallowed gravel of the Lakeland Academy for Girls and right in front of a reception committee. Three girls, one dark, one fair and one auburn, all of them tall and willowy and managing somehow to make the lumpen blue/grey uniform look chic, spoke at once. 'You must be Sandra.'

I never felt Sandra suited me as a name. Of course my parents were pleased with their choice. To show me what a great pick it was they pointed to Sandra Castle, Lady Mayoress of our town about a hundred years ago and to such luminaries as Sandra Dee (some old actress who anyway had actually been christened Alexandra, which wasn't so bad). I had never met people so pleased about so little as my parents were. Most of all they were pleased with me. They worshipped me from my thick ankles to the ends of my frizzy hair, or golden curls, as mother liked to describe it. My mother and Aunt Gina said I had style and character and that was worth much more than just a pretty face. And I had believed them, sort of, until I saw the princesses.

Then I heard myself say, 'I'm christened Sandra but everyone calls me Cassandra.' OK, so that wasn't actually true. But this was the start of my new life. Why shouldn't I be allowed a new name too, a name that suited me?

'Oh right?' The fair princess smiled politely. She was the tallest. She had sparkling blue eyes and honey skin. 'That's unusual, though, your nickname being longer than your real name. I'm Portia, by the way.'

'But if you prefer Cassandra,' the dark one said. She smiled too, a sort of all-purpose smile that might have been directed at me, or the minibus or a bird in a tree. 'I'm Rose.'

I took in the cascade of dark curls, the wide blue eyes and the peaches and cream complexion that looked as if it'd die of shock if it encountered a pimple. I wondered what it felt like going about the world being that beautiful.

'Why don't you like Sandra?' the auburn princess asked. She put her hand out, a long-fingered, rather large hand, and shook mine in a firm grip. 'I'm Eliza.'

Portia, Rose and Eliza; yeah, that figured.

The auburn princess seemed really to want to know the answer to her inane question because she asked again, 'Why don't you like Sandra?'

I shrugged. 'I'm used to Cassandra, that's all. I was only named Sandra to suck up to a rich godmother.' I smiled inwardly, pleased with my ingenuity.

'Miss Philips asked us to look after you, show you around and all that,' Portia said.

'I have a rich godfather,' Eliza said. 'But I won't get a bean from him because his avaricious daughter will inherit the lot.' At that all three of them laughed as if she had said something hilarious.

'Sorry, in-joke,' Rose said. 'It's my father, you see. My father is Eliza's godfather. And possibly soon to be stepfather.' She giggled.

I smiled back at them. In comparison with these girls Jessica and her family seemed positively conventional.

'So all she'll inherit is a stuffed fox,' Rose said. She turned to Eliza, 'Isn't that right?'

'Absolutely,' Eliza said. 'But I like the fox so that's OK.'
Then they fell into each other's arms and laughed some more.

I was shocked, actually. In my world you didn't start counting your inheritance while a person was still alive. At least if you did, you kept it to yourself.

'So,' Portia turned to me. 'Which one is yours?' She nodded towards the line of tuck boxes deposited at the back of the minibus. Stupid question. Mine was obviously the one without a single sticker. The brand-spanking-embarrassingly-new one. The one thing that would have been good to get second-hand my parents had insisted on getting new. 'Don't know what nasty dirty things someone might have kept in there,' my mother had said, wrinkling her nose at the very idea. I had tried to tell her how common it was to be bothered by dirt and germs. Jessica's place was a complete pigsty by my mother's standards but I wouldn't have been ashamed to take any of the girls from LAGs there. I bet the floors at the princesses' houses were a right health hazard.

Eliza helped me carry the embarrassing tuck box. As we walked along to the boarding house I asked her, 'So where's your real dad?'

'Dead.'

'And Rose's mum?'

'Gone. She lives on some Greek island somewhere. So Rose and I thought it would be really excellent if my mother and her father got married because then Rose and I would be sisters. We're making progress, aren't we?' She threw the last sentence over her shoulder.

'Certainly looks like it,' Rose said.

'So how rich is he, then?' I asked Rose, who had caught up. Next to me Eliza stiffened and her smile turned polite.

Rose said, 'I don't really think one asks people that kind of thing.'

I felt the heat rise in my cheeks. It was so unfair. They had talked about inheritance as if money and people dying were just some joke. They had opened the door but when I tried to step inside they had slammed it in my face.

At bedtime, Eliza came into my cubicle to see how I was doing. I decided I liked her after all. For a start she wasn't completely perfect-looking because of those large hands and feet and because of the slight bump on the bridge of her nose and the freckles. I thought we might become best friends.

Six

Eliza

WOULD HE ASK QUESTIONS first, or just shoot?

'Uncle Ian.'

Rose's father eased himself up from the chair and, as he reached standing, he wobbled, gripping the armrests for support. I had been about to step closer to give him a steadying hand but I had checked myself. When you were old the very last thing you wanted, probably, was to be treated as if you were. Instead I stood there, silent, while a quarter of a century's worth of words formed a disorderly queue at the back of my throat.

Rose and I had thought her father was old twenty-five years ago. To us then, forty, fifty, sixty ... was all much the same, a minor tragedy that was somehow never going to happen to us. And to Rose it hadn't. So just as Rose herself was frozen in time, for ever sixteen, Uncle Ian had been fixed in my mind the way he had seemed to me when we last met, old, so there was nothing much now to surprise me apart from perhaps the air of fragility. Like with a piece of porcelain filigree you would handle him with care and worry about breaks and cracks. That and the fact that I had found him reclining in a soft chair doing absolutely nothing seemed to me the only difference. In the old days you would be lucky if you interrupted him in one task, it was more usually two or three: speaking on the phone, reading through a pile of papers, signalling at someone to do something right then, that minute, no hanging about. But he stood tall still, he wore the same kind of wire-rimmed spectacles he had always worn, his hair, though thinner, was more sandy than grey and his nose, a good Roman nose that Rose had feared would sneak up on her one day, still dominated his face. Instead it was I who had changed the most, going from child to middle age in the time since our last meeting. I suddenly felt ashamed of my adult state, as if in having grown up I had done the wrong thing.

Uncle Ian held out his arms towards me and we embraced briefly, awkwardly, armour to armour.

'Eliza.'

I felt as if I had a face in two parts as my mouth smiled wide and my anxious eyes blinked. I knew of people who couldn't control their dogs or their children but not to be able to rule over your own face was quite frankly feeble.

'It's good of you to come.'

'It was kind of you to invite me.'

'Please,' he indicated the other chair. 'Sit down.' He began the process of lowering himself back down on his seat. I put my handbag on the small table between us. Then I picked it up again and placed it at my feet instead.

'It was good too, to speak to your mother again,' Uncle Ian said.

I was forty-one years old. My mother lived in Australia. I was used to managing without her, but right then I would have given a great deal to have her there.

'You'll want something to eat or drink after your journey?'

'I'd love some coffee.' I tried to think of something else to say, something inane, anything at all would do as long as it succeeded in warding off a meaningful conversation. I managed, 'It's quite early for snow, even for Sweden.'

Uncle Ian did well with, 'Quite early, yes.'

'Though it isn't as cold as one might have expected. Then again, it's true that it can be too cold for snow.' I gave a little laugh. 'People don't believe me when I tell them that but it's a fact.'

Uncle Ian nodded. 'Is that so.'

I thought I only needed to go on like this, spouting pointless little phrases, avoiding anything smacking of serious purpose, for three more days and then I'd be home and dry, back in my little flat.

'I've missed talking to your mother. We were good friends.'

It was my turn to nod. 'I know.'

'Do you get on with your stepfather?'

'Oh yes.'

'And he makes your mother happy?'

'Oh absolutely.'

Uncle Ian sat back and closed his eyes and for a moment I thought he might have dropped off but he opened them again almost immediately and said, 'When Barbro, that's my late wife, passed away I was still working. When that all came to an end, well, I've had time to think.'

'That's no good,' I said.

'What do you mean, that's no good?'

Just then Katarina entered the room. Either she knew people's minds or she had listened at the door because she was bringing coffee. As well as the coffee there was a plateful of buns and pastries. 'Seven sorts?' I smiled up at her.

Eva had told Rose and me about the custom of offering people coffee and seven varieties of cakes and pastries. Of course we had preferred the fairy tales over the niceties of entertaining. From the moment we had seen the picture of Näcken in one of Grandmother Eva's books we were in love with the beautiful naked boy who lived in the lakes and the rivers, playing his fiddle. Näcken's hair was a tumble of dark curls. His eyes, set into a face as pale as death, were filled with sorrow. Rose had thought Julian looked just like that picture. I hadn't seen the resemblance myself but that was infatuation for you; nothing but a mirror of your own deep desires. In the months after the accident I had told myself that Rose was with him, with Näcken, the beautiful boy with the fiddle, and that it was he who had brought her into the deep of the lake to sleep in his arms for ever. Those thoughts had been comforting at times and at others had driven me close to insanity.

'Not quite seven. Five, I think.' Katarina's voice brought me back.

'I seem to remember,' I said, 'that in Sweden, what we in England would call a biscuit counts as a cake. So it isn't quite as extravagant as it might at first appear to be. Of course a biscuit in America is what we would call a roll.'

'Really,' Katarina said. As she walked out of the room, the empty tray in her hand, I looked after her with long eyes and a sigh escaped me.

Uncle Ian said, 'I feel acutely at this stage, near the end of my life, that I have to settle with the past.'

I was biting into a moon-shaped butter biscuit when he said that and the crumbs caught in my dry throat. I choked and coughed. 'Sorry,' I said, 'frog in my throat. Do you ever wonder where that expression comes from? I mean, whoever would get a frog in their throat? And if we are dealing in unlikely scenarios why not go the whole hog and make it a toad. A toad sounds even more dramatic. Or a hog. I'm sorry, I've got a hog in my throat. Or would that just be silly? It would, wouldn't it? Because it is just about possible to swallow a frog or even a toad if it's small but a hog, never.'

'As I was saying,' he was speaking loudly and his sparse sandy eyebrows knitted together in a frown. 'I need to put things right before it's too late. That's what Rose was trying to tell me.'

'Rose?'

'I told you I had seen her.'

'Yes. Yes, you did.'

'Well then, there's no need to sound so surprised.' He changed the subject the way he always did when he was bored with an argument. 'Your mother filled me in on what has been happening in your life. Not that there was very much.' Uncle Ian always was one of these people who pride themselves on telling it as it is.

'Oh I don't know . . .'

'Don't be vague, Eliza. I can't be doing with vague.'

I had always irritated him. It had been good when that was the worst I could do to him.

'I'm sorry,' I said. 'I don't really know what to say.'

'Say what you think.'

Such an easy-sounding request yet almost impossible to acquiesce to. What would the world be like if everyone went around saying what they thought? Much like a city where all the traffic signals were broken and the cars had no brakes.

'I think not having had a lot happen is a good thing,' I said finally.

'I was in the bath this time.'

I took a gulp of coffee and scalded my tongue.

'It was a little awkward but luckily I had a towel to hand.'

'Sorry, I'm not quite following.'

'That's because you weren't paying attention. There were bubbles. Katarina insists on it. She says they're relaxing. I'm grateful now or it could have been embarrassing.'

I burst into a high-pitched laugh. I clamped my hand across my mouth, embarrassed. 'I'm sorry but it's just all been rather overwhelming. Your phone call, coming over to see you, Rose speaking to you. It's a lot to take in.' I decided not to say that I still had no idea where, in all of this, the bath came in.

Uncle Ian's frown relaxed. 'Your reaction is understandable. But as you get older you cease to be surprised because you realise how much there is out there and how little of it you could possibly know.'

I dabbed at my eyes with the little paper napkin. It had tiny blue forget-me-nots on it and lacy edges. 'We don't make such pretty paper napkins in the UK.'

'They're very keen on their paper in Sweden,' he said.

There was another silence. It was hard to make conversation when there was so much to say.

I drank some more coffee and my tongue stung from the earlier scalding.

'Ove, that's the new vicar,' he said finally. 'He explained that it's all about the need for closure.'

'Closure?' Hearing that particular buzzword from Uncle Ian's lips was as incongruous as finding him curled up with the latest issue of *Hello!*

'I'm not a well man.'

I forgot to be wary of him and reached out and touched his arm. 'I'm sorry.'

His gaze met mine. Then he smiled, a pale smile. 'It's Ove's theory that letting go will be a lot easier once I've put matters right with you. He says that most people struggle against death, not because of fear of death itself but because of leaving things undone, important things.' There was another pause as the gilt clock on the bureau struck three. Apart from that and the sound of the old man's laboured breathing it was quiet.

Are you really here, Rose? Darling Rose. I rested my head against the back of the chair and my eyes, staring at the ceiling, watered.

Uncle Ian spoke and I dabbed at my eyes and mimicked a smile before looking at him. 'I blamed you for what happened,' he said. 'And that was unfair.'

'It was entirely fair,' I said. I turned away, gazing out of the window. It was snowing. Thick fluffy flakes dropped and danced before the outside light like down from an eviscerated duvet.

Seven

I WOKE UP WITH a start to a landscape of silence. I had left the curtains open as, when I had gone to bed, there had been nothing to breach the impeccable darkness. It was still dark now so I switched on the bedside lamp to check the time. It was gone seven. There was no hurry to get up so I turned the light off again and lay back down against the pillow, closing my eyes. When next I woke there was noise; purposeful footsteps, water running, muted voices. Late dawn was spreading its rosy light across the sky, melding with the red of the barn opposite to lend the snow drifting against the wall a pink glow. I could smell coffee.

I threw on my dressing-gown and dashed across the landing to the bathroom, my sponge bag and some fresh clothes in my arms. There was no shower so I ran a bath. I lay back in the hot water feeling worn out, although the day had only just begun.

Before I went downstairs I checked the mirror. I looked grim, pasty-hued and puffy-eyed, with a tight little mouth on me. I patted on some lip gloss the colour and transparency of red currants and rubbed some more into my cheeks. I walked down the stairs like a small child or someone old, waiting to take the next step until both feet were firmly together on the one above. I studied the pictures running down the wall.

They were by a Swedish artist, Ivar Arosenius, a favourite of Grandmother Eva's. Poor Arosenius had died aged only thirty, at the beginning of the last century. He had known he was going to die young through an inherited illness that had carried away his two brothers. So in his thirty years on earth he painted and married and had a child and his paintings depicted life as a tender tragicomedy and his small daughter as a fragile source of light in a grown-up world of dark and giant objects. If I had been able to paint like Arosenius maybe then I would have deserved my place on earth even after what had happened. But I couldn't.

I reached the hall and in the kitchen they had heard my footsteps and Katarina called my name.

Uncle Ian was sitting at the kitchen table, eating porridge. He had been having porridge for breakfast for as long as I could remember. He said it made you live long. I knew there was a reason I liked Cheerios. Katarina poured me coffee which, like the day before, was black and bitter, and again like the day before I drank it down like medicine. I liked my coffee milky and best of all when sweetened with caramel syrup. I was sometimes told that I was lucky I wasn't fat when I had such a sweet tooth. I said luck had nothing to do with it; I simply cut back on real food. It was a simple enough measure available to anyone.

Looking out of the window, we all agreed it looked like it was going to be a lovely day and Uncle Ian and I retired to the glass veranda. My body had noted the word 'veranda' and anticipating cold, shuddered, but although three of the walls were glass it felt snug enough as we sat down side by side each in our white painted wicker armchairs that faced the snow-covered garden and the fields beyond. The sun had risen as far as it would go, hanging exhausted just above the tree line, shedding its pallid light.

'I have no one to talk to about her, about Rose. I speak of her and people look at me with a mixture of pity and boredom and I think that to them all she means is the social awkwardness of a long ago tragedy. The worst of it is, sometimes I can't remember. Talk to me about Rose, Eliza.'

Talk to him about her, my shadow companion. I closed my eyes. I searched my mind, but to my distress all I could see was my own guilt and shame like a grubby overlay obscuring the view of Rose herself.

He turned his head slowly as if he were pushing something heavy with the side of his face. Age was working against him, age that acted as a counterweight to everything he wanted to do. 'I know you remember.'

I felt so ashamed now at how hard I had worked *not* to remember. Ashamed of how I had skipped nimbly over memories that lay like jagged stones in my path. The lighter I stepped the less I felt.

I said, 'She was very beautiful.'

'Of course she was. That much is obvious from any photographs.'

'She loved parties,' I said. 'And dressing up. Do you remember the trunk full of old clothes and costume jewellery and hats and bags that Grandmother . . . your mother kept for us?'

He sighed impatiently. 'You could be talking about any one of a thousand sixteen-year-old girls.'

I closed my eyes. If I could just think of Rose up until that night and no further. If I could allow her to live in my mind how she had been up until that night then slam a door on what followed.

'What else do you remember?' Uncle Ian was growing impatient.

'She was funny.'

'Was she funny? I don't remember her being particularly funny. You were the funny one. You were precocious, quick. I'm afraid that used to annoy me. Rose's mother always accused me of turning everything into a competition and she was right.'

'I always knew I annoyed you.' I smiled. 'I just assumed it was because I was an annoying child.'

He gave a dry little laugh. 'Well, there was that too.'

'I don't mean she was particularly funny as in telling lots of jokes or saying funny things but she was so sweet, so other-worldly, in a funny way. She was funny-sweet.'

'Funny-sweet. I don't know what that means. What did she want to do with her life? What were her plans? Her hobbies? She liked ballet, I remember that.'

'She wanted to be an actress.'

He sighed. 'All young girls want to be actresses. Did she display any particular talent to mark her out in that field? And I don't want a whole load of polite waffling, Eliza. I don't have time for that.'

'I think she did.' I smiled as I did recall something concrete. 'Our drama teacher, Mr ... Oh ... Mr Whatever, I remember him saying that Rose reminded him of Vivien Leigh.'

'Did he really? Vivien Leigh.' He gave a delighted little laugh. 'You know now you point it out I can see similarities.'

'It wasn't just the looks but Rose had that same air of fragility. And these days people agree that Vivien Leigh was a much better actress than her contemporaries gave her credit for.'

'And she didn't like maths.' Uncle Ian's voice held a triumphant note as if he had found something he had lost and had been searching for. 'I remember her coming to me once when she was a little slip of a thing, crying and holding out this exercise book. "My head doesn't like sums," she said.' He was smiling. ' "My head doesn't like sums." You're right, she was funny.' But he was hungry for more. 'She was a good friend to you?'

'Of course she was. The best.'

'Was she kind?'

'To me?'

'Generally. Was she a kind girl?'

I thought about it. 'She was to me, of course. And she loved animals.'

'All young girls love animals,' he said.

'Kind?' I thought for a moment. 'I don't suppose you think about kindness very much when you're that age. You notice if people are kind to you directly, but I reckon that's about as far as it goes. I'm sure she was, though.'

'Why? Why are you sure? You just said you hadn't thought about it.'

I felt as if I were in court. 'I'm sorry if I'm not precise enough.'

'Don't be sorry, just be more precise.'

'I suspect, though, that we were all rather self-centred. It goes with being a teenager. It's not that you don't care about others, it's more that you forget that there *are* others. I think we were a bit like that, Rose and I and our friend Portia Dennis. You remember Portia?'

Uncle Ian nodded. 'What became of her?'

'You know, I have no idea.'

'You didn't keep in touch?'

I didn't know how to explain, to him or to myself for that matter, how, far from finding comfort in the company of someone else who'd known and loved Rose, I had done everything to avoid her until we had lost touch altogether.

'It was my fault. Being with her hurt. Looking at her I didn't see her, only . . . well, things I didn't want to think about.'

Uncle Ian nodded. 'I can understand that.'

Of course he could.

There was another pause and then Uncle Ian said, 'Rose wasn't very academic.'

I relaxed. 'Oh I don't know. She was very good at English Literature and her spelling was brilliant.' I nodded. 'Really excellent.'

'Of course, you were the bright one.' His face assumed a familiar look of puzzled irritation.

'Rose was perfectly bright. You can be bright without being academic. And anyway, it's what you do with your talents that matters.' Had I really say that? Had I said something so stupid, so insensitive?

I shook my head. 'I'm so sorry. I don't know how I could have said that.' I hid my face in my hands.

'It's all right.' I felt a hand on my arm, fleeting, a little awkward, as if it were the wing of a clumsy bird.

I looked up and our eyes met. The kindness in his took me aback.

'I'm very well aware that after Rose's mother left, Rose, without you and your mother, would have been a very lonely young girl.'

I swallowed hard and then I flashed him a quick smile. 'Would you excuse me, I'll . . . I won't be a moment.' I got to my feet, stumbling over a chair leg as I hurried from the room.

In the hallway I ran straight into Katarina. 'Eliza, are you all right?'

I nodded, avoiding her gaze. 'Fine. I'm absolutely fine.'

'You don't look fine.'

'It's just a headache. I get them all the time. I'll just lie down and shut my eyes for a bit. Would you explain to Uncle Ian, please?'

Katarina brought me a cup of sweet milky tea – she said she knew that was what all English people wanted when they were under the weather, and a plate of plain biscuits that looked like Rich Tea but were actually called Marie. She fetched an extra pillow and made me lean back against them like a poorly child so that I could sip my hot drink.

'Did you tell Uncle Ian?'

'I did and he's just sorry you're not feeling well. I'll come and see how you are at lunchtime. Do you want the blinds drawn?'

I shook my head. 'I like looking out at the snow.'

I finished the tea and as I looked around the little room with its yellow rosebud wallpaper and white lace curtains, as I saw a tiny distorted reflection of my face in the polished brass bed knob at the foot of the bed, I wondered how it was possible to feel so wretched and so comfortable both at once.

Over lunch we spoke politely of not very much until Katarina went through into the kitchen with the dishes, having refused my offer of help. 'You stay and talk to your godfather.'

'No, I insist.' I was halfway to my feet.

'Really, you have so much to talk about and you're not over for very long.' Katarina reminded me of our old housemistress, Miss Philips. At school we had been constantly amazed at the way she managed to get us to do what she wanted without resorting to shouting, threats, bribes or chasing people down corridors, all those methods favoured by other, lesser members of staff. Even Miss Philips's hair, golden blonde and back-combed, appeared to know better than ever to stray. It was certainty that did it, I thought now, a quiet unshowy conviction that you knew best. There was nothing that gave you as much easy authority. With an inaudible sigh, I sat back in my chair.

'You never wanted a family?' Uncle Ian asked.

I was used to people walking around the subject of children with me, especially once I had turned forty and there was an assumption that I was running out of choices. This straight question took me by surprise. Buying time, I shrugged. When he kept his gaze on me I shrugged again. Finally I said, 'We thought about it but ... well, we weren't married very long.' I took a bigger mouthful of the excellent white wine than I had intended. 'So it's all for the best.'

'You really think that?'

I looked at him over the empty wine glass. 'Yes, I do. I think.'

'Can you never be sure of something?' He was frowning at me.

I wasn't going to tell him about the way I had looked wistfully at toddlers on reins and babies in Bugaboos, or of the times I'd been loitering outside Baby Gap and Petit Bâteau. Nor was I going to explain that seeing as every time something went wrong in my life it felt like a victory for justice, it followed that it was best I never had what I could not bear to lose.

'I do find it quite hard,' I said. 'To be sure.'

'So what about your work? You enjoy it?'

'Oh yes. In fact I am sure about that.'

'You were very good at drawing and painting when you were at school. I asked your mother if you had done anything with it when we spoke the other day and she told me you turned down a place at art school.'

'I did History of Art instead. I went on to West Dean for my practical training.'

'You don't miss being the creator of works?'

I shook my head. 'As I see it there's enough mediocre art out there in the world to last for all eternity. Why add to it? I'd rather spend my time saving what's truly exceptional.'

'And who decided that what you would have produced would have been mediocre?'

'I did.'

'I see. And your mother tells me you're about to be thrown out of your flat.'

I frowned. 'For a woman at the other end of the world my mother says an awful lot. And I'm not being thrown out. It was always going to be a reasonably short-term rental. I'll find somewhere else nice.'

Uncle Ian sat back in his chair, a look on his face as if he were about to solve all my problems. 'Well, we'll see.'

It was still only half past one; meals in Sweden were early, so I went for a walk. I had wondered a little at Uncle Ian deciding to live by a lake. Myself, I avoided them whenever I could, lakes, ponds, even reservoirs; all those places more usually connected to sunshine and picnics and family fun. But as I gazed out over the tranquil water just the right blue shade of grey, I thought his might have been a good choice. The lake of my nightmares was a mere, as deep and as dark as despair. The trees did not stand guard as they did here but trailed their branches in the black water like skeletal fingers, the reeds reaching out from the depths as if begging for help. And always there was Rose,

Rose being dragged to the bottom, her hair heavy with weeds, her eyes wide open and begging me for help I could, would not give.

But here, in the pale winter sunshine, Rose was dry and safe and seated next to me on the trunk of the fallen tree. She was not Uncle Ian's visitation nor the vengeful Rose of those nightmares but simply a peaceful presence, my beloved old friend.

'I wish I knew what Uncle Ian wants from me,' I said to her. 'You didn't really come to see him, did you?'

Of course, I knew I wasn't actually speaking to Rose so I didn't expect a reply. I left all that to Uncle Ian. He was so much more convincing at it. But everyone knows that articulating a problem, even if it's only before an imagined audience of one, could be helpful. And it was, it has to be said, so very quiet in the woods by the lake with every sound muffled by snow or wrapped in cold, still air, that you felt that when you did speak your voice might easily carry through time and space, even beyond life itself.

I couldn't see to the lake's end but Uncle Ian had told me that to get to the far shore would take some twenty minutes of rowing or on skates if it were frozen over. I was wearing a heavy quilted jacket and a knitted hat and gloves but the cold was winning and it most certainly drove Rose away. As I said, I didn't believe in ghosts but someone/some*thing* had been there by my side and now it was gone I felt more alone than I could ever remember feeling before.

I wanted the presence back. I whispered to it to return. When nothing happened I sang 'Sweet Rose of Allendale'. It was Rose's favourite song. She'd sing it all the time. We had worked out the harmony, taking turns as to who sang the melody and who joined in on the refrain.

I sang quietly. I only wanted the dead to hear. I sang it twice and then I gave up. The lake stretched out before me, covered with a layer of ice that was just enough to lure the unwary, or stupid, out across, but too thin to carry the weight. I buried my face in my mittens. When I looked up again the setting sun was showing me a path across the ice. As I got to my feet I thought how easy it would be to walk out and never return.

Eight

Sandra/Cassandra

THE OTHERS WERE IN the sick bay so it was just Eliza and I hanging out. I was perched on the chair in her cubicle; I'd had to move a heap of clothes meant for the laundry to be able to sit. Eliza was on the floor, writing in one of her hundreds of A5 notebooks, her back resting against the bed, long ragdoll legs stretched out, big feet pushing up against the wall opposite. That's what she looked like, I had decided, a beautiful rag doll. She dressed like one, too. Today she was wearing red and black horizontal striped woollen tights, a floral print summer skirt with different coloured patches sewn on and a long black knitted sweater. Back when I first met her I had thought that she dressed the way she did for effect but I had come to realise that she actually thought those weird combinations looked nice. And on her, to be fair, they usually did.

'Shall I take your stuff to the laundry?' I asked her.

She glanced up as if she were surprised to hear from me, then she threw me a warm smile. 'Would you? That's really kind.'

As I went down to the basement I thought of Gillian Taylor saying that I should be careful not to let Eliza treat me like some kind of servant. 'She doesn't mean to,' Gillian had said.

'She just thinks it's completely natural that other people should run around doing things for her.'

So what? Gillian was jealous. Everyone knew she had the biggest crush on Eliza. She said she was over it but it didn't seem like it to me.

I returned to the cubicle. 'I'll hang it up later,' I said.

'Gosh, no, I'll do that,' Eliza said. I knew she wouldn't, though. She would forget about it until someone did it for her, either as a favour or because they needed the washing machine themselves.

'What are you writing?'

Without looking up, she said, 'I'm re-working one of Grandmother Eva's stories.'

Grandmother Eva wasn't actually Eliza's grandmother at all, she was Rose's, but because Eliza's grandmothers were both dead she was allowed to borrow this one. 'Can I look?' I asked her.

Eliza passed me the notebook. She had framed the writing with her drawings. She was a good artist but I didn't personally go for all that fairy tale stuff, although the huge ugly trolls were cool and the boy who played the violin by the lake.

'I wish I could draw,' I said.

'I'd love to be able to sing like you.' She smiled up at me. I don't know how she did it but she had a way, when she was paying attention, to make you feel special, chosen somehow.

'You would?'

But her attention had already wandered back to her notebook. The others wouldn't be staying in the San for ever and then who knows when I would get her to myself again. I was sure that if I could only spend enough time with her, just the two of us, we would become real friends. I reckoned she and

I actually had a lot more in common than she had with the other two. Like art and music, for example.

She was absorbed in her drawing once more. I knew she didn't mean to be rude. She just loved what she was doing. I was like that myself, passionate.

'It's funny how you got your artistic skill from Grandmother Eva,' I said. 'Because I've got the singing from *my* grandmother,' I said, kind of implying that I had forgotten Grandmother Eva wasn't actually Eliza's grandmother. She'd like that. I knew because a friend of Jessica's, a girl who was adopted, completely loved it when anyone forgot her parents weren't her real parents.

'Really,' Eliza said, but she still wasn't paying full attention.

'She was an opera singer.' That just slipped out but as it happens it worked because now she looked at me, actually looked at me and without those longing glances at her notebook. I didn't want that to end.

'Really? You never said.'

I shrugged. 'It never came up, I suppose.'

'Where did she sing?'

'Oh everywhere, all the big places. Covent Garden, The Metropolitan, La Scala, all of them.' I listened to myself say those things and I thought how right it sounded. It was how it should have been, my grandmother in a long velvet gown receiving a standing ovation, not standing behind the counter at Henson's department store in the regulation blue uniform. 'We were the first to use terylene, as it was called back then.' I remember her saying that as if it were an event. An achievement. And my parents had nodded and my father had said, 'My, is that so' and my mother had asked about the exact shade of blue. I didn't belong with them, with people like that. I belonged here, at LAGs with Eliza and the others.

And Eliza was looking at me with big starry eyes. 'Gosh. How exciting. I love opera. What's her name? Is she Mitchum too? I might have heard her. My mum certainly will have. She's a complete opera freak.'

I had to think fast. 'She died really young.'

'And she still sang at all the big opera houses. That's amazing.'

I felt my eyes flickering and I bent down pretending to do up my laces. Straightening up, I said, 'Sorry, what I meant was she was supposed to sing in those places if she hadn't died. It was really tragic. She was studying. In Italy.' I was able to look her straight in the eyes as I continued, 'In Florence. She was about to debut and she drowned.'

Drowned. 'How?'

'Swimming pool.'

Eliza looked at me and her eyes were almost completely round. For a moment I thought she might be laughing at me but when she said, 'That's dreadful,' she sounded genuine.

'Well, it was a long time ago.'

'Your poor mum. She must have been tiny.' She had finally put her notebook and pencil down. 'Or perhaps it's better that way. I don't remember a thing about my father and sometimes I think that's good because I'm not actually missing something concrete, although sometimes it makes me feel sadder for exactly the same reason. And your grandfather, too, he must have been devastated.'

I pulled a regretful face. 'Well, that's another thing. She wasn't married. She got pregnant by this Italian guy. He was a count or something.' I made my voice casual as if it made no difference to me if my grandfather was a count or not. 'Of course they weren't allowed to get married.'

'Why?' She was looking up at me, her large hands resting on her knees and her auburn hair streaming down her back and shoulders. Right then I would have killed to look like her, even with the big hands and feet and the freckles.

'Oh, all sorts of reasons.' I tried to think of some.

'I suppose him being Catholic?'

I nodded. 'That's it. It wasn't allowed on religious grounds.'

'So you're really the granddaughter of an Italian count? Cool.'

'Well, not officially, obviously. My grandmother had to leave the opera and she came back and married her childhood sweetheart.'

'But she went back to Italy eventually?'

'No, I don't think she did. She longed to but that was part of the tragedy, she never got back. She was stuck in this small town married to this guy she didn't love.'

'But she drowned? In a swimming pool in Florence?'

'Yeah. I mean, no, she did drown but it was back home in England. In a swimming pool, a public one, obviously, because they were really poor.' I noticed Eliza had picked up the pencil and notebook again.

'Anyway,' I gave a little laugh. 'Enough about my boring old family.'

'Hardly boring,' Eliza said, but by now she was looking at her drawing. I nodded at the large poster of Leslie Howard that she had blu-tacked to the wall above her bed. 'He died tragically young, too, didn't he? I know because my mum is always going on about him. Him and Cary Grant.'

I had got her attention back. 'He wasn't really young, forty or something, but too young to die, obviously. He was on a secret mission on behalf of Churchill when his plane was shot down. Everyone always goes on about Clark Gable in *Gone with the Wind* but I don't get that. I think Leslie Howard is just completely amazing.'

I wasn't going to point out to her that she was the only person I knew under the age of fifty who gave a toss about either Leslie Howard or Clark Gable because she wouldn't care anyway. She didn't seem to go for any of the things that the rest of the girls liked but she never got teased, not even the way she dressed.

'I sometimes think I too will die young,' I said. Actually I hadn't ever thought about it, but I just kept on saying stuff, any stuff, to keep her attention. She put her hand out and touched my knee lightly, for just a moment. 'Don't,' she said. 'That would be really sad.'

I sighed and gave her a smile. 'I won't, then. For your sake.'

Maybe I had gone too far because her tawny brows knitted together in a frown and her eyes took on a wary look.

'You always seem so, well, sure about stuff,' I said quickly. 'What you like and who you like and what you look like; everything.'

Now she looked more puzzled than anything. 'Do you think I am sure of everything?'

I nodded. 'You all are, Rose and Portia too.'

'Maybe we are. I hadn't really thought about it. I mean, I know what I know and that's it really. I expect it's the same with them.' She scratched her nose with the tip of her pencil and leant her head against the bed. Her face and body were covered in those tiny freckles but her neck, where her chin had shaded the skin from sunlight, was semi-transparent, blue-tinged like skimmed milk. She straightened up again. 'I think certainty is very restful.' She paused for a moment, her head tilted to one side. 'In fact that's what's so good about fairy tales. They rule in a realm of certainty. I mean you don't have "And the princess was quite pretty if you liked that kind of thing and the prince would follow many quests to gain her hand although he did draw the line at confronting the dragon. And they lived happily ever after, we hope." ' She grinned at me.

We exchanged smiles, two friends who understood each other. I didn't want the moment to end but I wanted even less for it to end the wrong way so I got up from the chair. 'I'll go and check on your washing.'

'No, don't you do it. I'll go in a minute.' She made a move as if to get up herself, but she remained where she was, her gaze on her drawing, her hand poised with the pencil.

We both knew she wasn't going to.

Her washing was finished and I sang to myself as I hung it up; her hideous tights, that black dress she loved that made her look just like a Victorian orphan, her knickers and her two bras. She had tiny boobs.

A little later I returned to iron her school dress.

I heard Miss Philips having a go at her. 'Eliza Cummings, the state of that dress is a disgrace. Surely you have been taught how to iron.'

I heard Eliza's cool voice. 'Yes, Miss Philips. I'm sorry, Miss Philips.'

'There's no excuse for being a slob, Eliza.'

'No, Miss Philips.'

Eliza was getting into trouble because of my crap ironing. The thing is, Mum always did that sort of stuff for me and at school I used the school laundry service. 'I'm not having you wasting your time on washing and such things,' my dad had told me. 'We can afford it.'

I think Rose and Portia used it too, but Eliza didn't. She'd mentioned that she and her mum had to be a bit careful with money. I remember being really surprised. I had imagined that everyone here apart from me was really well off.

My heart pounded as I stepped round the corner to face them. 'Miss Philips.'

Miss Philips stifled a sigh. 'Yes, Sandra?'

I pushed my shoulders back and raised my chin in defiance exactly like a young heroine in a film. 'It was me. It was my fault.'

'What was your fault, Sandra?'

'The state of Eliza's dress. I ironed it.' I caught Eliza's eye and gave a little nod to show it would all be OK.

'Is that true, Eliza?' Miss Philips asked. 'You let Sandra iron your uniform for you?'

Eliza shrugged and mumbled something.

'Miss Philips . . .' I began.

'That'll be all, thank you, Sandra.' Miss Philips didn't even look at me, keeping her pebble eyes on Eliza.

'But . . .'

'I said, that will be *all*.'

Menopausal cow. I stomped off but as soon as I was round the corner, out of sight, I stopped and listened.

'I simply will not put up with that kind of behaviour in Hill House, Miss Cummings. Getting another girl to act as your maid. It's especially distasteful seeing that Sandra Mitchum is here under the new Assisted Places scheme. I'm disappointed, quite frankly. And surprised. There are some girls from whom I'd expect no better, but from you, Eliza . . .'

The cool had left Eliza's voice as she repeated that she was sorry and that it wouldn't happen again. I couldn't understand why she didn't tell Miss Philips that I had done it without asking. As I dithered about whether or not to intervene again Miss Philips finished with Eliza and stalked back towards her flat. I poked my head round the corner and saw Eliza sitting on the stairs. She was crying.

The other two were furious with me. They cornered me in the supper queue. 'We thought you should know that Eliza's on cleaning duties for the rest of the month thanks to you having to be the Goody Two Shoes. "It was me, Miss Philips, I did the ironing." '

The way they looked at me, the way they imitated my voice, it was as if I were some lesser mortal. And it was so unfair. 'That's not how it was at all,' I said. But they had made their minds up. They didn't *hear* me. I felt my eyes tearing up. 'She was being told off for not doing it properly. I was trying to help her.'

'Sure you were,' Rose said. 'Great help running to Miss Philips to say you'd been left doing her laundry.'

'That's so unfair. I . . .'

'Save it for someone who cares,' Portia said. She turned to Rose. 'Let's join the back of the queue. Air's better there.' She swung around and her straight fair hair fanned out and danced round her shoulders.

'Rice or potatoes,' the cook asked me.

'Both,' I said.

'It's a choice menu, dear, so you have to pick one or t'other. The rice is good today.'

I looked at her, at her stupid red face, and then I fixed her with a princess stare. 'I said I wanted both. You're not a teacher.

You can't tell me what I can eat or cannot eat. Do you know how much we pay to come here?'

You wouldn't have thought it possible but she turned even redder. 'There's no need to talk like that, young lady. Just because you have money doesn't mean you can be rude, you know. Now what will it be, rice or potatoes?'

'Neither,' I said my voice calm and haughty. 'You can shove your disgusting food.'

Actually, I almost liked her for thinking I was one of *them*.

Nine

Eliza

THE DOORBELL RANG THE evening after my return from Sweden. I was sitting at the kitchen table working on a Staffordshire piece of Little Red Riding Hood and the Wolf that some misguided interior designer had made into a lamp. I was at a critical point of my work. It was the turn of the Wolf's grin to be retouched. The painter's vision appeared to have been of a wolf who grinned sheepishly. Not my take on the story, but I had no right to interfere with the creator's vision, so I would make sure it remained sheepish. I decided to ignore whoever it was. The bell rang a second time and for longer. Reluctantly I got to my feet and ran down the stairs. I looked through the peephole. It was Ruth. Ruth is my stepsister, my mother having married her father, Claude, the summer after I left school. Ruth, her husband Robert and their daughter Lottie, had remained safely on the other side of the world until six months ago when they had moved, rather suddenly, to London. My mother had muttered something about 'a fresh start', adding that her lips were sealed. She had gone on to say that it would be nice if I introduced my stepsister to some of my friends. After a pause she had added, 'Well, to Beatrice.'

'I have other friends.'

'Of course you do,' my mother had said.

'Eliza, is that you?' Ruth called through the door.

With a sigh I hoped she had not heard I unlocked the door. We touched cheeks. I realised I had paint on my fingers so I wiped my hands on the back of my dress.

'Oh I'm sorry.' She looked me up and down. 'Should I have phoned first?'

'No no, this is fine.' I stood by to let her through, as it appeared there was no polite way of stopping her.

She followed me up the stairs to the little landing. Looking around her she said, 'So this is where you live.'

'But you've been here before, haven't you?'

'No. Never. I told Olivia I understood if you were feeling a bit embarrassed. I've seen pictures of that lovely mews house you and Gabriel used to live in when you were still together.' She glanced around her at the narrow hall, which was painted in a 'neutral' colour like the rest of the place because the landlord had been watching too much *Property Ladder*. 'This is a bit different, isn't it?' She turned back to me. 'But I told Olivia, Eliza should know by now that I'm the last person to mind that sort of thing.'

Until then it hadn't occurred to me to be ashamed of my flat. It was perfectly comfortable and most importantly I could afford it without taking any of my ex-husband's money.

Ruth gave a skittish little laugh. 'Or else there's some other reason why you haven't wanted to invite me.' She led the way to the kitchen. 'At least there's no danger of getting lost.' She indicated the kitchen table that doubled as a workstation and at the brushes and pots of pigments and Little Red Riding Hood herself. 'You're working.'

'Yup.'

'Busy time?'

'Absolutely. We're preparing for the opening of the new gallery so we're flat out. All hands to the pump, that kind of thing.'

'Is that so,' Ruth said and sat down.

It happened quite a lot when I was working at home, that people phoned or visited unannounced, observed I was busy only to proceed as if they had caught me reclining on the sofa watching daytime TV with a box of Turkish Delight at my side.

People before porcelain, people before porcelain, I told myself and I thought of Uncle Ian's mopping-up operation, or search for closure as Ove the vicar had termed it. If I were to die tomorrow, did I want to go to my grave having added unkindness to a large woman with tiny feet and wistful eyes to my list of sins? I think not. So I moved my work to the far end of the kitchen table and lied with a smile, 'It's lovely to see you.'

'Well, I thought when you couldn't make our lunch . . .'

'I'm sorry.'

'But we saw you at our barbecue so that's nice.' She sat down, checking the floor before putting down her embroidered velvet bag.

'I cleaned up all the mouse droppings this morning,' I said.

'You have mice?' She snatched her bag up into her lap.

I sighed. 'Alas no. They are completely useless around here. Pigeons come to my window, though, and help me with my chores.'

Ruth put the bag down on the floor again. 'What are you talking about?'

'It was a lovely party,' I said, changing the subject back to her barbecue. I had turned up expecting family and a dinner of sausages and chicken legs on paper plates only to find at least fifty people in their garden-party best and a man in a chef's hat roasting a pig on a spit.

'You were so embarrassed.' Ruth laughed uproariously. I tried and failed to laugh with her.

'But honestly there was no need. I don't expect you to remember my birthday. Although Olivia might have reminded you. I did feel for you, though; turning up without a present and wearing that old cardigan.'

'It was cashmere.'

'Whoops.' Ruth slapped her neat little hand across her mouth.

'What is hateful to you do not do to your fellow man.' The Golden Rule as expressed by the great Rabbi Hillel. And it would be hateful to me to be thrown out of someone's modest but perfectly adequate flat by the scruff of my neck without as much as an offer of a hot drink so I assembled another smile and asked, 'Would you like some coffee?'

'I'd prefer tea. Peppermint.'

I shook my head. 'Sorry.'

She smiled the smile of one used to disappointment. 'Builder's will do.'

'I've got Earl Grey.'

'No really, builder's is fine.'

'Lapsang it is, then,' I said.

Ruth sipped her tea. 'Olivia told me your news. I wanted to make sure you were all right.'

'What news?'

' "What news?" she asks. You are a funny one.'

This made me none the wiser so I waited for her to continue. Usually, with Ruth, you didn't have to wait long.

'She told me your godfather had got in touch. The father of . . . you know, your friend.' She lowered her voice as if she were speaking of some fatal disease.

'Oh. Yes. He did.'

'Olivia said you went to see him, in Sweden. It must have been difficult for both of you. I mean, after all this time.'

'It was fine.'

Ruth looked disappointed. 'No awkwardness?'

'Not really.'

Ruth had a way of being interested that invariably resulted in me being determined to give away as little as possible. It was the way she looked at you, her eyes growing even larger, her head tilted, her ears back – no, perhaps not the latter, but there was definitely a quickening of the breath. It made me think she wanted to eat me.

'It was good to see him.'

'Really?'

Smile still in place, I shrugged in a non-committal way.

'Well, isn't he marvellous. After everything that happened.'

My smile disappeared. I could have sworn I heard it clanking as it hit the floor. Ruth took my hand across the table. I resisted the impulse to snatch it back.

'As I said, it was fine. We met. I said, "Goodness, we haven't seen each other since I suggested to your daughter that it would be a spiffing idea to go to an ice-cold lake in the middle of the night – doesn't time fly when one's having fun?" Then we moved on to talk about the weather.'

'Did you really?'

'No. No, not really. So tell me about you. How are you? And Robert? And Lottie?'

'I'd much rather hear about you than talk about boring old me. So he's stopped blaming you? I always thought that was so unfair anyway. I mean, how old where you when it happened? Nine?'

'Sixteen. We were sixteen.'

'Oh, that old?'

I wondered if she had intended to punch me in the gut or if she had been merely clumsy. With Ruth you never knew, just as you never quite knew if the stories she told you about her life were true or fabricated. This was made all the more disconcerting because of her voice, the way she had of enunciating each word with the perky, precise diction of a 1950s BBC presenter.

'But he's decided to let bygones be bygones?' She nodded vigorously. 'That's *good*. That's *really* good.' She leant back in the chair and sipped her tea. She wrinkled her nose then smiled as if she were about to go Over The Top before having another taste.

'Tea all right?' I asked.

'It's quite strong for Lapsang, isn't it? Anyway, your god-father is obviously a very generous-spirited man.'

I looked into her eyes, searching for the answer to the question: was it possible that, whereas I just didn't much care for Ruth, she might actively dislike me? But no answer was to be found in her polite visitor's gaze. I offered her cake. This was a pointless thing to do because there was no cake, I realised as I searched the larder cupboard.

'So sorry. Don't seem to have any biscuits either. Anyway, enough about me. I mustn't bore you with all that stuff. After all, you and I didn't even know each other when all that . . .' my voice trailed into nothing.

'Bore me?' Ruth's cheeks coloured. She was a handsome woman in her way, with her large deep-set eyes, fresh complexion and mass of dark hair. It was the kind of looks that made you think she would have felt right at home at some old sixties festival sitting cross-legged in the grass with a guitar, singing protest songs, rather than being what she was, a put-upon wife and mother and part-time PA.

'Bore me, you say.' Her voice rose half an octave. 'How could I possibly be bored? I mean, your issues have been my issues for the past twenty years. It's not as if I've had any choice in the matter.'

I shot her a questioning glance.

She raised her eyebrows. 'Take your first year at Leeds. Our parents had barely got married yet I appeared to have acquired not so much a stepsister as a goddamn case history.'

I couldn't help laughing, then I apologised. 'I'm sorry. It just sounded funny. Of course I know you're being serious . . .' my voice slunk back into my throat.

'And it didn't end once you'd got your degree, did it? How anyone could have that many accidents in the space of such a short time is beyond me. "I'm afraid we won't make Lottie's first birthday party after all. Eliza's collided with a wall and we need to fly over right away."'

'I never collided with a wall.'

'Actually, preposterous as it may sound, you did.'

'My car did hit a wall. You're right. I'd forgotten about that.'

Ruth looked back at me as if she were issuing a challenge. 'Then there was the time you gave all your savings to the Lifeboats? I'm not saying the Lifeboats aren't a worthy cause and I'm sure it made *you* feel a whole lot better but the result was actually that Daddy and Olivia had to bail you out for months afterwards. We were struggling ourselves at the time, with a young family and Robert's situation. We could have done with some help from my father and stepmother but no one thought of that. Oh no. Even when you were trying to sort yourself out, when you were at the clinic, even then everything somehow revolved around you.' She sat back abruptly, arms folded across her chest, causing the old chair to creak in pain. '. . . so when you asked if your affairs bore me, well . . .'

I didn't know what to say to her. I had had no idea that my behaviour during those years of misery and turmoil had affected my stepsister in this way. Or maybe I just hadn't cared enough to wonder about it. Now, what I heard appalled me. I looked up at her, helplessly, not sure what I might say or do to make it better. Ruth looked back at me. She was waiting. A pound of flesh might do, but I never had had much stomach for blood. 'I'm so sorry,' I said finally and uselessly. 'I didn't mean for it to be that way. Please believe me.'

She gave a little shrug. 'Maybe, but whether you meant for it or not that's still the way it was.' Her eyes narrowed. ' "I'm afraid we can't have Lottie this weekend. We're visiting Eliza in the clinic." And "We don't really feel like a big family Christmas with Eliza having had a setback, you do understand, don't you?" '

'No. No, I didn't. And I should have said so. I should have said, "No, I don't understand why my stepsister going off the rails instead of being grateful for the opportunities afforded to her by a first-rate education at a leading UK university should impact in such a negative way on me and my family." '

I gave a regretful shrug. 'At least you're saying it now.' I waited. I was pretty sure there was more to come. I really didn't want to hear it. I thought of sticking my fingers in my ears and singing very loudly, but apart from being unfitting behaviour for anyone over five it would also be no more effective at shutting out painful memories than had been the years of rude drinking and gentile drug taking and night-before-the-morning-after sex.

'You all right?' Ruth asked.

I nodded. She was still looking at me but her expression had changed and now her eyes were shiny with excitement, like those of a child who, having dropped a slug in an anthill, was sitting back to watch what would unfold.

'I'm fine,' I said.

'Good. And I'm sorry to go on but ...'

So don't, I wanted to cry. *Really, we can just leave it at this.*

'... but I think it's important that I tell you, finally, how I feel. I mean, I still don't think you fully understand. Take my fortieth birthday. I don't suppose you even remembered it was my fortieth? You managed to get yourself arrested. I assume you remember that. So of course your mother spent the whole evening in tears fretting about whether they should jump on the first available flight and Daddy spent the whole evening trying to comfort her. Quite the celebration that ended up being.'

It felt like being savaged by an old teddy bear, strangely painful and ultimately shocking. I tried to make excuses, at least for this last transgression. 'I really did believe I was witnessing a mugging. I couldn't just stand by and do nothing. The police could have been a bit more understanding. It wasn't at all obvious that there was filming going on. There was no sign or anything and I don't remember seeing any camera crews, so how was one meant to know?'

Ruth was shaking her head. 'That's all irrelevant.'

I hung my head. 'Yes. Yes, of course it is. I do understand what you're saying.' I looked up at her. 'Ruth, I'm sorry. I really am.'

'Well, good. Because what I am trying to explain to you is that your self-destructive behaviour doesn't only affect you.'

'I really am so sorry,' I said again. 'I never realised.'

Ruth paused. Then she said, 'No, I don't suppose you did.'

The silence had been expertly positioned. It might not have told more than a thousand words but it certainly managed about twenty. Some of these being: but you would have, had you ever shown any real interest in me or in my family. 'No man's an island sufficient unto himself, Eliza.' Ruth winced suddenly, straightened in her chair and arching her back.

'I'm sorry. Is the chair uncomfortable?'

'No, no, it's fine. It's my old disc problem. Just remember . . .'

I had been fingering the TV remote control and now I pretended to press the pause button, pausing Ruth before she could say anything else.

'. . . that if your godfather wants to help you then you should let him. It would be one thing less for your poor mother to worry about. She worries a lot about you, you know. Especially since you refused to take any of the money you were entitled to in the divorce.' As she spoke, Ruth was watching me the way a laid-back bird might watch a worm making its pains-taking way to the surface of the soil. Now she said, 'I haven't upset you, have I?'

I gave her a newscaster's smile. 'Of course you haven't.'

Next thing I knew she was crying. I stared at her. 'All right, you have. I am upset. There, you can stop crying now.'

Ruth looked up at me with tear-blurred eyes. 'What are you talking about?'

'You. You're upset. Because I'm not upset. But you needn't worry. I am. I just wasn't . . .'

'Will you listen. I think my husband might be having an affair.'

'Oh.'

'You don't seem very surprised.'

I gave a regretful shrug. It was hard to believe that anyone, Ruth included, could be truly surprised. Having affairs was what her husband did. Ruth herself had been an affair once when Robert was married to his first wife. I had thought that kind of a start to a relationship might give a person a clue as to what the future was likely to hold, but it seemed it seldom did. Then again, what did I know? Gabriel had never been unfaithful in any relationship before he cheated on me. There were some situations where being the first was not at all flattering.

'I had rather hoped that fresh start would be for us *together*,' she said.

'That's funny,' I said.

Ruth looked up at me, her fine dark eyes glittering with tears. Then she grinned. For a moment I felt comfortable with her. 'I'll get a tissue,' I said.

She blew her nose and tucked the tissue up the sleeve of her wine-red jersey. 'I'm sorry. I came here to talk about your problems not whinge about my own.'

'I don't have any problems,' I said. 'And I am just pleased you wanted to talk about yours with me. It seems I owe you.' I didn't add that I liked hearing about other people's troubles – as long as those people were ones I didn't particularly like. It perked me up. Until I remembered that wasn't very nice at all and then I got depressed again.

'No, really. I have not the slightest evidence against my poor boy. I'm being silly, aren't I?' She looked up at me as if she were expecting a reply.

'More tea?' I asked.

She shook her head. 'But thank you. I should be on my way. I just wanted to make sure you were all right. As I said, Olivia was worried.'

I fetched her coat and walked her to the front door. There she turned round and looked at me with a peculiar little smile. 'I don't know what I would do if it was happening again. And do you know, the worst of it is that I can feel people looking at me and then looking at him and thinking, "What else could she expect?" If they see me at all. Being large doesn't stop you from being invisible, you know.'

I felt suddenly defensive of her. 'You're worth ten of him,' I said.

Ruth frowned. 'Why do you say that? Most people think Robert's quite a catch. Maybe not compared with your Gabriel but then I don't set my standards quite that high.'

I put my hand out and touched her arm. 'I'm sorry. I didn't mean to dismiss Robert. I simply wanted you to see that you have no reason to feel grateful or inferior.'

Ruth clasped her shoulder bag to her side with her elbow and opened the front door. 'Well, don't be a stranger,' she said. 'Although now I know what you really think of Robert . . .'

I closed the door behind her, my head feeling like a snow-globe that had been given a good shake. I tried to get back to my work but when after several attempts the Wolf's sheepish grin still looked more like the smirk of a psychopath, I gave up and put my things away. Then Uncle Ian called.

He hoped he wasn't interrupting my supper and I told him not at all; the timing was perfect.

'Good,' he said. He went on to say that he had spoken to my mother, who agreed completely.

'I can't see how she could,' I said. 'She always gets the timing wrong when she calls.'

There was a pause. 'What are you talking about?' Uncle Ian asked.

'Timing. What were you talking about?'

I heard the impatient sigh at the other end of the phone. 'The house.'

It was like listening to the radio with only intermittent sound. I must have missed something.

I decided that asking, 'what house?' would irritate him even further so instead I tried an, 'Aha, the *house*.' Hoping this would lead him to reveal more.

'As I told your mother, people are apt to make their wills with the excitement of buying Christmas presents, forgetting they won't actually be there to witness the unwrapping.'

I paused, still confused as to where exactly this was all heading. 'Ain't that the truth,' I said finally.

'You're not an American.'

'Ain't . . . No, no, I'm not.'

'So what do you say?'

'Good-oh?'

'So you agree. Excellent.' The 'excellent' came out like the sound of a starting gun. 'I'll call your mother and tell her the good news. She'll be thrilled.'

'Uncle Ian.'

'Yes.'

'I don't have the faintest idea what you're talking about.'

There was silence. I crossed and uncrossed my ankles. I did good toes and naughty toes. Eventually he spoke. His voice was a model of enforced patience. 'Olivia told me your rental agreement on your current place runs out on the second of April. If we start looking now you might just get somewhere in time.'

'Ah, I see. And thank you . . . for caring, but I'm not worried. I'm on to it. I've got plenty of time to find another flat.'

'We think a house.'

'I wasn't thinking of a house.' This was not strictly true. I was often *thinking* of a house, a house like the one that Gabriel and I had lived in when we were married or some house in the abstract, a house just for me with a workshop and a garden where I could grow bluebells beneath a small pink magnolia. But in the sense of actually living in one I was not thinking about it. I wanted to stay in the area and the rental on even a tiny flat like this one was on the edge of what I could afford.

'With a flat you're always in the hands of other people, even when you own the lease. You have very little control over matters such as when maintenance and repairs are carried out, or by whom, or over the cost. No, your mother agrees, a house is a better idea.'

I reminded myself that age had had its way even with Uncle Ian and that he was now a very different man from the one I had once known. 'I can see a house might be better but then you're still in the hands of the landlord and the rental prizes around here are astronomical.'

'I remember you being much quicker, Eliza. Are you getting old? The whole idea is that we buy you your own place rather than wait for the money to come to you when I'm dead. It could still take a while, you know.' He laughed happily.

'No,' I realised that I had raised my voice. 'Sorry, I mean I don't know what Olivia said to you for you to make such an incredibly generous offer but really, no.'

'I have to go now; it's time for my pills but if you would be kind enough to think over my offer and maybe also have a word with your mother. Goodnight.'

'Goodnight.' My voice was a squeak and I stood holding the receiver long after Uncle Ian had put the phone down, right through the beeping and the schoolmarm voice telling me to please hang up and try again later.

Ten

THE DAY WAS COLD and brilliant with sun. It was the kind of day that lured pensioners outside to tumble and break, and children in mittens and hats to run across treacherous ice. The kind of day when fog or a slippery patch lay in wait on the road. The kind of day most commonly described as beautiful.

But I was safely inside the museum making my way through the opulent exhibition halls and up the dingy back stairs to the ceramics studio with its peeling walls and boiler-room decor.

Beatrice was at her workbench, dismantling the previous restoration on a Minton jardinière. She looked up with a smile and a wave of her free hand. Then she frowned. 'You look odd. Is everything all right?'

'Fine, thanks. It's just, well, you know, winter.'

'I do know. And it was winter last week but then you didn't look like you'd just come face to face with the Loch Ness Monster.'

'What made you think of the Loch Ness Monster? I hardly ever think about it.'

'Neither do I. Maybe it was your tartan scarf.'

'Oh,' I said. I took off my coat and the scarf and went off to hang them on a peg in the small back office. As I returned I said, 'My godfather seems to want to buy me a house.'

Beatrice looked up. 'Really. How wonderful.'

'Yes,' I said. 'As long as one isn't bothered by considerations like earning one's own keep and living within one's means and not profiting from one's sins, those kinds of details.'

'If he gives you the money, buying the house *is* within your means,' Beatrice said. 'The rest I wouldn't know about.'

I was working on a piece of Daisy Makeig-Jones Fairyland Lustre, retouching. The previous day I had applied the first coat over the untinted filler. The paint was not completely dry yet so I brought over the warm air fan, placing it at a safe distance from the bowl. The point was not to blast the fairies and birds from the blue-bowl-sky or the branches of the witchity-wood trees but simply to speed the healing with a warm caress. Lustre used to be the most problematic of finishes to replicate but with the arrival of some new fluid iridescent paints it was less of a challenge. Of course seamless perfection was not what we were looking for these days anyway. For us the emphasis was on conservation. Conserve, according to *The Oxford English Dictionary*: 'to keep from harm or damage, to preserve . . .'

Restoration was different. Restore: 'to bring back or attempt to bring back to the original state by rebuilding, repairing, repainting etc. . . .' A lot of people muddled up the two. But as I always told students, there were some basic rules to follow with both approaches.

The prime ones were:

Not to inflict further damage by misuse of tools or materials or by careless handling.

To make sure that each stage is reversible.

To carry out honest repairs without the intention to deceive.

Fairyland Lustre did not appeal to everyone. In fact it seemed not to appeal to quite a lot of people, including Beatrice. I could see why, but for myself I adored Daisy (we were on first name terms – my decision, had to be, she was dead), adored her ebullience, her revelling in colour, her fearless championing of fairies and elves and sprites and rainbows all in the face of received good taste. Looking at one of her pieces made me happy.

Beatrice brought me some coffee. 'How was your weekend?' I asked her.

'No one offered me a house but otherwise it was fine. My parents were over. They drove me insane while they were there and then I felt bad and missed them once they'd gone. So the usual.'

'My stepsister popped round. She drives me insane when she's there and I *don't* miss her when she's gone.'

I mixed burnt umber and Mars red pigment with some MSA varnish to get the dark bronze finish I wanted for the trunk of the tree, then I sat back, waiting and watching for the exciting coat of paint to dry. Contrary to common belief, it could be quite an interesting pastime. With some paints and pigments it was as if a veil were being slowly drawn across their surface, whereas others darkened and deepened during the process and others still simply got on with it, with no changes of tone or shade.

'Ruth suspects her husband's having an affair. I feel terribly sorry for her but he's always having affairs and I can't help feeling she should leave him. He's a jerk.'

'Maybe she loves him?'

I thought about it. 'Perhaps. Though I think it's more that she's allowed herself to be completely defined by him and by their relationship. She's so used to the role of bullied betrayed wife that she wouldn't know how to be if that all came to an end. She's always talking about all the wonderful things she would have done had it not been for Robert's work, or him making her move, or him playing around. Maybe in a perverse kind of way that works for her? Having an excuse on tap every time she feels her life isn't working out as she had hoped.'

'So true,' Beatrice said. 'People do that sometimes, don't they? Use something in their lives, a tragedy perhaps, as an excuse not to live fully.'

'That's so well put. It's exactly what ... Hang on a minute. You weren't just talking about Ruth, were you?'

Beatrice looked back at me with the kind of smile that was halfway between approval and exasperation, the kind of smile a teacher might give a particularly dim pupil who'd finally worked it out. But all she said was, 'So are you going to accept your godfather's offer?'

I frowned at my brushes. 'He says it would make him happy. If that's true, if that's how he really feels, well, then I should accept because in comparison my feelings aren't what's important here.'

Beatrice's smiled widened. For the class dunce I was doing well.

'Then again maybe he actually resents me as much as I think he ought to. Maybe the whole idea is some kind of elaborate punishment.'

Beatrice pursed her lips. 'You're quite perverse when you wish to be. I mean no one normal would have even thought of that.'

'What's normal?' I said. Not an original question but it was the only thing I could think of as a reply.

'Well, that wasn't,' Beatrice said. 'And if being given a house were a punishment then please can I be punished too, me and another few thousand recession-hit individuals.'

'That's unfair,' I said.

'Is it?'

'Yes. Because I believe that if you were in my shoes you'd rather stay where you were.'

Beatrice sighed. 'Perhaps.'

'And I know I'm about to lose the flat but there are plenty of rentals around. Anyway, I'd say I was doing averagely well in life these days but average isn't enough, it seems. If my godfather could acquisition Gabriel and arrange a re-merger he would be thrilled. And of course I should have a few children too. And because I was tolerably good at art when I was at school I was supposed to have gone on to become a great artist, so me doing what I'm doing, something I think is immensely worthwhile, he feels is somehow second best. And to be quite honest that pisses me off. And I'm not allowed to be pissed off with him because he's the good guy here. And why is he? Should I believe Rose told him to? And all that "closure" talk. Really, it makes no sense.'

'Oh Eliza, have you never heard of forgiveness?'

'Of course I have.'

'Well, there you have it. He's forgiven you. Would you like another cup of coffee?'

'I'll go.'

I walked off into the little back office where we hung our coats and made our coffee and where Beatrice did her paperwork. I filled the kettle and while I waited for it to boil I poked my head round the door. 'You know, no one's asked me if I *want* to be forgiven, have they.'

'It's not about you, though, Eliza, is it?'

'No. No, it isn't.'

I put two teaspoonfuls of instant coffee in each mug and added a spoonful of sugar to mine before pouring the water.

As I stirred the coffee I looked around me. I loved these shabby rooms with their peeling paint and engine room pipes running along the ceilings. I loved the fact that within such unprepossessing walls, work was carried out that brought what had been broken or neglected, forgotten and misused, back to life and usefulness by us, the conservators. All the tools needed for the transformation were to be found cleaned and neatly put away, each in its own place, or placed on the tables and desks ready for work in their overalls of paint and putty, pigment and wax. I liked the way the rooms felt safe even when I was working late on my own and the way they were peaceful even when all four of us were working there together. Just as I was thinking all this, as I waited for the paint to dry, my phone went ping, announcing that a text message had arrived. It was from my mother. It read: *I hope you have accepted your godfather's offer. Remember your father saved his life once.*

Years ago, when I was staying at the clinic, another thing they had taught me to practise was how to control and interrupt destructive thought patterns. When the repetitive thoughts come into your mind you should fend them off, telling yourself that they would all be dealt with at a set time and for a set amount of time, say ten minutes. That would be their lot. It had sounded too simple, too mechanical but I had come to realise that the human brain responded very well to simple repetitive commands. Of course it didn't always work, but when it did it was wonderful, like divesting yourself of layers of thick scratchy clothing, putting them all away in a wardrobe and emerging, light as a ballerina, to pirouette off into the light. I was scared that accepting the house would be like taking up residence in the wardrobe with no escape from that dark heavy clothing.

I texted back. *I should think that, after what happened to Rose, we're more than even, wouldn't you?*

My mother replied, *Remember Stalin.*

Years ago when my mother had first suggested that I see someone, a therapist someone, I had been very much against the idea.

'Therapists are paid to make people feel good about themselves,' I said to her. 'They would tell Stalin he wasn't to feel bad about himself.'

My mother had put her hand under my chin and raised my face so that our eyes met. 'Eliza, you're not Stalin.'

There was no doubt that, through the years, those words had proved strangely comforting.

The conservators in Sculpture had music playing all the time but on the whole here at the ceramics studio we kept it off, although we did have some iPod speakers on a shelf at the back. As it was just the two of us in today I asked Beatrice if she'd mind if I played something. She said she wouldn't so I put on some Celtic folk music, or as I liked to call it, Easy Throat-slitting.

'That's supposed to lift your mood?' Beatrice asked.

'I'm trying to bottom out.'

'Not here you don't. What else have you got?'

'Best of Mozart?'

'You can't take someone's money if they're potty,' I said after a while.

'Are you referring to your godfather?'

I nodded. 'I told you about the visits from,' I lowered my voice, looking around me, '. . . the dead.'

'You don't need to whisper. They can't,' she did a mock looking around the room, 'hear you.'

'Well, according to Uncle Ian it looks as if they can.' I straightened up and resumed my normal voice. 'Surely that makes one question his ability to make rational decisions?'

'Not necessarily. One of my great-aunts claimed to have had regular visits from her guardian angel. That apart she was as practical and down to earth as . . . as you or me, I was going to say, but let's just leave it at me.'

I raised an eyebrow to show I was not amused. Then I turned back to my pot and applied the bronze pigment to the trunk of the tree. It worked perfectly.

'Let's play the millionaire's game,' Beatrice said. 'If you could pick anywhere, where would you live?'

I told her I didn't want to play. She told me to indulge her. 'All right. There is this house up the road from my flat, in one of the tiny squares. It's like a Georgian doll's house. Small but perfectly formed with a front garden and a mulberry tree standing guard. It's up for sale for the first time in for ever.'

'Well, off you go. Make an offer.'

'No, absolutely not.'

'And what about your poor old dying godfather who only wants to make you happy?'

'I said no. It's not right. It's not right and it doesn't make sense. Any of it.'

'You know what doesn't make any sense?' Beatrice asked. 'That.' She pointed at Daisy's bowl. 'All those bloody fairies and elves and whatever else. Your godfather, on the other hand, makes perfect sense.'

I went past my stop right the way up to Hampstead Village to check out the estate agent's window. The house on the hill was still there and there was no sticker saying *Sold* or *Under Offer* plastered across the picture. The dark sky hung low, pregnant with snow, but I decided to walk home rather than take the bus. As I crossed over to the High Street I heard carols. A Salvation Army band had gathered round the Christmas tree. They were playing 'Hark the Herald Angels' and as the sky darkened the lights brightened to a heavenly blue. I stayed where I was, listening to the music, and as the last of the day was sucked into night a Salvation Army officer picked up his collection box and started his round.

I had my ten-pound note ready when I paused, and bringing out my wallet again, pulled out the cash I had drawn a little earlier: one hundred pounds minus the ten.

'It was easier when you had that cauldron thing,' I told the officer as I rolled up banknote after banknote and shoved each one through the narrow slit of the collection box.

'But not as secure,' the officer said. 'Thank you and happy Christmas.'

I didn't show it, of course, but secretly I was disappointed. I had expected a little more. An 'Hallelujah, thank the Lord,' or at least a 'Bless you, my child.' But 'Thank you and Happy Christmas' was exactly what he had said to the kid with the coin. Of course I knew that it was the thought that counted and most likely that coin represented the boy's entire week's income whereas I had just been offered a house as a gift. Seen in that light the level of gratitude had been absolutely right. Still, I was pleased when the officer returned and asked if I had a favourite as they wanted to play something just for me as a special thank you. He had not asked the kid.

' "Silent Night", please,' I said without hesitation. There was simply no limit to how many times I could hear that particular carol.

Eleven

Sandra/Cassandra

MY BLOODY PARENTS! THEY'D only gone and booked themselves a holiday over half-term. I couldn't believe it. I mean, they never went anywhere.

'We thought that now you were away at school . . .'

'But what about me?' I wasn't going to admit it but I had actually been looking forward to coming home.

They said they hadn't realised it was half-term when Des and Janet suggested the trip. Well, they should have; the calendar was right there over the phone, pinned to the corkboard. 'I'm sure Eliza, or one of the other girls you're such friends with, Portia is it, and Rose, will ask you to go home with them,' my mum said.

'I'd rather be here. I'm old enough to stay on my own.'

'No dear,' my mother said and she had that steely note in her voice that meant that nothing or no one was going to shift her. Apparently she had already spoken to Miss Philips, who had assured her their being away wasn't a problem. 'She said they haven't yet had a girl having to stay at school for half-term.'

So I would be the first, great.

'I might not get an invitation,' I said. 'You have to be really good friends with someone before they invite you home and I'm not.' I shut my eyes, waiting for the sky to fall in.

'Nonsense.' I opened my eyes to see my mother look at me, a mulish set to her face. 'You're always telling us what fun you're having, you and Eliza and your other friends.'

'I . . . I exaggerated,' I said. I couldn't bring myself to say out loud that even Eliza seemed to tolerate me rather than actually like me.

My mum turned to my dad. 'Have you heard such a thing. "I exaggerated"?' She shook her head laughing. 'Now I expect you've had a tiff, don't you think so, Daddy?' She turned to him.

'You make friends wherever you go,' my father said.

'I didn't at Lord Hanbury's.'

'You told us yourself that those girls were just jealous.' My mother had put on her patient voice. 'That's one of the reasons we sent you to The Academy, to get away from that kind of thing.' She pronounced Academy as if each letter was coated in honey. I wanted to tell her that the whole thing, me going off to LAGs, was a mistake, that actually I wasn't cut out for a place like that and that I wanted to come home. I wouldn't even complain about going back to my old school. At least it was a day school and I could go home at the end of the afternoon.

'Mum, Dad . . .'

'That nice Miss Philips told us herself that you had settled in very well. I'm sure she wouldn't make that up.' My mother turned to my father with a little laugh at the absurdity of the suggestion. 'I expect they've got lovely homes, those girls. We must buy some nice chocolates or soaps for you to bring. You can't come empty-handed.'

'Soaps would be best, I think,' Dad said. 'So many ladies are on a diet these days.'

'You might be right. Then again . . .'

Why had I lied to them? Why had I written those stupid letters home all about how I was hanging out with the princesses and how great everything was? Actually, it was their fault. I wouldn't have had to make things up if my parents hadn't been so needy, waiting like great big puppy dogs for the latest morsel of what they deludedly thought of as their daughter's glittering social life. My mother imagining that we were gliding around the corridors of LAGs with perfect posture and white gloves; a bunch of wannabe Grace Kellys. Mum was obsessed with Princess Grace, as she insisted on calling her. I would tell her, 'She's dead, Mum. Get over it.' But she still banged on about it. 'Princess Grace truly was this and Princess Grace truly was that . . . Grace by name and Grace by nature. A person like that never really dies. Did you know she always, without exception, wore white gloves to her auditions?'

As usual she had got all her information from the celebrity magazines. She'd always loved them ever since she was a little girl and they were just about her only indulgence now that every penny went on the fees for LAGs. I hadn't bothered to think about that side of things when I had first told them I wanted to go there. I suppose I'd been too busy just making sure I got my way.

'I think it's too much money,' I said to my parents now.

'What is?'

'Sending me to LAGs. It's too big a sacrifice.'

'You let me worry about that,' my dad said, giving me a pat on the head. 'And you're the clever young lady who got yourself a bursary.'

'That's like a tenth of the fees, and you had to pay for all that private tutoring first.'

'It's only a sacrifice if you don't make the most of it,' my mum said.

Then I asked if maybe I could spend half-term with Auntie Gina. You would never believe my mum and she were sisters, let alone twins. I always imagined that while they were still waiting to be born the foetus that became Gina took for herself all the fun and the get-up and go that was meant for two, leaving my mother this sad humble thing wobbling along in her sister's fizzing wake.

'I haven't seen her for ages,' I said. 'It's a really good opportunity to spend some time. You're always saying she's lonely.'

My mum said Auntie Gina was away on a cruise and wouldn't be back in time. 'Anyway, she's the last person who would want you to miss out just because of her.'

After that I gave up.

Gillian had told me that all three of the princesses had been called in to Miss Philips's soon after the incident with the dress. The door had been left ajar and Gillian had heard the whole thing. How they had been told to make a bigger effort with me. Miss Philips had noticed that 'poor little Sandra' was spending a lot of time by herself and that it was obvious I was finding it hard to settle in. She had finished off by saying that she would be extremely disappointed if she thought there was something as ugly as snobbism at work. So once I was back at school after the Sunday out I decided to use that to get an invitation. The princesses were going to Portia's family's holiday cottage in Cornwall for the half-term and some of her brother's friends from the boys' school were coming too. I imagined how excited my mum and dad would be if I were going. So I told them I was.

'You see,' my mum said over the phone. 'We told you, didn't we? All that nonsense about not having friends.'

I hinted quite a lot about wanting an invitation but either Portia was not as clever as she made out or she was being deliberately obtuse, because every time I said something about how much fun it sounded, them all going away together and how I didn't have anything organised, she just smiled in a vacant kind of way and changed the subject.

So I decided to just hang around with them as much as I could without being annoying. Eventually they'd get so used to me being there it would just seem completely natural that I come along on the holiday. I was helpful and cheerful and I was a good sport when Portia got *my* part in the school play. (Bloody Miss Barford said my figure was too 'womanly' for Hamlet. And Portia's DD wasn't?)

I put up with their patronising too. Rose: We're not taking the piss, you absolutely eat asparagus with your fingers.

Eliza: Unless they're in a gratin, obviously.

Rose: Actually Sandra, I mean Cassandra, the Spanish Steps aren't in Spain at all, they're in Rome.

Portia: Celia is Lady Celia Hennessey because her father is an earl but Katherine O'Hara's big sister is Francesca, Lady Turnbull because she married into the title.

Eventually, and with just ten days to go to half-term, I grew desperate. And Mum kept asking for Portia's mum's phone number so she could call up and have a 'chat' before I went. I had been watching Rose like a cheetah watched an antelope, so at break-time when she separated from the rest of the class and settled herself in the window alcove to read, I pounced.

As usual I just pretended not to notice the irritation flickering in her eyes as she saw me steer towards her and I called out a cheery hello. People talk about other people being thick-skinned as if we didn't notice stuff. It wasn't that. We were just people who had to try much harder to get what we wanted.

I asked her what she was reading. With her gaze lingering on a sentence she half looked up. '*Mary-Anne*.'

'Is it any good?'

'I don't really know yet. I haven't had much of an opportunity to read it. I was hoping to get some time now.'

If one's soul could blush mine would have done but instead I focused on the main goal and said, 'I suppose you'll have plenty of time to read in Cornwall.'

'I don't know about that. Portia's mum and dad are pretty into their activities.' Here she did in the air quotation marks and her book slipped off her lap and on to the floor. I bent down quick as a flash and picked it up, handing it back to her.

'Is it a big house they've got? I mean, it has to be with all of you staying?'

Rose closed the book round the magnetic Paddington Bear bookmark and looked up with a faux-patient expression. 'I suppose it is quite big.'

'How many bedrooms does it have?'

Rose frowned. 'I haven't counted them. One doesn't.'

My scalp began to itch. I hated her. She had a way of making me feel so small that even God couldn't see me. I hated them all and yet I wanted nothing more than to be their friend. Tears rose in my eyes, tears of anger, nothing else, and I began to walk off. Then I turned back, ignoring her sigh, and swallowing my pride like someone starving swallowing rotting food, I made one more attempt. 'I'm completely at a loose end this holiday. My parents are away too. They just assumed I would be able to stay with friends.'

Rose picked up her book. 'That's good then,' she said with a smile that showed that she obviously hadn't listened to a word I'd said.

I looked at her, imagined shoving her pretty face through the windowpane. But Rose remained oblivious, immersed once again in her reading.

Eliza was in her cubicle, sprawled on the floor as usual, sketching away in her notebook. Rose's grandmother Eva had sent her a tape of fairy tales that she had collected on a trip around Scandinavia and of course she wanted Eliza to do the illustrations. Then, Eliza had told me the other day, they were going to try to get the whole thing published. Her aim was to get a publishing contract by the time she went up to university.

There it was again, that serene certainty that her life was going to be charmed. They all had it. Portia was going to be an ambassador. Not just a diplomat, mind, but an ambassador. Straight to the top for our most regal princess. Rose was going to be a model and then she was going to be 'in films'. She wouldn't say film star. That would be vulgar. But she wasn't going to be a stage actress either because she said that only film and possibly TV was compatible with having a family. There were no question marks. No doubts. Just a wide golden road to the glittering future. If they ever discussed other careers, something normal, something most people end up being, it still always ended up being special. If they thought about teaching, it was in terms of Miss Jean Brodie or Mr Chips. If they thought in terms of retail, it was always floating around some art gallery or interior design shop, never manning the tills at Safeways or picking up after customers in Dorothy Perkins. I didn't even know if they were that talented, but their self-belief was such you couldn't help thinking they had to be.

'New story? Can I see?' I said. Eliza hated being interrupted and she hated showing her work unless she was ready to but manners maketh princess and she stifled her irritation and looked up with a tight little smile.

'Hi, Cassandra. I didn't hear you knock.'

'C'mon, let me have a peek.' I moved round so that I was standing at her shoulder. She shifted the notebook towards me. She had drawn a lake, smaller than the one nearby but overhung by branches of the trees in the same way and with a tiny island in the middle.

I pointed at the young man sitting on the island, a violin in his hands. 'He's cute.'

'Oh good. He's meant to be incredibly attractive.' She flashed me a quick smile. 'Enough to drive young girls like us to our ruin.'

I moved on to the subject of half-term. 'You must be looking forward to going to Cornwall with everyone.' I paused and then said with a little laugh, 'Can you believe I've never been. Actually, I've never been anywhere.'

She had escaped back into her story. Her gaze still fixed on the page she said, 'It's OK, travelling. But I like being home. It's where all my stuff is, like my desk and my notebooks and paints and books.'

I wanted to tell her the astonishing fact that everyone wasn't like her.

'I'm always home,' I said. 'So a change would be really excellent.'

Eliza peered at her notebook before adding a line to a clump of reeds growing on the shores of the lake. Without looking up she asked, 'Why don't you ask your parents to take you somewhere nice? You've worked really hard.'

I started to cry. Finally I had her attention. She put her notebook down and got to her feet. She put her hands on my shoulders and bent her knees so we were eyeball to eyeball, only I was looking away.

'Sand . . . I mean, Cassandra, what's the matter?'

'My parents are going away and they won't let me go with them,' I said. 'They want me to stay with my aunt but she's really horrible to me.'

'Have you told them, your parents?'

I hiccupped and rubbed at my eyes. 'They don't believe me.'

'But they have to.'

'Well, they don't.'

'I thought your parents were really nice to you. I mean your mum's always sending you stuff and . . .'

'That's easy, isn't it?' I said. 'Sending stuff. Beats having to actually spend time with me.'

'But you're always saying how clingy they are.'

Was I? 'Oh well . . . you know I suppose I didn't want to admit to what it's really like.'

'Oh. Gosh. I don't know what to say. Have you talked to Portia?'

I made my face a question mark.

'Haven't you told her you'd like to come?'

'Oh, she'd just say no.' I paused for a few seconds then I added, 'Maybe if you were to ask her?'

Eliza shook her head. 'I don't think so. It's not really done. Asking someone to invite someone else. Anyway, it's much better to be straightforward. What's the worst that can happen?'

I looked at her. She was so beautiful, so comfortable in her own skin, so pleased with the world and her place in it. I hated her and I wanted to be her. I wanted to be her more than anything.

Portia was standing in the milk queue. People were chatting but she was standing on her own. Had that been me everyone would have thought it was because no one wanted to speak to me. With Portia you just assumed it was because that's how she wanted it. My mother in a misguided attempt to be wise had told me that people like that are never as confident as they appear to be. It's all an act. Inside they're as scared and unsure as the rest of us. Well, she'd never met Portia Dennis, is all I can say.

Walking up to her, I pushed back my shoulders. The princesses all walked as straight as ballerinas, their shoulder blades practically meeting.

'I'd like to come with you to Cornwall if that's OK.'

Portia seemed at first not to have heard me then she turned slowly. 'Hi, Sandra.'

'What do you reckon? Can I come?' I could barely believe I was saying it. Then I spotted a flicker of uncertainty in Portia's eyes and suddenly I felt sure everything would work out. She couldn't just say no. Especially since Miss Philips had had that talk with them.

Portia had looked away for a moment, as if she were searching for someone. When she turned her gaze back on me it was clear-blue and steady.

'Gosh, I'm really sorry but you know, we just don't have the room.'

'Yes, you do,' I blurted out.

A small frown creased Portia's high forehead. 'We don't, actually. Maybe some other time.' Then she spotted Rose and Eliza and she turned and waved, 'Over here.'

I left my place in the queue, backing away from Portia, my eyes fixed on her back as if my gaze could rip it open. Then I turned and ran from the room.

'You are kidding? She actually tried to invite herself?' It was Rose and there was a giggle at the end of her voice

'I nearly said yes, I was so amazed. I mean has she *no* pride?'

'Poor old Sanders,' Eliza said. 'That might have been my fault.'

The princesses were smoking in Miss Philips's garage. It was where Miss Philips herself went to smoke – she was meant to be a good example to the girls so she had to sneak around just like we did.

'Your fault. What did you say to her?'

'Well, she came in and started on about how she had no one to stay with other than some mean old aunt or something. I felt sorry for her. Then she wanted me to talk to you and I told her that that wasn't the done thing and that she should ask you herself, straight out.'

'Thanks,' Portia said. 'Thanks a bunch.'

Rose said, 'She gives me the creeps, actually.'

'I know what you mean,' Eliza said.

My friend Eliza.

'I might be unfair,' she went on, 'but I always have this feeling with her that she's making stuff up. About her family and things. There's nothing I can put my finger on exactly other than the little inconsistencies, but it makes me uncomfortable.'

'As I said, she's creepy.' It was Rose.

'I still can't help feeling sorry for her, though,' Eliza said. 'She is what Grandmother Eva might term a most unfortunate girl and I think Miss Philips is right, we should all try harder to be nicer to her.'

'You would feel sorry for her,' Portia said. 'You felt sorry for Miss van Hagen, for heaven's sake.' Then they laughed.

'Anyway, I don't care how sorry you feel for her but thank God I steeled myself and said no. Can you imagine having her hanging around the place for four whole days? Can you imagine what the boys would say?'

The three princesses stubbed out their three cigarettes and buried the butts in the large bag of compost where Miss Philips hid hers. They pulled up the garage door and having checked that the coast was clear, left for class. Moments later I got up from behind Miss Philips's ancient Fiat and followed them outside.

Twelve

Eliza

I RETURNED TO SWEDEN the day before the festival of Lucia. Fresh snow had fallen the previous night and the air caught between each crystalline flake trapped sound and held it captive, leaving the world silent.

I had asked the driver to let me off at the bottom of the track leading up to the house. I only had a small overnight bag to carry and I needed some air. The pine trees looked like snow sculptures, some with their frosted limbs stretching towards me, others twisted as if they were trying to turn tail and flee. I thought one of them might be the Huldra in disguise, waiting for her doomed swain. Did she do girls? I wondered. I quite liked the idea of following a Rose-like beauty into the fathomless depth of the woods, unthinking, unquestioning until, exhausted, I lay down to sleep for ever on my mattress of snow.

'Eliza!'

Not the Huldra but Katarina, a more solid temptress, calling me to the house.

'Look at you,' she said as we met up at the top of the track. 'You're dressed for London weather.'

I dressed pretty well the same wherever I was, sticking to soft materials and muted colours. I particularly liked grey,

grey in all its handsome shades: sky, dove, sea, asphalt, granite, cloud, and black of course. Today I was wearing a grey and black dress in something silky that was not quite silk and a plain dark grey sweater that had cashmere in it, together with black woollen tights. 'My jacket's warm,' I said.

'But look at your shoes.'

I looked down at what I could see of the black patent leather shoes with bows on from under the snow. I liked those shoes because they made me think of Minnie Mouse. If you wanted to compile a list of Best Dressed Cartoon Characters, I thought as I followed Katarina to the house, Betty Boop would win, but only just, with Minnie Mouse coming a very close second. Olive Oyl would obviously end up with the booby prize in spite of her size zero figure.

Uncle Ian was in his favourite chair by the window facing the fields and the wood beyond. He must have been listening out for me because he was already halfway out of his seat by the time I entered the room.

Uncle Ian had always had a good smile. He did not deploy it much, but when he did, it was to great effect. It was a focused smile, not just for anyone. It made you feel favoured. He directed this smile at me now and held out his hands. I thought he looked markedly better than when I had last seen him, only a few days ago. His complexion was fresher and his eyes were clearer.

'So what have you decided about my proposal?'

I had forgotten his habit of launching straight into a subject without pausing for even a 'Lovely day, isn't it?' or 'Chilly for the time of year?' or 'My gout is playing up something terrible.'

'I am incredibly grateful for your generosity . . .'

97

Uncle Ian stopped me with a wave of his right hand. 'Let's have some coffee. You must be tired after your trip.' He eased himself down towards the seat of his chair, gathering speed as his arms gave way. As seat touched seat the look on his face went from surprised to relieved; one tiny victory in the unwinnable war against age and decrepitude. It had to take a lot of energy to remain true to the person you used to be once age made you grateful simply to have made it down on to your seat.

'Your mother tells me that there is a house you like up for sale.'

I was beginning to be in awe of my mother's ability to interfere across continents and time-zones. I nodded. 'They haven't dropped the price, though. It's incredibly expensive.' I sat down myself and for a moment I felt a strange mix of pleasure and embarrassment at the ease with which I, still a young woman, moved.

I said to him, 'I really don't want anything from you, anything material, I mean. Please.'

He frowned. 'I don't know why you have to make this so difficult?'

I closed my eyes for a second. I opened them again and looked out over the snow-covered ground and the small patch of light left by the struggling sun. 'It's money Rose should have had,' I said. 'Surely you can see how that makes me feel?' There was a pause and I relaxed a little.

'I can see that you are allowing yourself to be irrational.'

'Is it irrational not to want to profit from your best friend's death? A death for which you carry responsibility?' I realised that not only had I spoken out loud the thoughts that had filled my mind since he first made his suggestion but I had raised my voice as well. I sat back in my chair, my hands gripping the armrests.

'I'm a very wealthy man. What do you think I should do with my money? Maybe I should arrange to be buried with it like some long ago potentate?'

I couldn't help laughing at the thought. 'Of course not. But you could give it to charity. You could set up a charity trust in Rose's memory.' I felt excited by the idea. 'Wouldn't that be wonderful?'

Uncle Ian sighed. He used to sigh just like that when, as a child, I just would not stop arguing my childish point. 'I did that years ago, Eliza. The Rose Bingham Foundation. The money goes towards the education of girls on the Indian subcontinent.'

I felt stupid, put in my place. I should have known that anything I thought of Uncle Ian would have thought about already.

'I was born in India, did you know that?'

'I think I did but I'd forgotten.'

'The work with the foundation has been the most rewarding thing I've done. Although it took Barbro to make me see that it was the right thing to do.' His smile was wry as he continued, 'I went through my own period of irrationality and to me, then, helping others when I hadn't been there to help my own child seemed like a betrayal. Though, as I said, Barbro made me see that that was perverse thinking.'

'I can do perverse thinking,' I said.

I thought of how, after the accident, I had scurried around like some creature from Aesop's fables looking to others for answers. The school chaplain had told me that the best way to make amends and to receive forgiveness for one's sins was to dedicate one's life to God and to helping one's fellow man. I remember arguing with him. I had sinned against Rose. Was it not a false equation to think that you could make up to X for what you had done to Y? If it were me who had been sinned against I wouldn't like it. 'Oh Eliza, sorry to have cut off both your legs but you will be delighted to hear I've just given your next-door neighbour a couple of state of the art artificial ones *and* a turbo-charged wheelchair *with* cup holder.'

Of course the chaplain had not seen it that way. To him any sin was a sin against God and any good deed, a homage. That all made perfect sense. If you believed in God.

'I know you listen to the local vicar but do you believe in God?' I asked Uncle Ian.

'Yes I do,' he said. 'Do you?'

'I don't know. I think I'm with Woody Allen when he says "To you I'm an atheist; to God, I'm the Loyal Opposition." '

'I know the fellow,' Uncle Ian said, although it wasn't clear if he meant God or Woody Allen.

'You've done so much good with your life,' I said.

'You're a kind girl,' Uncle Ian said.

I shook my head. 'Oh dear no. Or perhaps in the little things that are easy. Were I a properly good person I would go and work for a charity in some war-torn hellhole or in a third world orphanage. I'd be feeding the starving, myself, with my own hands rather than simply sending a bit of cash now and then. But I don't. Instead I choose to sit at home in comfort and feel bad about not being good enough.'

'I could say the same. Most people could. You should talk to Ove. He's very good at putting things in perspective.'

I smiled in a non-committal way.

'Don't just smile. Do it.'

I stopped smiling. 'OK.'

'So you will speak with him?'

'Yes. No. I don't know.'

'Well, make your mind up.'

'Yes.' I nodded emphatically, hoping that would be enough for now at least.

And thankfully Uncle Ian let the subject of the Almighty drop, for then at least. 'It's waste I can't stand,' he said instead. 'And there's so much of it about. Wasted opportunities, wasted talent, wasted lives. That's what the foundation is for, to stop some of that dreadful waste.'

We were silent for a while. Then I said, brightly, as if I had just thought of it. 'Why don't we give the money you so generously want to give me, who doesn't need it, to the foundation instead?'

Uncle Ian gave me a long look. Then he got to his feet, leaning heavily on the armrests of the chair as he raised himself up. Then he sighed. 'Well, if that's what you'd prefer.' And he walked out of the room.

Thirteen

THE SOUND OF A heavenly choir filled my bedroom and for a while I stayed where I was, warm in my bed, listening to the high clear voices and waiting to wake up. When I realised I was awake already and that the music was coming from outside, I scrambled out of bed and over to the window. A procession of white-clad figures was making its way up the track towards the house, their voices high and clear in the dark still morning. The young woman leading the way wore a crown of candles on her fair head. She looked as if she were cut in two, and I thought again that I had to be dreaming until she came closer, into the circle of light from the porch, and I realised that it was the blood-red ribbon tied round her slender waist that had caused the illusion. The other young women were dressed in similar long white gowns and so were the two boys bringing up the rear, but instead of the crown of candles the other girls wore garlands of tinsel in their hair and the boys wore pointed white hats decorated with gold stars, like magicians in a Disney cartoon. Then it dawned on me, thirteenth of December was the festival of St Lucia, the coming of light in the season of darkness. I threw on a dressing-gown and hurried downstairs.

Katarina, also in her dressing-gown, was standing by the front door. Her usual calm seemed to have abandoned her. 'Jäklar ocksa. Damn.'

'St Lucia,' I said.

'Ian can't stand it. Happens every year. They go to the old folks' home down the road and then, not content and scenting further prey, they continue on up here.' She crossed her arms over her chest. 'They're ruthless.'

'Maybe they'll just pass on by,' I said.

'On the way to where?' Katarina asked. Then the doorbell rang. We looked at each other. Katarina remained where she was, an uncertain look on her face. There was a loud knock, followed by a young woman's voice rising above the singing.

I couldn't understand what she was saying but I expect it amounted to 'We know you're in there.'

Uncle Ian appeared on the stairs in a similar tartan dressing-gown to Katarina's, his thinning but usually immaculate hair standing on end. It was the hair of a baby just woken, a style that suited the plump freshness of a young child. On Uncle Ian, it made you feel embarrassed, as if you had caught sight of something private. I didn't recall ever seeing him unshaven either. The grey stubble growing in uneven patches made him look years older. I hurried up to him and ignoring the fact that one simply did not touch Uncle Ian, I smoothed down his hair. He barely noticed.

'Katarina,' he looked past me at her. 'What the hell's going on here?'

'Lucia,' she whispered.

'Bugger. I'd forgotten it was the thirteenth. Don't open. We'll pretend to be away.'

The sweet singing changed to something more rhythmic – the same words, 'Hej Tomtegubbar . . .' repeated over and over.

'Too late. They already know we're here,' Katarina whispered.

Uncle Ian came down the last steps on bed-stiff legs and with a sigh said, 'All right, let them in, but wait until I'm in my chair. Eliza,' he beckoned to me to follow.

We didn't make it in time. The door opened behind us and the hall was filled with singing and candlelight. Like bees to their queen, the maidens and star-boys swarmed round St Lucia, tall and fair, then formed a procession. I turned to see them come towards us, the tips and heels of their boots visible beneath their white gowns. Within moments we were surrounded.

Lucia took Uncle Ian by the arm and led him to a chair, the wrong chair, the one he found it hard to get up from. She turned to me. 'Har Ni en filt?'

'I'm sorry, I don't speak Swedish.'

She switched seamlessly to English. 'I think we need a blanket.' She turned back to Uncle Ian. 'Brrr. It's cold in here.'

'I don't like an overheated room,' Uncle Ian said.

I looked around for Katarina but couldn't see her.

'Say you're contagious,' I hissed in his ear.

'Tried that last year. It doesn't make any difference.'

St Lucia directed her steel-blue gaze at me. 'Blanket?'

I plodded off in search of a rug, the soles of my sock-clad feet getting soaked by the little puddles of melting snow from the boots of the choir.

I returned with a paisley silk throw to find the maidens bustling round the room, lighting every candle in the room with their own. It was a beautiful scene: the white-clad young people with their tinsel and flickering flames, the perfectly proportioned room with its soft colours and warm wooden floors. Feeling like a collaborator, I handed the throw to Lucia, who arranged it round Uncle Ian, tucking it in at the back. He offered no resistance. A star-boy tried to hand him a mug of coffee. Uncle Ian waved it away. The star-boy turned a questioning face to Lucia, who turned to me.

'It's the cream,' I said. 'Mr Bingham drinks his coffee black.'

'Cream's good for the bones, you know. Caffeine leaches away calcium, that's why we add the cream.'

'But he doesn't . . .'

'If you show me the kitchen I will make some tea.'

'I think he's fine. Really. We'll have some later. When you've left.'

Lucia signalled the maiden with the basket of buns. 'We'll try him with a Lucia bun,' she said. 'Ni skall val ha en lussekatt I alla fall?'

The choir sang 'We Wish you a Merry Christmas' in perfect English.

I spotted Katarina standing at the back behind the spare star-boy. I went over to her.

'We have to do something.' I whispered.

She shrugged helplessly. 'It's better just to let them get on with it.'

'Why are they so determined? I mean, what's in it for them? Do they get paid per pensioner or something?'

'I don't think that's the case. I believe it's all arranged through the council. As part of the care for the elderly.'

'Have you tried opting out?'

She looked at me. 'There is no opting out.'

Uncle Ian sat as far back in his seat as was possible, his own back pressed against the back of the chair, the saffron bun in his hand and his gaze fixed on the Munch painting above the fireplace. It was a favourite of his, an original etching, one of only three and made by the artist himself. Two faces, one red and one blue, leaning towards each other. They were the faces of Munch himself and of his mistress, a violinist. The sight of the painting seemed to give Uncle Ian strength and he heaved himself up from his chair. As he did so the throw fell from his knees and his dressing-gown came apart, exposing the gaping flies of his pyjama trousers. I didn't know what to do. Had anyone else noticed? It was impossible to tell. Katarina seemed to have disappeared again. Then Uncle Ian himself looked down and spotted the gaping flies and the tuft of grey curly hair. His gaze shot back to me and I looked away, pretending not to have noticed.

When I turned round once more Uncle Ian was back in the chair, the dressing-gown and throw wrapped tight around him. His face had no colour; it wasn't white or pink or even grey. His gaze avoided mine.

The choir sung 'Hosanna', their soprano voices singing the harmony and reaching the high notes with ease. I leant back against the doorpost and closed my eyes.

It was almost lunchtime and Uncle Ian, who had retired to his room the moment the Lucia choir had left, still had not appeared. I was in the kitchen with Katarina, helping to prepare lunch.

'It's hard when the phone stops ringing,' she said.

'But he has friends?'

She shook her head. 'He had business acquaintances. It was extraordinary – comical almost, the way the phone stopped ringing and the invitations stopped coming practically the day that he gave up his last directorship. Not being asked his opinion, I think is what he finds most difficult. People used to queue up to get his advice and now he can't give it away for free.'

'I'll be his friend. I'll phone. He doesn't need to buy me a house. Has he told you about wanting to buy me a house?'

She nodded. 'And I think it's a good idea. It'll give him something to do, something to think about other than the past.'

'I don't need him to wave his magic wand, that's the point. Of course I would love to have more money or to own my own home but not this way. Really not this way.'

'And is it all about what you want?'

I startled. I frowned. It's all very well for people to speak their mind but we barely knew each other.

Katarina didn't seem to notice my surprise or my disapproval; instead, she simply continued frying the meat patties as the kitchen filled with smoke. I wanted her to go on frying until we couldn't see each other, until I was enveloped in my own little cloud of veal patty haze.

Uncle Ian came downstairs at one o'clock just as Katarina was bringing the food through to the dining room. He had nicked himself shaving but his hair was slicked back and he was wearing a cravat tucked into his Vyella shirt. I wasn't sure what would be the best thing to do, to refer to the events of the morning or to say nothing and wait for his lead.

In the end I plumped for clueless gushing. 'What a stroke of luck to be able to experience such a typical Swedish celebration,' I said.

He frowned. 'You think so?'

'I expect they go around the whole neighbourhood.'

'No, just the old people,' Uncle Ian said. He gave the word 'old' an ironic emphasis that fooled no one.

I said, 'You're not old. Look at the Queen Mother.'

'She's dead.'

'There is that,' I agreed, 'but I meant before she died. She was over a hundred. So thinking back to when she was your age, well, she would have to go back almost fifteen years. Just imagine. Anyway, age isn't what it used to be,' I said, adding to my impressive tally of platitudes.

'Age is what it's always been,' he said.

I pointed to the window. 'It's amazing the way the sunshine makes the snow glitter silver. You would have thought gold. The sun being more yellow.'

Katarina had prepared one of Uncle Ian's favourites, a kind of hamburger named after a Swedish financier and made from prime cuts of veal, minced finely and mixed with egg yolks and thick cream. I could see that if you were tired of life, eating Wallenbergare would be a fine way to go. Katarina served boiled potatoes and peas and low alcohol lager with the Wallenbergare and for a while we ate in silence. I had been known to be a noisy eater so as not to embarrass myself I kept my lips firmly shut between mouthfuls and chewed as if my teeth were scared of meeting. I watched Uncle Ian surreptitiously. He might look all spruce and dapper but I could see in his eyes that he hadn't recovered from the morning.

Katarina asked if the food was to our liking and Uncle Ian and I both quickly assured her that it was delicious. 'I asked,' she said then, 'because you both look as if you're chewing cardboard.'

I turned to Uncle Ian, waiting for a response, irritation, a smile, a protest, but he just speared a piece of potato on his fork and raised it to his mouth, concentrating as if he were doing something important.

'If I phone the estate agent and ask him to email you the details of the house, would you take a look?' I asked him.

He raised his head and I saw a glint of interest in his faded eyes. 'Of course.' He speared another piece of potato and I thought I'd lost him again when he said, 'Make sure he includes a floor plan as well.'

Did I imagine it or had his voice grown stronger? He reached beneath his sweater for his shirt pocket. 'Have you got a pen, Katarina?'

Katarina got to her feet and returned with a piece of paper and a biro. Uncle Ian wrote down his email address and passed it on to me before running through a short history of domestic property investment. Maybe I was getting carried away by my imagination but by the time he got to the part where investing in a high-end area if at all possible was always a sound bet, even his sparse hair had begun to look fuller.

Katarina lent me a pair of fur-lined boots and after lunch I walked to the lake. By now the water was frozen solid and, pushed by the wind, the overhanging branches of the trees scratched the ice like fingernails.

We had loved skating, Rose, Portia and I. We hadn't been any good at it but that had not been the point. The point had been to wear white fur-trimmed skating boots and play at being Christmas card Edwardian young ladies and perchance to stumble helpless into the outstretched arms of Julian and David and – oh I could not recall the names of the others. They had been handsome boys and we had been pretty girls and that had been about the sum of it. Or it should have been. What it should not have been was a matter of life and death.

Fourteen

Sandra/Cassandra

THE PRINCESSES WERE ACTUALLY pretty rubbish at skating but they didn't know that until they went out on the ice with me. I'd been skating since I was three.

We weren't supposed to go out on the ice without Miss Jennings.

'Don't be pathetic,' I told them. 'Anyway, I know these parts as if they were my own pockets.'

'Oh very Worzel Gummige,' Portia said.

'It is a beautiful day,' Eliza said. 'C'mon, let's do it.'

'Very Mallory Towers,' Portia said.

'Oh belt up, Porsche,' Eliza said.

I turned and gave her a look. Nothing much, not nasty, only as if I were trying to remember who she was and why I should care. She liked to be liked, did Eliza, and I knew I was getting to her. It surprised me, quite frankly, to see how little it took. Not laughing at a joke she made, studying a picture she'd drawn for Art and then not saying anything about it, looking her up and down when she was all dressed up to go off into town then turning away with a tiny smile. Those kinds of things. In fact, I was beginning to think this was better than being her friend.

At first, after that time she talked about me with the others, I had thought of confronting her. To tell her how disappointed I was and that I had believed we were friends. Then I decided on this instead. As I said, she liked to be liked, even by people she didn't much like herself.

Snow fell across the fields and settled prettily in the hair and lashes of the princesses: Rose the cautious, Portia the waspish, Eliza the enthusiast. The three of them looked like some old-time Christmas card with their rosy cheeks and ridiculously unsuitable clothes. They had started a kind of fashion, rejecting practicality, so instead of wearing the jeans and jumpers and trainers most of us wore for mufti, they were at all times dressed in skirts or dresses and dainty shoes. Actually, Eliza's shoes could never be described as dainty due to the fact that she wore a size seven but the point seemed to be to wear something uncomfortable that needed polishing. They polished their shoes endlessly.

'I really don't think it's a good idea,' Rose said.

'Don't be so wet.' Eliza flicked some snow at Rose, who shrieked and jumped to her feet from her perch on a log.

'It's only an idea,' I said. 'You've all been banging on about how much you want to see the boys.'

'OK,' Rose said. 'I'll come. But if we get caught . . .'

Once we were out on the ice with the shore at a good distance either side and no sign of land behind or ahead, I speeded up. The princesses had been squealing and giggling as they lumbered and tottered out on to the frozen lake in their second-hand skating boots. I couldn't stand the noise. Part of the glory of being out on the ice was the absence of sound apart from the swish of the blades as you travelled.

I skated past the island, onwards towards the next turn, where I stopped for a minute, hauling some make-up from my bum-bag. I checked my face in the tiny compact mirror. My hair was hopeless, having gone frizzier still from the wet snow, but I had a good colour on my cheeks and no spots. I brushed my lashes with the mascara wand and put on some lipstick. It was the same colour, 'Pink plum', that Rose used. I'd always heard that gingers should not wear pink, but when I glanced again at my reflection in the tiny mirror I could see how the shade livened up my skin.

I stuffed the make-up back in my bag and sped off once more. Behind me the princesses were shouting for me to wait. I pretended not to hear, doing a pirouette and skating backwards for a good fifty yards before spinning round. I thought that if my life were lived on skates how different it would be. On skates I was fast and smooth. I was the one the others followed.

The boys weren't at the jetty when I got there. I had counted on having a few minutes with Julian before Rose came along, a few minutes for him to see me not past me or through me to someone more interesting, but see *me*, but by the time he and the other boys did arrive, sauntering down the snowy verge and out on the jetty, the princesses were already giggling and wobbling their way towards us.

Eliza waved and promptly fell on her bum. Rose clung on to Portia, who ran into Eliza, and then they lay there in a heap of long limbs and glossy hair and Julian skated over to help them up. No one had even noticed I was there.

When they did notice I wished they hadn't.

'Oh Sandra-Cassandra you've put on some slap,' Portia said.

I looked round quickly to see if Julian had heard but he was huddled with David and Matt, smoking.

I pulled a face at her. Then Rose asked, 'Is that my lipstick?'

I shrugged and lit a menthol. 'How should I know. I got it ages ago.'

I turned and saw that now he, Julian, was looking at me. Still with the cigarette between my lips I jumped back down on to the ice. I skated on for about twenty yards and then I did some pirouettes and some jumps. I just knew they were all looking now. I carried on, smiling to myself, pretending to be in my own world while actually, I was auditioning for a part in theirs. I could hear my blade on the ice as I skated past on one leg, the other in the air, outstretched. Another pirouette and I skated towards them at speed, finishing off with a jump and landing full square and steady right in front of them.

No one said anything and then they all clapped. The princesses clapped, and the boys, and then I heard Julian say, 'That was so cool.'

I don't think that I had ever been happier than I was at that moment.

It's funny how being happy makes you nicer. I even forgave Eliza. The next Wednesday I asked them if they were going into town. Portia looked at the other two. 'We're not, actually,' she said finally.

Rose said, 'Not with that Greek assignment.'

Eliza muttered something about being broke.

I saw them as they returned. I was sitting on the saggy old sofa in the common room trying to concentrate on *Tristram Shandy*. Eliza and Rose had read it during the Christmas holidays, so they said, although by now – page twenty-four – I was seriously doubting the truth of that. My eyes were wandering from the book to the French windows and back when I saw them ambling along the drive. Eliza was carrying a Miss Selfridges bag and Rose and Portia were pigging out on chips from a Wimpy box. They'd gone into town after all. It was me who had suggested going in the first place so if they'd changed their minds they really should have told me. Then I remembered how uneasy Eliza had looked when she said they weren't and the way they had exchanged little glances and I realised that they had been planning to go all along, they just hadn't wanted to go with me. I felt myself go clammy. Nothing was working out the way I had dreamt it would. Instead it was like my old school all over again, only worse, because then it was just about jealousy. I had known I was different from the others at the old place; better, to be honest. For a start I had plans for the future, plans that didn't include marrying the first acne-ridden loser who asked me and settle down five minutes from where I'd grown up. My parents said I had been like a bright-feathered bird amongst a flock of grey sparrows.

But at LAGs it was all meant to be different. That was the whole point of going. Of my mother not getting the conservatory extension this year either, in spite of having taken on that completely embarrassing part-time job, and of my dad sticking with his ten-year-old Cortina. Of Mum wearing the same dress every time she goes out anywhere and saying it's because she loves it so much. Of Dad having given up his membership of the club. That's why they were making sacrifices, so that I could be with girls like me, other bright-feathered girls. Finally I was going to fit in; the round peg in the round hole. Only that's not how it was, was it?

*   *   *

I got up and walked out through the French windows towards them. When Eliza saw me she startled and her cheeks grew bright pink as if someone had slapped her.

I made my voice all even and said, 'I thought you weren't going.'

Rose looked up at me with those huge blue eyes. Then she shrugged.

Portia said, 'We changed our minds.'

'I tried to find you,' Eliza said. She was lying. Again.

Portia and Rose started walking off as if what they had done didn't matter. I had been quite calm but now I felt the anger build up inside me, choking me, the way it had when I was little and Mum had to give me that cherry-flavoured sedative stuff. I knew I should pause and take deep breaths or count to ten or something, anything rather than what I did. Grab Portia by the shoulder and shriek, 'Don't walk away from me, do you hear. Don't you dare walk away from me. You said you weren't going in to town today.' I swung round and pointed at Eliza and her Wimpy carton, 'You said you had no money.' I stopped, breathless, as if anger and hurt had driven the very air from my lungs.

Portia assumed an air of theatrical concern. 'Gosh, you are in a state, aren't you?' She followed with Bafflement and finished off with Contrition. 'We're sorry. Really we are. Aren't we, girls?' She looked at the others and they nodded gravely and said they were indeed sorry.

I wanted to hit them all and I could do it too; if I spun round like a dervish with windmill arms, I could knock them down like skittles. I started counting in my head. One, two, three, four, five, six ... My arms dropped to my sides, but my free hand, the one not holding the book, was a fist still, clenching and unclenching. 'Really?' I had intended that 'really' to sound quizzical, somewhat superior, but instead it came out in a squeak as if I were a boy whose voice was breaking.

Eliza looked even more embarrassed. 'Are you OK? We're sorry. We didn't mean to upset you.' If Miss Doing the Decent Thing Eliza Cummings spent any more time sitting on the bloody fence she would split in two.

Rose put her soft little hand to her mouth to stifle a giggle. My forehead started to itch. I had got better at controlling my temper but I never could control the rash. It started at the hairline and spread down across my forehead; little tiny spots betraying me. I felt the weight of my Penguin edition of *Tristram Shandy* in my hand. I had forgotten I was holding it. My hand rose in the air as if pulled and then I did it. I lobbed the book, as well and as hard as I could, right at Portia's head.

Portia ducked, but too late. She cried out as the corner of the book hit her right above the left eye, cutting her eyebrow. I took a step back, stumbling on the edge of the lawn. I managed to steady myself but I was breathing as if I had run a race.

'Are you completely mad?' Eliza stepped in front of me.

I smirked. I had managed to knock her off that bloody fence at last.

'Seriously, have you gone completely mad?'

Portia, supported by Rose, had gone to sit down on the bench by the wall.

I looked at them then back to Eliza and I said, all calm now, 'You lied to me. You all lied to me and then you laughed about it. And I won't put up with it.'

I spent the rest of the afternoon waiting to be called into Miss Philips's study. Maybe I would be suspended, expelled even. If

I were, at least my parents' disappointment would be over with quickly, like the blow to the head of a twitching bird.

But nothing happened. There was no summons to the housemistress, no visits from Laura, our up-herself practically-perfect-in-every-way house prefect.

The next day Gillian explained that the princesses would rather swallow their tongues than tell on a friend. I was torn between the rather delicious image of them chewing and swallowing their tongues and the unexpected assessment that I was seen as their friend. Then I remembered that Gillian in her despised position at the bottom of the heap was likely to consider anyone who actually spoke to you a friend, so I concentrated on the tongue swallowing.

The following Wednesday I spent all my money on a huge bottle of 'Charlie' for Portia. I wrapped the bottle in red and gold paper – then I tore it off and went back into town and got some floral stuff in case Portia thought I'd been cheap and used Christmas leftovers. I bought a card too, with a punk standing in front of the guards at Buckingham Palace. I wrote saying how sorry I was and that I had never really learnt self-control but now I was learning through example and how amazing I thought it was to be a pupil at LAGs and how much their friendship meant to me. I drew a heart on the card.

The truth was I sort of meant what I wrote. The truth was I made myself sick sometimes by how I behaved. I felt sick now just thinking about it. In my mind my fists pounded the sides of my head until they were crushed bits of bone imploding into bloody mush.

But in the end Portia was actually nice to me about it all. She said she'd already forgotten about the 'incident' as she called it and that she just adored 'Charlie' and how did I know, seeing that she had never worn it? She even showed me some photos from her skiing holiday, including one of Julian. Portia talked about him all the time to people but only the inner sanctum were shown photos.

Eliza said my apology showed style. I looked at her.

'I live for your approval,' I said. Then I smiled, a nice smile as if I were being funny-friendly. She smiled back but I could see from her eyes that she felt uneasy.

Fifteen

Eliza

UP ON THE HILL the air was fresher. Up on the hill the small square opened up like a smile. Up on the hill life was easy. Up on the hill stood a house that looked as if it had been built on the piss. This was the house I wanted. I had wanted it ever since the day I first saw it, an autumn day seven years ago when out walking with Gabriel. He and I had met not long before, as I had staggered into the hospital A&E reception area bleeding all over the lino at the exact same minute as Gabriel was passing that exact same part of the reception area. He had taken my elbow to steady me before passing me over to the triage nurse.

('Why didn't you help me yourself?'

'I'm not an A&E doctor.'

'So if I'd been lying dying on the road would you have just passed by too?'

'Of course not. That would be completely different. And I didn't pass by, I handed you over to the appropriate member of staff. Anyway, if I had treated you I wouldn't have been able to have a relationship with you. So it was just as well, wasn't it?'

'Ah, but you didn't know that at the time. That you wanted to have a relationship with me.'

'How do you know I didn't?'

'You did?'

'No. But I do now.')

Gabriel, with his mind crammed full of matters of life and death was particularly unsuited to that kind of cringe-worthy banter but still he had risen manfully to the challenge, proving, on the way, that love was a true proponent of equality, making fools of us all with no regard to colour, creed, educational attainment or profession.

The second time Gabriel and I met was at the hospital fund-raising ball. The tickets had cost a hundred pounds, which was a lot of money for a ceramic restorer to spend on an evening out, but I felt bad for having taken up scarce hospital recourses when my injuries were self-inflicted as near as made no difference. I had also donated a lustreware cup to their raffle. It was not of museum quality but it was pretty and the best piece that I owned and I had thought long and hard before letting it go. In the end I had had to remind myself that the greater the sacrifice the more worthwhile the gift would be. (I'm never sure why it should be so, but it did seem to be the general understanding.) Also I liked thinking how pleased the lucky winner would be with the cup. In the event the man whose raffle ticket won him my cup had turned the gold and pink piece in his hand before passing it, with a laugh and a shake of his head, to his companion.

Then a voice behind me had said, 'Lucky guy. That's a beautiful prize.'

That had been Gabriel.

A little later that evening we won the karaoke competition for our rendition of 'Islands in the Sun' on account of our having elicited the fewest cat-calls according to the 'boo-rometer', and not many days after that, we had come upon the house on the hill.

It had been late October but the sun shone as if it thought it were summer. We had met for breakfast at a café before setting off for a walk on the Heath. As we crossed the road he had taken my hand, more, it has to be said, in the manner of a mother making sure her child didn't stop to tie her laces in the middle of the traffic than a lover, but either way, his strong warm hand holding mine had sent tingles down my chest to the pit of my stomach.

We had walked to Kenwood House and were returning to his car through the top of the village when I noticed the side street opening up into a small square. 'Pretty,' I said, and I pulled him along with me on the detour.

The house was not big, yet it stood back from the square in its own overgrown garden, guarded over by an avuncular mulberry tree. The house itself looked to be Georgian. Judging by its position I thought that it might once have belonged to a larger property that had since been demolished. Perhaps it had been the gardener's cottage or the coachman's quarters. Subsidence had given it an apologetic air as it leant towards its larger western neighbour, a tall red-brick, and a ramshackle one-storey brick and glass extension had been added to the eastern wall. The square itself looked like the setting for a television costume drama. Remove the cars, I had thought, and Emma Woodhouse would have felt quite at home wandering across the cobbles on her way to visit an annoying neighbour.

Gabriel put his arm round me. 'You like it?'

I nodded.

'Me too.' He kissed the top of my head. 'In fact, it reminds me of you.'

I looked up at him. 'Really?' I smiled. 'How?'

He tilted his head as he gazed at the house. 'It's got so much unfulfilled potential,' he said finally. 'All it needs is some TLC to bring it out.'

I decided that I was far too comfortable standing there in the autumn sunshine with his arm round me to worry about whether or not I had been patronised. I sighed, content, and rested my head against his shoulder. Maybe those shoulders were broad enough even for my baggage.

And now I was standing in that same tiny square gazing at that same house, but this time with Beatrice and an estate agent called Neil, and I thought of the time I had stood pretty much where I was standing now, imagining myself living here with Gabriel. What skill, what determination it had taken to loose such a man as he. I understood some of the reasons for why it had ended but not all. I'd never know, for example, what had made me grumpy when all I wanted was to smile. I winced as I remembered the times he had stepped through the door, his face elongated with exhaustion, yet still managing to put on a cheerful face and greet me like he was happy to be home. And I, who had usually been back for an hour at least, who had looked forward to seeing him, who had tidied up and maybe bought some flowers for the kitchen table, who had brushed my hair and re-applied lipstick and sprayed on scent and was ready to hear about his day and tell him about mine, what did I do? Well, more often than not I would find that the intended smile in return slipped into a pout and that all my stories of the day dried up into a dry little shrug and a sentence about the lousy traffic or uninteresting pot or the headache lurking at the back of my eyes.

Truly, I don't know how that had all happened, why I had felt this need to come down like a scoop of cold water over his lovely head. But I had. I remember him reaching for the bottle of red wine and, finding it empty (we had started trying to make one bottle last two nights), getting up from the table to open a new one.

'You shouldn't,' I said.

'Why?' He had sounded like a rebellious teenager. According to his mother, Gabriel had never been rebellious even when he *was* a teenager so I should have been warned. Instead, a little later, I told him off for dripping water on the floor when washing up – you walk in it and the floor gets all dirty. Then I rewashed the grill pan, sighing loudly as I went.

All in all I had managed to dampen his general enthusiasm nicely, but still he bounced back. We were watching the news and he told me that he had been so encouraged by the reaction to the publication of his paper on the developments of new therapies for Alzheimer's that although he had had his application for extra funding turned down twice he was going to apply again. 'They have to agree this time,' he said, and his eyes shone and he was barely able to sit still as he began listing all the reasons as to why he would be successful.

I have a memory for rhymes. I had felt it was a good idea to quote one of Fontaine's instructive fables so I did.

' "This world is full of shadow-chasers, most easily deceived.
Should I enumerate these racers, I should not be believed.
I send them all to Aesop's dog,
Which, crossing water on a log,
Espied the meat he bore, below;
To seize its image, let it go;
Plunged in; to reach the shore was glad,
With neither what he hoped, nor what he'd had." '

And my husband had listened to me, standing still and silent as the enthusiasm drained from his eyes and his shoulders hunched. That night, for the first time, he had slept wearing pyjamas. Now I know a lot of men do that, sleep in pyjamas. To those men and their partners that was fine, how it was and no questions asked. It didn't mean a thing. But to us, who had slept side by side for eight years naked as the day we were born (apart from the time the central heating went on the coldest night of the year and he had brought me his cosiest sweatshirt) that wearing of pyjamas had been as significant as if he had gone to work on a little brick wall down the middle of the bed.

'Shall we go in?' the estate agent asked me.

I paused by the gate, then I turned to Beatrice and whispered, 'Now, don't get carried away. Remember we're only here so I can tell Uncle Ian I've been but that I don't like it after all.'

'Speak for yourself,' Beatrice whispered back as I held the gate open for her. '*I'm* here because I've never been inside a house with this price tag before.'

I felt it as soon as I stepped inside: the sense of a place at peace with itself, and I found myself smiling without really knowing why.

'As you can see it's in need of updating,' Neil said as we walked though the ground floor.

I felt as defensive as if he'd been talking about me. 'I think it's lovely, nevertheless,' I said. 'It has lovely bones and that's what matters.'

'Updating?' Beatrice said as we walked upstairs. 'I think you mean rebuilding. And you're asking *how* much for this?'

Neil gave her a slow considerate look over before turning to me. 'Your mother?'

'You must be very confident of selling this property,' Beatrice said.

I ignored them and asked, 'It's listed, yes?'

'Grade two star.'

Beatrice turned to me with a helpful smile. 'That means you can't put up a spice-rack without the permission of English Heritage.'

Neil narrowed his eyes at her before saying. 'Of course, many people feel that it's a privilege to own an historic building.'

'Really?' Beatrice said. 'Of course, I wouldn't understand about that sort of thing, working as a museum conservator.'

I frowned at the bickering pair. Like a mother wanting to shield her infant from harsh voices and cross exchanges I wanted to shield the little house from discord. I was sure it was not accustomed to that sort of carry-on.

'I love it,' I said.

Neil spun round. 'Really? I mean, excellent.'

' "Ours not to reason why?" ' Beatrice muttered. She turned to Neil. 'Admit it, you think she's out of her mind?'

He shot her a steely glance. 'Not at all. There are many people who value character over convenience.'

Once Neil was out of earshot Beatrice asked me, 'I thought you weren't buying.'

'I'm not.'

'Of course you're not. You'll just phone up that Fairy Godfather of yours and say, "Golly gosh! House Charming is even more gorgeous than I thought it would be so I've decided most definitely to decline your generous offer." '

'Shall we go back to the office?' Neil asked. I hated to dash his hopes but I told him I needed time to think.

Giving me a firm handshake, the kind that speaks of honesty and integrity, he said, 'I'll give you a courtesy call tomorrow.'

As we crossed the cobbles we were forced back on to the pavement by a large black car coming round the corner at speed. 'What the hell?' I shook my head. The car swung into a tight space in front of Number 12, the house opposite.

'Meet the neighbours,' Beatrice said.

Sixteen

RUTH HANDED ME A booklet entitled *Free Yourself from Toxic Guilt* published by an organisation called The Living Life Group. 'Read it,' she ordered. 'It's all very well poo-poohing these kinds of things but in your situation I think you'd be wise to be open-minded.'

Ruth and I had been seeing more of each other lately. She said it was because we had 'cleared the air'. I assumed she was referring to the time she'd told me what a lousy step-sister I'd been for the past twenty years. I had laid in a store of peppermint tea for her and she was drinking some now, looking at me over the mug, as she told me she was now pretty sure that Robert was after all having an affair. She had no proof but all the signs were there, she said. Lottie didn't want to hear a word against her father and Ruth didn't trust her friends not to gossip so I was the only one she could confide in. I told myself that I should be grateful to be needed. I was alive and I was needed and if I wasn't careful I might end up with the house of my dreams, too. Any more to be grateful for and I might have to call my old friend Dr Herbert at the clinic.

'It's like living with a stranger,' Ruth said. 'He comes through the door at night and he doesn't look at me, he looks through me. Did Gabriel do that?'

I shook my head. 'But he left really soon after he'd started seeing Suki. In a way it was a relief. I couldn't have coped with any more of his torment.'

'His torment?'

'Not many people appreciate how hard it is for a good man to do bad things. He didn't sleep, tossing and turning and waking up soaked in sweat. He lost weight, he drank too much. It was awful.'

'I wore a red dress and red feathers in my hair the other night and I might as well have been wearing my jeans and a T-shirt.'

'Did you? Did you really. Good for you. You suit red.'

'Every time he's ... well, you know ... strayed, he's done the same thing, just removed himself from our life bit by bit.'

'Leave him.'

'I couldn't.'

'Why not?'

'Why not? You need to ask me why not? Well, I'll tell you why not.' She paused. Then she took another breath. 'Oh yes, I'll tell you all right.'

'You tell me,' I said.

'I couldn't do that to Lottie.'

'Lottie will cope better than you think. She's got her own life now. She's twenty, after all. Of course it will be upsetting for her but she'll cope. Anyway, she wouldn't want to see you be unhappy.'

'That's what people say when they want an excuse to do the wrong thing. "It's better for the children to have happy divorced parents than unhappy married ones." But it's not true, you know. They've found that out.'

'But Lottie's not a child any more, that's the point.'

Ruth frowned at me. 'And where would we live?' She gesticulated round the kitchen in my little flat. 'Somewhere like this?'

'Well, yes.'

'I'm sorry but I couldn't do that to Lottie. No, I'll have to soldier on. There's nothing else for it.' She was looking almost excited. 'I must say that Daddy and Olivia have been extremely supportive. They call all the time. Daddy even sent me flowers the other day. The last time I had this much attention was when I was expecting Lottie. You weren't there, of course, but it was wonderful. Like being a princess. Anyway,' she shook herself, 'I want you to really take a look at this.' She pushed the brochure from the Living Life Group towards me on the table.

'Each course lasts six weeks. The next one begins in a couple of days so it would work perfectly. Go on. It can't hurt.'

'No, no, I don't suppose it can.'

'So, how are things going with your godfather?'

I wondered if it would be mean to bring the subject back to her cheating husband. I expected it would be. So I just said, 'It's going fine. We get on very well.'

'And?' Ruth looked at me, her head to one side.

'And nothing else really.'

'That's not what Olivia tells me.'

'Isn't it? So what has my mother told you?'

'The house. He wants to buy you your own lovely home. I mean, how wonderful is that. Robert and I worked sixty-hour weeks for ten years before we were able to own our first home.'

'I can see that doesn't seem fair,' I said. 'When all I had to do was kill someone.'

Ruth shook her head. 'Really, Eliza, now you're being silly.'

'Yes. Yes, I am. I'm sorry.'

She got up. Nodding at the booklet, she said, 'So you'll go? For me.'

I picked it up once she had left and started reading. I learnt that 'most of the misery faced by affluent Western people these days was self-inflicted and therefore avoidable, caused by neuroses and illogical concerns and obsessions and that this was a kind of obesity of the mind'. And like obesity, the solution to the problem almost always lay 'in the hands of the individual concerned'. I also learnt that the Thirteen Steps embraced by the LLG were thirteen because it was a number feared by many and overcoming illogical fears was an important part in 'taking control'. Among other things, attendance at the 'workshops' would teach me to 'reverse ingrained assumptions and turn a negative into a positive'. That last one, I thought, they had just gone and pinched from Pollyanna.

The booklet went on to say that 'Everybody suffers from anxiety; anxiety is a normal and necessary part of being human. For some, however, it can affect us more intensely, occur more easily and more often, thereby giving rise to problems such as toxic guilt, persistent apprehension, obsessive thoughts, panic and depression.'

It finished by saying that 'Before we can truly cure these problems, before we can say goodbye to them for ever ... we need to know what happened to us and why. We NEED to know. To want to know is a basic human urge and we'll search for ever for the answers.'

Of course humankind is defined by its hunger for knowledge. That's how all the trouble started in the first place, allegedly. But knowing didn't always help. For example I knew exactly what had happened to Rose. If I hadn't known, if I thought that Rose was alive and well, living in New Zealand, there would be no problem. But Uncle Ian wanted me to be happy. And if that was what he wanted, however strange it was that he should, well, then I owed it to him at least to try. It would please Ruth too if I took her advice. Bossing me around probably gave her some light relief now she was going through a bad time.

The meeting was held in the basement of a large red-brick house not far from Dr Freud's house. This fact, also mentioned in the booklet, lent the whole enterprise a certain credibility, I thought, as I walked along Maresfield Gardens.

The large room was furnished like a mix between an opium den and a school assembly hall. A tall man seated on a floor cushion unfurled himself and greeted me.

'You must be Eliza.'

I was intrigued. 'How did you guess?'

'Everyone else's already here. Being late,' he paused, glancing at a large clock on the wall opposite, 'often indicates a reluctance to attend. I'm Marcus, by the way.'

'Really?' I said. 'Does it really?'

'Why don't you have a seat over there, next to Sam.' He pointed at a floor cushion with room for two.

Sam, a round-faced blonde woman in her thirties who looked as if the only thing she might have to feel guilty over was having second helpings, gave me a welcoming smile and patted a space next to her, so I smiled back and sat down. Looking around me, I noticed more smiles in my direction so I kept mine in place. If that's what guilt did to you, I thought, then death row must be one smiley place.

Marcus sat back down on his cushion. It too was a cushion made for two but he was there alone. I suppose no one wanted to be seen as therapist's pet.

'So what then is Toxic Guilt?' he began. I was happy to see him do those little quotation marks in the air thing when he spoke. I'd always wanted to see that done in real life.

'Toxic Guilt is inappropriate guilt – guilt that comes from self-judgement. Judgements that say you have done something wrong when there is no actual wrongdoing.' He paused and looked around him. There was a lot of nodding back at him.

'Do you feel responsible for everyone around you?' His voice was carrying and intimate both at once, like a trendy teacher saying; 'I'm one of you, just in charge, that's all.'

'Do you value the feeling of others more than your own? Do you have unrealistic expectations of yourself: then you may be trapped by Toxic Guilt.

'Trying to win the approval of others – parents, spouse, co-workers, friends, children can strain your relationships, drain your energy and dominate your life. The five easy-to-follow steps in escaping Toxic Guilt can liberate you from self-defeating patterns and put you on the path to living life fully, joyfully and on your own terms.'

I put my hand up. Marcus nodded at me. 'Eliza, yes?'

'I thought it was thirteen steps?' Actually, what I had wanted to ask was where the bit about how to deal with having caused, for example, a death, came in but I couldn't bring myself to do it – not yet. Maybe later, when we'd warmed up.

'Really? Why did you think that?'

'It said so in the booklet.'

'Maybe that referred to another of our programs. Either way, we use five, if that's OK with you?' The smile was not quite so friendly this time.

I told him that of course it was fine with me and that I was sorry for interrupting. Marcus told me I was not to apologise.

'In fact,' he turned to the rest of the room, 'over-eagerness to apologise is a typical response of someone suffering from Toxic Guilt.'

He went on to list the five steps. They were:

1) Recognize the difference between good guilt and Toxic Guilt;
2) Build boundaries around your time and emotions;
3) Weather the storm of people's disapproval;
4) Find freedom through forgiveness and relinquishing control;
5) Protect your sense of self while still caring for others.

Then it was everyone's turn to stand up, form a circle and share, one after the other, the focus of their guilt. Marcus nodded towards the woman opposite him. 'Daisy, why don't you start.'

Daisy looked around her and the others all smiled their encouragement. She stepped into the circle.

'Hello, everyone. I'm Daisy and . . . well, I just can't stop feeling guilty about the fact that I was sent to private school and my older sister wasn't. She's never forgiven me, or our parents. Everyone else tells me I have nothing to feel bad about, but I can't help it. I feel as if everything good that's happened to me since, my successful career, my marriage and lovely home, all stem from that lucky break. It makes it worse that my sister is struggling on a low income.'

Everyone clapped, and Daisy who was lithe and blonde and quite possibly drove a Porsche, appeared to be relieved of a burden as she seated herself back down in one smooth movement.

Alan was in his late forties and wearing clothes that looked as if he'd got them from the 'preppy' section of a catalogue. He had a buzz cut and a wide mouth that dipped at the corners.

'Hi, I'm Alan. I can't stop thinking about how I didn't visit my dying grandmother in hospital. We never had a chance to say goodbye. I was her favourite grandchild and she practically brought me up yet when she needed me I wasn't there for her.'

Again, everyone clapped. I wondered if I might suggest we drop the clapping. It took up a lot of time and the session only lasted two hours. It was the same in yoga class. I found the relaxation part difficult. I couldn't help thinking of all the things I should be doing, none of which involved lying on a mat imagining being a white feather floating to the ground.

Next it was the turn of a woman in late middle age with an elongated body and dry dull hair drooping around her thin face like branches of a weeping willow. She looked so distressed that for a moment I thought she might have done something truly bad.

'Hi, I'm Joan. When my dog died we found out that she was dehydrated because I rationed her water so she wouldn't keep peeing on the carpet. I didn't realise she suffered from diabetes. The vet said lack of water wasn't the cause of death but I can't stop blaming myself and thinking of how she must have suffered from thirst in those last few days of her life.' Joan started to cry and everyone clustered round and patted her on the back and shoulders and told her she was 'doing good work'.

I wanted to cluster and pat too. Instead I stood there, my arms hanging stiff at my sides, watching. I could feel Marcus's disapproving gaze. But I really didn't think the others would want me once they had heard what I had to say, any more than a gang of petty thieves would want an axe murderer to chummy up to them to say he knew exactly how they felt because, when it came to it, weren't they all in it together.

Joan appeared to have cheered up, and following her was Clare, who felt guilty the whole time but didn't know over what and Janet, who had the same problem. Then it was Zoe.

'Hi, I'm Zoe and I'm a working mother.'

There was an expectant silence from the group but the thin woman in her late thirties, whose stooping posture suggested that her guilt was perched right there on her shoulders, appeared to have said her piece and stepped back into the circle.

It was my turn. Marcus nodded at me. 'Eliza?'

'I'm not sure . . .'

'It's important that everyone shares,' he said. 'In fact it's pretty bad for the morale of the group if one member withholds.'

My heart was racing and I had to take a couple of deep breaths to steady my voice. I glanced over at Marcus. 'It's OK, Eliza. You're amongst friends.'

I stepped into the circle. 'Hi, I'm Eliza and my selfish and destructive behaviour when I was younger caused a lot of problems for my family, my stepsister especially.' I looked around me at the sympathetic faces. Marcus nodded his approval. I closed my eyes for a moment, before opening them again and giving Marcus a little nod back. 'And I killed my best friend.'

Everyone remained still vaguely in the formation of a circle, but looking awkward, a bit like party-goers when a fellow guest has said something really embarrassing before throwing up in the ice bucket. Then Joan and Zoe started up a conversation about begonias. This struck me as imaginative until I noticed the carrier bag with a pot of begonias on the floor by the door. I wished I could join in. Begonias were reassuring things. Looking around me I realised that by now I was standing apart although I hadn't moved.

Marcus called us to attention by telling us that our time was up; apparently the room was needed for the sex, drugs and alcohol addicts. I was collecting my jacket and bag when Marcus called me back. Could he have a word?

Once we were on our own he said, 'I'm not sure we are the right people to help you. As I explained at the start of the session we deal with toxic or as it could also be described, *imagined* guilt. Guilt with no real substance . . .' he carried on explaining as if I were not only really, really guilty but also really, really stupid '. . . with no basis in reality, is simply another kind of addiction and like all addictions it's about control. Your problem seems to be that . . . well, that you really do have a reason to feel guilty. Were you ever . . . well, punished for what happened?'

I didn't want to talk to him about it any more. I couldn't understand what had made me tell a room full of strangers in the first place. Perhaps it was the incense, or maybe the dimmed lights that made you think you were in the cinema or a theatre where nothing was quite real; maybe it was simply the act of forming a circle, which helped, in some curious way, to release inhibitions. I felt let down by Marcus and his clinic. I had told myself that I was only going along to please Ruth but I suppose I had hoped, too, that I would find some answers.

Marcus had been raking his fingers through his mop of dark curly hair and now he rolled his head from left to right as if his neck was hurting. 'I'm sorry,' he said finally, 'but as I said, we deal with . . .'

'I know. You only deal in guilt that isn't actually guilty.' I walked to the door.

'Wait.'

I turned round. 'Yes?'

'At least let me give you a refund.'

Earlier in the day I had sensed the promise of spring, but as I walked back to the flat through the dark streets the wind seemed to come straight from the north and I turned up my collar and shoved my hands deep into my pockets. I paused at the corner of the road, waiting for the bus to pass before I crossed. I was tired. I closed my eyes for a moment, thinking how easy it would be to just step into the road and be done with it. Dead and Done. Done and Dusted. They said a change was as good as a rest and there was no denying that being dead would be a change. One foot forward, one step down. I opened my eyes and jumped back on to the pavement. The bus passed.

I had done a good thing there, I thought as I walked on. Just think how late the passengers would have been had they had to stop and wait while the police came and the ambulance scraped me off the wheels. Being late home on a chilly March evening might not seem like such a big deal but it could be most inconvenient. Add to it that they could not exactly complain about it. I mean, what would it look like, coming through the door with a scowl and a sigh, saying, 'That's all I needed after a long day at work, some bloody woman getting herself run over by my bus.'

I had barely got through the door myself when the phone rang. It was Ruth, wanting to know how the session at the LLG had gone. I told her it had been very helpful.

'So you'll continue going? Excellent.'

'Not really.'

I heard her sigh at the other end of the phone. 'Why not, Eliza? I mean if I didn't know any better I would think you didn't even want my help.'

'I do. I do. But I really wasn't given the option to continue. Apparently mine was the wrong kind of guilt.'

Ruth seemed to think I was trying to be funny at her expense so she said goodbye in a tight little voice and hung up before I had had a chance to explain.

Seventeen

Sandra/Cassandra

'WHERE DO YOU THINK we'll all be in twenty years' time?' Rose asked.

'Old,' Eliza said.

Spring had arrived at last. We were sitting bare-legged in the grass on School Hill, looking out across the lake that not so long ago had been frozen solid. The sun had real warmth in it. I felt warm inside too. I didn't want to feel mean or harbour a grudge; I just wanted to be normal. There were times when I thought I might not be. And I don't mean not normal in a cute oddball way. I mean not normal in the way a sixth finger isn't normal, or a rogue cell. I knew too that Eliza sensed this about me and that that made her uncomfortable.

'Apart from old?' Rose said.

Eliza frowned in concentration. The breeze ruffled her auburn curls and the sun had brought out every last one of her freckles in spite of her wearing a sunhat. It was a battered old straw hat that looked like something your grandmother might wear when gardening and she'd fixed some daisies and forget-me-nots into the faded brown hatband. It was a pretty rubbish hat but somehow you ended up wanting one just like it. It was the same with that small enamel four-leaf clover she wore around her neck. It was nothing special, in fact had someone worn it back home I would have thought it was quite tacky even, yet, back when I had hoped we might be best friends, I had yearned for one exactly the same. I had described it to my parents, telling them I wanted it for Christmas. Of course they missed the point entirely and handed over this really expensive all gold one with a little diamond at the centre. 'We looked at a little enamel one like the one you were talking about but we thought this was much more stylish,' my mother had said, looking pleased with herself.

I wore it when I was home, so as not to upset them, but it wasn't what I wanted.

Finally Eliza replied. 'I'll be on my way to a meeting with my publishers.' She pushed her hat down securely on her head and sat back in the grass, resting on her elbows, a dreamy little smile on her lips.

'I'm eating a croissant as I walk. I'm too busy to sit down at a café. My first two books of fairy tales have been a success and now they want to discuss a third one but I'm not sure because I might want to focus solely on my art.' She laughed, so pleased with it all, and although I hadn't meant to, I found myself smiling back.

'What about money?' Portia asked. 'Are you rich?'

'No. No, I don't think so. But I have a nice flat and a good bicycle and I go on holiday to Italy once a year.'

'Then you're rich,' I said.

Eliza looked unsure. She was probably trying to work out if she had been tactless to those less fortunate, i.e., me.

'What about a family?' Rose asked. 'And a husband?'

'Of course. Eventually.' Eliza rolled over on her front and her hat slipped off her head and on to the grass. As she picked it up a sprig of forget-me-not dropped to the ground. 'What about you all?'

'I'll be preparing for the Oscars,' Rose said, straightening her back and tossing her dark curls, as if she were already on that red carpet. She giggled but I suspected that deep down she was deadly serious.

'You could play Snow White,' I said. 'You have the right colouring.'

Rose dimpled. 'You know, I don't think there's been a film with real actors as opposed to the cartoon version. It's actually a really clever idea.'

'Cassandra is a very clever girl,' Eliza said.

I wondered if she was taking the piss but she didn't look as if she was. She had the kind of face that showed everything she was thinking and right now she seemed to be thinking nice things. Her smile was friendly and her eyes were kind.

The sun had been sheltering behind a cloud but now it reappeared, just in time for us not to have to put our cardies back on. Portia passed round a packet of Philip Morris. She lit her cigarette and mine then Rose leant in towards the match. It made for a funny picture, Snow White with a fag hanging from her lips.

'Don't', Eliza said.

Rose drew on her cigarette. 'What?'

'Three on a match,' Eliza said. 'You remember, the First World War thing?'

'No,' Rose shook her head. 'Wasn't there myself.'

Eliza sat back up and as she hugged her knees to her chest I could see the back of her milky-white thighs all the way up to her knickers. I think she saw me looking because she pulled her skirt down really quickly. 'If three soldiers lit the cigarette from the same match the man who was third on the match would be shot.'

'Why? Why would he get shot?' Portia asked.

'What happened was that when the first soldier lit his cigarette the enemy would see the light; when the second soldier lit his cigarette from the same match the enemy would take aim and then, when the third soldier lit his cigarette from the same match, the enemy would fire. It's been considered bad luck ever since.'

'So who would cop it?' Portia asked. 'The guy holding the match or the guy lighting his cigarette from it?'

'Hm?' Eliza tilted her head to one side and rubbed the side of her nose with her middle finger. 'I suppose I always assumed it was the guy lighting his cigarette.'

'Bang bang,' I said. Pointing my pistol finger at her.

'Not funny,' Rose frowned.

But Eliza and Portia laughed so Rose laughed and then I laughed too.

Rose stubbed her cigarette out on a stone. She never smoked them to the end. Then she spat on it to make sure it had gone out before brushing it into the long grass. She looked up at the sky and then at all of us. 'God, we're so lucky,' she said.

'How do you mean?'

'Think if we'd been boys and it was back then. Two of my great-uncles died in the trenches. They were really young.'

'The average life expectancy of a junior army officer in 1914 was eleven days,' Eliza said. And her eyes grew round the way they always did when she thought about some interesting fact or was about to tell a story. 'They were so young and so brave and then it all ended, for nothing, face down in that stinking mud. They would have sat around just like we're doing now, talking about everything they were going to do and see and feel with all those lovely years. And then the war started and those beautiful boys put on their uniforms and picked up their guns and went off singing as if they were off on a great adventure.'

I thought of all the spotty spindly teasing youths I knew and I said, 'They weren't all beautiful, or brave either. And them dying made no difference to anyone other than their mothers.'

There was a silence. Then Eliza shook her head. 'No, I won't allow that. No one knows, that's the thing. Because they died before they could be much of anything, the world will never know what it missed or from whom.' Then she smiled. 'So that's why anyone who dies young gets to be good and beautiful. It's part of the deal.'

'Julian would be about to go off to war if now had been then,' Portia said, 'Or then had been now. It would kill my mother even if it didn't kill him.'

Julian, Julian who *was* beautiful and good, my Julian. My heart lurched.

Rose squeaked. 'Don't even say things like that.'

Eliza leant forward and patted her knee. 'It's OK, Rose. It won't happen again. At least not while we're young.'

'How do you know?' Rose asked.

Eliza shrugged. 'I don't. But I assume.'

Portia said, 'I can't make up my mind whether I'll be an ambassador or just live in a big crumbling house in the country with masses of dogs and horses and children.'

'What about a husband?' Rose asked again.

'Of course,' Portia said, just as Eliza had.

'You think you can just decide?' I said to them. 'You seem to think it's all just out there, just sitting there, waiting for you to go and get it.'

All three princesses turned surprised faces in my direction. 'How do you mean?' Portia asked.

I couldn't believe she had to ask. Eliza lay back down in the grass. 'What about you, Cassandra?' She touched my shoe with the tip of hers. 'Where do you reckon you'll be twenty years from now?'

I looked across at the lake that sat like crumpled foil at the foot of the hill. 'Oh, I expect I'll be working in some office somewhere.'

I waited for them to argue with me. Instead they seemed to accept this as a suitable limit, not only to my ambitions but also to my prospects. I looked at the sky, staring at the sun until my eyes stung. Then I looked at back them. They looked blurred. You know nothing, I thought. You don't know that twenty years from now all you'll be able to say is, 'To think we knew her.'

Eighteen

Eliza

'I HAD GREAT HOPES for you, you know, Eliza,' Uncle Ian said. 'You were such a bright lively girl.'

It was winter still in Sweden. At home I had left behind flowering cherries and green grass and, in the parts of London where pollution pushed up the temperature by a couple of degrees, even some precocious daffodils. It was different here. Heaps of packed snow still congregated in the shady corners of the courtyard and the grass was yet to green up.

Uncle Ian and I were sitting on the glass veranda drinking coffee; I had got used to Katarina's bitter black brew boiled on the stove.

'I remember soon after you were born, your father took me up to where you were lying in your nursery. And there you were, like a bug all tucked up. "A new generation," he said. "There's been enough latent talent and unfulfilled promise amongst the women of my family. This little one will be different."'

'All parents think that about their children,' I said, though the thought of my father showing me off with such pride to his friend made me ache to know this man I could not myself remember.

'Perhaps that's so, but as you grew up I began to think that in your case he had been right. Rose was a lovely girl but she was not intellectually or artistically gifted.'

'Everyone adored her,' I said. 'That's a gift. To be lovable.'

'Did they? Did they really?' He sat back, looking pleased.

I nodded emphatically although I'd realised as I spoke that I didn't remember whether or not Rose had been especially liked. I had loved her, of course. And she'd been close to Portia. And the boys had all liked her. But otherwise maybe admired would have been a better way of describing the way she was regarded, and envied, of course. Because you could not look like Rose and not elicit envy.

'The thing is, none of us know what she might have achieved,' I said. And I had to look away because my eyes had started to tear over suddenly, without warning. 'That's what I can't bear, that's the greatest wrong done to Rose, to those who die young, that they were never afforded the chance to be the best they could.'

We sat side by side, on our chairs, looking out at the garden, at the in-between landscape of yellows and browns and greys that was Sweden in not quite winter and not yet spring. Then I felt his hand take mine. We raised our twinned hands in the manner of two people striding, then lowered them down between our seats before letting go.

'And you, Eliza. Do you feel you're the best you could be?'

I looked at him. 'In the job I've chosen, yes, I'm pretty good.'

'That's very satisfactory, then.'

Katarina had gone shopping and in the silence of the house I listened to the old man's breathing: heavy, wheezing. It made me think he must find it tiring just to be alive. It was warm in the room and I thought he might be about to doze off but then he spoke again, asking me about his mother's stories.

'You were going to illustrate them, wasn't that the idea?'

I smiled, thinking about it. 'All those plans ... Though I expect she was just being kind.'

'Nonsense. And God knows she needed someone to sort out all those notes. She only ever published two volumes of her fairy tales. She spent so much of her time travelling around the countryside collecting the stories; that was the thing. Then she died. Awful waste. But you could do it for her, write them out and illustrate them. I've got her notes as well as many of the recordings she made.'

'I'm not good enough to be a professional illustrator.'

'Says who?'

'Says me.'

'Don't be so defeatist.'

'You sound like my ex-husband. Anyway, I call it being realistic.'

'Sometimes the two are one and the same.'

I gave a little laugh. 'No doubt. But then you can't build victory/success – whatever you think of as the opposite of defeat – on delusion.' I thought for a moment. 'Or perhaps you can. Anyway, I really enjoy the work I'm doing. I'm not looking for anything new.'

'So tell me then, what is it with mending old pots that you find so fulfilling?'

I frowned at him but he didn't notice so I tried to explain instead. 'I like it because so often ceramics, porcelain, are a combination of art and craft, of the decorative and the practical. I like the idea of someone taking the trouble to make something that is essentially a utilitarian workhorse of an object into a thing of joy. I think it's touching. And it makes me happy to think that instead of that thought and effort being thrown away and lost I can bring it back to usefulness.'

Uncle Ian said he could see the charm in that. He used that word, charm. I thought of the pieces that had passed through my hands; the refined Meissen and rustic Staffordshire, the intricate Willow Patterns and achingly sophisticated Sèvres, the humorous Tobys, the frail Minton, the joyful Wemyss, and I thought yes, charm was a good word.

'So have you thought some more about my offer?'

I was yanked back into the world outside work. 'Yes. Yes, I have.'

'And?'

'Uncle Ian.'

'Yes.'

'At the inquest I said I thought she was following.'

He looked at me, a question in his eyes, and then he nodded, slowly.

'And that I thought she was just mucking around when she called out.'

'Yes.'

I sighed and the sigh was so heavy I thought it might drag me with it to the ground. 'But that might not have been completely right. I might have realised she wasn't following. I was panicking, in a silly schoolgirl way; giggling and flapping both at once.' I paused and looked down at my hands, the fingers twisting and untwisting like crazed snakes, then I looked up at him. 'It's all such a muddle, but I might have realised.'

There was a long silence. I looked down at my hands again. Keeping my fingers still and flat against my thighs.

'Might?'

I nodded without looking up. 'I honestly don't know for sure. I realise that sounds just terrible because every second of that night should be seared on my mind, but the truth is I can't be sure.'

'Eliza. Look at me.'

I kept my head lowered but my gaze sidled towards him.

'Did you mean for any harm to come to Rose?'

My chin jerked upwards. 'Of course not. I loved her.'

'Well, then, that's all we need to consider, isn't it?'

'Is it? I mean, how can it be?'

'How can it not be? We lost Rose. No one meant for that to happen but it did. I'm quite sure that if you really had thought that Rose was in trouble you would have turned back to help.'

My snake-fingers began their twisting, folding, entwining once more. I looked into his eyes; I couldn't read his expression. 'I'm not,' I whispered. 'I'm not so sure.'

I was laying the table for dinner. Katarina had pointed me in the direction of the Royal Copenhagen Flora Danica china.

'We're using it today again?'

It was the same with the silver cutlery, George Jensen's Acorn, and the crystal, Orrefors; they used it all for everyday, but it was the china that took my breath away.

'Your godfather wants to enjoy his beautiful things,' she told me.

'How sick is he?' I asked.

'He's sick,' was all she would say.

As we sat down to dinner Uncle Ian acted no differently from the way he had before our last conversation. I looked at him when I thought he wouldn't notice, when he was busy helping himself to potatoes from the large Flora Danica bowl and butter from the cut crystal dish. I had laid out my soul on the ground before him and he had stepped daintily across while looking the other way. What was he thinking? Our eyes met for a moment. His were serious, considered. God knows what my own expression was like.

'Did you know that Flora Danica porcelain was intended to be botanically informative as well as beautiful and useful?' I heard myself say. I swallowed hard and continued. 'The imagery on the original set included not just flowers but roots and seed pods too.'

'I didn't know that,' said Katarina.

'Nor did I,' said Uncle Ian.

'You see, the painting of flowers on porcelain was common enough at the end of the eighteenth century but the ornamentation conformed to aesthetic criteria. The decorations on the Flora Danica porcelain, on the other hand, were not chosen for their aesthetics but instead, and in tune with the spirit of the Age of Enlightenment, it was decided to make exact "scientific" copies of the plates of the highly praised book *Flora Danica*. It was no easy task, however, to transfer the pictures from the engraved plates in the book. They would have been square, whereas the dinner service required oval or round shapes and sometimes compromises had to be made ...'

Nineteen

Cass and Ben

AS SHE LAY DYING, Cass Cassidy, the soap actress and runner-up in the last but one series of *Singing with the Stars*, handed her publicist the Dictaphone that contained the story of what really happened that night a quarter of a century ago.

'This will do it,' she said, her voice barely carrying. 'This will have the bastards fighting over my story.' She coughed and lay back against the pillows. Once the coughing had subsided she said, 'But you'll have to copy it out and add it to the manuscript yourself. I won't have time.'

Ben Sinclair told her not to say things like that. There would be plenty of time for her to finish her memoir herself.

She grabbed his hand and yanked him down close, surprising him with the strength of her grip. 'Promise me.'

He freed himself. 'Of course. All I'm saying . . .'

Her hand gripped his again. 'Promise.'

He nodded. 'I promise.'

They both knew her illness was terminal but her sudden decline still took him by surprise. It was only a few weeks ago that they had been having coffee together and then she had looked almost healthy. She had one of those square little bodies that even then had managed to give her a sturdy appearance. Her hair had grown back and was once again coloured her trademark fiery red, and skilfully applied make-up concealed the unhealthy hue of her complexion.

She had gone straight to the point as usual. 'So, how are we doing? How many offers have we had?'

Ben had stared past her out on to the street, as he replied, 'These things take time.'

'Look at me, Ben.' He turned his reluctant gaze back on her. 'Time, eh.' She gave a croaky laugh. 'Anyway, I told you I don't care about the money. I mean it's not as if I'm going to be able to spend it.'

'Don't talk like that.'

She sighed. 'I'm sorry, but shouldn't I be the one who's finding the truth difficult to deal with?' She looked around her. 'God, I hate this bloody smoking ban.' She pulled a placebo cigarette from her handbag and sucked on it as it were a tube of oxygen. 'So who's the top bidder?'

Ben's gaze slunk off back towards the window before being called back by a sharp, 'Ben, I said look at me.'

From inside the small Louis Vuitton holdall on the chair between them Chico gave a shrill bark as if to underline the command. Cass had threatened to leave Ben the damn dog, which was just one of the reasons he prayed she would live a long time yet.

'OK, OK. There is no bid.'

Her smile dropped and her mouth fell open. 'What do you mean, no bid? I was asked to do this, remember? They came to me.'

'It's the market. No one can remember when it was last this bad.'

'The market was bad when they asked me to write the damn thing.'

'Another latte?'

'No.'

A small child had come up to them and was staring big-eyed at the bag containing Chico. 'Shhh,' Cass smiled at the little boy. 'The doggie is our secret.'

The boy, eyes still fixed on the moving bag, nodded.

'Now run along back to your mummy,' Cass said.

The child remained where he was.

Cass sighed and turned to Ben. 'Anyway, I've heard the excuse, now give me the real reason. Is it the writing?'

Ben was able to be entirely truthful as he answered, 'No. The writing is fine. None of them could believe it wasn't ghosted.'

'So what, then?' As her voice rose she started coughing and he had to fetch a glass of water from the counter for her. As he returned he gave the small child a gentle shove. 'Do as the lady says now and run along.'

The child tilted to one side but his feet in their sturdy trainers remained planted in front of Chico's bag. 'What's the puppy's name?'

Cass sipped some water. 'Chico. Now off you go and bother your mum or carer or whatever like a good little munchkin.' She turned back to Ben. 'Spit it out. As we both know I don't have any time to waste.'

Ben was lucky that he had not had much experience with serious illness, but if he'd thought about it he would have imagined that the close proximity to death would have a soften-ing effect on the sufferer. Meek and mild were two adjectives that would have fitted his expectations. Neither of them was remotely descriptive of Cass Cassidy as she fought her losing battle against oblivion.

'All right then. I'm afraid the problem is with you.'

'I don't understand.'

Ben felt himself blush. He looked up and around him as if a reply might be found written on the walls of the coffee shop. Eventually he told her, 'You're not big enough any more. You can get away with a pretty uneventful life if you're a massive star but if you're not up there then there needs to be something major in your life to justify your place in the publishing schedules.' He paused, then he said, 'I'm truly sorry, Cass. I know how much this book meant to you.'

'Not meant, means. And it means everything. Everything, do you understand.' She sipped some more water. 'I'll be dead soon. Gone. What will I have to show for my life? I have no husband, no children. What will there be left of me? Of my time in the world? Some old episodes of a television soap.'

'Everyone loved Beth Howard.'

'Not enough to spend five quid at Tesco on my autobiography, it seems. So how long have I got?'

Ben shifted on his wooden chair. 'What have the doctors told you?'

'Oh that. I'm not talking about that. I mean, how long before they forget me? The public. My fans.'

'It's impossible to say.'

'Five years?'

He assumed a cheerful air. 'Anything is possible.'

'So not five?'

He shook his head slowly. 'I think even Princess Di was struggling a bit at five.'

'Three?'

Ben sucked in air between his teeth and shook his head.

'Don't. You look like a plumber facing a dodgy boiler. Two, then?'

Ben hated what he had to say but he had suddenly realised that the one thing he owed her now was the truth. 'I would say that anyone remaining in the public eye for more than a year after their . . . their . . .' He looked at her for help. He was young, and death, his own or anyone else's, did not become him.

It was her turn to shake her head. 'For heaven's sake, Ben, the word is *death*. My death. You deal in PR every day of the week. It's what you do. How long before they stop writing about me?'

'I'd say we'd be lucky to get twelve months.'

'Twelve months.' The toughness evident through the months of illness and treatment seemed to abandon her. Her voice fell to a whisper. 'So you think I might not even get a year before I'm . . .' she stopped, unable almost to say the word '. . . forgotten?'

Ben was more used to considering his own feelings than those of others; in fact, if he thought about it, which he didn't, he could only imagine the interior lives of others as sparsely furnished as a monk's cell from the vantage point of his own *House & Garden* extravaganza. What he did understand about was the hunger to be noticed. To die and for it really to be the end was as impossible to contemplate for him as it appeared to be for her.

'I have no family,' the actress said again. 'And as I've realised of late, nor do I have many real friends. I've got you, Ben, and,' she paused and hauled the little dog, tail-end first, out from the bag. 'And Chico.' Her pale green eyes filled with tears but she kept her gaze on his. 'This can't be it, Ben. It mustn't be. Do you hear?'

He felt his own gaze flicker. 'I don't know what ...'

Her hand clamped down on his. 'You must, Ben. You must help me. Promise me you won't let it end like this.'

He freed himself from her grasp only to clasp her hand again. It felt as light and as thin as an empty glove. And the distance between them even when touching seemed endless. His throat constricted. In his way he was fond of Cass. 'You're sure there's nothing else you can give them?'

At first he thought she hadn't heard, so he asked again. 'You're sure there's nothing?'

Her short bark of a laugh made him startle. She opened her mouth as if she were about to speak then shut it again. Contenting herself with just a shake of her head. He leant forward and fixed her gaze with his. 'Look, Cass, if you want to sell this book you need to have something worth selling.'

He glanced at his watch. 'Got to go, I'm sorry. Let me know if you come up with anything.'

They left the café together. Cass lit a cigarette while she looked around for a cab. Ben walked off to the Tube. He had reached the other side when he heard a scream and the sound of furiously beeping car-horns. It was Chico. The little dog was waddling across the busy road, hell-bent, it seemed, on ending it all. Cass was standing where he had left her, on the pavement outside the café, her bright red mouth open, her handbag and the dog's carrier on the ground by her feet. He let go of his briefcase and ran out into the road, dodging the traffic to scoop the little dog up in his arms. As he leapt back on to the pavement he knocked into a tall woman carrying a takeaway coffee. Muttering an apology, he looked into a pair of solemn eyes and he thought for a moment he knew her from somewhere. But her smile, as she stopped to fuss over a trembling Chico, held no recognition. Afterwards, when he had handed Chico back to Cass and had seen both of them safely into a cab he realised where he had seen her. The week before he had been at an exhibition of pre-Raphaelite paintings at the Royal Academy. It was in those pictures he had seen the auburn hair and the translucent complexion. It was there those same eyes had gazed back at him from the pale faces of the rows of solemn angels and limp and tragic Ophelias.

He did not hear from Cass for three weeks after that meeting, but when she did call, it was urgent. She wanted to see him. Right then. He had a meeting scheduled with a client who actually had a future but he cancelled and took the Tube to Hammersmith instead. He was out of breath when he reached Cass's apartment on the second floor. Her cleaner opened the door for him and Cass called out a greeting.

She was in bed, sitting up against a stack of pillows with Chico curled up by her side. When he heard Ben he raised his head from his front paws and pricked one ear before returning to his snoozing. This time no make-up could hide her pallor or the dark circles beneath her eyes, but she had wound some kind of bright scarf round her faded hair and she was wearing lipstick. The lipstick more than anything made him want to cry. He was still catching his breath and he had to haul out a handkerchief to wipe the beads of perspiration from his forehead. Cass asked him if he was all right and he felt sheepish for having panicked.

She was not feeling too good, she admitted. The doctor would be calling later. He would sort her out, she was sure. But just in case, she wanted to give him something.

Next to her Chico farted. Cass swore and weakly flapped a thin hand in front of her face. She pointed at an unlit scented candle and the box of matches next to it. Ben lit the candle and the sickly sweet smell of sandalwood rose in the air. A bluebottle, having survived the recent cold snap, buzzed and beat against the closed window.

She struggled to an upright position and twisted round to open the drawer of her ornate gilt-edged bedside table. From there she brought out a Dictaphone and handed it to him.

'This will do it,' she said, her voice barely carrying. 'This will have the bastards fighting over my story.' She coughed and lay back against the pillows. Once the coughing had subsided she said, 'But you'll have to copy it out and add it to the manuscript yourself. I won't have time.'

'Don't be silly. There'll be plenty of time for you to do it. You're having a bad day, that's all. You just told me the doctor would sort you out.'

Cass grabbed his hand and yanked him down close, surprising him with the strength of her grip. 'Promise me.'

He freed himself. 'Of course. All I'm saying . . .'

Her hand gripped his again. 'Promise.'

He nodded. 'I promise.'

A few minutes later he got up to leave, the Dictaphone safe in his jacket pocket.

She watched him leave and across the void, the voice of her old drama teacher rang out, *Girls, remember, eyes and teeth, eyes and teeth!* So Cass Cassidy opened her eyes wide and with a brilliant flash of her veneers she smiled her last smile.

Twenty

Eliza

I WAS WALKING FROM the Tube up the hill towards my pretty house, in the pretty square in this the prettiest, leafiest part of London. It was a quarter to six but there was still some heat in the sun and I took off my brown velvet jacket and stuffed it inside my bag. Feeling the warm breeze through the thin wool of my dress made me think of that first day each spring when, as a child, I had been allowed at last to swap the itchy woollen tights for knee-length socks and my bare legs had emerged into the sunshine like Cabbage Whites from their pupas.

As I neared the square the streets grew narrow and there were few cars and it was easy to imagine yourself in a country village. I skirted the churchyard, which was comfortingly obsolete. No fresh corpse had been lowered into its hallowed ground for over a century and the years since had served to soften the grief like the moss softened the gravestones, so you had to be right up close to think of loss rather than beauty. The sudden warmth after a cold early spring had prompted shrubs and flowering trees all to come out at once and the birds were singing.

Multi-tasking, I thought, was the thing. Or was it compartmentalising? One was meant to be female and the other male.

Either way, all I needed to do to enjoy my new life was to keep my mind firmly fixed on the present and the future. No looking right or left. No looking back. It was perfectly easy. A bit like walking a tightrope suspended across the jaws of hell. Of course there were many different versions of what hell might be like. Hot, seemed to be a generally held opinion. Uncomfortable, dark, hopeless. A place of endless torment, a place of nothingness. Different fears, different imaginings. To me it was a place of eternal What Ifs? What if it had been Virgil we had studied that term, not Ovid? What if the rain had continued instead of giving up around seven in favour of a huge moon? What if I had checked behind me? What if I had kept my nerve?

I thought of Pollyanna. She and I had had an uneasy relationship over the years. She ignored me. In fact you could say that she was entirely unaware of my existence, whereas I, on the other hand, alternated between ardent admiration and sullen contempt. At times I had tried to emulate her and played the 'Glad Game'. It almost always ended with me coming back with, 'I'm glad that I only abandoned *one* best friend to her death,' and of course that got repetitive after a while. I realised that like all true optimists Pollyanna was obviously unhinged. Of course she did have the excuse of living at a time when there was a dearth of news from outside the immediate community, which in turn meant that if it were a good year in Little Old Rock Bottom one could be led to believe it had been a good year all round and that there was nothing in this life that could not be cured by a positive attitude. And yet, and yet I wanted to believe she was right to be the way she was just in the same way as I wanted to believe that Uncle Ian really had received a visit from Rose telling him she forgave me everything and loved me still.

I had resolved to give as much of my salary as I could manage to Rose's Foundation. Of course the upkeep of my house would be considerable but if I were careful I should be able to set money aside each month. Rose herself had shown no great tendencies towards philanthropy, protesting more loudly than most when, in Sunday morning chapel, we were 'encouraged' to give a third of our pocket money to the needy in our community. 'Who are they, these Needy? Where are they? Not in town, that's for sure. The shopping centre's packed every time I go.' Yet who was to say that, had she been allowed to live, she might not have grown and matured into a dedicated helper of the poor. It had happened to her father. Uncle Ian had played his own version of the Glad Game when it came to philanthropy, telling me that he was glad he had never thought of making the kind of will which left all his money to charity should his heir, that was Rose, pre-decease him. When I had asked him why that was, he'd said it was because in his darkest moments he might have suspected God of letting his daughter die for the common good. I had told him I'd rather not believe than believe in a God who would think up something like that. His reasonable reply had been that he didn't think there was a choice.

I was on my doorstep when my phone rang. It was my mother. I was glad she called. The other day, over Skype, Uncle Ian had asked, out of the blue, 'And how is that nice ex-husband of yours?' This bore the nose-print of my mother, and I had wanted to ask her to please not put ideas into an old man's head.

'You're on your mobile?' my mother said. 'You shouldn't use those things.'

'You called me up to say that?'

'No, of course not. I just wanted to say hello and see how you were doing.'

'So you called on my mobile?'

'You never answer the other one.'

I decided not to argue the point. Instead I just said, 'Well, we don't need to talk long. It's very early for you to be phoning. Is everything OK?'

'You're always in a such a hurry. We haven't talked for days. Did I tell you about Joan? I did, didn't I? How are you? How is the house? Are you using earphones? You should at least be using earphones.' There were so many thoughts, most of them anxious, coursing through my mother's mind that, like a cat chasing its tail, she was forever going round in circles.

'What does Gabriel think about it? He must be pleased for you. I know he worried. He didn't understand why you wouldn't take what was after all your fair share . . .'

Of course I was grateful to have a mother, almost any mother tended to be better than no mother and my mother was better than most. I just wish she wouldn't insist on seeing the sun shining from my behind even when I was sitting on it. It made for unrealistic expectations. Any question posed by her, however harmless, made me determined to give nothing away other than name, rank and number. The answers to her questions now were, 'I am fine. The house is wonderful and Gabriel thinks so too.'

See, that wasn't so hard. But it was. Give away that much and what next? Would the massed armies of motherly love batter down the walls around my heart? Then there would be no telling where it would end.

'Did you say you were using your earphones?'

'No. What did you say to Uncle Ian about Gabriel and me?'

'About you and Gabriel? I don't think I've said anything at all other than that I always liked him and that I never did understand why you parted. Why do you ask?'

I sighed. 'You've encouraged him, Uncle Ian I mean, that's the problem. He's running out of work on my home and I'm worried he's planning on moving on to my heart. It's bad enough that he wants me to be happy without him asking me to be in love too.'

My mother's reply was drowned out by a man's voice bellowing, 'Fine. Good idea. Let me help you pack.'

I had met Archie Fuller at Number 4 and Jenny Howell at Number 5 and I had waved at a distance to a couple of other residents of the square, but apart from being nearly mown down by their large environmentally unfriendly car I was yet to be formally introduced to the family at Number 12. I had seen a dark-haired man with a face that, at least early in the morning, looked as if someone had slept in it, come out of the gate and get into the large black car, and once or twice I had spotted a blonde woman pottering in the small front garden or leaving with a tan briefcase that I had rather admired. There was a little girl too, but I had only seen her through the windows.

It was a woman's voice next and it was shrill with fury. 'You bastard! You complete and utter pig!'

The window slammed shut. A bird trilled. The soft breeze gave the cherry petals a ride across the cobbles.

'Are you there?' my mother asked. 'You really shouldn't be talking on your mobile.'

I turned the key in the lock and for a moment I remained on the doorstep. Like a vampire who had received a standing invitation, I still could not quite believe I had the right to come and go as I pleased. The builders had left for the day. Apart from a slight clanging coming from the radiator on the landing and some creaking in the wooden panels, residual noises like the gurgling of a stomach after an upsetting meal, the little house was quiet. Quiet and all mine. As I kicked off my shoes I admired the way the evening sun shone through the leaves of the evergreen clematis, reflecting on to the paler green of the walls, turning the hallway into a glen.

It had seemed an unnecessary expense to rent somewhere while the work on the house was being carried out so once the basics had been done I had camped in a small room at the top of the house. Builders like to start from the top and work down but I had persuaded them to leave that room be once the rewiring had been carried out. I liked it up there, apart but not isolated from the rest of the house. As I walked up there now I wondered who had lived in my room. The wallpaper was in bad shape and some of it was peeling but what was there was beautiful. Branches of flowering pink cherry trees reached skywards against a pale yellow background. Bronze-coloured birdcages hung from the branches but the birds themselves, pearlescent moon-white, were outside of the cages, flying free. My room had been shut up all day and the air inside felt depleted as if there weren't quite enough for a decent intake of breath. A bluebottle was panicking, buzzing hither and thither, bashing its unlovely body against the windowpanes. I walked across the worn floorboards and tugged open the sash window.

'And please arrange for your furniture to be removed at your earliest convenience; I never could abide white leather sofas.' It was that same loud voice that I had heard some minutes earlier, and, curious, I leant out of the window.

He was standing in the doorway of Number 12. From here it looked as if he were grinning in an exaggerated way. The pretty blonde who I had seen in the garden was marching down the short front path, pulling a suitcase. As she reached the gate she paused, as if she might be waiting for him to come after her, and when he spoke again she turned round eagerly.

'Are you sure you won't let me call you a cab?' he asked.

'Fuck you,' she yelled. 'Fuck you to hell and back.'

I could hear in her voice that she was crying. The man with the slept-in face looked as if he were about to go after her but then he seemed to think the better of it and went inside instead, slamming the door behind him.

I sat down at the small desk and switched on my laptop, dialling up Uncle Ian. Since the purchase of the house we had learnt together about the three subsections of the Georgian style: Palladian, Neoclassical and Regency, establishing that our little house came under the impossibly grand Palladian. We had learnt that the true determination of the style, whatever the size, was not pediments or pilasters or columns but the principle of proportion; the proportion of room length to height, of wall space to window space and of each individual façade. After that we had mugged up on Plato, having discovered in the course of our reading that his teachings lay at the root of much of the thinking behind the principles of the Georgian style. Recently our discussions had moved from the general to the particular. I had found some old slabs of marble of the kind you used to find in butcher's shops and around washstands in an architectural salvage yard and thought they would do very well for the kitchen, but Uncle Ian had cautioned me against using marble as it was porous and would stain too easily. Stainless steel was much better, he said. I told him I thought stainless steel would look brutal. In the end we had made a deal. I could use the marble slabs in the kitchen as long as there was a good area around the sink in stainless steel.

Katarina had assured me that no detail was too tiny, too humdrum for Uncle Ian. She told me that since the whole project had started – the project being me, apparently, rather than just the house – he had regained some of his old vitality. He felt 'affirmed', she said. I thought I knew what she meant by that. It was something to do with calling out into the wilderness, 'Can anybody hear me?' And having someone answer, 'Yes, yes, I hear you.' I had thought it strange that a man like uncle Ian could feel the need to call out in the first place but then I had realised that it had to do with age. If the past was another country then old age was another world, one to which few of us wanted to go even for a visit. When we were young and needed we resented the claims on our time and energy, yet as we grew old and people were looking past us as if we had already moved into the shadows, all we really yearned for was to be needed. So mindful of this I had taken to starting most of our conversations with the words, 'I need your advice . . .' But now the house was almost finished and I was searching my brain for something new to tell him, to ask him about, something relevant to the project but which preferably did not involve soft furnishings.

I dialled him up and Pow! I shied back as his face burst into close-up. I never got used to the way that happened. I imagined sometimes that he sat waiting, stiff and straight-backed in front of his laptop, that gaped open like a giant baby bird, always ready, always waiting for the next morsel.

'Good evening, Eliza.' His voice, as always when we spoke this way, was stately, as if he were appearing on television.

'Are the kitchen units in? And the stainless steel looks good, yes?'

'Really good.'

'I thought it would. Not too, how did you put it, brutal?'

'No. Quite pretty in fact. Maybe because it's brushed steel and that . . .' my words were interrupted by loud banging followed by a woman's voice. 'And this time it's it, do you hear? I'm not coming back.'

'What's that?' Uncle Ian asked me.

'Oh, just some neighbours calling to each other. As I said . . .'

'Come outside when I'm talking to you. I said, this time I'm not coming back. Never.'

The next morning was Saturday and I had only just shut the front door behind me on my way to get the newspapers when I heard my name called. It was Archie Fuller from Number 4. Archie had knocked on my door the day after I had moved in. It had been a quiet knock at first – the kind that made you wonder if you had just imagined it – escalating to the kind of loud banging normally associated with a fire. When I had opened the door, out of breath, having run from the top of the house, he had smiled blithely, and explained that he didn't like using the bell, 'in case it disturbed people'.

I had quickly realised that most people in the square avoided Archie Fuller. I guessed because he was old and lonely and never stopped talking and had unidentified stains down the front of his tweed sports jacket and insisted on planting busy lizzies in tubs made out of old beer-barrels outside his front door. At the same time, and as Jenny from Number 5 said, everyone agreed that he was 'real', 'a character' and 'old school north London' and there should be more like him to counteract the influx of 'bankers and non-doms and property developers'. I thought they should take better care of Archie or else they might have to start hiring in picturesque 'real' people.

'Off to get the papers?' Archie said. 'I wouldn't bother if I were you.'

I plastered on a smile and said, 'I'm sure you're right but I still like to see what's going on in the world.'

'Did you hear all that kerfuffle yesterday?' Archie's mouth was turned down at the corners in a show of disapproval but his small deep-set eyes shone as he nodded in the direction of Number 12.

'I did hear something, yes.'

'I would ask you in for a cup of tea but my kettle's given up the ghost and I haven't had the opportunity to replace it.'

'Oh. Well, why don't we have tea here.' I stifled a sigh and unlocked the door again. 'Come in.'

Archie bustled past me into the hall. 'Well, if you're sure?' He looked around him. 'My goodness, the place is a mess, isn't it?'

'Better than it was.'

One of the builders had put back an empty carton in the fridge, fooling me into thinking I didn't need to buy milk. I apologised to Archie, saying we'd have to drink our tea black, but he waved away my concern with an air of someone who had more pressing things on his mind than milk. 'I must say I wasn't expecting such goings on from the household of a hospital consultant.'

'I didn't know he was a doctor. What's his name again? Maybe my ex-husband knows him?'

'Dr Bauer. Jacob Bauer. Well he's Mr really I suppose, being a surgeon. Anyway, you might expect that type of behaviour over at the estate.' He lowered his voice when he spoke the world 'estate' as if uttering a swear word. 'But not here. Not in the square.'

Remembering the night I tipped the contents of Gabriel's underwear drawer out on to the street I felt unable to say anything much on the subject other than to ask if Mr Bauer made a habit of that kind of thing.

'I can't say that he does,' Archie admitted with evident regret. 'But I can't say that he is very neighbourly either. He's been here the best part of three years and he hasn't turned up to a single residents' association meeting. She came along once but he, never. As for that car he drives . . .'

'Big,' I said.

'A gas-guzzler.'

'Oh well,' I said.

'And I must say I was surprised to hear such language from her. She's always been very friendly to me but I suppose working in television you get inured to that kind of thing.'

I felt the morning slipping away from me and I thought of all the things I would like to be doing, none of which included sitting on a paint-speckled stool in my half-finished kitchen gossiping about people I'd never even met. Then again, Archie Fuller was obviously lonely. I was lonely too sometimes but it was easier to remedy that condition when you were young and didn't smell of mothballs.

'Of course I was just a baby when the war ended,' he said and I realised that I had missed a part of the conversation. 'Not many people know this but the bombing of Coventry was the inspiration for a very famous piece of music by Pink Floyd.'

'Really?'

'Yes, indeed. Which one was it now?' He began humming something that sounded nothing like Pink Floyd. After a while he gave up. 'Speaking of the entertainment business,' he said instead, 'That actress's died. Cass Cassidy.'

I looked blank.

'You know the one? She played Beth Howard in *Our Street*.'

'I never watched it,' I said. 'Still, that's sad. Poor old thing.'

'Oh no, not *old* at all, no, no. Cass was your age, I'd say, or thereabouts. Which reminds me, they said on the news last night that house prices are down again.' He studied me, his head tilted to one side.

'Oh dear,' I said. I knew I should offer him more tea but I was beginning to worry that the newspapers might all be gone by the time I got to the shop. Archie drained his mug then looked expectantly at the pot. 'Lovely tea.'

'I'm sorry about the milk.'

'Didn't miss it at all.'

'Would you like another cup, Archie?'

He glanced at his watch. 'No, no, I must let you get on.'

I was halfway out of my chair when he picked his mug up.

'Well, if you're sure.' He helped himself to a teaspoon of sugar then sat back, mug in hand. 'So where were we?'

I smiled brightly. 'Papers.' I realised I was sitting so far forward on my chair I might slide off so I pushed back on the seat, leaning back and crossing my legs in an attempt to look relaxed.

'Ah yes, the papers. Nothing in them. Apart from the sad news of Cass Cassidy's untimely passing away, of course. You can have a little read of my paper. Save you the bother of buying your own. I'll bring it over later.' He turned his head on its thin neck hither and thither like a telescope.

'And they're not cheap these days, the papers, are they. Yes, you must be feeling pretty dark about buying that house when you did. We none of us could believe you paid the asking price. I suppose you didn't realise the relatives were desperate to sell?'

'No, no, I didn't know that. Still, if they were desperate I'm glad they achieved a good price.'

This caught Archie on the back foot but he recovered fast and countered with, 'Julie, my daughter, and her husband, you haven't met them, have you? No, I didn't think you had. Well, Julie and Malcolm, Malcolm being her husband, you understand, sold their old property last autumn. They're renting for now, biding their time, waiting to snap up a bargain. There're repossession sales most weeks around where they live. She's very clever like that, Julie. She had a good old chuckle when I told her about you.'

'I bet she did.'

'Oh yes.' He laughed heartily himself.

'Well, bully for Julie, I say. But I'm still glad I didn't have to take advantage of someone in desperate circumstances.'

Archie frowned. 'Not everyone can afford to have scruples like that. Not if they want a fourth bedroom and a utility, that is.'

Now I felt bad. 'I'm sorry, that wasn't meant as a criticism of . . . well, of anyone wanting a fourth bedroom and a utility. And you're quite right. It's easy to have scruples when you can afford to.'

'Don't worry about it.' He turned towards the window. 'You wouldn't believe it was April, would you? I knew yesterday was too good to last.'

I looked out at the darkening sky. 'Oh, I don't know; it's quite mild. And at least it's not raining. I don't mind as long as it's not raining.'

Archie gave me a reproachful look. 'You're always very cheerful, aren't you? Very positive.'

'Do you think? Perhaps I am.' Unaccustomed as I was to accusations of excess cheerfulness I began to warm to the whole concept. 'I think it's a duty to anyone in this harsh and unforgiving world who is in reasonable health and not suffering from a recent loss or severe financial difficulties to try to be reasonably cheerful,' I said. It sounded good and I wished Uncle Ian had heard me.

But Archie was not that easily discouraged, and rising to the challenge he informed me that 'Malc's got a dreadful cough. Had it for months.'

'Has he seen a doctor?'

'He has.' He shook his head.

'Oh dear. Bad news?'

'No. Fellow insisted it was just a cough. But what do they know?'

'Quite a lot, actually.'

'Of course, you were married to one, you just said. Raking it in, these GPs.'

'Not all of them. Anyway, Gabriel isn't a GP.'

Archie winked. 'Earns enough to buy you a nice house, though.'

I was about to take exception to his blithe assumption that I had had to have some man buy me my home when I remembered that in fact I had. Archie had simply picked the wrong man.

So I simply told him, 'Actually, no. My ex-husband had nothing to do with it.'

It was obviously none of Archie Fuller's business how I had got the money to buy the house so I don't know why I went on but I did. Maybe it was those blinking bullfrog eyes eternally on the lookout for some new and juicy information. Maybe he lived on gossip, quite literally. I mean, had I ever seen him eat? No. Instead he was always around, by his window or on his doorstep or out and about on the streets, whether it were breakfast, lunch or suppertime. So I told him, 'The house is actually a gift from my godfather.' Archie's cheeks puffed up and I only narrowly resisted the temptation to add, 'My godfather from the Ukraine,' just to make the information a bit more gossip-worthy.

'A gift? He gave you a house? Generous, is he?'

'Very. He's not very well so he doesn't spend much on himself.'

Archie sucked his teeth. 'Cancer, is it? On the increase, you know. Of course they're trying to tell us that it's not an actual increase as such but more that we don't die of the things we used to die of, but that's just what they'd like us to think. No, it's the toxins, the toxins and the rays.'

He sounded perfectly happy about this, quite comfortable, as if the Toxins and the Rays were personal friends of his.

'Not that old is he then, your godfather?' he went on.

'In his eighties.' I looked at my watch and this time I made it obvious that I was. 'Oh well,' I said.

'Ah right.' Archie stood up. 'I'd better be off. Got a busy day.'

'I'll come out with you,' I said.

Out on the street a gust of wind, so wild and chill it seemed to belong to autumn, swept leaves and blossoms hurtling round our feet. Archie waved his stick at the clouds. 'I told you it was going to rain. If you were going out you've missed the best part of the day.'

I fled.

As I hurried down the street Jacob Bauer drove past in his anti-social car, slowing down just enough to allow me to jump up on to the narrow pavement.

Twenty-one

Sandra/Cassandra

HE WAS PLAYING THE piano, concentrating, looking down at his hands, his dark fringe falling over his forehead. I paused in the doorway, simply taking in the sight of him. He was only playing chopsticks and it made me smile that he still managed to mess it up. I loved him. I had decided I loved him that day out on the ice when he said I was amazing. I had only seen him a few times since then and never on my own. Then I heard Portia say he was coming over on Wednesday after games – he'd wait for her in the common room – and because I had stubbed my toe quite badly on a fence post (the idea just came to me as I was running after the ball) I'd been allowed off the field. But instead of going to the San I had gone straight to the common room, hoping he'd be there already.

Standing there watching him, everything having gone according to plan, I felt like this powerful being, able to arrange the world just as I liked it.

I waited another couple of minutes and then I went up to the piano. My toe was throbbing but it didn't feel like pain, at least not in a bad way. If there was something like good pain this was it because it had helped me get to where I wanted to be, alone with Julian Dennis.

I leant over his shoulder and put my hands on the lower keys and began playing the other part. Julian muddled up the notes and then he stopped so I stopped too.

'You're quite good,' he said.

'I'm OK.'

'What grade are you on?'

'Oh, I'm not doing any of that. I passed grade eight ages ago. I'm on to the certificates now.'

'Oh right. Cool.' His fingers wandered back to the piano keyboard. 'I'm waiting for Portia Dennis. I'm her brother.'

'I know who you are.'

It must have come out snappy because he looked up, surprised. 'Right. Anyway, I was told it was OK for me to wait in here.'

'Sure.' I smiled at him. 'We met skating. You thought I was quite good. At that too.' I didn't mind sounding cocky. Boys liked confident girls.

'Ah right.' He started jabbing at the keys in a tuneless manner.

'Shall I play something?' I asked him.

He stopped his jabbing and got up from the stool. 'Sure.'

As I took his place I felt the warmth left behind by his body against the back of my thighs. I pressed down further on the threadbare plush seat and struck the opening notes of the *Moonlight Sonata*. I was bored by that piece myself but everyone always seemed to really like it. As I played I noticed he was wandering round the room, hands in his pockets, looking at the paintings. We had put up a whole load of Eliza's cartoons on the bit of wall above the lockers. Then he wandered off and looked out of the French windows towards the playing field.

'It's pretty pathetic you've only got one,' he said.

I stopped playing. 'One what?'

'Playing field. Your fees are just as high as ours.'

'We have the theatre,' I said. 'And more music rooms.'

Julian shrugged. 'I suppose.' He seemed bored. He mustn't be bored. My toe was hurting. 'Music is really important to me,' I said. 'It runs in the family, actually. Music, I mean. My grandmother was a ...'

'How long do you reckon they'll be?'

'Oh. Not too long, I shouldn't think.'

I was right because just a few minutes later the door burst open and the princesses exploded into the room, followed by a whole group of other girls. Suddenly everything was chatter and giggles and movement and Julian was encircled and I started banging out *Rhapsody in Blue*.

'Jesus, Sandra,' Portia shouted. 'What has that poor piano ever done to you?'

Everyone laughed. But he, Julian, said, 'You're only jealous because you haven't got past grade three.' And then everything changed and now they were laughing at Portia. I didn't speak or look up, I just stayed where I was, playing, thinking if he told me to jump off a roof I would. I wouldn't even stop and ask why. I'd just do it.

'I need a ciggie,' Portia said, getting up from the saggy armchair. My mother would have a fit if she saw that chair. Its covers were filthy; I mean, you could only guess at some of the stains. The princesses never seemed to worry, though. Actually, they were quite unhygienic.

'I haven't got any left,' Rose said, but she too had got to her feet.

'Me neither,' Eliza said.

'Julian?'

Now I looked round. He shook his head. 'Nup.'

I swung round completely. 'I've got some. They're menthols, though.'

'That's fine,' Portia said. 'Beggars can't be choosers and all that.'

We went to the back of the tennis courts, behind the changing rooms. I pulled out the packet of cigarettes. As she took one Portia turned to the others and said, 'Sandra's the only person I know who has enough money to buy twenty.' The way she said it made me feel as if I'd stuffed up.

'I don't always,' I said. 'Anyway, you buy Philip Morris, for Christ's sake. In fact I clearly remember you buying a pack of twenty Philip Morris.'

Portia shrugged. 'Like it's important.'

'You started it,' I muttered.

Eliza smiled at me. 'Either way, thanks for sharing.'

I smiled back at her. We smoked for a while. I kept looking at Julian. I was reading this book where the heroine did that with the hero; just kept looking straight at him, not trying to get his attention in any other way, just this thing of calmly gazing at him until he got completely intrigued by her and asked her out.

Portia had smoked her cigarette right down to the filter and now she stubbed it out on the sole of her shoe before putting it in her pocket. No one was stupid enough to leave cigarette butts lying around to be found by members of staff. She looked at Julian then she looked at Rose. She had this little smile on her face and she said, 'Damn, I forgot, but I have to finish this essay.'

'Right, yeah, me too,' Eliza said. 'I have to finish a drawing for Grandmother Eva. Are you coming, Cassandra?'

I was still looking at Julian.

'Cassandra?'

I turned round slowly. 'No. No, you go.'

'And off we go,' Eliza said, and she took me by the arm and pulled me with her.

I looked behind me. Julian was saying something to Rose, who laughed.

'What about Rose?' I said to Eliza. 'Isn't Rose coming?'

Eliza gave my arm a little squeeze. 'For someone so bright you can be a bit dense sometimes.' She said it in a friendly way.

'Oh,' I said. 'I see.' That's all I said.

About an hour later, as I lay on my bed, writing my diary, I heard Rose scream.

Miss Philips said it was no laughing matter. It didn't stop everyone from thinking it was quite funny, though, Rose coming back to her cubicle to find her teddy hanged by her dressing-gown cord, a black plastic bag over his head.

Twenty-two

BECAUSE OF THE END of term play the boys were over at least once a week for rehearsals. And guess who got the part of Little Dorrit? Rose, of course. Then when Portia said she had persuaded Julian to audition for the part of Arthur I got really worried. But I ended up having the last laugh because he fluffed up his lines, twice apparently, and we both ended up working backstage; him on lighting and me on sound effects. Then I saw him in town. He was at the counter at Wimpy digging around in his pockets for enough money for the Coke he had ordered. I'd seen him through the window. Now I walked right up to him and just handed the cashier a pound. 'I'll take care of that,' I said.

He had smiled up at me under his long fringe. I thought he was actually quite shy. Portia thought she knew everything about him just because she was his sister but she didn't really. None of them did.

We had walked back towards the bus stop together. 'Why are you always staring at me?' he asked suddenly.

I thought I'd get all flustered and red in the face but I remained really calm. 'Why shouldn't I?'

He shrugged and it was he who turned red. It was two stops to LAGs and three to the boys' school. As I got off I turned and gave him a little wave. 'See you,' I said. I felt really light as I jumped down on to the verge. Not like me at all.

Then it was the First Night party and the boys had smuggled in some raw spirit from the biology lab, adding it to the fruit punch.

Julian was sick in the bushes at the far end of the car park and because I had followed him out I was there to help him clean up. That was when he kissed me. It was a bit gross because he tasted of sick but that wasn't important. He'd kissed me; that was what was important. I walked with him to the minibus and as he was about to board I said, 'If you want more you just have to ask.'

It was easy to keep Julian and me a secret from the princesses because it simply would not occur to them in a million years that someone like him would be interested in someone like me. It was hilarious, actually. I would find them in one of their usual huddles talking all about the big romance between Rose and Julian. Only there wasn't one.

That didn't stop them banging on about it, though, especially not Eliza. She herself fancied Julian's friend David but actually she seemed far more interested in matching up Rose with Julian, analysing every look or word from the poor boy. My poor boy. Of course, Portia, being his sister, was the guru. She pronounced on her brother's state of mind and how close he was to making a move. Rose simpered prettily and Eliza came up with suggestions as how to speed things up, typical Eliza ideas: 'How about if you go riding and your horse bolts just as he walks past . . . Why don't you go walking and when you get to LABs you fall and pretend to have hurt your ankle . . .'

So although it was kind of funny it was also getting quite annoying. I wasn't angry with Eliza, though, as obviously she couldn't know that I liked him. But enough was enough. I decided I would have to talk to her. Tell her to stop trying to push Rose on Julian.

We, Julian and I, did it in the meadowy bit behind the disused stables. I had told him to bring a picnic. I'd worked out exactly how it was going to be the first time. It would be perfect, like a dream or a film. We'd be sitting on a rug and he'd kneel in front of me and unpack the basket. There would be strawberries, of course, and cheese and bread and maybe some cold chicken and hardboiled eggs. No, maybe not the eggs. And some white wine. I would have loved it to be champagne but I didn't want to get my hopes up. And napkins of course, real ones, not paper.

In the event he arrived holding a rumpled paper bag. 'What's that?' I asked, pulling my outstretched legs up under me.

He grinned. 'You said you wanted me to bring something to eat.' He opened the bag and flopped down next to me opening the bag. 'Danish. I got two.' He gave me a look as if expecting praise.

I had a split second to decide how I wanted the afternoon to go. I could smile sweetly and stretch back down on the rug or I could complain. If I complained he'd leave. I thought of Miss Philips and Miss Gower forever preaching about the importance of us 'gals' valuing ourselves and of not selling ourselves cheap. Well, that was fine for the princesses, for Portia with her endless honey-coloured legs and her easy sense of entitlement. And for quirky-cute Eliza with her auburn curls and showy artistic talent. And it was absolutely fine for Rose, who looked like a Snow White who'd just lost her dwarfs. But for a me, when it came to someone like Julian, it was selling myself cheap or not at all.

'What?' Julian was looking at me from under that dark fringe. God, I loved his hair, loved the way it curled behind his ears and into the nape of his tanned neck.

'Oh nothing,' I said. 'Everything's fine.'

'Yeah, of course it is.' He reached out and then his hand pushed down inside my blouse, grabbing at my left breast. He was tweaking my nipple like it was the on button on my radio and it hurt. I tried not to but I couldn't help flinching.

'What?' he said again but now his gaze was cloudy under half-closed lids.

'What about our . . . our picnic?' I felt close to tears suddenly. If we were actors we'd be in different films.

His gaze cleared and he frowned. Then he said, 'Sure. If you're hungry?' He picked up the crumpled greasy bag and chucked it in my lap. 'Here.'

I wanted to get up and run away. 'C'mon. Have one,' he said, and now his voice and his eyes were kind. 'They're really nice. And you don't need to worry about calories. I like you the way you are.'

He leant forward and put his hand inside the bag, pulling out one of the pastries and biting into it with his even white teeth. I loved his teeth too. He had a gap – like Lauren Hutton – between his two front ones. He held the Danish out to me and I closed my lips around the same crumbling buttery sweetness as his lips had just embraced.

'Mmm,' I said giving him a hazy smile. 'Lovely.' I looked him straight in the eyes and stuck out the tip of my tongue and licked the crumbs off my lips the way they did in films, then, using my finger, I smoothed away the crumbs from his, that were dry and a little cracked but perfect just the same. I finished by licking the crumbs off my finger all the way, keeping my gaze on his. Everything changed in that moment. Suddenly I was the giver and he was the grateful receiver. I was the princess and he was my servant as I unbuttoned my shirt and slipped out of my skirt.

'You're amazing,' he said, and his voice had gone husky as if he'd got something caught in his throat.

In my moment of victory I felt a second's impatience. Did he ever say anything over and above the banal and the expected? I shrugged the thought away. I loved him; that was all that mattered.

He pulled his shirt off over his head. His torso was spare and tanned and smooth apart from the armpits and a line of soft fuzz running down from his belly button. I wanted to reach out and push my hand down the front of his boxer shorts but I stayed where I was, quite still, playing at being a goddess, waiting.

'I really like you,' he said, and that hazy, stoned look had returned to his beautiful eyes.

I had power. I could get up and leave him there, shirtless and excited. Or I could give him what he most wanted in the world right now and that, miraculously, was me.

He groaned and lunged forward and all at once I was sprawled on the rug with him on top of me.

It was over in seconds. I was disappointed but only for a moment because he stayed in my arms, his face nuzzled against my neck, and he was trembling. I stroked his naked back that was damp with sweat and I started murmuring all kinds of things that made me blush when I thought about them afterwards. Above my head a swallow circled, then a second one joined. They warbled to each other and I smiled up at the sky.

I don't know for how long we lay like that but my legs were beginning to hurt. I didn't mind, though. I could have stayed like that with him on top of me, inside me, for ever. But then he pulled out and he raised himself in a one-armed push-up as he pulled his pants and trousers up before rolling off and on to his back. I could feel him trembling again and I was about to pull him towards me when I realised that he was laughing.

'What?' I asked. 'What?' And I giggled because I expected he was laughing with happiness.

But he kept on laughing and it seemed like an ugly sound all of a sudden, like the rattle of the magpie that had driven away the swallows a few minutes earlier.

'What?' I asked again, my voice turning shrill. 'What's funny?'

'There,' he pointed at my left breast. He was giggling now.

My mouth had filled up with saliva and I could barely swallow as I looked down. My left breast and my right looked normal. Smallish but nicely rounded with average-sized nipples.

'There,' he pointed again and then I saw it, a curly red hair.

I brushed at it. 'It's from my head,' I said, my voice tight. 'It's just a hair from my head.'

'I know,' he said. 'It just looks as if it's growing from your tits.'

Twenty-three

Eliza

I ROSE FROM THE Underground, emerging into the twilight of the high street. It was Friday night and I had been to the ballet with Beatrice and our friend Katherine. My mind was still on poor doomed Giselle, who loved not wisely but too well and ended up a woodland spirit for her troubles. I had wept, as I always did, right through the bit where, turned mad by her lover's betrayal, she danced herself to death in front of him and I had wept anew when that feckless lover pirouetted before the avenging Queen of the Willies, begging forgiveness, clutching his own breaking heart. As I rode home on the Tube, the music filling my head, I rewrote the ending, changing it to one where Giselle is released from the spell and lives happily ever after with her remorseful prince. It didn't matter how many times I saw *Giselle*; I still always hoped that was how it would turn out. It was the same with *Romeo and Juliet*. Each and every time I sat there hoping, praying that the Friar's messenger would reach Romeo in time. I never could figure out how that worked: what spell a story cast to make us think that each time it played out was the first, and that there might, after all, be a different, happier ending.

I stepped out on to the corner of the high street and turned left without looking, so I didn't notice the long jeans-clad legs stretched out on the pavement until I stumbled over them. I steadied myself and looked down. The legs belonged to a teenage girl slumped across the doorway of an art gallery, a grubby rucksack and a can of Red Bull next to her. I muttered an apology, stepping round. She didn't reply and I was about to walk on when it struck me she might not be stoned or drunk, but unwell, in need of medical attention. I might walk on by only to wake in the morning to the news, no doubt delivered by Archie, that a young woman had been found dead in the comfortable heart of the Village. There would be the comments by the police, made more in sorrow than in anger, that it appeared that the poor young girl had been lying there dead, or at the very least dying, and no one did anything to help. In fact one person, a woman, early middle age, grey dress, brownish reddish hair, actually stepped right over her yet did not bother to check if the girl needed assistance . . .

So what could I do but kneel down by the slumped figure and put my hand, lightly, on the sleeve of her arm. The girl gave me a hazy look under half-closed eyelids. I asked her if she was all right. Which was a pretty stupid question when directed to someone slumped in a doorway in the middle of the night. 'I mean, do you need help? Are you sick?'

The girl didn't reply.

'Are you hurt? Shall I call an ambulance?'

The girl's eyes snapped wide open. 'No. I'm fine.'

I wanted to walk away. But she didn't look fine. She didn't smell fine either.

'I'll call an ambulance,' I said. I was about to get back on to my feet when my wrist was grabbed by a grubby hand. 'I said no. If you do I'll only walk away.' All at once she was crying. 'I'm all right,' she said again, in between sobs.

'I can help you to get home?'

'No. I had a fight with my boyfriend. He threw me out.'

'Have you nowhere else to go? What about your parents? How old are you?'

The expression in her eyes as she looked back at me said I was just as clueless as she had expected me to be. 'Seventeen. And that was my home.'

'Oh.' I shifted my weight from one knee to the other. 'What about your parents?' I asked again. 'Are they not around?'

'Ha,' she said. 'Ha', and nothing more.

'How about a hostel? We can call the police and ask them where the nearest hostel is?'

'Just go away, will you. Leave me alone. Go home.' The word 'home' sounded like a reproach. As well it might. I had a home. She didn't. I didn't deserve mine. I expect she didn't deserve not to have one. I got to my feet and then I reached down and took her by the wrist. 'Come on. You can stay the night with me and then we'll see what to do in the morning.'

I regretted it the moment I had said it. But it was too late to take it back. The girl was looking at me now, and she was actually smiling. The smile made her look about twelve. 'You mean that?'

I nodded. 'Absolutely. I live just around the corner.' I had to force the words from my mouth because by now all I wanted to do was run off. I mean, what was I thinking of, asking a stranger into my home at night?

'Nice place,' the girl said. She had dropped the rucksack on the hall floor and was looking around her.

'I'm very lucky. It's a bit of a mess still, though. The builders have only just finished.' I switched the light on and smiled at her. 'I don't even know your name.'

'Chloe,' the girl said.

'I'm Eliza. Would you like something to eat?'

I scrambled some eggs as Chloe slumped on the kitchen chair. It felt quite normal; the kind of thing people did, scrambling eggs for a monosyllabic teenager in the middle of the night. In fact it felt great. I thought of the J.B. Priestley play, *An Inspector Calls*. I thought about no man being an island. I thought of the Big Society. The more I thought, as I scrambled the eggs, the more pleased I felt.

'What do you do?' Chloe asked me as I put the eggs and toast in front of her.

I joined her at the table. 'I'm a ceramic restorer.'

'Right. What about your husband?'

'I'm not married.'

Chloe looked around her, chewing on her food. 'Right,' she said again. 'Boyfriend?'

I knew the answer should be 'that's personal' but it would sound rude. I just shook my head.

'So you live here alone.'

What was I doing telling her these things? I shouldn't have said anything. I most certainly shouldn't have told her I lived alone. I wondered if it were too late to invent a housemate. A man. A man who played rugby. Or practised karate. I could slip it in. I could look at my watch and say, 'Steve should be home from karate any minute now. I'm so proud of him now he's a black belt.' Chloe interrupted my thoughts. 'Do you have anything to drink?'

I got to my feet. 'Of course. Sorry. What would you like?'

'Orange juice or milk or something like that?'

I hurried across to the fridge, feeling shabby and cross with myself. I was being prejudiced, judgemental, instantly assuming that this poor girl was up to no good just because she was on the streets. I was being the kind of person who was lampooned in television satire and possibly even beheaded come the revolution. 'Here you are.' I smiled as I handed her a large glass of orange juice.

'Thanks,' she smiled back and her pale drawn features lifted, making her almost pretty. Her gaze was clearer too. If she had been stoned, she was coming down. 'You're pretty amazing, asking me in like this?'

I felt ridiculously pleased. 'Oh, I'm only doing what anyone would have done.'

'I've been on the streets before. This is the first time anyone's bothered.'

'Really. That's too bad.' I was beginning to warm to this helping business. 'Well, if one's lucky enough to have a lovely home,' I gesticulated round the kitchen. I was pleased with how it had turned out. The walls were the colour of crème anglaise (not custard, as I had explained to Uncle Ian, custard being too yellow, but the soft sunshine-on-cream colour of its French cousin) and the wooden kitchen units painted in two shades of fresh green that might have clashed as one contained yellow pigment and the other blue, but somehow didn't.

'It's really pretty. Colourful,' Chloe said.

This was cosy, the two of us at the kitchen table talking interior decor.

I lent Chloe a pair of pyjamas and made sure she had a glass of water by her bedside. Once I was in bed myself I lay staring at the birds flying free across the tattered yellow wallpaper of my room and I felt happy. Who knows what might have happened to that girl out there on the streets, if it hadn't been for me.

A little later I got out of bed and walked up to the door, turning the key in the lock. Just in case. After a few minutes I got up once more and unlocked it.

Twenty-four

I WAS WOKEN BY the insistent ringing of the doorbell. I checked the time. It was half past six but somehow I still felt perky. Half past six, I thought, glancing out of the window, and a sunny day in North London. The doorbell rang again; two short bursts and one long one, the kind where the ringer had a finger pressed hard against the bell and a pissed-off look on his or her face. I threw on my dressing-gown and hurried downstairs. I was halfway down when I remembered the guest in my spare room. The din must have woken her but being a teenager she had most probably just rolled over and gone back to sleep. I'd check on her in a moment, perhaps even bring her a cup of tea in bed. She was most likely not used to being spoilt.

Bang bang bang!

'Who is it?' I shouted through the door.

'It's Archie from Number 4.'

'It's six thirty in the morning, Archie,' I said as I opened up.

'You take a look outside.' He flung his arm out, gesticulating towards his house and the two either side.

I looked. It took me a moment to take it in but then I saw it, the graffiti scrawls across the doors and brickwork. I turned back to him. 'Goodness.' I was about to step outside to check the damage done to my own place when Archie held his hand up in a policeman's stop. 'Nothing on yours.' He looked severe. 'For obvious reasons.'

'What do you mean?' I pulled the dressing-gown closer round my neck. Spring was dragging its heels and it was a chilly morning.

'Seeing it's the handiwork of that young guest of yours? I saw you both coming back last night as I was closing my shutters.'

Again? I thought. That man was always closing his shutters. I frowned at him, disappointed by his attitude. 'Why on earth should that,' it was my turn to gesticulate, 'be her handiwork? Did you see her do it? Anyway, even if she had managed to sneak out without me noticing she wouldn't have been able to get back in without a key. The poor girl is asleep upstairs. Exhausted, no doubt, from having been thrown out on the streets by an abusive boyfriend.' My voice was rising with my mounting outrage. What chance did young people like Chloe have when everywhere they went they were treated with suspicion? I myself had been guilty of it last night. Why should misfortune make someone more prone to bad behaviour, I wanted to know.

Archie was pointing a thick finger over my shoulder at my hall and I turned round. 'What?' Then I saw my bag on the floor, some of its contents spilt. 'Oh. It must have got knocked off the chair.' I went back inside, leaving Archie in the doorway, and picked the bag up. Looking inside, I saw that my wallet and keys as well as my phone were all missing, so I took another look around the floor, but all I could find were my lipstick, a hairclip and a tampon. I quickly put my foot on the tampon as I searched inside the bag once more but it was empty bar a blister pack of ibuprofen. 'Excuse me.' I closed the door in Archie's face. Then I walked into the kitchen, slowly. Looking around me, and even with one eye closed, as if that would help, I realised that my friend, my beloved laptop, was gone as was the television and, of course, my tin of pound coins. I opened both eyes, as it couldn't really be much worse. And at least the place was still clean and tidy. No vandalism, no graffiti here. I had another thought and with a little yelp I ran out into my workshop. Thankfully, nothing in there had been touched.

I ran upstairs and knocked on the spare room door. There was no answer so I knocked again. Still no reply, so I turned the black iron doorknob and opened the door. Chloe was gone as was the small silver button box that used to sit on the dressing-table. On the bed lay a note scrawled on a scrap of paper. *Sorry but my boyf need money. Thanks.*

I sank down on the bed. Then I started to laugh. The doorbell rang again. I expected it to be Archie and much as I didn't want to see him right then I owed him and pretty well everyone else in the square an apology.

'Since brick and stucco are porous and the pores tend to catch and hold the dirt,' I was telling Archie, 'they are the most difficult surfaces to clean.' I had achieved a good result with the front doors using Graffsolve liquid. It was biodegradable and non-toxic, thereby avoiding the need to block off windows and doors, although I had placed a special mat on top of the storm drain. For the brickwork I was using Graffsolve gel and a pressure washer and I had ensured that Archie, Jenny Howell and Terry Neil, the neighbour on the other side of Archie, kept at a safe distance. I myself was wearing protective goggles and heavy-duty rubber gloves. I applied the gel to the affected areas and agitated the surfaces with a stiff brush. Stepping back approximately three feet, I pressed the trigger. I kept the water pressure low as I worked the hose from top to bottom in overlapping strokes.

The paint washed off reasonably well although it was too early to tell if some repainting might be needed. Once I had achieved as good a result as was possible with the equipment to hand, I went back into my studio to put my materials away and to take off my overalls. Archie had told me he wanted a little word when I had finished but I was in no hurry to speak to him. It was a strange thing but in my experience 'little words' were exactly the ones that spelt trouble. People who had something disagreeable to say never began with, 'I'd like to have some really big words with you.'

No, it was always 'little' words.

As it happened I got a mug of weak tea with my words. I don't know which I minded most. I really dislike weak tea.

'I've had a little word with some of the neighbours.' There it was again, the L word. 'And it was agreed that I should be the person to speak to you, seeing as we already know each other.'

I sipped the tea and tried to look nonchalant.

'We understand that your intentions in taking this young woman in were good, but here's the thing, with the privilege of living in a place like our little square comes – well – certain responsibilities.' He paused, looking expectantly at me. A passage from the Bible would have come in handy right now, I thought, something about Samaritans, for example, but my knowledge of Scripture was sketchy.

'In short, and to be blunt, we all hope you're not going to make a habit of bringing young undesirables into the neighbourhood.'

'I'll try not to. Although if one just attaches herself to me and won't let go, then I can't be held responsible.'

Archie looked confused. 'Surely that's not likely to happen.'

I had to admit that it was not.

'Well then, we're agreed.' And he offered me another cup of tea. Feeling I'd been punished enough I told him I had to get back home and make some calls.

I could not blame my neighbours for being angry, though, and later that evening I went round the neighbourhood like an overgrown Easter bunny, delivering boxes of chocolate, each with a note of apology.

Twenty-five

I WAS WORKING ON an exquisite Famille Verte plate, its design based on the 'The Three Kingdoms' – I was applying a filler made with Araldite and talc to a bad crack that ran from the edge of the plate right through Guan Yu while actually decapitating poor Zhang Fei – when Beatrice asked me if I would mind being interviewed for a newspaper feature. A friend of hers who worked for a Sunday supplement was doing a piece entitled 'Make Do and Mend Beats Chuck Out and Spend'. Beatrice had suggested to her that I might be just the right kind of artisan craft person needed for the piece, especially now I had my own studio.

I looked up reluctantly from my work. I was intrigued at the contrast between the gentle colours and the coarse caricature features of the male characters. Even the great heroes of the stories frequently had faces that even a mother might find hard to love, and great hulking bent bodies to go with those faces. In Europe the fashion was altogether different; for us it was all depictions of bland-faced knights and pretty princes whose flawless features were clearly meant to indicate a flawless soul.

'I mean, the builders are gone, right?' Beatrice said.

'Builders are never really truly gone,' I said. 'Anyway, I don't know. I was brought up to believe that the only times you should appear in the papers were for birth, marriage or death and possibly on receiving an honour from Her Majesty the Queen.'

Beatrice, quite reasonably, told me not to be a twit. 'Think what a thrill it would give your godfather. Your poor old generous godfather? One minute you're living your quiet little life where nothing exciting ever happens and the next, voilà, you're a media star and all thanks to him.'

I shot her a mean look as I decided where to start with my objections. 'First of all, one little newspaper article hardly makes one a media star. Secondly, for some of us "a quiet little life" is a blessing. Thirdly and,' there I had to add, 'absurdly' because it made such a nice rhyme and nice rhymes are not as easy to come by as one tends to imagine, 'I derive plenty of excitement from my work.'

Was it my imagination or did Beatrice look at me pityingly?

'Well, I think our work is exciting,' I said.

'Of course it is,' Beatrice said.

But in the end I agreed to be interviewed on the grounds that it would perhaps provide good bangs for Uncle Ian's bucks.

The journalist, arriving precisely on time, was accompanied by a photographer. On my way to open the door I checked myself in the mirror. My hair was tied back. I was wearing a Liberty print tea-dress that the shop assistant had assured me was 'of the moment', although on closer inspection I felt it might be more of my grandmother's moment. My make-up was OK although perhaps a bit too light on mascara, and in the sunlight I could see that pink and tangerine, in many cases a beautiful and underrated combination of colour, did not work so well if on the same face at the same time. There was no time to do anything about it now, though. They would just have to describe me as 'interesting-looking' or, possibly, 'different'.

'Isn't this just the most perfect doll's house?' Edwina Perry, having introduced me to Jodie, the photographer, stepped past me into the hall.

'And the location. I didn't realise there was so much money in broken pots.'

'There isn't,' I said.

I turned to Jodie, who was carrying two cameras, a tripod and what looked like a folded foil screen. 'Let me give you a hand.'

Jodie said she was fine; she was used to lugging equipment around.

I was just about to make some coffee when the doorbell rang a second time.

It was Gabriel. He too was laden down, balancing a large cardboard box between his raised knee and his chin, while using his right hand to ring the bell. 'I'm not interrupting anything, am I?'

I smiled in a welcoming way. 'I've got a couple of people from a newspaper here at the moment but that's fine. Come in.' I had found that it was only within a marriage that showing basic good manners appeared to be a problem.

'I nearly got run over by one of your neighbours,' he said nodding sideways in the direction of the big black car being manoeuvred into a too tight spot. Jenny Howell was watching from her front door, frowning, no doubt as a warning to Jacob Bauer not to scratch her brand new baby Fiat. He didn't. He was a good parker at least.

'That would be Jacob Bauer,' I said. 'In fact he's a colleague of yours. You probably know each other.' I raised myself on tiptoe and kissed him on the cheek, just beyond the corner of his mouth.

'Jacob Bauer, sure,' he said, putting the box down in the hall. 'I know him.'

'You look exhausted.'

As if to counter the suggestion that he might be human after all he straightened his shoulders and plastered on a smile. 'I'm not exhausted, I just haven't slept much.' I noticed that he had nicked himself shaving and I stopped myself from reaching out to touch the cut.

'What's in the box?' I asked instead.

'Your pig. The Wemyss pig.'

I had asked Gabriel to look after my pig until I had somewhere appropriate to put him. My flat had not been the place for a large and valuable china pig painted all over with shamrocks.

'Thank you. I would ask you to stay but . . .' I made a vague gesture in the direction of the kitchen just as Edwina appeared in the doorway. On seeing Gabriel she did the kind of things women tended to do when introduced to my ex-husband: she touched her hair, pushed back her shoulders, slipped the tip of her tongue across her lips. Then she suggested that 'my friend' might like to join us.

'This is Gabriel,' I said. 'He's gay. Gabriel, this is Edwina. She's a journalist.'

I made them all coffee while Edwina told Gabriel about the people who were going to be featured alongside of me for the newspaper piece. One was a 'celebrity cobbler' who actually mended shoes as opposed to designing them. It appeared he had been working away unobtrusively for thirty years at the back of his shop in Primrose Hill, deriving most of his income from making duplicate keys for home-alone teenagers and mugging victims, when one morning Jude Law was spotted bringing a pair of ankle boots into the shop. Not long after, a celebrity from *Strictly Come Dancing* brought in some Louboutins. Now the business was booming.

The third in our triumvirate of make do and menders was a woman who unravelled old unwanted knitted items and remade them as 'colourful and imaginative throws, blankets and cushion covers'.

While Edwina and Jodie were arguing about where the best place would be for taking the first photograph, Gabriel asked me why I had said he was gay.

I shrugged. 'It was the way she looked at you. I thought you were safer that way.'

'How very kind of you.' He looked around him. 'It's a great little house. Really beautiful. I didn't like you living in that other place. It was damp.'

'It wasn't.'

'It smelt damp. I never did understand why you wouldn't let me help.'

I just shrugged and smiled. With Gabriel's talent for nurturing and mine for screwing things up it was no wonder that, for a while, we had made a perfect couple.

'I still think the kitchen is a good starting point,' Edwina said.

'Boring,' Jodie said.

'How about putting her here? She could gaze out across the street, framed by those floaty white curtains.'

'Nah,' Jodie said.

'So anyway,' Gabriel said to me, 'Well done.'

'For what?'

'For having the courage to accept your godfather's money and for creating this lovely home.'

'You think?'

He nodded. 'I do.'

My smile grew wider. It might be a somewhat absurd thing to get praised for but praise was in short supply in this world so I reckoned sometimes you just had to take it when you could.

'I thought maybe the roof.' Jodie said.

'The roof?' Edwina asked.

'I'm sure there's access.'

'She's a ceramic restorer not a builder. Why would she be on the roof?'

'I was thinking Humpty Dumpty.'

I had been inching closer to Gabriel, wanting only to continue right on until I was pressed right up against his chest. Now I turned to Jodie. 'Humpty Dumpty does spring to mind when you think of ceramic restoration. And it's possible to get out on the roof but it involves ladders.'

Jodie said she'd have a look if I told her where to go. Edwina turned her attention back to Gabriel. 'So how do you two know each other?'

'We used to be married,' I said.

She frowned. 'I thought . . .'

I gave her a tragic look as if to say, 'Need you ask why it didn't last?'

'Isn't it great that you can be friends,' she said instead.

Gabriel and I smiled bland smiles.

'It was the most extraordinary thing to find that there was a studio here already just waiting for me to equip,' I said. 'It looks like just a lean-to, but it's light and bigger than you might think.'

Once in the room, I pointed to the two trestle tables placed in an L-shape at the entrance. 'That's the reception area. Behind us, with the two sinks, is the wet area. And the bench and chair over by the window is my main workstation. I've used kitchen units because they tend to be the right height. I use a little fridge for storing materials like the silicone and polyester rubbers and, of course, the hydrogen peroxide.'

Gabriel, standing behind me, put his hands on my shoulders and I felt the heat of his skin through the thin material of my dress. 'Of course, the majority of the chemicals are stored safely in the flameproof cupboard. And over there, behind the curtains, is my retouching area. That ugly thing on the wall is the vent extractor.'

Jodie had returned to say that she had gone off the idea of the roof. 'There is a wall out at the back,' I told her. 'I can sit on the wall. For that authentic Humpty look.'

But for now she contented herself with some shots of me at my workbench while Edwina asked me technical questions. I found that I was enjoying myself. There were proper answers to be given to proper questions when talking about my work. Answers like, 'No, we are conservators or restorers, but not conservationists.' And 'We only use gloves in the late stages of the process and then it's to protect the piece, not our hands.' And 'Yes, that is indeed an old satay stick rolled in cotton wool. That way you get the exact thickness you're after and also it's much cheaper. We have a very tight budget at the museum.' And 'You just use water and ordinary detergent unless you're removing old adhesives in which case you use acetone.' And

'Actually, it's "sherds" not shards if you want to be absolutely correct.' When I gave lectures to students of my subject, there was always a part of the audience who appeared bored out of their minds. It was possible that I was very boring or that they simply had those kinds of faces, faces that looked very bored, but you could never be sure, so it ended up being quite off-putting. But Edwina took notes and smiled and looked up and asked more questions and all the while Jodie was snapping her pictures. And it was all right to enjoy the attention because it was all for Uncle Ian's sake, to show him what a positive effect his interest and generosity were having.

Gabriel had been out in the small back garden but now he stepped into the workshop again, wiping his feet on the mat. I gave him a cheery little wave. The kind he could have done with, I thought, back when we were married.

'Shall I put my hair up, for some of the pictures?' I turned to Jodie.

'Why not,' she said.

I twirled my hair into a rope and fixed it to the top of my head with a pencil. 'Like this?' I swung round

'Great,' she said. Gabriel was smiling at me; he always did like me with my hair up.

Edwina asked me if there was any real difference between the work I did for the museum and the work I did for private clients. I told her, 'A museum is concerned mostly with conservation, the long-term health of a piece and you don't usually disguise the mend completely. It's about authenticity. Restoration is more about making pretty.'

Gabriel bent down, his hands on my shoulders, and I felt his warm breath against my bare neck. 'I'll be off but thank you for the tour.'

As he strode off, disappearing into the main house, Edwina and I both heaved a sigh. Then our eyes met and we exchanged a smile instead.

'It must have been really hard?' she said. 'When did you find out?'

'Find out? Oh, *find out*. Only recently. And yes, it was hard. But he's such a great guy.' I was struck by a thought. 'You're not going to write about this, are you?'

'No, of course not. It's not that kind of piece.'

We went back to talking about restoration and I felt comfortable once more, back in my world of broken things.

'Say I'm dealing with a severely damaged vase. I haven't got anything at that stage of the process here at the moment so you'll have to imagine. The first thing I would do would be to make a drawing of each sherd on a piece of paper, positioning them in the correct order.' I scrabbled around the drawer. 'Here. You see this. It's like an exploded view ... It's pivotal that each sherd is in true alignment, or as you near the top ...'

A little later we moved upstairs to the sitting room, partly in order to have somewhere comfortable to sit while we finished off the interview and partly to give Jodie a change of backdrop.

'Please, sit down.' I indicated the sofa. I followed Edwina's gaze. 'The stains are just glue and stuff.'

'I was just curious. Everything else in here is so ... well, pristine.'

'Edwina has germ issues,' Jodie said. 'Do you mind if I have a snoop round your bookcases?'

'I don't have "germ issues",' Edwina said, turning to Jodie. 'Just because I don't rummage around other people's dustbins ...'

'Skips,' Jodie said.

'Skips, then.' Edwina tuned back to me. 'I'd love to be one of these people who find treasures in skips and bring them home and use them as plant stands and all that but I just can't do it.' She shuddered. 'You see what people drop in other people's skips. In fact I don't really do car-boot sales or flea-markets either. I mean, "vintage" handbags, for example. People could have put snotty old tissues and all kinds of things inside . . .'

'Told you,' Jodie said. 'She's got issues.'

I gestured at the sofa. 'I can understand that. Stains are personal things. Rather like children. Your own are fine but other people's can be really disturbing. But the sofa really is perfectly safe. Actually, it comes everywhere with me. Well, not everywhere obviously. I don't take it shopping or on holiday. But we have been through four moves together.'

Edwina asked me if I ever carried out what one might term 'ordinary' mending? I told her that I did. 'Mainly as a favour to friends or when my own things meet with an accident. I feel as if I'm the last chance saloon for all these chipped teapots and cracked plates that not long ago would have been tossed in the bin or on one of Jodie's skips. And people are changing the way they regard their possessions. It's not just about saving money. They are mindful of what it is that's gone into producing even the humblest item and they feel that it's a kind of wanton wastefulness, a disrespect almost, to write something off without at least trying to save it.'

'That's exactly what this piece is about,' Edwina said. 'Make do and mend is becoming sexy. Caring for your things; polishing furniture until it shines; mending your cashmere, or is it darning? Anyway, looking after your stuff is no longer seen as being an anal-retentive fifties throw-back but a badge of honour. It shows you care about the environment, that you're in tune with the planet.'

Jodie picked up a Daisy Makeig-Jones pot, looking at it as if it were a particularly deluded participant in a talent show.

'You don't like it?' I asked.

'Not really. I prefer artists like Brenda McMahon and Beate Kuhn.'

Edwina said, 'I'm always fascinated by what makes people dedicate their lives to a particular line of work. So what was it that made you go for restoring porcelain as opposed to, say, picture restoring?'

Suddenly I felt tired. I had not slept well for weeks, years, decades, possibly. When I did sleep my dreams were raw and dangerous, leaving me drenched in sweat and with my jaws clamped as if I were trying to hold in water. Of course I loved my house on the hill, I just wished I were living there with someone other than myself. In short, I could not be bothered to give her a thought-out answer.

'What attracted me to restoring porcelain?' I repeated the question. 'Well, I suppose it breaks easily.'

Twenty-six

Sandra/Cassandra

WE WERE IN THE common room. The princesses were fussing around the two-ring stove, heating milk for hot chocolate. We had only just been given the privilege of making ourselves hot drinks this term and you would have thought we had been granted the freedom of a city or something, the way they carried on. 'How about it, girls,' one of them would say in the corridor as a group of juniors passed. 'Shall we go and make ourselves some tea/chocolate/coffee?' And then the other two would say, in equally loud voices, 'Let's,' and off they'd trot with little glances all around, hoping no doubt for envy. And they got it. The juniors couldn't wait until their lives got that glamorous. It was pretty pathetic when you thought about it, the way the smallest, most day-to-day treat became a huge deal in a place like this. No one at my old day school would put up with a single week here. Cubicles with curtains instead of doors would be unacceptable not to mention sleeping in beds with two-hundred-year-old mattresses made from unwashed horsehair or whatever it was. No privacy, no wardrobe space. And now this, thinking it was the biggest deal being able to make yourself a hot drink.

'Aren't you having one?' Eliza asked me.

I told her I couldn't be bothered. This obviously puzzled her. Then her brow cleared. 'You can have some of my chocolate if you've . . . run out.'

'Sandra, sorry I mean *Cass*andra, has a humongous tin,' Portia said. 'Her mum sent it by return.'

It was obvious that my mum had got it wrong again. Around here you could go on a Kenyan safari for your Christmas holiday but if you wanted some chocolate powder you saved up or waited until your birthday. If I lived until I was a hundred I'd never work out all the little snobby rules of the princesses' existence. I couldn't believe how much I used to care, too. Before it happened. Before my life changed.

'Porsh, is Julian going on the excursion?' It was Rose asking.

I had been rummaging in my satchel for my cigarettes but now I looked up.

'He said he was.'

'Looks like it's you and me sitting together then, Porsh,' Eliza said, grinning at Rose, who flushed beetroot.

I tried to stifle the grin spreading across my face but it was impossible so I pulled out my hankie and pretended to blow my nose. My heart was beating faster the way it always did when they mentioned his name. I had been trying to find a reason to say it myself, to suck the sweetness from each letter. J.u.l.i.a.n. I wanted to tell someone about us. No, I wanted to tell everyone. I wanted to shout it out and sing it out and for everyone to know. To know about how it was true that love made you go weak at the knees, literally. How it was true that love hurt and how it was as if a band were tightening around your chest until you felt breathless. How it made you wake each morning so full of energy you wanted to dance instead of walk. And how it made you feel sorry for everyone else in the world simply for not being you. I wanted to tell everyone all of that. But I couldn't. I had promised Julian. He said it was extra special only us knowing. Like we had a private world. Anyway, he couldn't stand PDA – public displays of affection. It cheapened a relationship. But we wouldn't keep it secret for ever, obviously. Maybe the trip would be a good time to go public. The princesses would be in their seats, Portia and Eliza next to each other and Rose would be across the aisle with an empty seat just happening to be next to her. We'd stop at LABs to pick up the boys. Julian would climb on board, pause and look around. Rose would blush all cutesy and Portia would call him over in that bossy proprietorial way she had with him. And then it would happen. Julian would push his fringe back the way he did when he was determined about something and then he'd saunter down the aisle, past the empty seat next to Rose, and, ignoring his sister, right on down to where I was sitting. Then, and in full view of the entire bus, he would smile that slow lazy smile that showed the dimple in his right cheek before slipping into the seat next to me, next to poor old Sandra/Cassandra.

'Cassandra, you look weird. What's up?' I was so deep in my daydream that when Rose spoke to me I flipped my arms back, knocking the mug of chocolate from her hand. It was almost empty but what little was in there splashed across the wall as the mug crashed to the floor and broke.

I couldn't believe it but Rose, seeing it there in pieces, started to cry. And not just any crying but she cried like a little kid, open-mouthed and wide-eyed, not even bothering to look away.

'Shit,' Eliza said. 'Her mother gave that to her.' She put her arms round Rose and hugged her close. They looked like little girls, all foal-legged and lost.

'Sorry,' I said. 'I'll get you a new one.'

'That's not the point,' Eliza hissed at me. She turned to Rose and her expression changed. 'We'll get it mended, Rosie,' she cooed. 'It'll be as good as new.'

I wanted Eliza to speak to me that way, and look at me so sweetly. Maybe she would once she knew about Julian. Maybe then she would see that I was more than just the annoying bumpkin hanging around the perimeters of the group.

Rose had stopped crying and was looking at her with those big blue eyes. 'Promise?'

'Promise.'

We were on the bus, waiting for the boys to board. My heart was beating so hard I felt as if my blood were being whisked, bubbling up to my brain, and I imagined my head lighting up red like a beetroot or a lamp in a prostitute's window. But no one seemed to notice anything different as I made my way to the back. It was amazing, the princesses were sitting just the way I had imagined they would with Portia and Eliza next to each other and Rose on her own with an empty seat next to her. Both Gillian and Celia had been about to join her but Portia had stopped them, literally throwing herself across the aisle. I was actually beginning to feel a bit sorry for Rose. She would feel completely humiliated when Julian walked past her to sit with me. I used to wish I were she, with her perfect looks and Eliza for her best friend. But after today she might be wishing she were me.

As the engine of the bus idled I thought of Julian limp and grateful in my arms. He had chosen me, just the way I was. I had been tempted to ask him, why me? But I always held back. I didn't want to break the spell. Because maybe that was what it was, a spell. Some fairy godmother bored with princesses who had it all had rolled up her sleeves and got down and dirty, making so that Julian, when he looked at me, saw perfection. Maybe that was the spell. 'Whenever Prince Charming looks at you, my thin-lipped, frizzy-haired child, he shall a perfect beauty behold.' Or some crap like that.

Then I spotted him on the forecourt with his friends. Julian was actually shorter than the others, which was weird because his sister was so tall, but he'd told me his father had been the same but then he'd had a late growth spurt. I told him he was just right the way he was. Anyway, taller men didn't live as long. I'd read that in the paper just the other day. The spring sunshine was turning his chestnut hair copper and when he turned his face towards us it was as if the whole bus shivered with a moaning sigh. In front of me Portia twisted round and grinned at Rose. The two of them made me sick, behaving as if he were a piece of prime steak to be divided between them.

The doors opened. I sat back in my seat as if I were about to go to sleep and half closed my eyes while I looked out for him coming towards me. I had my hand ready to pat the empty seat next to me in a gesture that only he would see. I watched, from under lowered lids, as he hung back with his friend David, the boy Eliza liked, letting the others pass, and he was looking round as if searching for someone. I sat up straighter and lifted my hand just a little in a tiny wave. But he wasn't even looking in my direction, having spotted his sister. I realised that someone was talking to me and I looked up to see Gareth Penning.

'Is this seat free?' he asked again. Gareth was the only boy I could think of who would ask and not just plonk himself down. He was a complete loser, unfortunately.

'No, no, it isn't,' I said. And he lumbered off to sit on his own somewhere. If I hadn't been so excited I might have felt sorry for him.

I craned my neck in time to see Eliza and then Portia signalling to Julian and David. Julian was coming up to Rose's row. I couldn't stand it any longer so I got to my feet.

'Hi,' I called. Julian turned and looked in my direction. I gave him a smile and a wave.

It had gone quiet. Everyone was watching. I held my breath as I waited. This was when it was going to happen. This was when they were all going to find out. I exhaled and relaxed my shoulders and the air escaping through my lips whistled like a steam-train.

Slowly Julian raised his gaze and looked straight at me. I widened my smile, God, I must have looked as if I were about to swallow him, and gave another wave. But Julian let go of my gaze with no flicker of a smile back. David said something to him and then they laughed. Eliza turned round and looked and as our eyes met she went pink and looked away. I realised I was still standing. As I sank back on to my seat she turned to look at me again. She seemed to be asking me if I were OK. I pretended not to notice. She half rose to her feet but Portia grabbed her arm and said something and she sat back down. Just as well, because if she had come over I would have smashed her stupid face through the bus window.

The bus pulled out and as I turned away my heart exploded into little shards that went all over the place, piercing my throat, my breasts, my stomach, my groin. I breathed in and out, slowly, rhythmically, the way Dr Curtis had taught me when I was little. The bus turned on to the main road.

Twenty-seven

Eliza

THE NEWSPAPER ARTICLE APPEARED with my picture beneath the open-to-misinterpretation headline of 'Old is the New New'.

My mother, having got hold of a copy somehow, phoned to say that she thought the new haircut was flattering but that she did not quite see why I had felt the need to dye it black. As I had not had a haircut nor had my hair coloured I was as much at a loss as she was.

Uncle Ian was happy. He Skyped, having read it online. As I listened to him talk all about the way my life seemed to be taking off I felt happy; Frankenstein could not have been more proud of his monster than Uncle Ian was of me. He finished the conversation by saying that Rose was as pleased as he was. That unsettled me all over again. I couldn't make sense of it, the way he seemed completely rational in every way but for this insistence that he spoke to Rose. I had asked Katarina about it. She said that in her view there were more things between heaven and earth. I had felt she could have tried to come up with something a little more helpful and anyway she'd got the quote wrong. Because I was annoyed I told her. 'I think it's "in", actually. As in "there are more things *in* heaven and earth." 'Then, feeling bad for being rude, I had added that it did seem odd. I mean who says 'in earth'? None of this, of course, had got me any closer to the truth about Uncle Ian and Rose.

Ruth phoned to tell me she was so sorry about the photographs.

Archie, lying in wait in his usual spot, felt compelled to tell me that I was not the first celebrity they had had in the area. Not by a long shot. I had assured him that I a) knew that and b) never imagined that an appearance in a Sunday supplement made me a celebrity. Archie had countered with the warning that I might nevertheless be stalked and murdered on my doorstep especially as I lived on my own and had some 'unfortunate acquaintances'. I told him my stepsister really wasn't that bad, which had made him choke and splutter and apologise.

My five minutes of fame also brought a small, dark-haired child to my doorstep. I found her there when I returned from work, a girl of about eight or nine, all knees, teeth and eyes, seated on my doorstep with a plastic crate in her lap. As I approached she struggled to her feet, the box in her arms.

Her name was Annie Bauer, she told me, and she lived in Number 12. 'Sometimes,' she added. She had read about me in the newspaper and she wondered if I could mend her jug, or rather her father's jug.

I stifled a sigh. On the bus ride home I had been thinking of nothing else but a glass of wine, a bowl of salted almonds and sitting with my feet up in front of the television.

'I'm a bit busy right now but I'm working from home tomorrow so why don't you come back then?' I unlocked the door and was about to step inside when I realised that the child had not moved away. I gave her house across the square a meaningful look. She looked at me.

'I can't. Daddy is home tomorrow too and I want it to be a surprise.' She sighed theatrically. 'I can't go anywhere when he is around, without him knowing.'

'So why don't I take it in with me and then we can talk about it once I've had a chance to examine it. Tomorrow.'

But the child Annie somehow managed to sneak past me into the hall. She was quick, you had to give her that. 'I don't think I should leave it with you just like that,' she said. 'I don't mean to be rude or anything but it's a nice jug and I don't even know you.'

I sighed again. 'All right. We'll take it to the studio and have a look.' I paused. 'Actually, you should not get into the habit of going into strangers' houses.'

'You're not a stranger. You're the woman who moved into Number 2 and we hope hasn't tarted it up beyond all recognition.'

I gave her a long look. 'I am, am I. Still, as you said yourself, we don't *know*, know each other so you should really have an adult's permission.'

'I do,' she said. 'You're an adult and you've given me permission.' She stepped further into the hall.

Good try, I thought. 'I mean a proper adult. Of course I am a proper adult. What I mean is an adult belonging to you.' Warming to the subject, I went on, 'In fact I think that according to the latest regulations you need a permit in order to entertain strange children on your premises.'

'I'm not a strange child,' Annie said. She looked offended. 'And I'm not asking to be entertained.'

I sighed again. 'When I said "strange" I meant simply a child unknown to me, *previously* unknown to me.' I corrected myself before the child did. 'And when I said entertain, I didn't mean as in juggling or telling jokes, I meant hosting.'

'Hm.'

'I don't think we're really getting anywhere,' I said.

It was the child's turn to sigh. 'I'll get Sheila,' she said. 'She'll sort this out.' She was still holding the crate. She gave me a look as if to tell me she was on to me, put the crate down and walked out. I closed the door and thought of bolting it. I didn't think a simple string of garlic would work with that child. Then again if I didn't let her back in she would probably call the police to say I had stolen her broken pot.

A few minutes later the child reappeared, this time with a blonde woman in tow, a different blonde woman from the one who had walked off with the suitcase. This one was older. How much older was difficult to say as she belonged to the old-fashioned school of middle age, the one that still favoured elasticated waistbands over a work-out and who believed sun was good for the skin.

Her name, she said, was Sheila Wilkinson and she was Mr Bauer's housekeeper. The fact that she was anyone's house-keeper, she managed to imply, was one of life's little ironies.

'It's so lovely to finally meet you,' she added. 'I would have had you over but my little quarters don't really lend themselves to entertaining. Although Mr Bauer has of course said that I must treat the place as my own. He's . . .'

'He only said that,' the child interrupted. 'But I don't think he really meant it. It's because he works with Dr Wilkinson that he feels he should.'

Sheila Wilkinson's cheeks coloured. 'Well, that's just silly. Whom my ex-husband works with should have nothing to do with it. I shall have to have a word with your father.'

I felt for her. She wasn't someone I instinctively warmed to, but I had to sympathise with anyone who had to spend her days battling the child Annie. I glared at the girl. I might have imagined it but I thought she looked a little ashamed.

'Well, all I can say is that you don't know how lucky you are to have your own place until it's gone.' Sheila made sweeping movements with her arm, taking in my little house and the pretty garden.

'I am lucky, I know.'

Sheila peered at me. 'There's no need to look so upset about it,' she said.

'Would you like to come in for a moment?' I asked her.

As we walked though the hall to the kitchen I apologised for the bag slung on the floor and the letters still on the mat, explaining that I had just got back from work and hoping she might take pity on me and remove the child without too much delay. Sheila said she was used to untidy houses, going on to tell me all about the mess created by Annie's father. 'It makes you wonder,' she said, 'it really does. How he can be so organised in his work, I mean.'

I opened a bottle of white wine and poured two glasses. I offered the child a glass of apple juice. She said that she would rather have coffee. I turned to Sheila, who said that Annie would love some apple juice.

I never could understand people who yearned for their childhoods. It was a time of powerlessness, a time when you couldn't even pick your own drink. I shot the child an apologetic glance.

'Yes, people who meet Mr Bauer at the hospital would be amazed if they saw him at home. It's like two completely different people.'

'Really,' I smiled.

'Oh, absolutely. All those little nurses and his female patients who think he's some kind of god. "Yes, Mr Bauer, No, Mr Bauer, three bags full, Mr Bauer." ' She must have realised how sour she sounded because she rearranged her disappointed features into a smile. As smiles went it wasn't very successful. I thought I would tell Uncle Ian about her. 'She's just like Grandmother Eva's sister,' I would tell him. 'Your Aunt Berit. The one who never forgave the world.' I realised that I had no idea for what Berit could not forgive the world. Maybe Grandmother Eva had never got around to telling us.

'Yes, they should see him at home,' she was saying, 'creating chaos, slopping round in those awful old jogging bottoms.'

It was odd, I thought, this need some women appeared to have to infantilise the men around them by sharing quasi-embarrassing little facts around. Maybe it was a way of claiming ownership? 'Daddy says he knows where everything is unless some interfering busybody has moved it all around.'

Sheila coloured, starting from the neck. Then she proceeded to talk about the weather. It was un-seasonally seasonal, we both agreed. She drank up her wine. I didn't offer her another glass. I reckoned it was best to take this good neighbour thing one step at the time.

Turning to Annie, Sheila said, 'You're not to be late.'

'Annie's not going with you?' I realised I was speaking rather loudly and they both looked at me, surprised.

The child said, 'I want to show you my jug.'

'She wants to show you her jug,' Sheila said.

I closed the front door behind her and picked up the box. 'All right then,' I said to the child. 'Let's do this.'

Once inside the workshop I put the box on the table in my reception area and picked out the largest piece. Having inspected it I looked at Annie with renewed respect. 'That's some jug,' I said. 'Or bits of jug. How did it get broken? Did you drop it?'

Annie shook her head. 'Daddy did.'

'Oh dear.'

'He threw it at the wall.'

'Oh *dear*.'

She looked up at me with huge dark eyes. 'Andrea gave it to him. I think he is sorry he broke it. Please can you mend it?'

'It's an expensive business, a proper restoration.'

'Andrea gave it to him,' she said again. Tears welled up in the brown eyes.

I stifled a sigh. Then I thought, why not? Thanks to Uncle Ian I could afford to do a bit of *pro bono* restoration. 'All right. I'll see what I can do. But it will take time. It's not simply gluing a few bits together.'

The tears dried so quickly she might have used a blow dryer. 'Thanks.' She beamed a smile at me.

'No worries,' I said. 'And tell your father that if he's going to throw china around to throw something a bit less like eighteenth-century Spode.'

The child told me that he had not thrown it 'around' but straight at the wall. 'He's a very good fast bowler.'

'I suppose you should be running along back to your place,' I said, thinking of supper. And television.

The child had made herself comfortable, cross-legged on the chair. 'It's all right. Daddy won't be back for ages yet. I might as well stay here.'

I was used to guests taking a hint. Then again I was used to adults.

'Sheila doesn't like girls, she only likes boys.'

'Well, then, she's very unfair. And she's missing out.'

'Actually, she really only likes Daddy. She says all he needs is the love of a good woman. I think she means herself. She says he needs to be mothered because Granny was in the jungle.'

'What was your granny doing in the jungle?'

The child shrugged her scrawny shoulders. 'I don't remember. I think she's still there, though.'

'Really?'

Annie shrugged again. 'We think so. I've certainly never seen her. Anyway, all the women tell me that Daddy needs to be mothered.'

'All the women?'

'Andrea and before that it was the French lady, Yvonne, and even Mummy. Well, she used to say he needed mothering but she doesn't say it any more because she's got two babies to look after now so she hasn't any time for a big one. She barely has time to look after me, actually.'

I gave the child a quick glance. She sounded relaxed enough but that didn't mean she felt that way. But she had her face turned away so I couldn't tell for sure.

'I liked Andrea.' She sounded wistful.

I had felt a niggle of concern as we spoke and now I felt I had to voice it, but casually. Or as casually as one could when dealing with such a potentially serious issue. 'Your daddy doesn't throw things at you, does he?'

The child looked at me, surprised, then she burst into peals of laughter. 'Daddy? Of course not.' She turned serious again. 'I'm sorry Andrea moved out and I think Daddy is too although he won't admit it. It had taken me ages to get used to her.'

'So where's your mummy now?'

'She's on a divorce cruise with Auntie Megan.'

'A divorce cruise?'

'Yes,' Annie nodded. 'Auntie Megan got divorced from Uncle Tony and Mummy got divorced from Dan.'

The child's eyes misted up. 'I didn't really like Dan to start with because he wasn't Daddy and I didn't like his boy Will either, or the new babies, but Mummy told me I had to love them because we were a family. So I did and then Mummy and Dan got divorced and now she says I shouldn't mind because Dan isn't even my Daddy. I don't even see Will any more.'

'How long's your mummy away for?'

The child shrugged. 'I can't remember.' She looked around her. 'So what shall we do now?'

The obvious answer was, '*I'm* going to pour myself a large glass of wine and have my supper in front of the news and *you* are going home to bed or homework or to practising being Paris Hilton or whatever little girls do these days.'

But Annie looked up at me as if it was a given that I could think of nothing better than to spend my evening in her company. The nuances of social intercourse worked fine when it was between children. As none of them ever took a hint they could be straightforward. 'You have to go now because I'm having my supper.' It usually worked well, too, if both parties were adults and one might say, 'Goodness, is that the time?' And the other replied, 'Oh, I'm sorry, you must be wanting your supper.' It was mixed company that didn't really work.

Stifling a sigh, I said, 'Well, seeing we're here, why don't we take a closer look at your jug?' I moved the box across to my worktable, where I laid out the sherds.

As I studied the pieces, Annie stood by my shoulder, breathing heavily in my ear. I wondered if she was asthmatic or maybe it was just a child thing.

'Yup, it's early Spode, possibly even designed by the man himself, Joshua Spode.' I turned round to look at her. 'You've done brilliantly rescuing it.'

The child straightened and her tight little mouth widened in a controlled smile. She said, 'Sheila was going to chuck it out. She said it was just old junkshop tat not worth mending.'

Sheila would think that. I knew one's not supposed to be quick to judge but in my opinion she was typical of the kind of woman whose soul had been left to soak for so long there was nothing of any interest left.

'Do you know the story of the Willow Pattern?' I asked instead.

She shook her head.

'Once upon a time ...' I began, the way I knew one should with stories, '... there was a very rich and very mighty Mandarin of China, Mandarin being a minister or some such thing, who lived with his beautiful daughter Knoon-se in a great palace in a garden filled with trees and flowers. One day a young man named Chang came to work for the powerful Mandarin as his secretary. Chang was poor and lowly.'

'Like Lowly Worm?'

'I don't know. I don't think I've ever come across him.'

'He's a worm.'

'Right. Yes, I suppose a bit like a worm, but brighter and probably more handsome.'

'Lowly Worm's quite nice-looking. In a wormy sort of way.'

'I suppose then Chang was quite nice-looking in a human secretary sort of way. Anyhow, he fell hopelessly in love with the beautiful Knoon-se and Knoon-se fell right back in love with Chang. They met in great secrecy every evening beneath a willow tree by the river. But the Mandarin found out and got furious because he thought that Chang, though not a worm, was still too lowly for his daughter so he told Chang to go away and never come back, ever. Then he locked poor Knoon-se in a pavilion overlooking the river and built a crooked fence all around.'

'Couldn't he get it straight?'

'Good question and the answer has to be no, he couldn't. Silly old Mandarin. Anyway, if you look at this piece here,' I pointed, 'you can see a bit of the fence.'

Then the doorbell went. It was Sheila. 'Annie really has to come home now,' she announced, as if she expected some kind of argument from me, something along the lines of, 'No, no, please don't take this child who just appeared on my doorstep and wants me to do major restoration work for free while stopping me from having my supper, awaaaay from me!'

'I'll call her,' I said.

The child came skipping along the passageway at the back. 'Is that my daddy?' When she saw that it was Sheila her little face took on a sullen look and her skips became a shuffle. But Sheila didn't seem to notice. She patted her hip the way you do to get a dog or a small child to follow. 'Come along now, dear.'

From the way Annie was skipping along at her side I deduced that things were not quite as bad between them as all that. I was about to close the door behind them when the monster car drove into the square and parked on the far side. As he got out and locked up I thought Jacob Bauer had had a tough day. I recognised the signs from Gabriel: the tense, hunched shoulders, the downturned gaze, the hand raking through the hair. Then he spotted his daughter, who had pulled away from Sheila and was running towards him, and he straightened up the way Gabriel used to do when he realised I was watching him, and gave her a big smile. She hugged his waist and he ruffled her hair and then they walked, hand in hand, up to the gate of Number 12.

I don't know whom I envied the most, him for having a daughter or her for having a father or both for having someone to take by the hand.

Twenty-eight

Sandra/Cassandra

I MADE MYSELF SICK enough to be sent home. When I returned to school a week later I knew they had all been talking about me. Gillian and the others tiptoed around me as if someone had died. Rose and Portia were nice in that exaggerated, self-satisfied way everyone was nice to the smelly old people the school made us all visit once a term. Eliza was all right, though. She didn't say anything much and she didn't give me pretend sorry looks, she just gave me a drawing of Näcken that she knew I really liked. 'You don't need to put it up or anything.' I blu-tacked it on the wall above my bed. Quite apart from anything else, it was generally believed around the school that Eliza would make it big as an artist one day so who knows how valuable something like that might become.

I wanted to tell Eliza everything. I wanted her to know that I wasn't having some silly unrequited crush on Julian. The others could believe what they liked but Eliza was different. I wish she'd see how alike we really were, she and I. Much more so than Rose and she. We had the same interests. We were both musical, both artistic. She was nowhere near as good on the violin as I was on the piano but I wouldn't mind accompanying, even.

I had thought about all those things when I was at home lying in the gross faux-rococo bed in my room and with my mother hovering anxiously outside, listening for sounds of puking. So they'd leave me alone I told them I had a stomach bug and even just talking made me feel sick. In fact I ended up having to call for Mum to come and keep me company, they left me so alone. When I did see her she looked at me in a funny way, though, almost as if she were frightened. I shouldn't have got so angry. I regretted it now, having smashed up my collection. Not because it was worth very much because it wasn't, but because I'd been collecting those little animals for ever and there were some really pretty ones like the unicorn. I was sorry the unicorn was gone.

Most of all, as I lay there, I had thought of Julian. J.U.L.I.A.N. I had forgiven him. It's what you did when you loved someone. I'm not stupid. I'd worked out that he lied when he had said he was keeping us secret because it made it more special. He was ashamed of me. I knew that now. But I saw too that it wasn't his fault. It was his sister and Rose. They were behind it all. He was totally under Portia's thumb, that was obvious. Their parents were always favouring her. They were all complete over-achievers and Julian was always having to think of things that would win their approval. I suppose bringing home little Miss Perfect Rose Bingham would get him that. But it was me he wanted. I just had to make him see he didn't need to be ashamed. I had to help him.

The first night back at school, and after she'd given me the drawing, Eliza brought two cups of hot chocolate into my cubicle and asked if I felt like hanging out. She chatted about nothing much and then she said, 'You know, boys aren't really so important. It's easy to think they are but there's so much else in life. I mean, think about it; we're young and healthy and we're getting a brilliant education and we have dreams we're going to fulfil. Boys are just a part of that. If I had to choose between my work and a boy my work would win every time. And you're good enough to become a professional musician if you work hard and don't get distracted.' She had drawn her long legs up under her and was sitting there at the foot of my bed, her eyes all shiny. 'I think of the future as this big room filled with wonderful things and all we need to do is open the door and walk in. So,' she gave me a big grin and a friendly buddy-buddy punch on the shoulder, 'who needs boys?'

I know she was trying to help. And although I was pleased that she recognised that I was talented I wished she'd understand that Julian was *my* room full of wonderful things and so I couldn't allow him to leave me.

Two days later we were playing the girls from Skipton Ladies' College at lacrosse and as we used the LABs playing fields for interschool matches it was obviously a possibility that I was going to see Julian. Eliza looked all worried. 'You're sure you're up to it?' she asked as we waited for the minibus.

I gave her one of my blank looks. 'What do you mean? Why shouldn't I be up to it? I told you it was just a tummy bug.'

She looked uncertain but she persevered. 'I wasn't thinking of that. You know Julian might be there?'

I kept my blank look. 'So?'

She did a little shrug and I thought I might have gone too far. I quickly smiled. 'It's nice of you to care.'

She was all sunshine again. 'That's OK.' She bent her long neck and gave me a quick kiss on the cheek before turning away to speak to Rose, who had come up behind us.

I insisted I wanted to sit on my own at the back. When no one was looking I raised my hand to the bit of my cheek that she had kissed. Eliza confused me. Just as she was about to seriously annoy me she did something sweet, like she actually cared.

But as we drove up the driveway to LABs I felt sick. Not sick with nerves this time because I was feeling perfectly calm. I'd been feeling like that a couple of mornings since getting back and at first I thought Miss Philips was right when she warned us against faking illness, saying it was tempting fate. But then, as I sat there on the bus, the thought occurred to me that maybe it was something else. Maybe it was morning sickness and I was pregnant. Julian had definitely used a condom. But they weren't a hundred per cent safe. Accidents happened. A grin spread across my face as I thought of telling the princesses. Especially Portia, or should I say Auntie Portia. We would be sisters. Family. She wouldn't be able not to invite me on her holidays now, would she? Rose would learn that beauty wasn't everything. And Eliza? My smile subsided as I tried to work out what Eliza would make of it. She might even be happy for me. Or she might hate me because of Rose. No, not hate me. Eliza didn't hate people. But she might not be at all pleased. What about Julian? I decided not to think about that just yet.

Some of the boys were watching the match but Julian didn't get there until the end of the first half. I was queuing up for a drink and when he saw me he raised his hand in a little wave and smiled an upside-down smile that I suppose was meant to be apologetic. I thought a moment about ignoring him just to give him a scare but before I knew it I had waved back. He nodded in the direction of the pavilion and started walking.

I was really thirsty but I left the queue anyway and followed him.

'So?' I looked at him, my chin raised. He didn't know it yet but now I was the one holding the cards.

'Sorry, about the other day.' He gave me his naughty little boy's smile, half-sorry, half-cheeky. 'About not saying hi and all that.'

'It was pretty pathetic.'

Just like Eliza he didn't seem to know what to do when I wasn't all meek and grateful and his smile grew uncertain. 'I bottled out, that's all. You know, with everyone there and everything.'

'You said we would tell people.'

He pulled that downward face again. 'I really am sorry, all right.' He pointed his finger like a gun at the playing field. 'You looked good out there.'

'I didn't think you were watching.'

I looked around me and realised that it was a beautiful day with the sun high in the sky and birds singing. I wondered if I should tell him now, about the baby? Or wait until I was sure. He nudged me gently with his shoulder.

'C'mon. Say you forgive me.'

I smiled. It came out bigger than I meant it to. 'OK. I forgive you.'

'Good. Are you around this weekend?'

'Might be.'

'Shall we meet up?'

'I suppose.'

' "Our place"? After prep Saturday?'

'OK.' I sighed and that sigh opened up something inside me and let out the poison. 'See you then,' I said and I walked off, leaving him to watch after me.

Twenty-nine

Eliza

I GOT BACK FROM work to find a curt message on my home phone from Ruth. She had not called for a couple of weeks and to my surprise I had found myself minding. It was that old story about needing to be liked even by people you didn't particularly like yourself. I poured myself a glass of Sauvignon and took it out into the front garden amongst the sweet woodbine, jessamine and briar-rose. Dusk was settling and the square was quiet. I sat down on the white wrought-iron bench and sipped my wine.

A few minutes later the door of Number 12 opened and Jacob Bauer stepped outside in his white shirtsleeves, a cigarette in his hand. I always thought it incongruous, seeing a doctor smoke. He must have felt me looking at him because he turned my way and then he raised his hand in a small wave, the glow of his cigarette rising in the air like a firefly. I waved back. Behind him the view looked like a Japanese painting; dark-shadow trees against a blush-pink sky with shades of blue darkening above. He disappeared back into the house only to reappear with three large fat black bin bags that he placed outside on the pavement. I had forgotten that the next day was bin day. There was no sign of a recycling box outside

Number 12. The other week, Archie told me, he offered to give his spare box to Mr Bauer as he, Archie, seemed to have been given two. It had been Archie's way of telling him we all knew he wasn't recycling. But Jacob Bauer had simply thanked Archie and said he was fine.

You had to ask yourself, did this man even care about the future of the planet?

I finished my wine and with a little sigh I went back inside and phoned up Ruth.

'I'm all right,' she assured me, before I had had a chance to even ask. 'It's only a bruise.'

'What's only a bruise?'

'Olivia didn't tell you? Oh. I thought that's why you called.' She had put her brave voice on.

'I called because you left a message telling me to. And because I wanted to speak to you, of course. So what's going on, Ruth?'

'Nothing. I told you, nothing. Obviously, Olivia didn't think it was worth telling you about. Anyway, I'm sure he didn't mean to.'

'What did who not mean to?'

'It was an accident, I'm sure of it. Robert's never been violent before.'

'Robert hit you?'

'No, no, of course not. It was more of a shove. As I said, I'm sure he didn't mean for that to happen.'

'Oh for heaven's sake, did he mean to hurt you or not?'

Ruth began to cry noisily. 'Don't shout at me. I can't stand being shouted at.'

It took ten minutes of apologising and cajoling to calm her down.

'Where's Lottie?'

'She's gone to Greece with some friends.'

I choked back a sigh and said, in my best games mistress's voice, 'Tell you what, why don't you come over?'

She was there within such a short time I could almost believe she'd been hiding in some nearby shrubbery waiting for the invitation, a ridiculous thought, of course. Apart from a faint bruise on the left cheek she looked fine.

'Where is Robert?' I asked as I ushered her inside.

'Oh, he's at home playing around on his computer.'

'But did he hurt you? If he did you have to call the police. Oh, you've brought a suitcase?'

'I'm sorry. I thought that's what you meant. For me to stay over. But if I'm going to be in the way . . .' She raised her hand to her cheek.

'No, no, of course you're not. It won't take me a minute to make up a bed. Have you eaten?' I picked up her case.

She gave me an offended look. 'I couldn't eat a thing. Not after what happened. But you go ahead.'

As I cooked I cast little glances at her as she sat, quite calm, at the kitchen table reading the newspaper. I wished I didn't always harbour a faint suspicion that she was making things up. It wasn't that I had ever caught her in an outright lie but simply that weird little things always seemed to happen to her. The milkman chasing her round the kitchen table, her mother-in-law paying her cleaner to spy on her, those kinds of things.

I had eaten a couple of mouthfuls of my pasta with broccoli and Gorgonzola cheese when Ruth leant across and picked at the pasta spirals. She had a dainty way of using her fingers, as if they were tweezers.

I put my fork down. 'Would you like your own plate?'

She gave me a coy little smile. 'If you insist. But only a teeny amount, mind.'

'There isn't that much left so it'll have to be, I'm afraid.'

As I put the plate down in front of her she looked around the kitchen.

'Is there something you need? The parmesan is here.' I shoved the little peony-patterned china bowl with grated cheese towards her.

'I was just thinking that a small glass of wine might be just the thing.'

I got up. 'Sorry. I should have offered. Is white OK?'

'Sure. Unless you've got some red.'

I shut the fridge door. 'I'll check in the dining room.'

'Gosh, you have a dining room. Very posh.'

'I didn't put us in there tonight because you said you weren't going to eat.' I tried watering down the defensiveness in my voice with a smile.

'I'm so sorry, I've put you out. I should have eaten at home before I came but . . .'

'Goodness, no, of course not. I mean, you were fleeing.' Even as I said it, it sounded absurd. Robert was a toad but he wasn't, I was sure of it, a belligerent toad. Yet the consequences of disbelieving Ruth if she were telling the truth would be far worse than believing her even if she were telling fibs.

I returned with a bottle to find Ruth shovelling the food from my plate on to her own. When she saw me she said, cheerfully enough, 'Waste not want not. I'm so hungry all of a sudden I could eat anything. It must be delayed shock.'

I cut myself some bread and sat down again. 'Tell me what happened.'

'I can't talk about it,' Ruth said.

Only because you've got your mouth full, I thought sourly.

'I really can't bear to talk about it,' she said again with an encouraging glance at me.

'Oh right.' I did my best to return the encouraging look. 'Please try.'

'No, I can't.'

I stifled a sigh. 'If Robert is ...' I paused. The thought of Robert ever daring to lift his hand against anyone bigger than himself, and Ruth was a good couple of inches taller and at least a stone heavier, seemed increasingly unlikely the more I thought about it. Then my gaze fell on the faint bruise on her cheekbone and I felt sick. Terrible things happened when you failed to take a cry for help seriously. 'If he's hurting you, you must go to the police.'

She had stopped looking encouraging and assumed a mulish expression instead. 'I told you I don't want to talk about it.'

'No, no, I'm sorry, but you can't just come here and tell me your husband hit you and then expect me not to do anything.'

'Leave it for now,' she said. 'Please. We'll decide what to do in the morning. In fact what I want now is a tour of the house. I can't believe you've been here for two months and I haven't been allowed a proper inspection.'

'You saw it just after I bought it.'

Ruth gave me a conspiratorial little smile it?' She winked. 'Well, I won't tell if you don

'You saw it just after Uncle Ian bought it, point is, it's been a building site until recent must be exhausted. I'll show you around tomo

'I'm not ready to go to bed yet,' Ruth said. surprised if I sleep at all tonight.'

I waite

Then I

after

upsta

'H

She

wha

dece

She told me that the inky blue made the dining room look 'quite dark'.

'SC 224 from Papers and Paints Traditional Colours collection,' I told her.

'You memorise these things? Goodness. It's an unusual colour but it does sort of work with the rose pink and china blue of the curtains.'

'The Georgians didn't really use blue for their dining rooms,' I said, sounding even to myself as a voice-over for Wikipedia. 'Green being the more common choice. In fact, blue generally was a rare colour up to the mid-Georgian period because of the cost of producing it, but I just felt this was a blue room.'

Ruth told me she thought the table was lovely.

'Uncle Ian picked it out online from an auction house catalogue.'

'God, you are lucky.'

'Aren't I just,' I said. Maybe I didn't look that lucky just then because Ruth said, 'I know, I know. Having all of this, being given it by, of all people, Rose's father, it must make those feelings of guilt worse.'

'Excuse me for a moment.' I hurried out into the hall where
 d just long enough to assemble a convincing smile.
 returned, reminding myself that I had to be nice. Ruth,
 ll, had just been duffed up by her husband. 'Let's go
 rs to the sitting room.'
 w sweet. Adorable,' Ruth said standing in the doorway.
 stepped inside and looked around some more. 'You know
 , you could probably knock through the wall to get one
 nt-sized room?'
 Not allowed to. English Heritage. Great idea, though.'

'Oh, pity. Still, I do love those sash windows. And that simple wooden mantle is lovely. Is it original?'

I nodded. 'They didn't start installing the more ornate projecting chimneypieces in simple homes like this until the end of the nineteenth century.'

'Simple? Hardly simple.'

'At that time it was seen as a simple house. It would have been the home of an artisan or possibly even built as servant's quarters. Of course, I know it isn't nowadays.' I was beginning to feel exhausted.

'You've really gone into all this, haven't you?'

I smiled, genuinely this time. 'Uncle Ian and I together. I suppose we're pretty expert by now.'

'Of course, the rooms will have a cosier feel to them when you get the curtains up.'

'I'm not having curtains in the sitting room, only the snug,' I said. 'Because of the shutters.'

'Really? You can't have both?'

'I could probably but I rather like it like this. I'll think about it, though,' I added, not wanting to seem to be turning down all her suggestions out of hand. 'I'll live with it as it is for a bit longer then I'll see how it goes. But you might well be right.'

Ruth gave me a big smile back and there was no hint of martyrdom. 'I do have quite a good eye, you know.'

'You do. And thank you for being so interested.'

She shrugged. 'I love decorating but we don't have any money to do our place up. This is almost as much fun, though.'

'Right.' I was impressed, not for the first time, by the way Ruth had of making me feel like a child with special needs while at the same time maintaining her air of humble diffidence.

'The early Georgians were very keen on quite dark drab colours,' I said. 'But as the period moved on towards Regency the decor got lighter and brighter. Pea green, that is SC271, became a popular alternative to, for example, sage.' I walked out on to the landing.

'Let me show you your room.'

Ruth followed me into the bedroom with the look of a person whose hotel didn't live up to its star marking. 'I suppose the master bedroom is bigger?'

'This is the master bedroom. I'm in the smaller room upstairs.'

'It's very pretty,' Ruth said. 'The whole house is delightful. I just find it extraordinary that they can charge what they did for a place this size. No disrespect intended.'

I shrugged and said, 'Well,' in a non-committal way, while wondering how she had found out how much we paid for the house. 'The bathroom is over here.' I turned round and pointed to the door opposite on the landing 'It's not en suite, I'm afraid.' I got that in before Ruth did. It was like when you're small and they go through the football scores on television and you have to get through them before the newsreader does:

Portsmouth1Arsenal3BirminghamCity0ManchesterUnited2 AccringtonStanley0Tottenham7 ... faster faster as if the words were chased by wolves.

Once Ruth had gone to bed I brought my new laptop up to my room. *Dear Uncle Ian*, I wrote, *I thought you might like to know that my stepsister Ruth is staying with me at the moment. She's going through a difficult patch in her marriage. I didn't even have a spare room in my flat so it's very special to be able to put her up like this.*

I couldn't sleep so I picked up the book on my bedside. I was rereading *Wuthering Heights*. It had been Rose's favourite novel. She had told me Heathcliff reminded her of Julian. That had made me laugh then and it made me smile now. Julian Dennis had been no more like Heathcliff than a cross kitten was like a tiger. I closed my eyes, suddenly unable to focus on my reading. Rose should be living in this house. She should be here with Julian who had grown up to be her husband and their two adorable little girls who could play with Jenny's boys next door. It should all be Rose. I wished I could believe Uncle Ian when he said she had come to him. I wished I could believe that she wasn't angry. I wished she would tell me herself because I was so very tired of feeling bad.

Me: I can't believe I'm living in this wonderful house and all because you're dead.

Rose: I can't believe I'm dead. Especially with you all talking to me the whole time.

Me: I feel so bad.

Rose: How do you think I feel?

Me: You're supposed to tell me to forgive myself and move on.

Rose: Whoops, sorry. Who's a bad little corpse, then? I'll start again. Eliza, do stop beating yourself up about the fact that I'm dead and you are living like a queen off my old father's money.

Me: You were always so sweet and kind. What's happened to you?

Rose: What's happened to me? Let me think. Oh yes. I'm dead. You'd be surprised how that affects one's mood. I'm sorry but if it's a comfort corpse you're after, get someone else.

I got out of bed and went downstairs to the kitchen. I heated up some milk in the microwave and then I added some brown sugar. I thought for a moment and then I went to the drinks cupboard and brought out some dark Jamaican rum and added a good slug of that to the sweet milk.

'You can't sleep, either?' It was Ruth, standing in the kitchen doorway in a Victorian-style long white nightdress.

I shook my head.

'What are you drinking?'

'Sit down,' I gestured at a chair. 'I'll make you some.' I moved around my kitchen, enjoying every touch of a surface, every smooth opening of a cupboard and drawer. I thought of previous occupants of my house on the hill, especially my lady painter, Marguerite Stephens, and her sister Anna, who lived here for over forty years during the reign of Queen Victoria. I wondered if they too had comforted themselves with a hot drink and perhaps a slug of rum or brandy on nights when the world seemed dark and wild. Their kitchen would have looked very different of course but behind the layers of paint the walls were the same walls. Their feet would have touched these same dark pine boards as my bare feet were touching now, and years from now when I too was gone, and Ruth and everyone I knew were gone too, some other woman would move around this room, her feet caressing the same warm smooth wood. I couldn't make my mind up as to whether that was a comforting thought or just very depressing.

'Mmm, nice,' Ruth said, sipping her rum and milk. The dark circles under her eyes were more vivid than the faint bruise on her cheekbone and she looked suddenly old. It hit me then that Ruth might have had higher hopes of life than most of us. Life not living up to your dreams perhaps did not rank highly in the league of sorrows, but it was a sorrow nevertheless and a common one at that. And as sometimes happened when I was tired or drunk or both, that particular sadness joined all the other sorrows in the world until it seemed to me as if the entire universe were crying. I wanted to block my ears and sing something silly really loudly because it was all too much to bear. Instead I reached out and put my hand on hers. She looked surprised and that too upset me.

'Couldn't you please try and tell me what is going on?' I asked.

Her eyes welled up and she was shaking her head, swinging it from side to side like a mournful donkey. Then she said, 'Robert didn't actually hit me.'

'Ah', I said.

'But he did shove me out of the way and that's when I stumbled and knocked into the door–post.'

'He shouldn't have shoved you.'

'No, he shouldn't have. It was pretty frightening.' The memory seemed to cheer her up a little.

'Of course it was.'

She wiped her tears and gave me a timid smile. 'Thank you for taking me in.'

I waved her words away. 'Don't be silly, least I could do.'

'I really am very comfortable in my little room.'

'It's the biggest one, I promise.'

'I know. I just don't understand why you insist on being in that horrid little attic one?'

'I like it.'

'Fair enough.'

She smiled again, that timid little smile. A very un-Ruthlike smile. Then she grew serious. 'I shouldn't have alarmed you. It wasn't such a big deal.'

'I expect it felt like a big deal. Being shoved by someone you love and trust and ending up hurt must be a shock.'

She put her hand on my arm. 'I knew you'd understand. That's why I wanted to come here. After all, there's nothing like family.'

In the past, the assumption of closeness would have made me feel uncomfortable, but not now. Now I felt strangely pleased.

'We had a terrible row. Lately, we seem to be having them all the time. He tells me I'm being paranoid. And I know I'm not. And I tell him, please just admit it. Just tell me the truth. I can cope as long as you're straight with me. And he looks at me, always the same look, as if he's a parent dealing with an hysterical child. And then I begin to wonder if I really am imagining things, if I really am paranoid.' Ruth drained her mug. 'But I know I'm not. Eliza, I know I'm not.' She got to her feet, heavily, leaning for support on the table.

I didn't know what was better, to agree with her that her husband was probably cheating on her again or to agree that she was probably paranoid. So instead I just said that either way she was welcome to stay here for as long as she needed to.

She bent down and flung her arms round me. 'Thank you. Thank you, Sis, it means a lot.'

'Oh, don't mention it . . . er, Sis.'

I finished my drink standing by the window, looking out at the square. It looked particularly pretty at night. I suddenly longed for winter. This place was made for Christmas wreaths and snowflakes falling in the golden light of the street lamps. Across at Number 12 a dark figure stood framed by an upstairs window. Like me, Jacob Bauer, because I expect it was he, seemed to find comfort in the view.

Thirty

I LOOKED UP FROM my work to find a small face with big dark eyes under heavy brows peering in through the studio window. I walked out of the side entrance. 'Annie, what are you doing?'

'Looking,' she said. 'What are you doing?'

'Working.'

'Can I come in?'

'Not really. I need to concentrate.'

'You're not working on my thing, I saw.'

'You shouldn't peer through people's windows.'

'Why?'

'Privacy.'

'But windows are for looking through.'

'Only from inside out. You wouldn't like it if people were spying on you through your window. "What is hateful to yourself do not do to your fellow man," ' I quoted.

She squeezed past me into the studio. 'Daddy is always saying that to me.'

'He is?'

'But they can't anyway because my window is on the third floor in Daddy's house and even higher in Mummy's flat.'

'I was talking of the principle.'

'Ah,' she said.

'How old are you, did you say?'

'Nine, almost.'

'How almost?'

She glared. 'My daddy says it's impolite to ask someone's age.'

This sign of awareness of social niceties from Jacob Bauer surprised me as much as it surprised me that he had been endeavouring to teach his daughter Rabbi Hillel's Golden Rule. If we could only get him out of that anti-social car and into recycling he might become a valued member of the community after all.

'What are you smiling about?' Annie asked.

'Was I smiling?'

'Yes.'

'I've forgotten,' I said. 'Anyway, it's only rude to ask someone's age if they're grown up. When it's a child, it's obligatory.'

'Ah,' she said again. 'I'll tell Daddy.'

'Do,' I said. 'Don't you have school?'

'It's half-term,' Annie said, making herself comfortable in the saggy armchair in the reception area. 'That's why I'm staying with Daddy.'

It was my turn to say, 'Ah.'

'So what are you doing?' she asked again.

'Making use of odds and ends.'

'What do you mean?' She got back up from the chair and went to stand behind me at the bench. 'It's broken,' she offered helpfully, pointing to the yellow china budgerigar lying on its side, one red china leg in the air.

'I know.'

'Are you going to mend him?'

'No.'

'Why not?'

'Because to mend him, give him back his leg and his wing and fill in all the chipped bits, would be a vast amount of work and he's too ordinary a bird for that.'

'Daddy has to mend everyone, even, he says, people who are utterly loathsome.'

'Of course he does. But he's a doctor. And he's talking about people, not porcelain. Anyway, I'm not discarding the little bird, I'm simply giving him a different function.'

'Different from being a bird?'

'Well, he isn't really a bird, is he, at least not in the way of flying and hopping and chirruping and stuff. He's a china ornament whose function it is to be pretty and I'm going to make him pretty in a new way.'

'How?'

I sighed. 'You must have stuff to do.'

'No. I like being here.'

'Fine, stay then.'

'Why are you putting the bird on the plate?'

'Because I'm interested in exploring objects and their roles as both functional tools within the domestic environment, and as the means by which we express or define ourselves.' I would have quite liked to have added, 'so put that in your pipe and smoke it,' but one didn't talk like that to children, probably.

Annie, however, seemed perfectly happy with the explanation. 'Fair enough,' she said.

'You're sure you're not *fifty*-eight and a bit?'

Annie frowned. 'Of course I'm sure.'

'Fair enough,' I said and I went to put some water on a cloth, and as I passed Annie I wondered if I should tell her not to pick her nose but I decided against it. I seem to remember finding that kind of thing quite hurtful when I was a child. Instead I passed her a tissue.

After a while she said, 'So you and my daddy are the same in a way.'

'In what way?'

'You both mend things.'

I looked at her. 'That was a very Hollywood-profound thing to say.'

'But Daddy tries not to leave people without their legs. Or wings, if they have wings. Which they never do.' She sounded as if she regretted the fact. I knew how she felt. It would be nice to think there were people coming into the operating theatre with great big white feathery wings to be put back together by a skilful orthopedic surgeon.

'Anyway, I might come to live with Daddy all the time.'

'Really? What about your mother?'

'She's going away. To America. She said it's better for me if I stay here because my school and all my friends are here.'

'You'd soon make new friends in America.'

'That's what Daddy says. But Mummy says it would be difficult and anyway she has to work and she doesn't have anyone to look after me there and she might come back after a year anyway and then I would have to start again with friends and things.'

I nudged the bird on the plate a centimetre off-centre. 'But when you come back your old friends would still be here.'

'That's what Daddy says.'

I felt suddenly grateful for the literalness of children. Without it Annie might have realized that her parents were trying to palm her off on each other.

'Why don't I leave this to one side,' I said, moving my bird on a plate to a shelf. 'And I'll show you what I've done to your jug so far?'

'It's almost ready,' Annie said, pleased with her inspection.

The door opened. 'And who have we got here?' It was Ruth. She had been for a walk.

'This is my neighbour, Annie Bauer. Annie, this is my step-sister, Ruth Perkins. Ruth is staying with me for a while.'

Ruth smiled down at Annie. 'You're Mr Bauer's little girl.'

'Do you know my daddy?'

'Not exactly. But I've seen him around.'

'Have you been looking through our windows?'

'What's that?'

'Long story,' I said.

Ruth went on muttering about how she would never look through anyone's window but Annie and I both ignored her as I carried on explaining the various steps entailed in restoring her jug, finishing with, 'All I need to do now is the touching up along the lines of the mends.'

On my way to put the jug back on the shelf I said to Annie. 'It must be your teatime.' I was keen to return to work on my broken bird and I needed solitude and silence.

Ruth ended up walking Annie home. She absolutely insisted. 'I never allowed my daughter to go anywhere, not even the few yards to the sweet shop until she was much older than you are now.'

Annie looked at me and I raised my palms to the ceiling. 'Best to let her,' I said.

Annie shrugged her bony little shoulders. 'OK.'

Ruth returned half an hour later, flushed with news. 'Well, I've met your charming neighbour.'

'Who?'

'Anne's father, of course. Mr Bauer. Why don't you like him?'

'I don't *not* like him, I simply don't know him.'

'You've lived here for two months and you don't know your neighbours? I am surprised. I would have thought this was just the kind of place where old-fashioned community values were still to the fore.'

'I do know most of them, just not Jacob Bauer. He's not the neighbourly kind.'

'Well, he was very nice to me.'

'Good.' I cast a longing look at my bird.

'I asked him if he knew Gabriel. He said they had met. He was really interested to hear that you were Gabriel's ex-wife.'

'Really, why?'

'I don't know. He was being friendly, I suppose. Chatting.'

'I didn't think he was the chatty type.'

Ruth tossed back her hair and smiled coyly. 'I suppose I have a knack of bringing people out of their shells.'

And that knack would be a pincer, I thought.

'He's rather a handsome man. I'm surprised he's single.'

'He wasn't until recently,' I said. 'Anyway, he has a touch of the gorilla about him, don't you think?'

'I thought you said you hadn't met him.'

'I have seen him across the square a few times.'

'Well, I've actually met him, and close up there's nothing gorilla-like about him. He's got a perfectly good forehead, for a start.'

'If you say so.' I thought of Gabriel. I supposed that compared to him most men looked coarse.

'He obviously dotes on that little girl.'

'Ruth,' I said. 'Why are you so interested in my neighbour?'

She looked stung. 'I'm a people person. There's nothing wrong with that, is there?'

'No, no, of course not.'

'You're still hung up on Gabriel, aren't you?'

'Why don't you run yourself a nice hot bath?' I said. 'I'll be done here in a minute.'

I laid supper in the dining room. I had left the shutters open to the street and as the light faded I lit the candles on the table and on the small sideboard. I had prepared a chicken and mushroom and cream casserole and once I'd added a quarter of a bottle of sherry and some garlic it tasted good. I served it with mashed potatoes and green beans.

'It's all right for you to add butter and cream to everything,' Ruth said. 'You don't need to worry about your weight. Although you've put on a bit, haven't you? What are you now? A 14? Not 16, surely?'

'12,' I said. 'If it's a dress or a skirt and cut loose over the arse.'

'Exercise would fix that,' Ruth said.

'Well, isn't this cosy,' I said. I looked across to the sideboard and the photograph of Rose and me on a family holiday. If Rose hadn't died our parents might well have married and she would have been my stepsister. Instead there was Ruth.

Ruth traced my gaze to the photograph. Her fine dark eyes were bright like a bird's. 'You can always talk to me, you know that, don't you?'

'I know. And thank you.'

'I don't want to push but I've always heard that grief is best let out into the open.'

'Oh for heaven's sake, Ruth, it was twenty-five years ago. It's not exactly raw.'

Ruth stared at me, her mouth open in a little 'o' of surprise. She shook her head. 'Still, if you've finally moved on.'

'Moved on?' I realised I had banged my fist on the table and I withdrew it and rested it in my lap. 'Have some chicken.'

'I wish you'd stayed with that course, the toxic guilt one. They would have taught you that guilt has no purpose beyond teaching us not to make the same mistakes again.'

I stared at her. 'That's so true.'

'You don't have to be so surprised. I do make sense sometimes, you know.'

I laughed. 'I know you do. Anyway, I told you, they kicked me out.' I poured us both some more wine. Ruth was looking at me with an expression I couldn't read.

'What?' I smiled, a little uneasy. She shook her head.

'Is it Robert?' I asked. 'Is there something you haven't told me?'

After a pause she said, 'Yes, but it's not anything to do with Robert.'

I lifted my glass of wine to my lips and drained it almost before I was aware of doing so. 'So what is it?'

She sighed. 'There's been a barrier between us, Eliza. And it's my fault.'

'Really?'

She gave me a rueful smile. 'I fear so. I'm ashamed to say that I've been harbouring this . . . well, this resentment.'

I sighed. 'I know. You told me about it the other day, remember. About your birthday party and the lifeboats and . . .' I gave a helpless shrug. 'I really am so sorry.'

She shook her head. 'No. No, that's just part of it.'

My shoulders slumped. 'There's more?'

'You don't get it, do you?'

I shook my head, feeling despondent. 'I'm sorry.'

'You don't have to keep saying that. It's not all your fault. It's not your fault that you're a favoured person. But you are. People *see* you. Have you thought about that? Even as you spend most of your time trying *not* to be seen, they see you. You walk into a shop and within moments an assistant has come up to you and offered to help. You enter a restaurant and you're shown to a table by the window. At parties people come up to you and they ask you about yourself. And all this, not because you've done anything in particular to deserve it but because you were born that way, you were born *visible*. You even had Gabriel, for heaven's sake. But me, I walk into a shop and the assistants continue to swap notes about their night out. I step into the restaurant and I wait by the door until eventually someone notices. Usually because someone like you has just come in behind me.' She gave a little joyless laugh before continuing.

'At a party I work my butt off and I still end up with the red-faced fat man who is there only because I'm the only other person who seems to find the topic of him as fascinating as he does. And I got Robert.'

It was hard to know where to start so I started at the end. 'I thought you adored Robert. At least until now.'

She gave me a look that was both kind and a little contemptuous. 'You would assume that, wouldn't you. Robert with his ingratiating manner and sleazy charm. Robert with his too thin neck and his too long hair and his mannequin good looks. Robert with his big plans and small achievements. Robert with his desperate attempts at being a ladies' man. Would you have wanted him?'

'So why?' I said quietly.

She gave me a small smile. 'Because he was the best I thought I could get.'

'That's nonsense,' I said because I wanted it to be. 'And if you weren't in love with him why did you act as if you were? Why did you marry him? Ruth?'

'Because I wanted to be crazy about him. I wanted that whole romance thing that girls like you get and I didn't want it with nice steady paunchy Joe Willmott, that's why.'

'Oh Ruth.'

She smiled again, that small knowing smile. 'Anyway, that's what's been making me so angry; the way you keep being given, yet unthinkingly waste, what I would kill to have.'

Then the phone rang and I got up to answer, grateful for the interruption. It was Katarina telling me that Uncle Ian's health had declined further. She thought I might wish to come over to see him. Unsaid were the words, 'while you still can'.

I went online and found a ticket for the following morning. Then I told Ruth that she was welcome to stay. I emailed Beatrice to tell her there was a family emergency and that I would make up the time on my return. I hoped she would understand. I packed my bag. I prayed Uncle Ian would still be alive the next day.

Thirty-one

Sandra/Cassandra

WE DID IT AGAIN, in the pavilion, during match tea. We had to be really quick, obviously, but Julian never took very long anyway. I didn't mind because it was afterwards that I liked. It was what I did it for, what I lived for; those brief moments when he lay all trembly and grateful in my arms, his eyes glazed and his hair damp with sweat. Because during those moments he was truly mine. But this time, because everyone was around and the coach was waiting he just pulled up his pants and gave me a peck on the cheek. 'Can you get rid of this?' He handed me the condom.

'Where?'

'Your sports bag or something.'

I took the sticky rubber dripping with mucousy sperm, holding it between the tips of my thumb and my middle finger. Then I thought that made me seem uptight, like I was disgusted, so I folded my palm around it instead and put it into the pocket of my games skirt. He didn't seem to care either way as he opened the shed door to check that the coast was clear. I wondered if I should tell him about being late and feeling sick and all that. Then I decided to wait until I was sure.

'So when will I see you again?' I had meant the question to come out casual but instead it sounded like a plea and I saw a flicker of irritation on his face as he turned to me.

'I don't know. Soon.'

I couldn't bear that he should be annoyed by me just as we were saying goodbye so I tried desperately to think of something to say that would make him think I was cute or funny or something, anything but desperate and needy. But I didn't have time.

'I'll be in touch.' He turned in the doorway and my heart lurched as I prepared a smile. 'Just wait for a couple of minutes before you follow,' he said. Then he was gone.

I still hadn't had my period. I hugged my secret close, smiling to myself as I listened to Rose banging on to Eliza about what a perfect match she and Julian were. How completely stupid they would look. While they were fantasising about kissing in the woods like the silly little girls they were, he and I were proper lovers and soon maybe we would have a baby together. In fact smiling was not enough. I wanted to laugh out loud but instead I just asked Rose if she had actually *seen* Julian. As I knew the answer would be no, I turned away before she had the chance to reply.

'Actually, I have.'

I swung back and faced her. 'You have?'

She gave a little shrug with her dainty shoulders. The princesses all had really narrow backs, even Portia, who was athletic and Eliza, who had those big hands and feet. I was a barn door compared to them, even though I was quite slim. It was how I was built. Like a brick shit-house.

'I didn't know you'd been to LABs. Why didn't you tell me?' I realised my voice had gone shrill so I took a breath and started again. 'I mean, I have friends there too. Like, like Miles Boyd, for example.' Rose was still looking at me as if she thought I was loopy so I finished with a lame, 'I would have gone with you, that's all.'

Then she giggled, her creamy-white cheeks blushing pretty-pink and her forget-me-not eyes sparkling. She was so beautiful she could be everything she wanted, a model or a film star or a real princess even, like bloody Grace Kelly.

'Actually, he came here.'

Portia was in the San. And she was infectious so she wasn't allowed visitors. He would have known that, so he must have come over to see me. I wondered why he hadn't let me know in advance. I had checked the usual place for messages but there had been nothing. But all I said was, 'I didn't think Portia was allowed visitors.'

Rose did her little giggle again. 'She isn't.'

'Oh. So he came for nothing.' I prepared to walk off again when Rose said, 'Actually, he came to see me.'

I snapped round. 'To see you?'

Rose pointed at Eliza, who was sitting on the floor as usual, her black exercise book resting against her knees, drawing or scribbling. 'Liza set it up.'

I turned and looked at Eliza. '*You* set it up?'

She didn't respond at first. She was too busy sketching. But I asked again and my voice must have been sharper than I had intended because now, when she looked, I saw I had startled her. Then she frowned. 'I just told him Rose might like him to come over, that's all.'

I stared at her. The anger came slowly, starting in the pit of my stomach and swelling until I thought it would choke me. I tried to speak but it took two attempts before I managed.

'You just thought you'd interfere, did you?'

Eliza blinked. 'C'mon, there's . . .' But Rose butted in. 'Look, Sa . . . Cassandra, we all know you had a crush on Julian but that doesn't mean you own him. Anyway, you said yourself that you like Miles Boyd.'

That would be right. They would think that would be just the perfect match. Me and Miles; the two second-raters, the hangers-on. But my voice was steady as I told her, 'I didn't say I *liked*, liked him. I said he was one of my friends. We're in the debating team together and that's all.'

Rose looked bored now the topic had switched away from her. Eliza was obviously feeling uncomfortable. She should do.

Then Rose turned back to me. 'We kissed, actually. And I'm sorry if that upsets you but you will have to get over it. You can't just lay claim to someone because you like them. It's not as if you're a couple or anything.' The way she said that was as if the very thought was absurd.

I clenched my fists so hard my nails dug into my flesh. 'Proper kissing? Or a peck on the cheek?'

She opened her mouth to answer then closed it again. She shook her head.

'Tell me.'

'Look, if you're going to be weird about it . . .'

I practically ran the four miles to LABs. I didn't care that it wasn't a half-day. I didn't care that I'd get detention for the rest of my life if anyone saw me, I only knew that if I didn't get to see him, talk to him, I might die.

I found David sitting smoking behind the cricket pavilion. 'I need to see Julian,' I said.

'Are you all right?'

I thought I'd scream if one more person asked me that. But I needed to calm down and I imagined my voice tied to a balloon so it would come out all light and unbothered. 'I'm fine. I've been walking really fast, that's all. So where is he?'

David shrugged. '*I* don't know. Maybe he's doing prep.'

'Please can you go and find him. Tell him I really need to speak to him.'

He smirked. 'Take it easy.' But then he looked at me again and with a little shake of his head he stubbed out the cigarette, putting the butt away in his shirt pocket, and lumbered to his feet. 'Wait here.'

I sat down in the grass. Time had nothing to do with the moving of the hands on a clock. I learnt that while I waited for Julian. I have no idea how long that wait lasted but it gave me a taste of what eternity would be like in hell.

At last I thought I saw him as a figure moved towards me from the direction of the main school building, but as I stumbled to my feet I saw it wasn't him. I had been playing with a stone and now I lobbed it at the magpie that sat laughing in a nearby tree. But I didn't even come close to hitting the damn thing; it just cackled even louder, taking lazy flight, circling overhead before returning to its perch.

There he was, ambling towards me. But I was wrong again. They all walked the same way, as if their legs were too long and needed folding.

Finally I saw him, sauntering across the grass as if he had nowhere in particular to go, hands in his pockets, looking down at his feet and then up at the sky, kicking at a can or something as he went. I felt hot and my watch felt too tight. I took it off and chucked it on the grass next to me. I wanted to run towards him but I forced myself to stay put. He didn't seem to have spotted me.

A lifetime later he was standing in front of me, his hands still in his pockets. I scrambled to my feet. 'Hi.' I was amazed at how in control I sounded.

'Yeah. What is it? David said it was really urgent.'

I opened my hand and showed him the silver charm on a chain inscribed with his star sign, which was Taurus. 'I got it for your birthday but I couldn't wait to give it to you.' I tried to smile.

'Right. Thanks.' But he kept his hands in his pockets.

'Don't you want to put it on?'

'We're not allowed jewellery.'

I wanted to scream at him that they weren't allowed to smoke or fuck either but that hadn't stopped him. 'You can wear it under your shirt.' I undid the lock of the chain and made to put it around his neck but he shied away.

'I'm not really into . . .' he paused and I thought I saw a tiny smirk on his face '. . . medallions.'

I knew that big heavy gold chains and stuff like that were totally out of the question but this was more like a good luck charm. 'It's not a medallion,' I said.

'Right.' He thought of something. 'Actually, why don't you wear it yourself? Like a memento-type thing.'

'I bought it for you.'

He shrugged. I wanted to throw it at him, hard, and watch the blood as the chain slashed his cheek. Instead I just placed my gift in its little box and put the box back in my dress pocket. 'What do you mean, memento? A memento is to remember something once it's gone.' As I spoke I kept my gaze fixed on him. His face seemed to shrink as if I were sucking the air out of it but I went on. 'Rose says you kissed.'

He blushed right up to his hairline. Then he shrugged again. 'Well, did you?'

He looked straight at me, challenging me. 'What if we did?'

My heart, that had been hammering away in my chest, now seemed to have stopped beating altogether. I felt myself go cold and I felt sick. 'You can't have.'

'Oh, come on, Sandra,'

'Why did you call me that? It's Cassandra, not Sandra, you know that. You completely know that.'

'OK then, *Cass*andra. But c'mon, you and I, we weren't serious. I never said we were serious. And you've been practically stalking me since you arrived at LAGs.' He smirked again. 'So what did you expect?'

I stared at him and I don't know what he saw in my face but whatever it was it seemed to scare him. He took his hand out of his pocket and touched my shoulder, a quick touch as if I burnt. 'Don't freak out. I'm sorry, all right. I'm sorry if you thought it was more than that.' Then his face melted into the sweetest smile and my heart came back to life.

I smiled back, putting my hand out towards him. It was going to be OK. I didn't know what had been going on but now it was going to be OK.

'But you know ... Rose ...' he blushed again and still with that sweet smile on his face he shrugged like a coy little boy. 'Well, it's Rose. She's a goddess.' He shook his head in wonderment. 'I honestly never thought I was in with a chance and then it turns out she liked me too. I mean. What would you have done?'

I started screaming and as I screamed I ran at him, hammering my fists against his chest. He tried to push me away but I was stronger than he was and I pushed him to the ground and threw myself down on top of him, screeching and pounding as if I were trying to propel myself down though his thin body and right through to the centre of the earth, where I would lie, quite still.

I must have blacked out because the next thing I knew I was lying alone on my back on the ground, looking up at the laughing magpie. I turned my head and watched Julian lope off into the distance. Maybe he felt me looking at him because he turned and yelled out, 'You're crazy, you know that? Off your fucking head.'

I lay there for a while and then I picked up my watch and got up from the grass.

Thirty-two

Eliza

KATARINA TOLD ME THAT Uncle Ian had insisted on getting up and dressed to greet me. I followed her into the house, that seemed quieter than I had ever found it: no pipes singing, no floorboards creaking as I crossed, no wind whistling through the single-glazed windows. It was, I thought, a respectful, watchful silence as if the house were waiting, not for me, for something altogether more momentous. In the silence my steps grew exaggerated and Uncle Ian called out to me before I had reached the sitting room.

He was in his usual chair by the window. I thought he had lost weight in the weeks since I'd last seen him. His face had the look of an ancient child, his hair stood up in tufts and his eyes were huge behind the reading glasses.

'I'm sorry,' he said. 'She scared you into coming, didn't she?' He nodded towards Katarina. 'Interfering old woman.'

Katarina ignored him like you would a naughty child.

I touched his tissue-paper cheek with my lips. 'I had planned to come over about now anyway. I wanted to see the woods. I remember Grandmother Eva telling Rose and me about the woods in spring.'

'Katarina won't let me go for a proper walk,' he grumbled.

'She's always been bossy but now there seems to be no stopping her.'

Katarina sighed and shook her head. 'I think it's too far and I've told him so but you know, he's a stubborn old man.'

We talked back and forth and eventually it was decided that I would go with him after lunch but that we would turn around the minute he tired.

The sun's rays spread like fingers through the branches of the trees and the air was filled with cracking, snapping sounds. I turned to Uncle Ian, who was walking toddler-stepped by my side.

'Is it really the trees making those sounds? Eva told us about this but we never quite believed her.'

'It's the beech leaves.' He raised a shaking arm an inch or two, pointing towards the canopy of young leaves that seemed to float above our heads like a pale green veil. 'After the long freeze of winter, when the warm sun comes out, the buds burst into leaf like a series of tiny explosions.'

We stood still for a few minutes, listening. Then, as we walked further into the woods we came upon a sea of tiny white star-shaped flowers. 'Vitsippor?' I said. I bent down.

'You can't pick them,' he said, just as I was about to do just that. 'They're protected.'

As we went further into the woods I was careful not to trample the little white flowers underfoot – if you weren't allowed to pick them I was pretty sure you weren't supposed to crush them to death either – but they formed such a dense carpet that I soon had to give up. A bird, a wood warbler perhaps, struck up its song amidst the snap-crackling leaves.

'Let's have a break,' Uncle Ian said. He leant heavily against the trunk of a tree and fished out a couple of plastic cylinders, of the kind used to keep camera film, from the pockets of his jacket. 'Here,' he handed me one.

'I only have a digital camera,' I said.

'It's drink. Film canisters make excellent containers for akvavit.'

As I drained the canister my eyes watered. 'Christ,' I said. 'Let's sit down.'

I took off my anorak, spreading it out on a bit of grass that was more or less free of flowers. I helped Uncle Ian down and then I seated myself next to him on the coat.

'Here, have the second half.' Uncle Ian hauled another couple of film containers from his pockets.

Rose never got to walk in the woods when the leaves opened. Her visits to her grandmother having taken place in either winter or in summer. The thought made me feel like a cuckoo – a great big cuckoo who had taken her place.

'What are you thinking about?' Uncle Ian asked me.

I shrugged. 'Nothing in particular.'

'You were thinking of Rose, weren't you? You know, Eliza, there has to be a line drawn between remembering the past and living in it. She knows you haven't forgotten her.'

I turned and faced him. 'You really do see her?'

He nodded. 'I do.'

'I'm sorry but I find that so hard to believe.'

'I know that too.'

'You're sure it – I mean she – is not some kind of hallucination?'

He smacked the ground with the palm of his hand, crushing a whole host of the protected little white flowers. 'Do you have to argue the toss about everything?' He turned his head as far as his neck would let him, glaring at me sideways. 'Eh?'

'No,' I said. 'Sorry.'

'Then, skal,' he said, raising his plastic cylinder of akvavit to his lips and draining it.

'Skal,' I replied. As the warmth spread down through my chest and stomach I looked around me. 'You can see why people living in a place like this believed there were trolls and elves and huldras. In fact, I would not be at all surprised if there were some of the creatures here now, hiding behind the trees and in the dead tree stumps, watching us.'

'Now who's fanciful,' Uncle Ian said.

I lay down, making a pillow for myself with the palms of my hands. I might have dozed off but just for a moment or two. '"Briar Rose",' Uncle Ian said. And my eyes snapped open. 'That's who you look like.' He sounded triumphant. 'Exactly like Burne-Jones's "Briar Rose" lying there on your bed of flowers. My mother always said that we named you girls wrong. You should have been Rose, she said, and Rose should have been Lily. Briar Rose and Lily White.'

'Like the fairy tale. She had the most wonderful complexion, didn't she? Translucent. Or perhaps pearlescent is an even better word.'

Uncle Ian smiled. 'I never ceased to marvel at how a combination of her mother's and my genes could have produced someone like Rose.'

'I don't remember what Rose's mother looked like.'

'She was striking, I think one would say, rather than beautiful.' He shifted uneasily and made a little grimace.

I asked him if he was all right and he said he thought it was time we moved on. I got to my feet and reached down to help him. He snatched at my hand like a fish snatching at bait and I bent down lower until he got a firm grip of my wrist. I gave a little tug. He remained seated. I pulled harder, gripping his arm with my other hand. I pulled as hard as I dared and he lifted an inch or so off the ground before collapsing back down with a small groan of discomfort.

'One more time,' I said, but still I couldn't get him to his feet. I avoided his gaze. I knew he would feel embarrassed. It was just no good having to be helped, no, worse, *failing* to be helped to your feet by someone you had once dandled on your knee. Or perhaps not dandled exactly, but he had most certainly sent me to my room on at least one occasion. For the purpose of embarrassment it was much the same thing.

Above our heads a pair of magpies squabbled.

'How about I get behind you,' I said and I did just that, hooking my arms under his. I thought my back would go as I heaved him a few inches off the ground and I had to let him slip back down.

'Actually,' Uncle Ian said. 'Why don't we sit here a while longer? It is a beautiful day. The sun still has plenty of warmth in it.'

Sitting back down myself I said that it was indeed a beautiful day and one that it was a shame to waste. 'Anyway, we need to sober up before we face Katarina.'

He smiled a young man's smile. 'You're right about that.'

Of course we would have to get up and leave eventually but how I was going to get him to his feet I did not know. I was thinking that I might make some excuse and sneak off with my mobile to give Katarina a call when Uncle Ian said, 'Was she happy the night she died?'

I started. 'Was she happy?'

'It's a simple enough question, is it not? All I've heard about that day is how she died. I want to know how she lived in those last hours.'

I found myself smiling suddenly. 'I think she was. She was excited about the dance, of course. We all were. And we had decided we were in love. Not that the boys were very important in the scheme of things.' I laughed. 'I would say they were more like extras in our little drama. The main players were Rose and I and of course Romance. She was wearing the dress you had bought for her. Do you remember that dress? And she had flowers in her hair. You should have seen her . . . We had all helped to decorate the assembly hall . . .'

He was asleep. Uncle Ian was asleep, his back against the trunk of the tree, a sweet smile on his face like a child who'd been told his favourite bedtime story. I touched his cheek. It was warm, as were his hands. I decided to let him sleep.

Rose *had* been happy that night. Happy in that fulsome, reckless way you can be when you're very young and everything seems possible and when you really do believe that you are the centre of the universe while all else spins worshipfully around you.

And then there was Ovid. 'Blame it on Ovid.' Had death been a comedy that is what this particular one might have been called, *Blame it on Ovid*. We had been high on nymphs and gods at the time, an ancient menagerie of illusionary creatures to add the already familiar ones given to us by Grandmother Eva.

We had worked it all out. If the boys had not played their part, that is, danced with us, kissed us, done whatever the perfect hero in the perfect romantic novel would have done, by the time the dance was drawing to a close, we would go off to the lake. Portia was going to follow a little later, bringing them with her under some pretext or other. And there we'd be, Rose and I, nymphs as naked as the day we were born, splashing playfully in the dark waters of the moonlit lake. Overcome by our innocent beauty the boys would rush into the water and take us in their arms to be our adoring slaves for ever, or at least to the end of term.

But by ten o'clock the boys had done nothing much more than glance in our direction a few times. Mostly they had just hung around the buffet table, sneaking outside now and then, to swig from some bottle stashed away in the shrubbery. So Rose and I signalled to Portia and then the two of us went ahead to the lake.

We were undressed, ready to get into the water, when we thought we heard them. And I, the begetter of the whole stupid thing had, faced with the reality as opposed to the pretty picture fantasy of appearing naked in front of two boys, lost my nerve.

I grabbed my dress and ran off in the opposite direction.

And then what happened?

I think I called to Rose to come with me and, as I ran off in a muddle of laughing panic, I *think* I believed she was following. Did I hear the splash? I don't know. I might have or else I had simply been told that I would have; either way I no longer knew what was memory and what was supposition. And if I had heard the splash I must have assumed that she had decided to go ahead as planned without her feckless friend. Then she called out something. I do remember that she called out something and I believe that what I heard was her laughing and calling me a wimp. That was what I believe I thought I heard at the time. So, Uncle Ian, I didn't stop. I kept on running.

Then they found her and details that would otherwise not have merited a second thought became weighted with terrible significance and I ceased to be sure of anything at all. I went over and over those moments in my mind, playing out different scenarios until I thought I would go crazy, because in the end both the 'real version' and the 'supposed version' were as familiar as a memory. But the police told me they believed she had been intending to follow when she slipped and fell. No one said but we all knew that while that was happening, I, her best friend, I who loved her, had kept on running.

Thirty-three

Sandra/Cassandra

THE WAY EVERYONE CARRIED on you would have thought they were preparing for the second coming, not a school dance. I wasn't going. In fact I had thought I might kill myself. Hanging most probably, blue tongue lolling, eyes popping; or slitting my wrists, the blood creeping along the bathroom floor, seeping through the gap in the door. Or I could set myself on fire in the hall. Any of those options would have stopped the dance. And I would have made sure everyone knew why I had done it. I would write a letter and I would pin it to my chest. My last words would be a judgement on those who had betrayed me.

What stopped me was the realisation that I wouldn't be around to see them suffer. I think people forget that bit when they go off and kill themselves, I think they forget that they won't actually be around for the fun. But I remembered. Just in time.

And there was something else, a part of me that would not accept that Julian had meant what he said and that he still wanted me. It was a blow when my period arrived, because a baby would have solved everything, but I still could not believe that I wouldn't get him back, one way or the other.

Auntie Gina had sent me a dress for the dance. There was a note too. *Trust your old Auntie Gina; this will knock the socks off the competition and make that boyfriend of yours eat out of the palm of your hand. I wish I were your age again. Have fun for the both of us.*

The dress was a gorgeous metallic blue. It was perfect except for the shoulders. Auntie Gina was a huge fan of *Dynasty*.

Eliza passed my cubicle as I unpacked. I should have drawn the curtain. She poked her head round. 'That's beautiful. Did your mum send it?'

I shook my head. 'My Aunt Gina.'

'Bad Aunt Gina?'

'She's got nicer.'

'May I?' Eliza stepped forward and took the dress, holding it out, inspecting it. 'It's real silk.'

'I'm not wearing it,' I said.

'Why on earth not?'

'Because I'm not going.'

'But you must.' She sat down on my bed, the dress still draped over her arms. 'You mustn't miss the dance.'

'I mustn't do anything.'

'OK, obviously you don't *have* to go but I think you'd be mad not to.' She knitted her tawny eyebrows together in a frown. 'Oh Cassandra, you're not still hung up on ... well, you know, a certain person?'

I forced myself to smile. 'No. Of course not. It's simply that dances and parties and stuff have never been my thing.'

'But ...'

'So what are you wearing?'

That deflected her. 'I'm not sure. I've got the material. It's velvet and sort of moss green. It's from an old dress of my grandmother's. But I haven't decided on the style yet.'

'I'm surprised you haven't gone for the curtains in the common room,' I said. That made her laugh.

'And Rose?' I bit down on the name and had to turn away so that she wouldn't see my grimace.

'Oh, it's lovely. Uncle Ian let her . . .' It seemed to dawn on her that she was being tactless because she stopped herself, saying instead, 'But yours is heavenly too. You're completely going to be the belle of the ball.'

There was no dress in the world that would make me the belle of the ball, not with her and the other princesses around, and we both knew it.

She put her arm round me. 'Do come. It'll be such fun. And there'll be heaps of other people.'

By people she meant boys. I thought for someone so smart she was really very slow. She really had no idea what it meant to properly love someone. None of them did. They were virgins, for a start, even brash, confident Portia. I knew because I'd heard them all talk about it. I asked her, 'Has Rose seen Julian again?'

Her cheeks coloured, clashing with her hair. 'I don't know.'

'Of course you know. How stupid do you think I am?'

'Cassandra, please.' She placed her big hand on my arm.

My face set hard. 'So she has seen him.'

'That's not what I said. I just don't think we should be discussing it. It's their business whether they see each other or not.'

'Them, their.' She spoke like they were already a couple. I slept with him, I wanted to tell her. I might have had his baby. What is Rose's pathetic little flirtation compared to that? But

I didn't say any of that. Because she would tell Rose and then Julian might hear and he'd get even more furious with me and I wasn't going to risk that, not while there was still hope. Instead, I picked up my dress and held it out. 'You're good at stuff like this. Could you do something about the Krystle shoulders?'

She pinched and tweaked at the dress and studied the seams of the sleeves. She looked up and smiled that wide open smile she had which made me think no one had ever been mean to her in her life.

'I could take the sleeves off altogether. It would make it younger and get rid of the shoulder problem.' She stepped back, looking at me now. 'You've got good arms. Yup, that would do it, I reckon.'

I smiled back at her. 'That would be great.'

'So you'll go.'

I nodded.

'Good.' She walked off with the dress in her arms, turning in the doorway to give me another beaming smile.

She brought the dress back the next day. 'Try it on.' She looked excited.

I shook my head. 'I'm sorry. I mean, after you've taken all that trouble and everything, but I've decided not to go after all.'

Her face fell. She looked as if she had failed at something. She held the dress out to me. 'At least try it on. I think it'll be lovely on you now.'

'It's not about the dress. I'm just not feeling well, that's all. The curse. Cramps, nausea, the lot.'

'Rubbish. As Grandmother Eva always says, "Only house-maids have period pains." '

'Well, there you are,' I said. It was quite funny to see how embarrassed she got.

'I didn't mean ... Oh, c'mon.' She stuttered on, turning bright pink again.

I shrugged and gave her a brave smile. 'It's fine. I'm not ashamed of my roots.' That made her blush even more. 'Thank you for doing the dress for me, though.'

As she left she said, 'Maybe you'll change your mind again. I hope so, anyway.'

I drew the curtain across my doorway – the crazy old biddies that ran this place thought proper doors were 'isolating' – and tried on the dress. It was difficult to see because the mirror was so small but what I could see made me realise that she had been right, taking the sleeves off had made all the difference.

I found out about their plan by accident. I was going past Eliza's cube when I heard low voices behind the closed curtains. I checked that there was no one else around and then I listened. That's when I heard the three of them hatching their clever little plan to snare Julian, to take him away from me once and for all. I knew Rose was my enemy but what really hurt was how I had been taken in by Eliza yet again. I know I'd told her I was over him but if she were really my friend she would have known that I was just saying that. She would have known that I still loved him and she would never ever have betrayed me this way.

None of them, not even she, even mentioned me once during their little scheming session. I think that was what made me really hate them, the way I was airbrushed out of the equation. Had they even acknowledged the possibility that I might be a rival – then maybe I wouldn't have had to get so angry.

Thirty-four

Eliza

KATARINA CAME MARCHING THROUGH the fairy-tale woods in a state of high agitation. 'It's damp on the ground. The warmth's gone out of the day. What were you thinking of?'

She got Uncle Ian to his feet with ease and I looked at her and then at me, wondering where the secret of this woman's strength lay. She read my mind and gave me a small smile. 'Training,' she said. 'There's a knack to it like with everything else.'

Once home, she called Hans, the district nurse. He checked Uncle Ian over and pronounced that no ill effects were apparent from the afternoon spent in the woods. I didn't believe in God but that didn't stop me thanking him with all my heart.

I was due to leave the next morning but I was reluctant to go.

'Don't look so worried,' Uncle Ian said.

'We have a very busy period coming up at work and I don't know when I will next be able to take time off and come over.'

'I might come over to see you,' he said to me, with a look at Katarina. When Katarina didn't rise to the bait he said again, louder this time. 'I said, I might go over and see Eliza.'

'I heard you.'

'So why didn't you reply?'

Katarina paused in her dusting and looked at him, her hands on her hips.

'Bloody woman,' he muttered.

'Pay no attention. I certainly don't,' Katarina said to me. 'I'll be in the kitchen if you need me.'

Uncle Ian gave her a long look as she left, then he turned back to me, saying in that same loud voice as if he were hoping she could still hear him, 'Yes, I'd like to see that house of yours.'

'Why are you two bickering?'

'Who's bickering?'

I thought of the stories I'd heard of defenceless old people being mistreated by the very people charged with their care. It was hard to see Katarina in that light but I had to ask. 'She's not bullying you, is she?'

Uncle Ian looked at me as if I'd gone weak in the head. 'Ha. I should like to see her try. No, of course she isn't, poor woman. She gets on my nerves, that's all.'

My shoulders relaxed and I sipped my coffee. I never would have thought it when I first came to the quiet house by the lake but I'd grown to like that bitter brew they served.

'Anyway, where were we?' Uncle Ian said. 'Oh yes, me visiting.'

'There was a time,' I told him now, 'when I thought I might not carry out any of the repairs but just live in the house and give the money to charity.'

He laughed. 'Did you really? So what changed your mind?'

'The realisation that you might do just that, come and visit. Plus I got seduced by the appeal of soft furnishings.'

He started to laugh and then the laughter turned into a coughing fit and I got scared and called for Katarina, who came rushing with a glass of water. 'Drink this, Ian dear,' she said and she held the glass to his lips with one hand, stroking his thinning hair with the other.

The coughing subsided and Uncle Ian sat back in the chair, his eyes closed. When he opened them again he frowned and said, 'Both of you, stop looking at me as if you're measuring me for my coffin.'

'Best to get these things done,' I said.

He glared at me. 'You don't have much of a bedside manner, do you?'

I had been glancing surreptitiously at my watch. The cab was not due for another twenty minutes. It was always the way, it probably was for most people, but however much I dreaded a parting, once that parting was inevitable I just wanted to get on with it, so that I could lick my wounds in peace and start counting down the days until the next meeting. The difference this time was that I feared that for Uncle Ian and me there would be no next meeting.

'I said, don't look so worried. I'll be fine. And Eliza, will you promise me something, me and Rose?'

I had grown used to him speaking as if Rose were only in the next room so I simply told him, 'Of course. Anything.'

'Don't waste any more of your life on regrets.'

I opened my mouth to speak but he raised his hand to stop me. 'To my mind waste should be counted as the eighth deadly sin.' He leant forward and peered at me. 'You think I'm exaggerating?'

I shrugged like a child. 'No. Yes. Perhaps.'

He fell back against the chair. 'You think you owe me something, Eliza? Then you owe me not to waste your life. War, inequality, discrimination, poverty, in the end those things are all about waste. As is failing to live the best life you can. No more, Eliza.'

I put out my hand and took his. Uncle Ian, like my mother, was not much for touching and usually his hand slunk off back to his side like an embarrassed schoolboy, but not this time. 'I promise,' I said. 'At least, I promise to try.' After a couple of minutes we let go of each other's hands and I said, 'But it's an unusual situation; you give me a home and you tell me to have a lovely life and then you somehow make it sound like by accepting your gifts and following your advice I'm doing you a favour.'

'You are. I've come to believe there's a particular hell where all the unused gifts, the wasted opportunities, the ill-spent hours end up, and if you listen hard enough you will hear a terrible wailing and gnashing of teeth.'

I smiled weakly. 'I think I've got it.'

It was his turn to take my hand. 'And don't look so worried. I'll still be here when you come back.'

Now I did smile. 'A bit of a pointless visit if you're not.'

He gave a dry laugh. 'So,' he said. 'Off you go.'

'The car's not here yet.' I had no sooner said that than it arrived, beeping its horn as it came up the drive. I got to my feet and Uncle Ian lifted himself an inch off the chair before sinking back down again. I busied myself checking I had my tickets and my passport.

'Eliza.'

I looked up at him. 'Yes, Uncle Ian.'

'Be happy.'

I nodded.

'You can be a black hole, Eliza, or you can be a candle. Which is it going to be?' I must have looked surprised because he laughed. 'One of Ove's little bons mots.'

'Ah. Still, it makes a corny kind of sense.'

'That's what I thought.' We kissed and I picked up my handbag. Chopin's Nocturne Number 2 was playing on the old-fashioned CD player as I walked from the room. When I got to the door I turned round and we looked at each other. I thought, he knows it too; he knows this is the last time that we'll see each other. I wanted to run back to him and hug him but I knew that if nothing else the shock of such a display of emotion would surely kill him.

'Goodbye then.' I gave a little wave.

He raised his hand. 'Goodbye, Eliza.'

Thirty-five

I RETURNED TO FIND my house on the hill empty of Ruth. She had left a note. *I know you won't approve but I've gone back home. I felt so lonely, that's the honest truth. (Now you're not to feel bad for having left me here. Your godfather has to come first.)*

I went from room to room checking, just to make sure that she hadn't changed her mind and was in fact hiding in some drawer somewhere. Then I phoned her. 'Ruth, are you OK?'

'I'm fine. Everything's fine.'

'Should you have gone back? He might do it again. Is he there with you now?'

'Eliza?'

'Yes, Ruth.'

'I might have overreacted.' She rushed out the sentence as if she half hoped I wouldn't catch it.

'You can't overreact to something like that.'

There was a pause, then Ruth said, 'You can if the whole thing was really an accident.'

It was my turn to pause. 'Right,' I said finally. 'Well, as long as you're all right.'

'I am. And, Eliza.'

'Yes, Ruth.'

'Thank you.'

I put the phone down and went out to the workshop to check on my patients. There were the ones about to be discharged: Annie's jug, an early Staffordshire lion with a bubble-bath mane, and a Moorcroft vase that was my equivalent of Jacob Bauer's 'completely loathsome' patient, hard to care about, yet accorded the best treatment available because that was what the job was all about, doing your best to put right what was broken because it was not your place to judge but to mend. Then came Recovery, objects bandaged with tape, bits held in place with staples, wounds covered but not fully healed: an eighteenth-century Meissen Harlequin figurine playing bagpipes, a large cockatoo with a splendid lemon-yellow comb, a Minton bust of the young Queen Victoria in a sickly shade of blue. Finally came Intensive Care, the pieces that had reached me in the most sorry state, some arriving in bits in a box, some cracked and flayed of whole fields of enamel, and all of them written off by other restorers and sent to me; the last chance saloon for the cracked and the broken.

Once I had finished my inspection and satisfied myself that nothing untoward had happened to my charges in my absence, I telephoned Gabriel and invited him to dinner.

The following day I hurried back from work, practically running from the Tube, so that I would have plenty of time to get everything ready for my dinner. I had told Beatrice, over a Willow Pattern jug not dissimilar to Annie's, about inviting Gabriel home. I expect it was obvious from the way I looked and the way I sounded that it was more than just a dinner, because she had rushed over to me and given me a hug, saying, 'Oh Eliza, I'm so pleased for you.'

I had looked over her shoulder at a set of tiles that I found particularly hideous, just to stop myself from crying. 'I do love my work,' I said.

'That's somewhat of a non sequitur,' Beatrice had said, letting go of me. 'But I'm pleased you feel that way.'

'Oh I do,' I'd told her as I smiled at my poor harried willow lovers.

Back home, as I showered and washed my hair, I thought how proud Uncle Ian would be of me for taking life and all its promise by the scruff and – well, doing whatever you did with a scruff.

I stood in front of my wardrobe, looking in at the rows of dresses. I had taken to wearing dresses in preference to any other clothes back at university. I had realised how convenient life became once you did not have to worry about finding a top. I'm sure that there were people for whom matching a top to a bottom did not constitute one of life's major hurdles but for me the whole thing was a problem I could do without. Tops, were they T-shirts, blouses, sweaters or cardigans, seemed to assume a malevolent life of their own, appearing and disappearing at will, like the Cheshire Cat, never being in the place where I thought I'd left them. They even seemed capable of subtle colour changes so that what was, for example, a sensible navy, turned lilac or violet or heather or some other skittish floral shade that managed to clash with whatever else I tried to match it with. But with a dress you had no such worries.

In the end I plumped for a grey Liberty-print tea-dress. It had short sleeves, and as the evening was turning chilly I added a brown cashmere cardigan. It looked nicer than one might have thought, because there were little brown spots in amongst the grey and white flowers of the dress.

I had already prepared supper, a lamb casserole, and I had some meringues that the packet promised no one would believe were not home-made, waiting in a tin. I would mix those with cream and berries to make an Eton Mess.

I looked out of my bedroom window but of course he was not there yet. He wasn't due for another quarter of an hour. Then I thought Gabriel might find it odd that I'd picked for my bedroom the small room at the top of the house with its peeling paint and wallpaper when there was a comfortable and freshly decorated one on the floor below. So, with my heartbeat speeding up like the steps of a lover, I grabbed the bedding and rushed down to the room where Ruth had slept. I remade that bed and then I hurried downstairs and out to the front garden to pick some early roses to place on the bedside table. As I searched for the blooms Jacob Bauer drove up in his big bad car and barely a minute later I saw Gabriel approach on his bicycle. He had a determined look on his face as well he might; there was a long steep hill to negotiate before you got to the square. I waved at him with my secateurs but he wasn't looking in my direction but at Jacob Bauer, who had got out of his car, stretching and pulling a face as if his back hurt. He should follow Gabriel's example, I thought, and cycle for a change. That would get rid of the beginnings of a belly as well as make him more popular in the neighbourhood.

Gabriel jumped off his bike and called out something and Jacob Bauer turned round, and seeing who it was he raised his hand in a wave and came over. The two men were standing not twenty feet from my garden. I wondered if I should join them but I decided not to. I enjoyed watching Gabriel. I used to do it all the time, not spy on him or stalk him, just sit happily at a restaurant table or wait in some foyer at the theatre or the ballet, watching him stride though the throng, so tall, so handsome, so mine. Of course he was mine no longer. But who knew but that after tonight he might be mine once more. Jacob Bauer had to feel a bit short and plain and heavy-featured when standing next to Gabriel. Though if he did, it didn't seem to concern him. He had a nice smile, though, I noticed. He was smiling now as he was telling Gabriel about something, describing with his hands, even doing a little walk about with a put-on limp. It was work talk, obviously, and I grew impatient, wishing my neighbour would stop monopolising my guest. But Gabriel listened and nodded and smiled back and shook his head and interjected and I thought that at this rate the evening would be halfway over before he had even stepped over my threshold. It used to drive me mad, the way Gabriel would be endlessly polite and attentive to someone he barely knew at the expense of someone close to him, someone like me, for example, who was waiting for him.

Next Gabriel pointed over his shoulder to my house and they both turned round. I ducked and walked, knees bent, head down, to the door, and slipped back inside. I went and sat down at the kitchen table. I started counting to a hundred, thinking that by the time I had got there Gabriel would have torn himself away. But there was no ringing of the doorbell so I thought I'd write my email to Uncle Ian. I had spoken on the phone to Katarina earlier in the day. She had told me he was reasonably well, though tired and spending the day in bed. So I wrote and said I hoped he would be up and about soon and that everything was fine with 'our' house. I finished by telling him that following our last conversation I had invited Gabriel for dinner as getting back with an ex-husband had to count as first-rate recycling, the very opposite of waste.

Once I'd clicked on 'send' I shut down the laptop and went back to the window. It was getting dark but the two men were still chatting. I was about to go the bathroom – not because I needed to but because usually when you waited for the phone to ring or for someone to arrive, you only needed to get into the shower or sit down on the loo and there it was, the ringing phone or the knock on the door – but then I saw Annie running down the path in the twilight. Her father turned round and waved at her, a wide grin on his face, and then he gave Gabriel a pat on the shoulder before hurrying off. I smiled to myself as he picked his daughter up as if she weighed nothing at all and carried her back up the path to their house.

I had seen the back of Jacob Bauer but I half expected Archie to appear and possibly have some sort of seizure just so that Gabriel would be further delayed. But nothing like that happened and at last the doorbell went.

'I'm sorry I'm late.' He pulled off his helmet and tossed it on a chair. 'I got chatting to Jacob Bauer. It's funny how these things happen. I mean, before you told me he was your neighbour I had hardly exchanged two words with the guy but now we seem to bump into each other all the time.'

He leant down and kissed me on the cheek. 'I hope I'm all right like this.' He looked down at his jeans. I assured him that he was.

'I said to Jacob that I can't believe you two haven't met properly yet. In fact I suggested he come over and have a drink with us now but he said he had to help his daughter with her homework. I told him to pop over later if he felt like a nightcap.'

I was on my way into the kitchen and I said, over my shoulder, 'Well, I hope he doesn't.'

'Do you have to be so antisocial?' Gabriel said. 'You never want to see anyone.'

I swallowed and blinked away the hurt. 'White wine all right?' I asked. 'Or would you prefer a vodka and tonic?'

He told me wine was fine.

I grabbed the bottle from the fridge and led the way upstairs to the sitting room.

'No, he's a nice chap.' Gabriel sat down on the sofa and accepted the glass I handed him.

'He's not terribly popular with his neighbours,' I said. 'He drives that great big car and refuses to attend the Residents' Association meetings, plus I know for a fact that he doesn't recycle.'

'Neither do you.'

'Yes, I do.'

'You put batteries in with the normal rubbish.'

'No, I don't.'

'You take them to the recycling point, do you?'

'Almost certainly,' I said. 'His daughter's nice, though. A bit pushy but with a father like that . . .'

'Jacob Bauer isn't especially pushy. Why do you have to be so judgemental? You don't even know the man.'

'All right,' I said, trying to get the evening back on track. 'Fine. I'll wait until I do know him and *then* I'll be judgemental.'

Gabriel didn't look amused. I thought I might tell him that it was only with him that I appeared so critical. There was something about his unreserved enthusiasm that made me want to counter by being negative. It was one of our little ying and yang things, I suppose.

'As I said, the man's actually quite shy.'

'Really.'

'Yes, really.'

A silence followed. I looked down at the rug, counting the embroidered flowers. I got to thirty-three before Gabriel spoke.

'I'm sorry,' he said. 'I didn't mean to snap.'

I smiled at him. 'It's all right.' And my smile grew bigger. 'It's nice to see you.'

He laughed softly.

'What?' I said.

Gabriel shook his head.

'What?' I said again, coming over all coquettish, looking up at him sideways, giving a little shrug.

'Oh, it's just something Jacob said.'

I sat up straight on the sofa and put my feet back down on the floor. 'Jacob?'

Gabriel nodded, and still chuckling he started telling me a seemingly endless story involving a geriatric patient, the man's son, a motorcycle helmet and a very angry staff nurse. I wasn't really listening. Instead, I watched his face as he talked and gesticulated. He was very beautiful. Not many men could be said to be beautiful but Gabriel really was. My mother had made me angry by saying he looked like a male model when she first met him but in the end she had to admit that he had character as well. I realised that Gabriel had finished his story and was looking at me expectantly.

I laughed, assuming the ending of the story had been as amusing as the beginning was supposed to be.

'You think that's funny?' Gabriel looked puzzled. 'I think it's terrifying. If it hadn't been for the staff nurse God knows what might have happened.'

'Did I laugh? Sorry. I do sometimes when something's really sad or terrifying. Don't you remember?'

'No, not really. Anyway.'

I waited but nothing followed. I was growing desperate. Here I was, all set to make the most of life, grab it, hold it, kiss it, remove all its clothes and jump into bed with it, yet nothing was going my way.

'Don't waste any more of your life, Eliza,' I heard Uncle Ian's voice. 'Be a candle not a black hole.' That wasn't much to ask, was it? No, but could I do that one little thing for him? No, it appeared I could not.

Gabriel sat back against the cushions. 'As I said, Jacob and I have been seeing quite a bit of each other lately. We're both involved in a study on bone density. The holy grail, of course, is to encourage bone regrowth rather than just halting the decline and we've had really very good results.'

'I think Uncle Ian might be suffering from osteoporosis,' I said. 'People don't always realise that it can happen to men as well as to women. You do, of course. It's your job, knowing those kinds of things but generally I don't think people are aware of it.'

Gabriel listened politely before asking, 'And how is he doing apart from that?'

I looked away, feeling tearful all of a sudden. 'Not so good. When I left yesterday I suddenly had this overwhelming feeling that I wouldn't see him again. At least not in this life. I don't know what it was exactly but he seemed to grow smaller even in those last few minutes, as if he were disappearing already.' I shook myself and cleared my throat. 'I'm sorry, I don't mean to be morbid. Katarina mentioned an operation but . . .' I shrugged.

'Surgery on the elderly is fraught with risk; that's the problem. In fact that was exactly what Jacob and I were talking about just now.'

'Gabriel.'

'Yes.'

'Can we please stop talking about Jacob Bauer?'

Gabriel frowned. Then he shrugged. 'Sure. What do you *want* to talk about?'

I swallowed an urge to say, 'Me,' and got up instead. 'Why don't we have some dinner?'

On the way to the dining room I checked myself in the hall mirror. I thought I looked like someone dressed for the funeral of a distant relative, suitably glum while not all in black and upstaging the real mourners.

I served the food and sat down. I wanted to be light and cheery, gay, in the old-fashioned Nancy Mitford sense. I wanted to be a woman as light as air in a light as air frock, a cocktail in one hand and a cigarette in the other, throwing back my face and laughing. Then, when I was old I would tell our grandchildren, 'Oh daalings, we were so frightfully gay, Grandpa Gabriel and I.'

I tried to think of something of interest to say. Something uncontentious. 'You know Mrs Turnbull who lived next to us at number five? Well, she died last week.' And I threw back my head and laughed, so frightfully frightfully gaily.

'Are you all right, Eliza? Forgive me for saying so but you've been rather odd all evening.'

I drained the red wine, hoping that following the two glasses of white, it might render me unconscious. 'I'm fine. Just a bit tired, perhaps.'

'This is very good.' Gabriel raised his fork on which was speared a piece of lamb.

'I forgot the green beans,' I said, getting up from my chair. 'I'll go and put them on now. They only take a minute.'

'Really, don't bother. There are vegetables in the casserole. And we've got the delicious bread. Really, this is lovely.'

So I sat back down again. 'Uncle Ian gave me several of his mother's notebooks,' I told him. 'They're filled with stories: fairy tales, myths. He wants me to illustrate them. I never liked the man she used for the published volumes. His work was very seventies brown and orange and almost Stalinist in its lines. You know, the prince sticks his chin out and raises his sword to the skies. And the trolls look rather evil, which I think is wrong. Ugly, yes, cross, yes, but misunderstood I'd always say, rather than evil.'

'Maybe you should do it,' Gabriel said.

'Do what?'

'The new illustrations.'

'I'm too rusty. My technique's not up to it.'

'Don't be defeatist.'

'I'm not. I'm realistic.' But then I remembered Uncle Ian and I said, 'Though I could go back and do some evening classes.'

'That's the spirit,' Gabriel said.

I beamed at him.

Silence fell.

After a while I asked, 'So how have you been?'

'Fine. Busy busy busy.'

'I don't suppose it can be much fun coming home late to an empty flat after a hard day's work and having to cook and . . .'

He looked down at his hands and then back at me. 'Actually, I'm not coming back to an empty flat.'

'You're not.' I swallowed hard. The odds on Gabriel having got a cat were low.

'I'm seeing someone.'

'Ah.'

'She, Isobel, is a registrar at the hospital.'

'Ah.'

'She's divorced, too. She's got a little boy, Edward.'

'Edward,' I repeated. 'Is it serious?'

'We're not living together yet, not officially, but they stay over most of the time. We're looking to get a place together.'

Now he'd got over the hurdle of breaking his news to me he seemed unable to stop talking. They were hoping to find a house in this very neighbourhood as that would be the most convenient both for the hospital and for little Edward's school. Edward was a real bright spark. Just like his mother. Who had this amazing energy and *joie de vivre*. In spite of the fact that her life had not been easy.

I had tried to keep a neutral to interested expression on my face while my heart lurched and twisted in my chest. In the end I couldn't stop myself. 'So she needed you,' I said. 'She needed rescuing.'

He frowned. 'I can see where you're going with this but you're wrong. She's very independent.' His face softened. 'Well, she's had to be, poor little thing.'

'Orphan, is she?'

He looked puzzled. 'No.' Then his brow cleared. 'I'm sorry. I've been banging on rather, haven't I? It's just, well, I'm happy. I've told Isobel, by the way, that you are and always will be very important to me. And she completely accepts that.'

Good old Isobel. In the midst of my misery and my anger I felt this tenderness towards him as he sat there, all excited and pink-cheeked and sparkly-eyed, and so utterly without any understanding.

'In fact, she really wants to meet you.' He relaxed in his chair. 'I can't tell you how relieved I am that you understand.

Then you always were understanding.' He put his hand out across the table and searched for mine.

'Was I?' I fished my right hand up from under the table where it had been scrunching my napkin into a little sweaty ball, and reached out to him. We held hands for a minute or so. Then I eased my hand out from his grip, but reluctantly. I had always loved the touch of his hands, that were warm and dry and a little bit rough. I stood up.

'Pudding.'

He picked up his plate and was about to follow me but I told him to remain seated.

'You're a guest,' I said.

'You've been crying?' he said as I returned. He stood up, taking the bowl of Eton Mess from my hands. 'Oh God, I'm sorry. I thought we were OK. I thought we . . . I mean, it's been three years.' We stood there, looking helplessly at each other. Then I shrugged and turned away but he took a step towards me and hugged me close. I tensed up as I tried hard not to press up against him and my arms remained limp at my sides.

'I really am so sorry,' he said again. 'I didn't realise.'

I freed myself from his awkward embrace and like actors after hearing the word *Cut*, we simply assumed our places. Pushing the bowl towards him I said, 'Don't be sorry. As you say, it's been three years.' Then a little vial of poison burst inside me. 'Anyway, Isobel needs you. Not to mention Little Edward.'

He gave me an uncertain look as he helped himself to the Eton Mess.

I smiled politely. 'Of course, I myself I have gone and contracted leprosy, silly me, careless as ever, but you know how it is? One minute you're fine, then the next your nose is falling off. Plus we've got this termite situation. You know termites, the little guys who chomp their way though large timber structures in the time it takes you or I to eat a spoonful of Eton Mess. They came across with a consignment of bananas apparently and then they were brought to me by Ocado. But it isn't all bad. No, not at all. In fact they could turn out to save everyone a lot of trouble and expense now the council has applied to demolish every house in the square to make way for that much needed bypass.' I gave him another quick smile. 'But enough about me.'

Gabriel was staring at me. Now he put down his spoon and said. 'What are you talking about?'

'Nothing. Only you speaking of poor Isobel reminded me of my own small troubles, that's all.'

'You're being very silly.'

'Sorry.'

'Maybe I should go.'

'Isobel waiting, is she?'

He got to his feet. 'No, as it happens. She's at her own place this week. Half-term.'

'Well, sit down, then, and finish your pudding.'

I watched him clear his plate. He had always had a healthy appetite. After a few minutes I said, 'You mustn't worry, though. I exaggerated when I said my nose might fall off. Your extremities don't actually just fall off when you've got leprosy. No, what actually happens is that you lose all feeling because of the damage to the nerve-endings so you simply don't notice when you chop a finger off while cutting up the carrots or that your nose is being scorched while you bend down to stoke the fire. But as I hardly ever chop carrots, preferring to eat them raw and whole, and as I can never get a fire to take, I'm glad to say that I should be safe.' I got up from the table. 'Coffee?'

He sighed and shook his head. 'I think I'm fine.'

'I've got an espresso machine.'

Once he had gone I went into Ruth's room and stripped the bed, taking the sheets back up with me to my own room. I didn't wash or take my clothes off but just crawled into bed and lay flat on my back, staring at the ceiling and pretending I was counting stars. After a while my eyes were too wet for me to see properly so I closed them and tried to go to sleep.

Thirty-six

THE NEXT EVENING, AS I sat down to write my email to Uncle Ian, I found it hard to know what to say. Should I lie and tell him that the evening had been called off? Or lie and say that the evening had in fact been a roaring success and that Gabriel and I were back together? Or should I not mention the previous evening at all and hope he wouldn't remember that I had asked Gabriel over in a fit of hopelessly hopeful excitement? The one option I couldn't contemplate right then was telling him the truth; that once again I had failed to get my life back on track. 'Be happy, Eliza,' he'd said. Could I not at least do that for him?

The phone went. It was Ruth. She sounded odd. 'Ruth, are you OK?'

'I'm fine.'

'You don't sound it.'

'It's probably the reception. I'm in the car. I'd like you to come over please.'

'Come over where? I thought you said you were in the car.'

'I am. But I'm in the car at home.'

Robert's silver Mercedes was standing in front of the garage, the engine running. It took me a couple of seconds to register that two people, Robert and a woman I didn't know, were pinioned to the garage wall by the front bumper of the large silver car. I ran up and pulled open the passenger door. Ruth was in the driver's seat, her hands clutching the steering wheel, her foot hovering above the accelerator pedal.

'Get her out of there.' Robert's voice was high-pitched with terror, but at least he was alive, as was his companion, because she kept opening and closing her mouth.

'Ruth,' I said, as calmly as I was able. 'Ruth dear, why don't you . . .'

'Brrrm brrrm,' said Ruth, as her foot played above the accelerator.

'Brrrm brrrm, indeed. Absolutely, but why don't you reverse, *very* slowly and carefully away from the garage door.'

Ruth poked her head out of the window and yelled to the woman. 'You hear that, you stupid tart, it's garage. Ga-ra-ge not garridge.' She pulled her head back and smiled at me. 'Sometimes you simply have to make a stand,' she said.

I nodded. 'Of course you do. But why don't you just reverse ever so slowly . . . No, don't touch the accelerator until you've put the gear in reverse. I said don't . . . That's right. Gently. Gently does it.'

It took some doing but I managed to persuade Robert and the woman not to call the police. Instead I got him to pack Ruth a small bag and then I told him that I needed to take the car to drive Ruth and me back home as I didn't think she was in the right frame of mind for public transport.

Ruth did not say one word as we drove though the summer streets of London. I thought she was about to as we passed Camden Lock; for some reason Ruth had it in for Camden Lock, and just then I would have welcomed a comment or two about tattoos and graffiti and perhaps a small follow-on mention about the idiocy of the contemporary art scene. But nothing. Ruth sat bolt upright in her seat, her hands clutched in her lap.

'Goodness,' I said trying to entice her back to normality. 'Will you look at that wall. I wouldn't be surprised if they took it down and rebuilt it as an exhibit at Tate Modern.' When still she said nothing, I pulled out my trump card. 'It'd get the Turner Prize, I bet you anything you like.' But still nothing.

Once back home I helped the silent Ruth into bed and brought her a mug of warm milk with honey. I was about to close the door behind me when she finally spoke. 'Eliza, what shall I do? Where shall I go?'

I swallowed a sigh. 'Don't worry about that. You're obviously welcome to stay here for as long as it takes. Would you like me to call Lottie?'

Ruth shook her head. 'No, absolutely not. Anyway, she's in Chile. What can she do from Chile?'

'All right. I won't.' I took a step back into the room. 'Do you feel like telling me what happened?'

'No.'

'Right. Fair enough. You try to get some sleep. We'll talk it all through in the morning.'

I went out into the front garden. The night was warm and heady with the scent of mock-orange. I stood there for a while, my face raised to the sky, as I attempted and gave up counting the stars. I thought of the lady painter, Marguerite, and her sister Anna. I wondered how much of the garden and the view of the square were the same now as when they had lived here. I wished I could step though a gate in time and visit them. We'd have a cup of tea, discuss the artists of the day and comment on the beauty of our surroundings. 'This is our house,' I'd say. Yours and mine and everyone else's who called it home. We all live on in the fabric of the house, our essence melded with the paints and the varnishes and the very bricks of the walls. Then, and before I took my leave, I would assure them that I would take the greatest care of our little house and pass it on, eventually, in the best possible state.

A lone saxophone began to play, a mellow, lazy blues. At first I couldn't hear where the sound was coming from but as the music rose into a melancholy A flat I realised it came from Number 12. I couldn't tell if someone was playing an actual saxophone, or just a recording, but the sound was good.

I turned my head at the sound of a window being thrown open and saw Archie Fuller's head popping out from his third-floor window with such speed and vehemence I half expected him to call out 'cuckoo'.

Instead he shouted, 'I say, do have some consideration for those of us who are trying to sleep.'

The saxophone responded with a mocking riff – either Archie had made his protest at just the right moment or the music was live. There followed a few last lingering notes and then there was silence. Archie's head was gone, back to bed with the rest of him, I assumed. The lights of Number 12 went out and I walked back inside.

Thirty-seven

Sandra/Cassandra

TO ROSE, JULIAN WAS just the icing on the cake. But he was my lifeblood. Rose didn't love him. She didn't know what love was; she was a child playing an adult game. She would soon get bored with it but by then it would be too late.

The day before the dance, and after nights of lying unable to sleep and with my thoughts whizzing round my head like comets, I felt dizzy with anxiety, but I still had no idea what to do. I just knew that there had to be something.

'If you want something badly enough you'll get it,' that's what my parents always told me. And I'd thought, well, they can't have wanted anything very badly at all. I wanted Julian so bad it felt like my insides were on fire. And it came to me that maybe I should just talk to them, the princesses, be straight, tell them what Julian meant to me and appeal to their better nature. I'd say to Rose, 'Look, you can get any boy you want, so please – don't take him.'

The princesses were crowded into Portia's cube with Celia Hunter and Hannah Maitland. I stood in the doorway, a goblin peering in. Eliza looked up from pinning some kind of crazed corsage to the waist of Celia's frock, and tried to give me a smile with a mouthful of pins. She finished the job and spat out the rest of the pins in the palm of her hand.

'Aren't you going to get ready?' she asked me then turned to the others. 'Cassandra's dress is absolutely gorgeous. Brilliant colour, too.'

I smiled back. Oh, it was easy to be nice, I thought, when you have everything. 'I wanted to have a word,' I said. 'With Rose mainly.'

Rose, who was plucking her already perfect eyebrows, turned round. 'Sure. Shoot.'

'Can I have your tweezers when you're done?' Celia asked Rose.

'C'mon everyone, it's only two hours to show-time,' Portia said. 'I haven't even done my nails. Have you done yours, Rose?' Rose held out a dainty foot. 'You haven't. Well, hurry up then. At least I'm wearing sandals but yours will have to be completely dry.'

'I wondered if we could have a word in private,' I said, looking at Rose. My voice was casual enough but I was looking at her intently, hoping she'd pick up on it being important. She didn't. Nor did anyone else. Not even Eliza.

'Look, Sa . . . Cassandra, can it wait? I've got masses of stuff still to do. We'll talk tomorrow, OK?'

I actually looked quite good once I was dressed and ready. I had used the heated tongs Aunt Gina had given me for my birthday and for once my frizz did resemble golden curls. I used almost an entire can of strong-hold Elnette so as long as it didn't rain the look should last the evening. Beads of sweat kept rising to the surface of my armpits and the palms of my hands. I dabbed them away with a tissue and sprayed on some more of the Fenjal deodorant. It was really expensive and I knew only one shop that sold it, but Julian loved the smell, he had told me.

The party committee had turned the assembly hall into a glittering grotto with the aid of some old sails and a load of fairy lights. It looked pretty cool, actually. Miss Grant, Miss Robbins and Mr Loftus, the three members of staff in charge, were wandering around trying to look as if they were comfortable. Mr Loftus looked ridiculous in a pink shirt and a black knitted tie. Miss Grant and Miss Robbins just looked like they always did but in brighter colours. The boys' coach had arrived but I couldn't see Julian anywhere. I couldn't see the princesses either. I pushed through the throng to the far side of the room but still they were nowhere to be seen. 'Oi, watch where you're going.' It was Celia. I hadn't even realised that I'd bumped into her.

'Have you seen Rose and Eliza anywhere? Or Portia?'

'No. You look weird. Well, weirder. What's the matter?'

I narrowed my eyes at her and she rolled hers and we walked off in opposite directions. I saw Hannah by the drinks table. I waved and called out. 'Have you seen the others?'

'What others?'

I swallowed my annoyance. 'Eliza and Rose and Portia. Why aren't they here?'

'Are you all right, Sandra? You look ...'

'Don't call me Sandra.' The correction was automatic because just then I didn't care what anyone called me as long as by the end of the night he, Julian, was back to calling me his baby.

Hannah shrugged. 'Sorry. Always forget. Anyway, I don't know where they are. Have a glass of punch. It's almost as revolting as it looks.'

'No, thank you.' I continued on until I got to the emergency exit right at the other end of the hall. I slipped outside and the next thing I knew I was face to face with the three of them. 'Hi, Cassandra.' Eliza gave me a big smile as if seeing me was just the best thing that could have happened to her at that moment.

'Don't you look great. Doesn't she look great, guys?'

She, of course, was looking amazing in a medieval-style green velvet dress that trailed the floor. She was wearing a garland of pale yellow flowers and her Titian hair tumbled halfway down her back. Portia had gone for public-school tart in a sleeveless short black dress and sky-high gold sandals and her blonde hair was arranged in an artfully messy up-do. And Rose . . . I found myself smiling at her before I realised what I was doing, because she was so beautiful it was impossible not to. She too was wearing flowers in her hair, white ones to match her dress, that was gauzy and fitted as perfectly as if it had been stitched straight on to her.

As I stared at her my smile died away. She was perfect and there was no boy on this earth who would say no to her. I felt the tears rise in my eyes and I muttered something and hurried off. I heard Eliza call after me but I didn't stop until I was out of sight. The Folly was out of bounds for pupils at all times and for the evening they had gone so far as to fence it off with the kind of tape they use to fence off a crime scene. As if that would stop anyone.

I sat there on the cold stone floor listening to the laughter and the music, which seemed to come from so far away it might have been another planet. The princesses' planet. It wasn't fair, I thought. Rose was not particularly clever or funny or even nice. Other than for the way she looked she was ordinary. But if you were that beautiful people forgot to look for anything else. It was like being royalty. You smiled and everyone felt like the sun had come out just for them. You spoke, and even the most commonplace of your utterances was noted and savoured and brought out again and again to impress at dinners and family celebrations.

I don't know how long I sat there but when I next checked it was ten thirty and the moon was high. I got up and went back into the throng of the assembly hall. I wanted to find Julian. I wanted to see him so badly it hurt but I couldn't see him anywhere. On my way out again I spotted the princesses huddled in the corner by the door. I realised they must be going over their plan, their stupid, unfair, bad plan. Next, Portia peeled off, going off towards the dance floor. It seemed I wasn't the only one looking for Julian. Rose and Eliza waited a couple of minutes before going outside. Another few minutes went by and then I too left, following them.

Thirty-eight

Eliza

THREE WEEKS AFTER THE incident at the garage Ruth went off to stay with her late mother's cousin in the country. 'But don't worry. I'll be back in a couple of days.' She raised her hand out of the car window and gave a little wave as she drove off.

It had taken her several days to be able to tell me exactly what had happened. It was the old story. She had found a receipt in the pocket of a pair of his chinos she was washing. As often as that seemed to happen it struck me that the first rule of conducting an affair would be to do your own laundry. The receipt was for a pair of pearl ear studs. Ruth didn't have pierced ears. This, added to her earlier suspicions aroused by his furtive manner around his mobile and his many work 'dos', convinced her that her husband was indeed guilty. That evening, when Robert got home, she informed him that she was going to stay the night with a friend from work. A friend who could do with some company. 'Her husband's been having an affair,' Ruth told Robert, enjoying the sight of his little old boy's face appearing to crumple and shrink.

Of course, Ruth was not going anywhere. Instead she had collected a blanket, a thermos of coffee and a bag of Devon cream toffees, and gone to hide behind the wheely bins. There she waited. She waited for what seemed like a very long time – how long she wasn't sure as it was too dark behind the bins for her to be able to read her watch. Finally the silver Mercedes drove up with a woman Ruth recognised but didn't know, in the front passenger seat. The woman had the kind of short perky hairstyle given to middle-aged women on makeover programmes. Now Robert was not the kind of man to leave his car out overnight when there was the prospect of rain, so the woman, who had brought an overnight bag, got out to open the garage door. But the door was stiff and heavy and Robert had to get out to help her. That's when Ruth had sprung out from behind the bins and leapt into the car with a speed and agility that had taken even her by surprise.

She didn't regret having given them a fright, she said. But she did mind having driven over a very handy thermos flask. Apparently it matched their cold-box. 'The trouble is,' Ruth had told me, 'that they don't sell them any more, not even at John Lewis.'

I managed to persuade her to see her doctor. He had referred her to a counsellor and already she was much more like her old self.

I spent the rest of the morning, a Saturday, working in my studio. At lunchtime I made my usual cheese sandwich and sat down at the kitchen table with the papers. I was just thinking how nice it was to have silence (Ruth liked to have the radio on right throughout the day) when I heard it: a loud piercing scream and it sounded like Annie. I jumped to my feet and ran towards the front door. There was another blood-curdling scream and I hurtled outside, down the path, out of the gate and on to the square, running towards Number 12. I didn't see the car until it was almost on me.

*   *   *

I came around to find myself on my back on the cobblestones, my head resting on something soft. My neighbour, Jacob Bauer, was kneeling over me, prodding at me, bending my right leg at the knee then twisting it gently at the ankle.

I winced.

He gave me a quick smile. 'Sorry.' He stared into my left eye and then he stared into my right eye. He raised my head very slowly a couple of inches off the ground and rested it back down again.

I remembered. 'Is Annie all right?' I tried to sit up but he stopped me.

'Annie? Why shouldn't she be?' He leant down and peered into my eyes again, as if checking for leaks. 'At least she was a moment ago. I asked her to go and fetch a blanket.'

'But she's OK? She was calling for help.'

His dark eyebrows knitted together. 'Annie is fine. How is your vision? Blurred at all?'

'No.' I tried to shake my head but it hurt.

'You hit the back of your head when you fell.'

'It *was* Annie. I'm sure of it. And she was calling for help.'

'How many fingers?' He raised his right hand and held up three, no, four fingers. It was a well-formed hand (you learnt to study hands at art school as they were amongst the most difficult parts of the human anatomy to depict). Both hand and fingers were covered in fine dark hair and the nails were clean and very short.

'Three,' I said.

He nodded, then he turned round. 'Ah, there she is.'

Moving towards us at a stately pace down the Bauers' garden path was a large white cloud with Annie's head on top. I tried to sit up but was stopped yet again by her father. As the apparition got closer I realised that it was only Annie carrying a large duvet. Her father relieved her of her burden.

'You couldn't find anything larger?'

Unaware that she was being teased, she shook her head. 'No. This is the biggest and softest.'

He gave her a quick smile before growing serious once more. 'Annie, did you yell out for help just now?'

'No.'

'Only Mrs . . .'

'Eliza,' I said. 'Eliza Cummings. I recently moved into Number 2.'

'That's a good sign, isn't it, Daddy? That she remembers her name and where she lives?'

'Absolutely. Anyway, Eliza says she's sure you did.'

'Oh.' Annie shifted from one sandalled foot to another. 'Maybe, then. Maybe I was playing.'

'Ah, playing.' He glanced up at her while taking my pulse. His hand was dry and pleasantly cool.

'I might have been playing Muggers.'

'God in heaven, Muggers? Is that a game?' He rolled his eyes. They were rather beautiful eyes, I thought, as he let go of my wrist. Grey-brown, deep-set and very clear, and his gaze was straight on steady. I was beginning to see why Gabriel liked him.

'Goodness gracious me, that was a lucky escape.' It was Archie Fuller steaming towards us, breathless with excitement.

I gave him a broad smile, 'Well, hello, Archie, how nice of you to join us.'

Jacob Bauer swallowed his obvious irritation over the arrival of our neighbour and gave him a curt nod before saying to Annie, 'Remember the little boy who cried wolf?'

'Yes.' She was looking at her feet and kicking at a small stone but her cheeks were colouring and I had a feeling she was near to tears.

'Well, then, remember it better. Mrs Cummings had a nasty accident, running to your rescue.'

'If you hadn't managed to brake,' Archie Fuller said. He shook his head emphatically enough for me to fear it might come off and roll down to lie next to mine on the cobbles.

I managed to sit up. 'Don't make her feel bad,' I hissed at Jacob.

'Lie back down, please. Anyway, why shouldn't I?'

'She's upset,' I mouthed. 'Don't make it worse. You mustn't make her feel guilty.'

'A little well-earned guilt never hurt anyone. Anyway, there looks to be no sign of spinal injury and I'm fairly sure you're not concussed so I don't think we need an ambulance. Still, Annie and I will drive you down to the hospital just to make sure. And I should call the police.'

'Why?'

'Any accident involving injuries has to be reported to the police.' He picked up his mobile.

'No need,' Archie said. 'You had managed to brake; a sharp swerve followed by an emergency stop, very impressive bit of driving, I must say, so in effect your car was already stationary when Eliza ran into it. I saw it all from my window. I don't mind telling you that for a moment there I thought we were going to have a death in the square.' He sounded so regretful that this had not been the case that I felt I ought to apologise for disappointing him.

But he carried on, 'If only Eliza here had been able to execute those same manoeuvres on foot, eh.'

Jacob Bauer frowned. 'I don't care about that. The thing that matters is that Eliza hasn't come to any serious harm.'

And he phoned the police anyway. 'May I sit up now?' I asked him as he dialled.

'No,' he said.

It did not take long for the police car to arrive and despite Jacob Bauer having told them it was not an actual emergency the car had its blue light flashing. I found that quite exciting. ' "Therefore, send not to know for whom the blue light flashes, it flashes for thee." '

'What's that?' He glanced down at me, that small frown knitting his dark brows together.'

'John Donne,' I explained. 'Or at least, John Donnish.'

Next, a policewoman was kneeling at my side, asking me questions. She took my details and those of Jacob Bauer. She asked if there were any witnesses to the accident other than us. Archie stepped forward with the air of a sergeant major presenting his troops.

'That would be me, ma'am.'

The WPC got to her feet. 'Right, sir.'

Archie told his story with a great deal of dramatic flurry. 'Shooting out of her gate ... first-class driving ... Angels watching ... bump ...'

Annie was crying properly now and finally her father noticed and took her in his arms. 'It's all right, darling. It's all right.' He kissed the top of her dark head. 'Don't worry, little one. You weren't to know.' It made me smile. I was amazed that someone as gruff-looking could sound so soft.

The WPC shot them an enquiring glance and I quickly explained that I had simply mistaken childish play for a call for help and had rushed blindly out on to the road. 'It was no one's fault but my own,' I said. At this Archie nodded vigorously and I felt a moment's irritation with him for being so ready to leap to Jacob Bauer's defence, however rightly, when he had done nothing but complain about the man since the first day we met.

The WPC looked even more puzzled and I explained further, saying that I had been feeling a bit tense of late, as I had a sick relative in Sweden and . . .

Having established that Jacob Bauer did not wish to make a complaint about me hurling myself at his car and I did not wish to make a complaint about his car being in my way as I hurled, she left.

Jacob Bauer helped me into the front seat of his car, having first blocked Archie as he tried to get into the back. As we set off, Annie, strapped in at the back, seemed quite recovered, going so far as to say, in the manner of a hostess handing out the sherry, 'Well, isn't this nice?'

'How did you manage to stop like that?' I asked him. 'I mean you usually drive quite fast.'

'Cat,' he said, keeping his eyes on the road. 'It came shooting out of nowhere just before you did.' He turned briefly and grinned at me. 'I reckon we owe that cat.'

'I'll erect a statue in the square,' I said.

The triage nurse greeted Jacob Bauer with a cheery 'Can't keep you away from the place, can we, Mr Bauer?'

'Daddy ran Eliza down in his car,' Annie informed her.

'Why, thank you for sharing that,' her father said. Annie looked offended.

'He didn't really,' I said to the nurse. 'At least, it wasn't his fault. Luckily, there was a cat.'

'Right,' she said and I saw her glance at Jacob Bauer. I decided that maybe I was feeling a little tired. It had been a shock after all.

As I was taken through to X-ray Jacob Bauer asked if he should phone Gabriel. I told him not to. I must have spoken more vehemently than I had intended because he shot me a curious look but he didn't argue. Instead he said he and Annie would wait and take me home when I was through. 'I'll tell them to let me know when you're done.'

'I've taken up enough of your time,' I said. 'I'll get a taxi.'

'We won't hear of it,' Annie said.

'That's right,' Jacob Bauer said. 'Annie and I won't hear of it. Anyway, I've got some paperwork I can get on with.'

'Me too,' Annie said.

As I waited I picked up the newspaper left on the chair next to me. It was not a paper that I usually read, preferring as I did my death and mayhem in a more respectable packaging. The front-page headline shouted, 'Soap Star in Posthumous Murder Confession!' I turned to the back pages to do the Sudoku – I could never manage the broadsheet ones. This one, though, I managed in ten minutes. I started to flick back through the pages, each one making an art out of highlighting the personal above the general, the minor misfortune above mass suffering. I got to the story behind the front-page headline. It turned out that the actress responsible for the 'beyond the grave confession' was none other than Archie's soap star, Cass Cassidy. I wondered if I could take the paper away with me to show him. I didn't think he usually read this particular newspaper.

Then my name was called and I quite forgot about Archie and left the paper behind on the same chair from which I had picked it up.

Thirty-nine

JACOB BAUER HAD BEEN right to believe there was nothing much wrong with me: some bruising to the back of my head – no concussion, though – and some more and heavier bruising on my right foot and ankle.

I couldn't see him or Annie as I limped back out into the reception area, when I heard a child's voice call my name. It was Annie, of course; little mosquito girl, all eyes and knees and feet, appearing to skim the floor as she ran towards me.

'We told you we'd wait,' she shouted. 'Daddy's got the car ready outside.'

It made me feel warm inside to have someone waiting to take me home.

'I'm sorry,' Annie said, putting her hand in mine. It was so thin I feared my fingers might meet through the soft flesh as I clasped it back.

'What are you sorry for now?' I asked her.

'For scaring you and making you run out in front of Daddy's car.'

'We've been through that. It's my fault if I don't look where I'm going.'

Back at the house, Jacob Bauer and Annie insisted on helping me inside. I assured them yet again that I was perfectly able to manage by myself, but he made me sit down in the kitchen with my foot on a stool. Next, he removed the bandage, and having found the freezer without asking, which was cleverer than it might sound as it was built into a kitchen unit, brought out a packet of peas and placed it on my naked foot. I winced and Annie started giggling.

'Would you like a cup of coffee?' I asked her father.

'I'll make it,' he said. 'You stay exactly where you are.'

'There's apple juice in the fridge,' I said as I watched him move round my kitchen as if he had a map. 'For Annie.'

He didn't need to ask me where anything was but just went about finding it all, mugs, milk, spoons, and he seemed to have no problem working the espresso machine. 'Espresso? Cappuccino?' he asked me.

'Cappuccino, please.'

'Yes please, Daddy,' Annie said. At least the one he made for her was mostly milk.

'You've done a brilliant job on this place,' he said as he sat down. 'It's quite an undertaking refurbishing a house like this while retaining its character.'

I felt ridiculously pleased at the compliment. 'I did it together with my godfather,' I said. 'He's got excellent taste. And lots of money,' I added. Then I regretted having sounded tacky, but Jacob Bauer didn't seem to have noticed.

We had barely started on our coffee when the doorbell rang. Annie ran to get the door. 'It's Archie,' she shouted from the hall.

Jacob Bauer leant across the table and whispered, 'I could say you're not allowed visitors.'

I gave him a quick smile and shook my head. 'Come on in, Archie,' I called. 'We're in the kitchen.'

I asked if he would like a cup of coffee, if Jacob wouldn't mind making him one. He told me that considering the hour he would prefer tea if there was a pot going.

He was holding a copy of the newspaper I had been reading earlier. Following my gaze he handed it to me. 'It's for you. Funny how it was only the other day we were talking about her. Terrible story. Dreadful. Thought it might cheer you up. Who would have thought.'

'That's so kind of you. Actually I read part of the article at the hospital but I didn't have time to finish it.'

'That's what happens when you've got friends in high places,' Archie said, looking at Jacob Bauer. 'The rest of us would have had time to read the whole newspaper. Speaking of which, I'm hoping to get hold of a copy of the book today or tomorrow.'

'The autobiography? How? It isn't out yet.'

Archie touched the tip of his nose. 'Old Archie's got his contacts,' he said. 'Friend of mine's in the second-hand book business.'

'Do you know who they're talking about? Jacob Bauer asked Annie.

Annie shrugged. 'No idea.'

My head was beginning to hurt again and my foot was throbbing and I wanted to go and lie down but that would leave poor Archie with gossip interruptus and that would be unkind. 'Do tell us more.' I gave him an encouraging look.

Archie sat down, his legs splayed, and a look about him as if he were settling down for the evening. 'Most of his stock are review copies but this one was very hush hush, for obvious reasons.' He winked at me.

Out of the corners of my eyes I saw that Annie too was attempting, but failing, to wink. 'Daddy, how do you do it?'

Jacob Bauer winked.

'Embargoed,' Archie said. He tasted the word and seemed to like it. 'Oh yes, embargoed,' he repeated. He sat back in the chair and looked at me expectantly.

'But Daddy, how do you do it?'

The sun was pouring in through the south-west-facing window and the warmth, combined with the effect of the strong painkillers, was making me sleepy. I opened my eyes wide, imagining that each of my eyelids was being held up by a very small, very helpful imp. One had a green hat on and the other one's was red. 'Gosh. So how come he's able to get hold of a copy?'

'Ah,' Archie sat back in the chair. 'You may well ask. But you see he in turn has a contact who works in a warehouse. For books,' he added.

Jacob Bauer was fidgeting, tapping his finger on the table, twisting round to look out of the window and Annie, I realised, had left the room. With an uncharacteristic sensitivity to moods Archie seemed to realise that he was losing the attention of his audience.

'Anyway, he's getting it for me.' Then he shook his head and said, as he had when he had first arrived, 'Terrible story. Dreadful.'

'Well, well,' I said. I was about to nod off again but seeing the way Archie seemed to shrink before our indifference I gave myself a little wake-up shake and tried to look alert and interested, 'So you really think it's true? She actually killed someone?'

Archie straightened up and he looked purposeful once more. 'I fear so, Eliza. I very much fear so. And now it turns out that Cass Cassidy was not even her real name.'

'That happens all the time with actors, though, doesn't it,' I said.

'It'll almost certainly turn out to be some kind of a stunt to help sales,' Jacob Bauer said. 'So I really wouldn't worry one way or another.'

Just then Annie returned. Walking up to me she hissed in my ear, 'It's finished, isn't it, the jug?' I felt a little shower of spittle hit my skin and some puffs of hot heavy breath and for some reason this made me smile. I whispered back. 'Just need a final clean-up. You didn't touch anything, did you?'

'Of course not.'

Jacob Bauer had grown alert once more. 'What have you been doing, Annie? Have you gone somewhere you shouldn't?'

'Not at all,' I said. 'We've got a little project going, that's all. Annie was just checking on its progress.' I turned back to Archie. 'I'm so sorry, we never got you that tea.'

Before Archie could reply Jacob Bauer made a great show of looking at his watch and said, 'And now it's too late. Well, there we are.'

Archie opened his mouth to speak when Jacob Bauer continued. 'Eliza must rest. Doctor's orders.' He got to his feet and Archie followed, but reluctantly.

'How's Julie?' I asked him, wanting to finish the visit on a bright note.

He didn't quite look me in the eyes when he replied. 'Oh, she's very well, thank you. Both of them are. Of course, they're extremely busy. I was to have visited but . . .' His voice trailed miserably.

'Well, thank you again for bringing the paper,' I said. 'Just what I needed to cheer me up.'

'Murder has that effect on some people,' Jacob Bauer said as he opened the front door. I frowned at him. He really should stop tormenting poor old Archie.

'That's not what we meant and you know it,' I said. Then I couldn't help smiling because he was pulling funny faces behind Archie's back. 'I was of course referring to the thoughtfulness of the gesture of bringing me the paper,' I said. 'It's what I love about the square, the neighbourliness.'

Archie got back some of his swagger. 'Community spirit doesn't happen by itself, of course. We all have to do our bit.'

Having managed finally to shoo Archie out of the door Jacob Bauer walked back with me into the kitchen to clear away the cups and to ask if I needed help with supper or getting upstairs or anything else. I assured him I was perfectly able to manage on my own and he looked relieved.

'I'm so sorry,' I said. 'This business has taken most of your day. I'm sure you had other things planned for your day off.'

'Nothing at all,' he said.

Annie nodded. 'I like it when things happen.'

'Fair enough.' I held her back for a moment as her father walked out into the hall. 'I'll bring the jug over as soon as I've done that last little bit.'

'You'll bring what over?' Jacob Bauer asked.

'He hears everything,' Annie said.

'And I heard that too,' he said. 'Now come on, Annie, we must get back.'

We joined him in the hall. 'Foot raised, continue with the ice and phone if there's anything. Anything at all. I mean it.'

The doorbell went again. This time the visitor was Sheila. I noticed that her cardigan was buttoned the wrong way. 'There you are.' she stepped inside and grabbed Annie, pressing her close. Annie squirmed and broke free.

'Is there a problem, Sheila?' Jacob Bauer asked. His voice was friendly enough but I detected irritation behind the even tones.

'Well, thank God, you're both all right. I had no idea anything was wrong until Mr Fuller told me just now. Someone could have phoned, you know.'

'It's your day off,' Jacob Bauer said.

Sheila's flat cheeks coloured and she swept at her hair. 'So I shouldn't care, then, should I? That's how it should be from now on? Oh, it's my day off so I don't care.' She glared at me. 'What were you thinking of? I mean, really? Anything could have happened.'

Before I had a chance to reply Jacob Bauer turned to me and said, 'I'm very sorry about this. I'll explain to Sheila how this was not in any way your fault.'

And they were gone, Annie being the last out of the door and giving me a thumbs-up sign as she left.

I sat in the kitchen as dusk fell, watching as the lights came on in the windows of the houses around me. For a moment I felt happy, part of the world around me, rather than some undeserving hanger-on. Then I thought how stupid I was, how clumsy. Sheila had been right to be angry with me. Anything could have happened. Jacob Bauer could have driven straight into a lamp-post or into another car in his efforts to avoid the madwoman running to the rescue of someone not at all in distress. And if Annie had needed help, and if I had managed to save her rather than endanger her father, would that have wiped my slate clean? Of course not. Rose would still be dead. Rose was always still dead.

The next morning I was woken by the phone. It was Katarina. She was calling to tell me that Uncle Ian had passed away in the night. 'There was no pain, no trauma,' she said. 'In fact, I think he was talking to Rose.'

Forty

Sandra/Cassandra

IT WAS LIKE SOME cheesy film; moonshine and laughter and dancing. I had followed Rose and Eliza to the part of the lake where the shore became a tiny cove. If they really went into the water after the winter we'd just had, they'd be crazy.

I hid behind a clump trees and watched. I didn't have a plan. I didn't know what I would do when the boys turned up. I just knew that I needed to be there. To put things right.

'What about here?' Rose called to Eliza, and she stepped into the old wooden rowing boat that lay stranded amongst the reeds. 'Lady of Shalott.'

'You're a crap swimmer. If you drift off don't expect me to jump in to save you.'

'I'm not a crap swimmer.' Rose disappeared inside the boat; next, her pale arm dropped over the side and her little hand gave a feeble wave. Then she laughed. Now her dress flew over the side like a big flappy white bird, landing on the low hanging branch of a birch tree. I felt like calling out to her not to be so careless. That dress must have cost a fortune. Now Rose's head appeared. 'Your turn, Eliza.'

Eliza was standing not that far from where I was hiding.

She was laughing so hard she was barely able to reach the zip at the back of her green dress.

I felt like two people. One, the one I longed to be, wanted to laugh with them and be angry with no one. That me was all pink and soft inside. The other me, the one that made sure we stayed hidden behind the clump of trees, was mud-dark and foul like a smoker's lung.

'Look out,' Rose threw her shoes over the side of the boat followed by her bra.

Eliza stepped out of her dress, folding it and placing it on a flat stone. She took off her shoes and put them next to the dress. She had stopped laughing.

Rose stood up in the boat and I almost cried out. All she had on was a tiny pair of pale blue lacy knickers and that garland of flowers in her dark hair. Her body was perfect. Her breasts were high and round with pink nipples. Her waist was tiny, her legs were long and shapely and her skin was pearlescent. My stomach churned. I knew I was about to lose everything. Once Julian saw her like that, he would never want me again.

'Hurry up,' she called. 'They'll be here soon.'

Eliza still had her watch on as well as her knickers and bra. Her garland had fallen off when she took her dress off. She checked the time. 'Not yet.'

'I'm getting goose-pimples,' Rose said. 'That won't be a good look. C'mon. Strip.'

Eliza giggled as she slipped off her bra. She sounded nervous which was unlike her. I hadn't had her down as a prude.

By any standards but those of her friend, Eliza was beautiful, but because Rose was perfect Eliza's flaws showed up more. Her breasts were too small and I'd never noticed before but she was a tiny bit knock-kneed. The nice me liked her better for the fact that she wasn't perfect. The other me had to cover her mouth to stifle a giggle of pleasure because of it. Then she stepped into the moonlight and I hated her because she was still ten times lovelier than I'd ever be.

Rose jumped out of the boat and they ran towards each other and took each other's hands and danced round and round like demented fairies. When they got out of breath they flopped to the ground and lay there laughing. I closed my eyes and imagined running them over with the school lawnmower.

I must have stepped on a twig. I ducked back behind the trees but Eliza had sat up. 'Hush,' she said to Rose. 'It's them.' She reached out and grabbed her dress and got to her feet.

I made sure I didn't make another sound.

Rose listened for a moment. 'No, must have been an animal or something. What's the time now?'

Eliza checked her watch again. 'No, not yet. Anyway, Portia's always late.'

Rose grabbed her hand. Nodding towards the lake, she said, 'Let's go.'

Eliza held her back.

'What?' Rose turned round.

Eliza was bobbing up and down, crossing and uncrossing her legs.

'You can't go to the loo now,' Rose hissed.

'I don't need the loo.'

'So what's the matter? You look bonkers.'

'I'm scared. No, not scared, well . . . I feel silly. This is silly.' She gesticulated at her near-naked body.

'It was your idea,' Rose said.

'I know, and I'm sorry but I don't want to now.' She sounded close to tears. 'I don't know what got into me. I'm not a naked sort of person.'

'Well, I am,' Rose said. There was a pause and then she said, 'Do what you like but I'm going through with it.'

Eliza started walking off towards the path. To scare her some more I took a couple of steps on the spot before crouching down behind the clump of bushes. Eliza's steps hastened to a run. She called over her shoulder to Rose to follow. But Rose stayed where she was, stretching and pirouetting. Then she laughed and called back. 'You're such a wimp, Eliza Cummings.'

With that she ran back to the boat and stepped inside. A moment later her hand appeared, holding the blue lace knickers. I watched as they dropped over the side and on to the ground.

I looked around me but there was still no sign of Portia and the boys. I took a deep breath and stepped out from my hiding place. 'Rose.'

Her dark head popped up, her mouth open in surprise.

I walked closer. 'Don't do it,' I said.

'Don't do what? Anyway, what are you doing here? This is private.'

'I know all about your stupid little plan. So don't.'

'Don't what?'

'Don't take him. Don't take Julian. You can have anyone. You don't have to have him.'

'Oh Sanders, don't be so melodramatic. Anyway, you can't *take* people. They either want to be with you or they don't.'

'Julian wanted to be with me until you started chasing after him.'

'Me chasing him? My God, coming from you.' She laughed her pretty, bell-clear laugh. 'Don't be silly, Sanders. And could you please hand me my dress?'

'Don't call me Sanders. Or Sandra. And you don't know anything.' I felt close to tears but I fought to hold them back.

'Oh for heaven's sake, *Cass*andra, you don't think doing it with you meant he *liked* you.'

I felt cold. Not ordinary cold but corpse cold. 'You know about that? You know we . . .'

Rose interrupted. 'Of course I know. Everyone does. Now please go away or at least hand me my dress. They'll be here any moment and we'll look pretty suss like this.'

'You're lying.' I walked closer. 'You're just guessing. Julian . . .' I paused, drawing comfort from saying his name '. . . Julian didn't want us to tell anyone until we were ready.' I grabbed the dress from the branch, not caring that it snagged. 'Here.' I walked right up to the boat and stared down at her. She reached out for the dress. I pulled back.

'Admit you lied.'

Rose's face grew sad. 'Oh fuck, I'm sorry. You really like him, don't you. Shit.' I could hear the pity in her voice.

'Don't take him,' I said again.

'Oh God. Oh for heaven's sake.' She paused. When she spoke again her voice was low and perfectly kind. It was the kind of voice you employed when explaining something completely obvious to someone completely dense. 'Don't you get it? He doesn't even like you. I mean, he really doesn't like you. Look, Cassandra, I'm not being mean. I'm telling you so you don't make an even bigger fool of yourself than you have already.'

I think there were mosquitoes. It was early for mosquitoes but they were there, I could feel them all across my forehead.

'Dress please, Cassandra.' Rose put her hand out. She was beginning to look worried.

'What do you mean, me making an even bigger fool of myself?'

Now Rose got angry. She made an attempt to get out of the boat but I got there first and I kicked the side. It rocked and she stumbled backwards ending up on her behind.

She looked pretty silly sitting there, butt naked and with a surprised look on her face. 'For Christ's sake, what do you think you're doing?'

'What did you mean?'

She got back up again. 'Just give me a hand out of here and then we can talk.'

'No.' I gave the boat another kick.

'All right, all right, you asked for it. Julian's been telling everyone. About your special underwear and how you moan and cry and cling to him and how after the first time he actually felt sick.' She stopped, her eyes widening as if she realised that she had gone too far.

But I felt calm. 'He said he felt sick. He felt sick after we had made love.' I gave the side of the boat one more kick and this time she fell hard. I heard the thud as the back of her head hit the deck. I went up to the water's edge and peered down at her. She must have knocked herself out because she was lying stock-still, looking paler than ever and kind of silly with the garland of flowers slipped down over her nose. 'You want to be the Lady of Shalott,' I whispered softly. 'Well, you're welcome.' And I gave the boat one more shove. As it floated away I looked around me, listening, but there was no sign of anyone coming.

I took off my shoes and tights and after a moment's hesitation, my dress, and waded into the water. It was ice-cold but I didn't mind. Instead I ducked under the boat and with the water taking much of the weight, turned it over.

I didn't wait around. Instead I got back on land and I used Rose's white dress to dry myself off. I put my clothes back on and without a backwards glance I ran off into the woods.

Forty-one

I WAS IN MY cubicle, already in my pyjamas and reading in bed, when the screaming and wailing began. I noticed, with interest, that I wasn't deemed worthy of having the news told to me until practically every member of the lower sixth and most of the upper sixth had been informed. It was Gillian Taylor who told me in the end. She practically tore the cubicle curtain off the rail in her excitement.

'You haven't heard?' She stared at me as I sat calmly turning the pages of my book.

I took my time looking up. 'Heard what?

'Oh my God, you *haven't* heard? It's Rose.'

I sighed. 'What about Rose, Gillian?'

'She's dead.'

I waited a moment or two before saying, 'Rose is dead. Are you sure?'

Gillian flung her arms out. 'Of course I'm sure. It's just awful. They found her in the lake.'

'In the lake? What on earth was she doing there?'

'Apparently she and Eliza were going for a late night swim.'

'A swim? The water's freezing.'

'Exactly.'

'And what about Eliza? I mean she was there, you say.'

'She's hysterical.' Gillian drew out the word for maximum effect. 'They've had to give her something to calm her down. Anyway, it looks like Rose stayed behind on her own, mucking about in some leaky old boat and it capsized and she drowned.' Gillian's eyes were bright with the excitement of it all. She didn't actually seem that upset, though. She was about to sit down on my bed but I gave her a look and she straightened up.

'That really is terrible news,' I said. 'Poor little Rose.' I reached for a tissue and blew my nose. 'Just terrible.'

'I know. And her father is out of the country and they haven't been able to get hold of him so Miss Philips is going mental.' She looked at me, her head to one side. 'You're in shock, aren't you? My mum says that when people are in shock they often act really calm.'

I nodded and dabbed at my eyes. 'Yeah. I think I am. Do you mind, Gillian, but I'd like to be alone now.'

'Are you sure? I can stay if you like. I'm really good in a crisis.'

By now I had managed to squeeze out a couple of tears. I gave her a brave smile. 'Thank you but I think I just need to be left with my grief.'

Gillian nodded, a self-important look on her face. 'Well, if you're sure. But you know where I am if you need me.'

'Thank you,' I said. She was still hesitating so I waved the tissue at her. 'Bye, Gillian.'

'Oh, right. Night, then.'

Of course no one bothered to ask me if I knew anything, not the police nor any member of staff, nor any of the girls. It was really quite funny. I mean, I was the one person who knew exactly what had happened but no one thought to ask me.

Eliza was allowed to go home. When she got back a week later she looked like her own ghost. Her hair had lost its shine. Her complexion was grey-looking and her freckles stood out like a rash. I didn't go up to her at supper but waited until we were getting ready for bed.

'May I come in?'

She was sitting on the floor, her back against the bed. She looked up. 'Sure.'

I sat down next to her. After a while she said, 'I never mended her mug.'

'Oh well. I don't suppose that matters now.'

She turned her big, pink-rimmed, puffy eyes on me. They had a really weird look in them; like she was watching a horror film. 'I promised her I'd do it.'

'I wouldn't worry about it,' I said.

Eliza kept staring at me and I was beginning to feel spooked. 'I promised her,' she said again and then she started crying, sobbing; grating sobs that made her whole body shudder.

I looked at her for a while. Then I said, in my nicest voice. 'What happened? What happened down at the lake? I mean, I thought you were there with her.'

Eliza yelped in distress. I didn't want anyone to come in and check on us so I tried to calm her down, stroking her hair and telling her 'hush'. For a moment, as she rested her head on my shoulder, I wished I really were her friend. But it was too late for that now.

'I'll get you a clean tissue,' I said, getting up. I knew she kept a box in her bedside locker.

'We were just mucking around,' she said. 'We wanted the boys to find us.' She suddenly looked embarrassed. At least she was aware enough to realise that her stupid little plan to snare Julian for her friend might not be exactly popular with me.

I smiled what I hoped was a gentle understanding smile. 'Don't worry. None of that matters now.'

Eliza looked at me as if we were on the same page and reached over and put her big hand on mine. 'No, no, it doesn't.'

I waited another moment before asking. 'So how come you weren't there when it happened?'

She groaned and buried her face in her hands.

'You don't have to talk if you don't want to but everyone says it helps,' I said, my voice brisk and helpful like Miss Philips's in a crisis.

She didn't look up. 'I left.'

'You left? Right. So the others had arrived.'

'No.' The word was a whisper.

'Okaaay. So you just left her there – on her own.'

Eliza took her hands away from her face and stared at me. She looked as if she were about to start screaming and I thought I might have gone too far. But she simply nodded, mute.

'You mustn't beat yourself up about it,' I said in my nice brisk voice. 'I mean all right so it was dark and everything but you weren't to know she'd capsize.'

'I wimped out,' she said in a voice that was so small I could barely hear. 'I've never been naked in front of a boy. I suppose I panicked.' She looked at me as if she were begging me to understand. I looked back as if I didn't.

'You know how when you're little and you're playing tag and you're being chased and you know perfectly well that there's no one frightening behind you, and you're laughing but somehow you're scared too and you're running really fast?'

In fact, I was amazed at how calm I felt, and how utterly without pity. It was as if that part of me, the part capable of feeling what other people felt, had disappeared. It felt nice. Peaceful. 'Didn't you say she called after you, though?'

She was frowning now, as if she were trying to recall. 'I think so. Yes, she did, because I remember thinking the boys might hear us. She was just mucking around, though.'

'Oh. Right.' I paused. Then I said, 'No. No, it can't have been.'

'What? What can't it have been?'

I looked at her under lowered lids. 'No. It's nothing.' I made a worried face. I always was a good actor.

'Please,' Eliza said. 'What is it?'

I sighed as if I found what I was about to say really hard. 'I just wondered, seeing what happened soon after, if she might actually have been calling for help? I mean, that would explain why she wasn't worried about anyone hearing, wouldn't it. If she were in trouble. And she was, wasn't she? Sadly.'

'You think she might have been calling me for help?' Eliza spoke as if each word had a full stop after it, as if the words were so huge that they couldn't fit in the same sentence. And the way she looked at me. People talk about eyes filling with horror but hers drained. They went blank like I imagine a blind person's eyes. It was actually quite scary. I got up from the floor.

'Of course you would have been able to tell the difference between someone calling for help and someone just mucking around.' I paused. 'Yeah, of course you would have. However much you were panicking and running.'

She made a weird little moaning sound, burying her face in her hands once more. Honestly, it was a relief not to have to look at her. Now she was saying something. I had to bend down close to hear.

'I thought she was mucking around. We were laughing.'

'Well, if you're sure,' I said, as if that were the end of it. I looked at my watch. 'Gosh, it's lights out. Try to get some rest, won't you?'

Back in my own cube I was too excited to sleep. The past week had seemed, not like a dream exactly, but like a film. I was watching everything, myself included, with interest, but none of it really touched me. That was it; I was untouchable, out of reach not only of those around me, but myself.

As the days went by I kept expecting to feel something, guilt, shame, regret for what I had done, but nothing. In fact, I had never felt better. It was as if every itch I ever suffered had been scratched and every hunger satisfied. I walked around feeling light on my feet as if, had I wanted to, I could have floated up in the air. I was free, free of all those troublesome feelings. To be honest I didn't even care much about Julian. I suppose I wouldn't have minded if he had come crawling, begging me to go out with him again. It would have been quite amusing to see the reaction of the others, the remaining princesses, if he had, but otherwise I really didn't care. And the less I cared the better things became. Eliza needed me. She was looking to me for reassurance, which was pretty funny when you think about it. And I gave it to her, for a bit, then I took it away and confused her all over again. She kept looking mournfully at me with those great big red-rimmed eyes. The bags underneath were massive by now. She really wasn't looking very pretty at all.

Then one morning she was gone. I didn't see her again. Miss Philips told us during assembly, three weeks after Rose died, that Eliza Cummings was not coming back to LAGs.

Forty-two

Eliza

'IT'S LATE,' JACOB BAUER said. 'Don't you think you should go to bed?'

'I'm reading.' I waved the Cass Cassidy autobiography at him. 'Archie got me a copy, just as he said he would. Good old Archie.'

'Aren't you tired?'

'Not really.'

'You must be cold.'

'Not as cold as Rose.'

It was a quiet night and his sigh could be heard all the way up to the roof.

'Don't do that,' I said. 'I hate it when people sigh at me.'

'Then please come down. I'm cold even if you're not.'

'Then you must go inside.'

'I won't leave until you're down.'

It was my turn to sigh. 'I told you, I have to work this out.'

'So work it out inside. Where it's warm. And not so, well, high up.'

'I like it here.'

'Fine. Then I shall stay until you come down. In fact, I shall get a ladder and climb up and get you.'

'Don't be so melodramatic.'

'You're the person sitting on your roof in the middle of the night yet you accuse me of being melodramatic. How can I be sure you won't jump?'

'Jump? Don't be so silly. Of course I won't jump.'

'I don't believe you.'

'All I want is to be left alone to read my book. Is that so strange?'

'Yes, quite frankly. If you're reading it sitting on a roof.'

'Roof schmoof, what's with the locality?'

There was a pause, then he said, 'Well then, if you're going to jump, jump. I can't hang around here all night waiting.'

I snorted. 'Ha, that's what they say in films, isn't it? "Do it then. Jump if that's what you want," they say, thinking they'll shock the person back to their senses. Which would be fine had I taken leave of them, but I haven't. They're all here. Next to me, all neatly lined up.' I patted the bit of roof by my side.

'Well, I'm sorry. I mean, forgive me if I don't see the funny side, but I'm cold and I'm tired and quite frankly I'm bored. It's all very well for you; you at least have something to read.'

'You could *read* at a time like this?'

There was a pause as he tethered his voice to patience, then he said, 'You're the one telling me everything is fine and that sitting on your roof in the middle of the night, reading, is just something you do.'

'And you *believe* me?'

His sigh reached all the way to the sky. 'You've had a shock,' he said. 'You're not in your right mind.'

'That would imply that there's a choice, don't you think? Like in "What mind shall I be in today? The right one? Nah, boring, done that. What about hers next door? No, it's busy;

she's using it herself. Ah well. I know, how about the one walking by outside the window? It's the wrong one but it doesn't do to be too fussy these days." ' As I spoke I gesticulated and the torch beam weaved its way across the garden like a drunk. For a moment I thought I might be about to topple. Jacob Bauer drew a sharp breath as he lunged forward, arms outstretched as if to catch me.

Once I was steady again he tried another tack. 'If you do fall you probably won't die straight away. Not for you a speedy and becoming death. Oh no. Most likely you'll simply be horribly injured and then left disabled, in pain and confined to a wheelchair for the remainder of your life. You do know, don't you, that the body implodes? It doesn't go splat, which is what most people imagine happens, it implodes, meaning . . .'

'I do know what implode means.'

'So get down from the *bloody* roof!'

'There's no need to yell at me. You're a great yeller, aren't you? When in doubt raise your voice . . . Anyway, I printed out this article from the Web about how to survive a fall from a great height. Just in case I changed my mind on my way down.' I pulled some folded A4 pages from my pocket, and leaning over the edge, waved them open.

'Careful . . .'

'It's very good advice. Useful. I'll read it to you. "*The Rockefeller Center in New York City. A survivable fall? Probably not, but stranger things have happened.*" '

'This is . . .'

'Please don't interrupt. "*What can you do if you slip off the scaffolding 10 stories above the ground or, worse yet, if your parachute fails while you are skydiving? The odds are not on your side. Is it possible to survive a free-fall from 50, 250, or 25,000 feet (15, 75, or*

7,500 m) above the ground? The answer is yes. There are hundreds, maybe thousands of people who have fallen from such heights and lived to tell the tale. While most of it comes down to luck, there are ways you can influence your velocity, the duration of your decelera-tion, and the distribution of the impact forces upon your body, and ultimately increase your chance of survival. Steps: The arch position: Slow your fall using the arch position. Unless you're falling from an airplane, you won't have enough time to try this step. Maximize your surface area by spreading yourself out . . ."'

'Enough.'

I put the paper down. 'Fine. I just thought it was interesting.'

'Anyway, I thought you said that you had no intention of jumping.'

'Damn,' I said. 'You got me there.'

There was another pause, then Jacob Bauer said, in a much softer voice, a voice I had hitherto only heard him use when speaking to Annie, 'What is this all about? Is it Gabriel? I know he's seeing someone.'

I laughed heartily. 'Good heavens, no. You think I would go and sit on my roof over something like that?'

'So what is it?'

I sighed. 'It's complicated.'

'I hate is when people say that.'

'Well, I'm sorry but it is.'

'Try.'

I thought about it. 'The thing is, I've spent my whole life since my best friend died thinking that I was responsible. We got into this situation and it was all my idea but I bottled out and left her there on her own. Now I find out she was murdered. By Cass Cassidy the soap actress. Who is actually Sandra/Cassandra from school. Which is all pretty surreal. It's in here, though,' I waved the book at him again. 'In her bloody autobiography.'

There was a long pause. Then Jacob Bauer said, 'OK, I can see how that could be upsetting.'

'Thanks.'

'I still don't believe that sitting on your roof is going to help.' There was another pause and then I heard him say to himself, 'Oh, to hell with it.'

I looked down as he strode out of view. Then I lay back against the chimney-stack and looked up at the star-strewn sky. A few minutes later I heard banging. The roof hatch flew open and Jacob Bauer's head appeared. I sat back up. 'How did you get here?'

'Same way as you did.'

'But how did you get inside?'

'I'm afraid I had to break a window. I will pay for it to be replaced, of course.' He pushed a heavy shoulder through the hatch. 'Damn! Damn it, I'm stuck.'

'Like Pooh in Rabbit's hole,' I said.

'I'm glad I'm amusing you.'

I got to my feet and peered down at him. 'How about if you make your shoulders round? Like this?' I showed him.

There was a lot of grunting and shoving and then the rest of Jacob Bauer emerged. I went and sat down, dangling my legs over the edge.

'Would you mind coming back from there?' Jacob Bauer said.

'I'm fine.'

'Well, I'm not. I suffer from vertigo.'

'So you don't like this kind of thing?' I leant over as far as I was able.

'For God's sake!' He stepped forward and his foot slipped and for a moment I thought he might tumble off the roof. I threw myself backwards to try to grab him but he had managed to regain his balance.

'Christ,' I said. 'What are you trying to do?'

He was pale and his eyes were wide and frightened.

'I'm sorry. I forget you're not comfortable with heights.'

'Would you mind coming over here.' He pointed a trembling finger at the chimney-stack.

'OK.' I got to my feet and went to sit down next to him. Then I started to laugh.

'There's something amusing you? A little joke you'd like to share?'

'I'm sorry,' I said. Then I started to laugh again.

'For fuck's sake.'

'OK, OK, I'm sorry. It's just that it would have been pretty funny if, having just found out that I had not, after all, caused Rose's death I should cause yours.'

'Hilarious. Absolutely side-splittingly hilarious.'

'Rose chose to stay. She hadn't tried to follow me and she hadn't called out for help.'

There was a pause then Jacob Bauer said, 'I'm afraid I don't have the faintest idea what you are talking about.'

I started crying.

I felt his hand on my shoulder. 'There, there.' He handed me a large red and white spotted hankie. 'It's a bit bright, I know. Annie picked it out for me. She picks out my ties too. Go on. It's perfectly clean.'

I took the hankie and dabbed at my eyes.

'That's it. Good girl. And it's going to be all right. It really is.'

I handed him back his hankie. 'At first I just felt this huge relief. We'd been silly schoolgirls doing what silly schoolgirls do. I shouldn't have chickened out, that's true, but Rose could have come with me. She chose to stay. And she hadn't called out to me for help. Then I remembered: Uncle Ian is dead. He'll never know now.'

I looked out across the roof. The light from the street lamps didn't reach that far up but there were plenty of stars in the sky and a diffident moon hanging back behind a large yew.

I went on speaking. 'And it hit me that the truth was worse, much worse. Someone did that to Rose deliberately, with malice, with hatred. In an accident there's no malice, no bad intent. But here, there was evil.' I slapped my hands over my eyes as if I could shut out the image of Rose, frightened, fighting for her life while that girl, a girl whose face I could barely picture, whose voice I couldn't remember, had stood there, watching.

'Time to get down from here.' Jacob Bauer's voice brought me back. 'We can make a nice hot drink and then we can talk, all night if you like. It's much easier to make sense of things when you're not in imminent danger of toppling off a roof.' When I didn't move he said, 'Annie will wonder where I am. I really don't like leaving her on her own. I know I'm only a roof away but still . . .'

I looked up. 'Annie's alone? Where's Sheila?'

'Visiting her sister.'

'Goodness. Right. Well, then, you must go back home immediately. I mean, think if she wakes up and finds you gone. She might have woken already.' I grabbed his arm and shook it. 'She might be out, on the streets, looking for you.'

'I locked her in.'

I was surprised at him. 'You really must go and check on her.'

He scrabbled to his feet. He wasn't terribly agile. 'Here.' He held out his hand. 'I will, when you come down with me.'

I shook my head. 'Please go.' I waved in the direction of the sky. 'It's pretty up here.'

Jacob Bauer sat down again.

'What are you doing?' I asked. 'And don't say, "sitting down".'

'I wasn't going to. That would be to insult your intelligence.'

'So what are you doing?'

'Sitting down?'

'This isn't funny. Nothing is funny. And your little girl being home alone in the middle of the night isn't funny either.'

'I can see her window from here.'

'But you can't see or hear *her*. To be honest I think you're being irresponsible.'

He sighed and pushed his hand through his hair. 'I don't know what choice you're giving me. I mean, I leave to go and look after my daughter and you throw yourself off the roof. Or I stay with you . . .'

I heaved myself to my feet, heavy as an old woman. 'OK,' I sighed. 'Very clever. Very physchologically something or another.'

'You're coming down?'

'You haven't given me any choice, have you?'

Jacob Bauer insisted that I come with him to Number 12. 'I won't leave you on your own, it's as simple as that.'

I told him to wait while I went out into the studio. 'I'm just getting something.'

338

I returned, holding a box with the restored Willow Pattern jug. He didn't ask any questions, which I appreciated, but simply offered to carry the box for me. As my front door shut behind me we walked out into the silent square that was doubly lit, by the stars and by the street lamps.

'You look pale,' I said.

'So do you,' he said.

Having made me sit down at the table, he moved around the industrial-looking kitchen, that was all black granite and stainless steel, making tea. He used loose leaves and warmed the pot.

'Shouldn't you check on Annie?'

He placed the pot and two mugs on the table and sat down opposite me. 'She'll be fine.'

'I thought you were such a good father.'

'I am. Now tell me everything. Slowly. And in some kind of order.' His heavy stubble showed up black against his pale skin and his kind eyes were tired, but he managed a small smile. And I wanted to tell him yet I hesitated. It was as if I needed to keep it all away from him the way you keep dirt away from a clean white sheet.

I was still thinking about what to say when the kitchen door was flung open and Sheila appeared, standing in the doorway, wrapped in a kimono the colours of a gas flame.

'What on earth?' she said.

'Sheila, did we wake you?' Jacob got to his feet. 'I am sorry. I would offer you a cup of tea but I know you'll be keen to get back to bed.'

I stared at him. 'But you said she was away? You ...' He hushed me with a glance.

Sheila took a step inside. 'I might as well stay up. I'll never get back to sleep now. It's almost morning, after all.' She gave me an accusing look as if it were my fault another day was dawning.

'Try,' Jacob Bauer said. Something in his expression must have made her realise it would be useless to argue. She wrapped herself close in her kimono and umbrage and stomped off out of the door. We could hear her angry steps moving up the stairs and along the landing above our heads.

Then I said again, 'You told me Sheila was away. I only came down because I thought you'd left Annie on her own.'

He grinned at me. 'Clever, eh?'

I got to my feet. His hand shot out and took mine. 'You're not going to go back up on that roof, are you?' He let go again. 'It would be rather silly, don't you think?'

I pulled a face and sat down. 'Yes, I suppose it would be.'

'Good.' He smiled and the relief in his eyes made me smile too. 'Now tell me the whole thing from the beginning. You'll find I'm a much better listener when I'm not in fear of my life. And you never know, I might be able to help. Not many people know this but I almost chose psychiatry as a speciality.'

'Almost.'

'Absolutely almost.' He put his hand on mine. 'Now tell me.'

I took a deep breath. 'It all began at school when this new girl, Sandra, joined the lower sixth . . .'

Epilogue

MY LIFE HAD BEEN like the shadow of the one I was meant to have lived. I suppose that was what Uncle Ian had been trying to tell me. It had been a life of 'if onlys' and 'what ifs?' Of trying not to take too much because I deserved nothing.

Having found out what really happened to Rose, I could have added a hundred new what ifs and a hundred more if onlys. If only I had seen how mixed up and unhappy that new girl was. If only I had taken her feelings for Portia's brother seriously. What if I had bothered more, tried harder, been less self-absorbed. What if I hadn't persuaded her to go to that dance? What if I hadn't altered her dress?

Jacob Bauer said that none of us knew what misery we might inadvertently have caused. It was just the way life worked. Everything was connected.

He said, 'You step on to a pedestrian crossing, causing a car to slow down and stop. The tiny delay makes it get on the motorway a fraction of a moment later than it would otherwise have done but just at the moment a lorry pulls out without signalling, causing a crash. Is that your fault?

'You get the last pint of milk in the store, which forces another guy to go somewhere else for milk, which in turn makes him late to pick up his girlfriend, who ends up accepting a lift from a stranger. Is that your fault, because you bought some milk? And how do you think it works for Gabriel and me? We do our best but there are times when we get it wrong when treating a patient. So what should we all do about it? Lock ourselves away in a small attic room and do nothing for fear that our butterfly wings beating may cause an earthquake in China?'

A young girl had died and all that she might have been was left undiscovered and all that she might have done was left undone. That was the tragedy of Rose and the tragedy of every life cut short.

The rest; well, it should be silence.

Yet mercifully for me, it was not. Because finally, and with a little help from my neighbours, I had begun to look around me and to ask, not 'What if,' but 'What now?'

Acknowledgements

A huge thank you to Victoria Oakley and her team at the V&A for taking the time and trouble to show me around the wondrous Ceramic Conservation Department and for being so patient in answering my endless questions and also to Alex Patchett-Joyce for all her advice about ceramic restoration. Any mistakes on the subject are entirely my own.

As always I want to thank my editor Alexandra Pringle who never stops caring and everyone at Bloomsbury, especially Alexa von Hirschberg.

Thank you also to Georgia Garrett and Linda Shaughnessy at A.P. Watt.

I also had excellent support and advice from Jeremy Cobbold and Michael Patchett-Joyce.

Finally, huge thanks to Harriet Cobbold Hielte without whose brilliant advice, help and support I don't like to write anything much other than a shopping list.

ALSO AVAILABLE BY MARIKA COBBOLD

A RIVAL CREATION

Tonight I will speak to you about The Failure. The yearning in man to do more than just survive is the making of both the greatness and the tragedy of being human.

Once upon a more prosperous time, Liberty Turner was a published writer, bursting with creativity. Now, aged 39, divorced and pulverised by relentless rejections, Liberty is forced to face the truth that she has long been hiding from: that, despite all her bright-eyed ambition, she no longer has the talent to be a writer. That she is, in fact, a failure.

With nothing but time on her hands, Liberty tries to put her life back together and begins to involve herself more in the lives of her friends and neighbours in her village. But Tollymead is far from the middle-class idyll it appears to be, and everyone seems to have problems to solve and secrets to hide. When the handsome Oscar Brooke arrives in the village, Liberty prays that happiness might just be within her reach . . .

'Undoubtedly one of the funniest novels you'll read this summer'
DAILY MAIL

'Hugely entertaining . . . all human life is here'
DAILY EXPRESS

'Charming, funny and finely observed'
WOMAN AND HOME

BLOOMSBURY

THE PURVEYOR OF ENCHANTMENT

A life lived in fear is a life half lived

Clementine Hope, thirty-something and newly divorced, lives in a small Hampshire town, teaching music and working on a collection of fairy tales left to her by her Great Aunt Elvira. But mostly she worries. She worries about the rising crime rate. She worries about disease and illness, about offending God and, in the rare moments when she is at peace with Him, about upsetting the man in the carpet shop. When her sister Ophelia asks her if there's anything she is *not* frightened of, Clementine has to think for a while before replying, 'Doris Day.'

But when she falls in love with Nathaniel Scott, the son of her next-door neighbour, her neuroses threaten to destroy her hard-won happiness. Determined to take control of her life, Clementine resolves to transform herself from victim to heroine, slay her personal dragon of fears and phobias, and rescue her very own Prince Charming.

'Wonderfully funny, with a strong undertow . . . a joy to read'
DEBORAH MOGGACH

'I strongly recommend *The Purveyor of Enchantment*'
DAILY MAIL

'Cobbold's brilliantly witty and blackly comic writing manages to both point fun at the absurdities of life and, at the same time, to celebrate them'
ELIZABETH BUCHAN

BLOOMSBURY

FROZEN MUSIC

My name is Esther Fisher and I'm about to walk out on the only man I've ever loved . . .

Esther has been angry all her life – angry with her impossible parents, and at a world that just won't play by the rules. Now working as a tabloid journalist, she takes up the fight once more – this time on behalf of a couple who are being evicted from their home to make room for an opera house. The architect on the project is Swedish-born Linus, a successful, yet dreamy man who is also trying to put his childhood anxieties behind him.

When circumstances force them both to spend a summer in Linus's family home on an island off the west coast of Sweden, the growing friendship between the two soon turns into something more. But with Esther's professional integrity at stake, she begins to wonder if ultimately this is a fight with no winners . . .

'*Pride and Prejudice*, Scandinavian style'
SUNDAY EXPRESS

'A deliciously descriptive novel . . . beneath its charm lie serious truths'
SHE

'Her writing is dreamy yet dextrous . . . Like Conrad and Nabokov, she has conquered a language that is not her own'
OBSERVER

ORDER BY PHONE: 01256 302 699; BY EMAIL: DIRECT@MACMILLAN.CO.UK

DELIVERY IS USUALLY 3–5 WORKING DAYS.

FREE POSTAGE AND PACKAGING FOR ORDERS OVER £20.

ONLINE: WWW.BLOOMSBURY.COM/BOOKSHOP

PRICES AND AVAILABILITY SUBJECT TO CHANGE WITHOUT NOTICE.

WWW.BLOOMSBURY.COM/MARIKACOBBOLD

BLOOMSBURY